Desired

Also by Virginia Henley

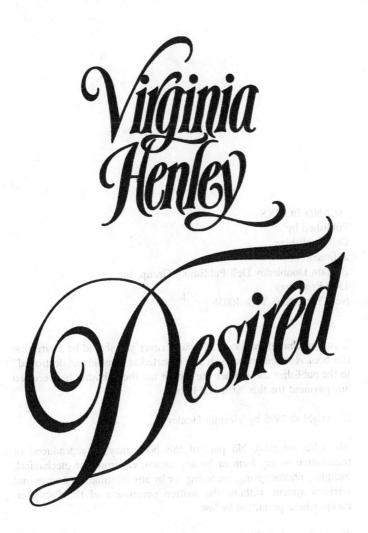

Island
BOOKS

ISLAND BOOKS
Published by
Dell Publishing
a division of
Bantam Doubleday Dell Publishing Group, Inc.
1540 Broadway
New York, New York 10036

ISBN: 0-440-21703-2

Printed in the United States of America

Published simultaneously in Canada

For my mother-in-law Marjorie.
Thanks for putting up with
me all these years.

Desired

🦢 1 🦢

The first time he ever saw her she was naked. Perhaps that was the reason he felt such a raging lust, yet he doubted it. He had seen many naked females in his twenty-odd years. But she was the most beautiful maiden he had ever glimpsed. Her flesh was the color of cream, her lashes lay upon her cheeks in dark crescents, while a tiny witch-mark sat on the high point of one slanting cheekbone. Her golden hair, brightly burnished as newly minted coins, fell below her knees, cloaking her in a nimbus of red-gold.

He had no idea who she was, knew nothing whatsoever about her, save one thing: he coveted her.

The problem was these persistent visions of his "lady" came at the most inconvenient moments, like now. Christian Hawksblood cleared his mind with effort, then focused his total attention upon his lance. It took only a moment for his pulse beat to merge with the rhythm of his charger, for his powerful arm to become an extension of his weapon, and for his fierce eyes to fix upon his opponent. In one fluid motion he couched his lance, lowered his visor, gripped his charger with his knees, and swung his shield to cover his body.

The baton fell and as clods of earth flew into the air, Hawksblood visualized his lance point striking the hostile shield with such force his challenger was flung from the saddle. A split second later it happened exactly as he had envisioned.

His opponent did not lie in the dust, but was on his feet with drawn sword within a minute, an amazing feat considering the impediment of his armor. This was the reason Hawksblood had challenged the Frenchman. He wanted his opponent's sable armor and his dappled gray charger.

Hawksblood was out of the saddle in a heartbeat. It was

within the rules for him to remain mounted, but his pride was too great. The honor of chivalry was at stake. He drew his sword, advancing with such deadly intent his challenger measured his six-foot length prone in the dust and lay still.

A woman screamed.

"Dead!" cried the spectators.

Then the French champion's squires ran onto the field, managing to carry him from the lists, thankful he had only been stunned by the Arabian Knight.

By the time the dust of the tourney field had begun to settle, Hawksblood sat in his tent soaking the kinks from his body. One of his squires had removed his armor, bathed him, and was now massaging the hard, rippling muscles of his arms and shoulders with oil of almond and frankincense to keep them supple.

Ali, an Arab who had been with him since birth, thrust the stopper into the aromatic bottle and held out the towel for his master. As Drakkar rose from the tub to his full height, the water cascaded down his limbs, leaving his dark skin glistening. Ali thought his master's Arabian name suited him much better than Christian. He had royal Arabian blood, jet-black hair, and the swarthy visage of a fierce hawk. Only the light turquoise eyes suggested he was not a pure-blooded prince. Ali's glance ran down the magnificent body. *Nay, I delude myself. His great breadth and long limbs proclaim him Norman.*

His other squire, Paddy, was out collecting the tournament prizes of horses and armor. Hawksblood and his squires had magnificent warhorses but trained chargers needed for tournaments were in short supply and a pliable hauberk of finely tempered steel cost as much as a piece of manor land.

As Paddy led the dappled gray and a light bay toward the pavilion, he realized how vividly it stood out from the other tents. Brilliant red and purple silk topped by a gold minaret made even its shape differ from the rest, hinting at Moorish, Turkish, or Arabian opulence.

Paddy staked the horses beside what amounted to a small mountain of armor. The pattern had been repeated wherever they had journeyed, through Morocco, Spain, and now France. Hawksblood was still undefeated.

Paddy lifted the silken flap to enter. "Christ, Ali-Babba, get this bloody water shifted. There's a mountain of armor for himself to sort through."

"I left it there on the off chance you'd take the hint to use it, Paddy's Pig. I can smell you across the tent."

"No bloody wonder with a hooter like yours, boyo. I've run bowlegged today, you lousy lump of camel dung!"

Hawksblood's eyes narrowed against laughter. His squires indulged in a continual contest of name-calling, yet on the battlefield they thought nothing of risking their lives for each other.

"Enough," Christian admonished. "I want the brass armor and the sable. Ransom the rest back for money."

"In that case, Lord Drakkar, *I* had best do the haggling while Paddy cleans up the tent."

"Since yer ancestors were rug thieves from the bazaars of Baghdad, I concede ye'r better at cheatin' knights from their livelihood than meself."

"I doubt that, Paddy," Christian murmured, pulling on a cream shirt that emphasized the darkness of his sun-bronzed skin.

Paddy grinned, pleased with the compliment, threw off his clothes, and slid down in the now tepid bathwater. "I'll have this outa the way in a jiffy, m'lord, long afore the joy girls arrive."

The evening of a joust was intended for revelry. After fasting all day, campfires would be lit, game would be roasted, and the flagons filled to overflowing. Whores, or women of joy, would dance about the fires laughing, teasing, touching, disrobing, and finally coupling for a penny or a pint or a bellyful of warm food.

"Enjoy the gorging and guzzling, Paddy," Christian said, stroking the ruffled breast of his gerfalcon on its perch. "Don't forget to give Salome a few succulent morsels. I've an invitation to visit the castle tonight."

"Ho, watch out fer the noble French fillies. The ones I saw from the lists today all looked like they were sufferin' from night starvation."

"I'll try not to overtax my strength, Paddy," Christian said with a leer. Hawksblood felt a sense of anticipation. He had glimpsed more than one lady who from a distance looked as if she might have golden hair. Once again he had been lucky in the lists. *Who knows? Perhaps this is the night I shall meet my vision.*

The Royal Court at Windsor was a haven for at least a dozen young heiresses. Edward III, married to Queen Philippa, was the most spectacular Plantagenet king England had ever known. His court was brilliant because he lived and spent lavishly. He gathered orphaned heiresses into his vast household, then bestowed these coveted young royal wards upon the families who gave him the most loyal service.

One or two of the older girls had been chosen as ladies-in-waiting to young Princess Isabel, whose every whim was indulged by her doting father. Though Queen Philippa was sweet and motherly, her *raison d'être* was giving birth to Plantagenet princes and princesses. It seemed that whenever Edward spilled his seed in her, her fecund womb ripened it. She had just whelped her ninth Enfant Royale. As a result, the queen's household grew apace until now it overflowed with nursemaids, nannies, serving women, laundresses, ladies-in-waiting, chaperones, and tutors.

Lady Brianna of Bedford and Lady Joan of Kent picked up their skirts and ran like hoydens through Windsor's gardens. They were both seventeen, both orphaned, but there the similarity ended. Joan was petite with silver-blond hair the color of moonbeams. She enhanced her dainty looks by wearing pink or other pastels, and entwining her hair with seed pearls. She looked innocent as a child and was never, ever blamed for the mischievous tricks she was always ready to instigate.

Brianna was a beauty. Her ripe breasts and generous mouth proclaimed to every eye that she was all of seventeen and on the brink of womanhood. Her hair cloaked her in golden splendor, falling below her knees in shining waves ending in hundreds of silken tendrils. One glimpse foretold she would become that rare object of desire: a man's woman.

The two girls stopped running the moment they saw the group of females gathered about the fountain in the privacy of the walled garden where Dame Marjorie Daw instructed them on etiquette each afternoon. They could hardly be punished for being late when Princess Isabel had not yet arrived. All the royal wards were now present, ranging in age from seven to seventeen.

Little Blanche of Lancaster sat decorously by the fountain. Though she was motherless, her father was Henry, Earl of Lancaster, who had been head of the Regency Council for King Edward before he took the reins into his own hands. Though Blanche was heiress to the vast Lancaster fortune, she was pale and ethereal. Her lack of vitality made her almost timid.

The dragon-faced woman with eyes like agates tapped her long stick impatiently on the flagstones as she awaited Princess Isabel's arrival. The afternoon was extremely warm and as Dame Marjorie removed the black cloak she always wore, Joan's eyebrows elevated with delight as she looked meaningfully at her friend Brianna, then imperceptibly inched toward the discarded mantle.

Isabel and her entourage finally arrived with her greedy little pug yapping at her heels. They disposed themselves upon the fountain's ledge while the fat little dog removed itself from the vicinity of the dragon and lay down on Joan's pink skirt, which billowed upon the lawn.

"Ass-licker," Joan whispered to Elizabeth Grey, Princess Isabel's best friend.

Dragonface glanced sharply in the direction of the whisper. Her agate gaze passed over an angelic Joan and settled fiercely upon Brianna. The birch rod lashed out like a whip. In its fright the little dog immediately produced a turd, missing Joan's skirt by half an inch. Brianna lowered her lashes to keep from whooping with laughter.

"Ladies, I admonish you all to be both courteous and meek." Dragonface looked at Joan and Blanche with approval. "A young demoiselle looks before her with her eyelids low and fixed. Each one of you will have the status of a minor until you are wed. All words of authority belong to your lord and a wife's duty requires she listen in peace and obedience. Submissiveness is the best way to disarm a husband's anger." Dragonface glanced at Princess Isabel and hoped some of her words would be heeded. In truth she gravely doubted they would.

Joan's quick fingers trickled a vial of lemon juice down the back of the black cloak. She had procured it to bleach the curls at her temples, but she could get more from the castle stillroom.

Dragonface droned on. "It is a wife's duty to bear children and manage her servants. *However . . .*" Dame Marjorie paused for dramatic effect and rapped her stick upon the flagstones, "you stand little chance of becoming a wife if you fall from grace. You must keep the body modestly covered at all times. Never allow yourself to be alone with a man, never allow a man to touch any part of your person except your hand. A kiss upon the cheek is permitted after a betrothal, but kissing on the mouth is forbidden until after marriage." Again she paused. Isabel looked quite flushed and eager at this talk of kissing. Dame Marjorie reminded herself the girl was a Plantagenet, a passionate brood who came over-early to sexual maturity. She cleared her throat and moved to less titillating nostrums.

"No running or trotting, never trail your mantle, do not scold in public, never overeat or get drunk. Young ladies should not tell lies. Never repeat gossip, never indulge in games of chance. Take no pleasure in low songs or the antics of the jongleurs. Rather, you should go to chapel every day."

Brianna hid a yawn. Dragonface would next be telling them to use their serviettes rather than wipe their hands on the tablecloth. Her mind drifted off to contemplate her betrothed. She hadn't the vaguest idea who King Edward would choose for her, but she knew it would happen before she reached the age of eighteen. She had begun to have the most deliciously disturbing dreams of a phantom knight who would come to claim her. The dreams were so intense they felt real, yet when she awoke she could never quite recall his face. Brianna shivered with anticipation, knowing the most exciting time of her life was almost upon her.

She was abruptly brought back from her daydream by a roar from the dragon. Dame Marjorie, upon concluding her lesson, laid down her stick, then swept her cloak about her ramrod back. Then she heard the ridicule of laughter.

The lemon juice combined with the bright sunshine had left a yellow streak all the way down her black cloak.

"None of you may leave until the culprit is found." The light of battle was in her eye and the lines of her face were rigid, showing she was not amused one iota. The silence stretched out as the Dame's agate eye fixed upon each girl.

Blanche of Lancaster paled and looked as if she might faint. Princess Joanna, Isabel's younger sister, shrank back in alarm. Joan, however, was busy sticking a sharp rose thorn through the birch rod just at the place where the dragon would grip it.

Isabel tossed her dark hair back over her shoulder and said with malice, "It was Bedford, and her friend, Joan of Kent." Isabel was jealous of the girl's beauty.

Brianna's mouth fell open.

Joan had been absorbed in poking the birch rod's handle into the dog turd but as Isabel's words reached her ears, she stood up to confess all. Brianna quickly took hold of Joan's hand and squeezed hard to stop her friend's words. "I did it, Dame Marjorie. Joan had naught to do with it." Brianna was used to Joan's mischievous, childlike behavior. Joan never gave a thought to the consequences of her irresponsible actions and Brianna always felt a need to protect her.

The Dame's face went still. "Lady Bedford, you will follow me." The words were like a sentence, dooming Brianna. She would be purged of her evil ways. The dragon bent dramatically to retrieve her stick. The thorn pierced her thumb, which immediately flew to her mouth so she could suck upon the injured digit. Joan of Kent was entranced at the look that came upon the dragon's face when she realized she was sucking shit.

Brianna followed Dame Marjorie from the formal gardens of the East Terrace with reluctant steps. As she walked through the Upper Ward past the State Apartments, she glanced longingly across the Quadrangle to her own rooms in the York Tower. She had hoped to finish painting a page to illustrate the Legend of St. George and the Dragon she had laboriously scripted. She sighed with resignation and followed the rigid back of Dame Marjorie to her lodgings, located beyond the cloisters that housed the clergy.

Joan of Kent, racked with guilt, trailed after her friend. She watched Brianna enter the dragon's lair and knew she must gather her courage to intervene. Joan drew herself up to her full five feet one inch and knocked resolutely. When the door was flung open she forced herself across the threshold. Not daring to look at Brianna, she blurted, "Dame Marjorie, I am to blame for the wicked prank—"

The older woman swung to Brianna immediately. "This is beyond the beyond. To drag Lady Joan of Kent into this is unconscionable." She turned back to Joan. "My dear, you are to be commended for such a noble gesture. Royal blood will out, I suppose, but this time Lady Bedford will suffer the consequences of her depraved actions."

Joan knew it was futile to argue. She was making things worse for Brianna. As she turned to depart she was rewarded by a smile of thanks from her friend that warmed her heart.

Brianna decided in that moment not to let Dame Marjorie victimize her. Before she held out her hands for the birching, she would challenge her woman to woman. "Dame Marjorie, we both know I wasn't responsible for the mischief today. Princess Isabel wrongly accused me out of spite. But since you cannot punish the princess royal and are loathe to chastise Joan of Kent because of her royal blood, that leaves me." Brianna's eyes lit with mocking laughter. "If you really feel the need to vent your spleen, be my guest." She held out her hands and the Dame knew immediately that Brianna of Bedford didn't give a tinker's damn about a few strokes from a birch rod. The Dame decided on a more subtle punishment. She looked with distaste at the pigment stains on Brianna's hands.

"The devil makes work for idle hands. The stains upon your fingers lead me to believe you fritter your time away unwisely in useless endeavors. Your hands are intended to ply a needle. It is shameful to do otherwise when so many garments are needed in the royal household."

In fact, the queen and her ladies had insisted just the opposite. They excused Lady Bedford from sewing duty so she might pursue her God-given talent. Brianna kept a wise silence.

The dried-up old spinster felt even more outrage at the girl's upthrust breasts and long golden tresses. "I shall advise the queen to betroth you to an older man who will rule you with an iron hand."

Brianna's heart sank.

"You are dismissed, Bedford."

Brianna's heart lifted slightly.

"Go straight to the chapel and confess your sins to Brother Bartholomew."

Brianna's heart sank hopelessly. She would have to attend vespers and wait until he had finished the service before she could confess.

All the light had gone from the day before Brianna could seek the refuge of her chambers. With every step she plotted her revenge. She would paint her dragon with Dame Marjorie's features!

Her mother's sister, Adele, who had accompanied her from Bedford as her waiting-woman, opened her chamber door. She was Irish, but it had been Brianna's mother who was the beauty of the family. Adele was covered with freckles and her hair was the color of straw. She had resigned herself to being an old maid though she was only twenty-nine. "Oh, my lamb, wherever have ye been? Someone's been in here doing mischief while I was visiting the royal nursery to glimpse the new baby princess."

Brianna flew to her worktable beneath the leaded window. Her parchment lay in ruins. Spilled paint obliterated the exquisite sketch of her dragon and the carefully scripted legend of St. George. She gazed through the darkened window with unseeing eyes, angry at the injustice of life. She had taken the blame for her friend and been rewarded by having her artwork ruined. In a moment of self-pity her eyes flooded and a lone tear rolled down her cheek. A minute later she dashed it away with impatient hands, her Irish sense of humor coming to her rescue. "No good deed shall go unpunished." Her laughter bubbled out irrepressibly. "Remember that, Adele."

Brianna often used laughter to mask her sensitivity and vulnerability. Laughter was a most alluring quality in a woman. Men were attracted to her because of her laugh, which gave them a delicious foretaste of her innate sensuality.

As she drifted off to sleep, a smile curved her lips as a tall figure stepped into her dream and beckoned. Desire overwhelmed her. This knight who came to her dreams was utterly irresistible. She went to him willingly, wanting him to touch her, to kiss her, to carry her off to a secret place. As the distance between them closed, she realized they were on the parapet of a strange castle. He reached out a powerful hand and lifted a tear from her cheek with the tip of his finger. Brianna laughed up into his face, and as she had hoped, he could not resist the sensual curve of her smiling lips.

His mouth on hers felt glorious. She had never experienced anything to equal the deep pleasure she received from the touch and the taste of him. When he enfolded her in his arms and pressed his hard body against hers, she thought she might die of joy. She sighed with longing as his image began to dissolve, then moved restlessly in her sleep. Her palm cupped her full breast where the hand of her phantom knight had touched her so possessively only a moment before. She sighed again. This time she had seen his eyes. They were a startling aquamarine!

❧ 2 ❧

At the castle of St. Lô, Christian Hawksblood kept his mouth closed and his ears and eyes open. The talk was all of war with England. Though there was a truce, it would be broken the moment that the King of France had assembled a large enough fleet.

He had been taught his fighting skills by Norman knights who had imparted history and hatred for the French in equal measure. Hawksblood was a mercenary at the moment, until now selling his sword to the highest bidder. Because he had ambivalent feelings toward France and England, two lands he'd never seen, he had decided to visit them before he pledged his sword in the inevitable war that had been threatening for years.

England had held all the western and southern provinces of France since Eleanor of Aquitaine wed Henry Secund, two centuries ago, and there had been fierce fighting along the borders ever since. Philip of France was Edward III's grandfather, so when Philip died and his sons followed him to the grave without male issue, the King of England decided to claim the throne of France. Recently he had quartered his coat-of-arms with the French lilies along with the leopards of England. This did not endear him to Philip of Valois, who had inherited the French crown. He openly declared to help Scotland invade England and began to pirate English ships.

When in France the English Royal Court was headquartered in Bordeaux. Christian understood why the moment he had visited the beautiful, sunny, flower-filled city on the curving river Garonne. He fancied living there himself and to that end purchased a white stone palatial villa next to the property owned by the infamous Earl of Warrick. The thought of confronting the father who had abandoned his mother before his birth was fleeting. Perhaps Guy de Beauchamp, Earl of Warrick, was not his sire after all. He had no proof. He was convinced, however, that he had Norman blood, yet now that he was in Normandy, he felt strangely alien.

At the castle of St. Lô, Hawksblood's glance caressed each lady it fell upon, eliciting open invitations from a dozen willing women. When he was absolutely certain "she" was not of the company, he relaxed and sampled the rich wine Baron St. Lô proffered him.

"I will pay double what Philip will pay for your sword," St. Lô said expansively. "All his money is going into ships at the moment, but you and I know it is land battles that are decisive."

Hawksblood's lids shielded his eyes as he listened without committing himself. He knew St. Lô had observed him in the lists—knew he was already counting the fortune Hawksblood could earn him ransoming the English nobles he would capture. "You seem very sure France will be victorious."

St. Lô laughed as if Hawksblood was jesting. "Philip already has a hundred ships with over twenty thousand Normans, Bretons, and Picards. He even has Genoese bowmen. In the last few weeks he has mounted coastal forays against English ports and captured three of their best ships."

"Have the English not retaliated?"

"They've tried." St. Lô was still amused. "An English army at Lille was defeated only last month. The Earl of Salisbury, rumored to be a personal friend of King Edward, was taken prisoner." St. Lô's eyes gleamed. "Can you imagine the ransom he'll fetch?"

A husky voice interrupted them. "Bernard, you must introduce me to the dark champion, chéri."

Christian looked down into eyes heavy with sensuality.

"Behave yourself, Lisette, or your husband will snap that fine neck of yours one of these nights."

The resemblance between the two proclaimed them brother and sister. Both were uncommonly attractive. Lisette cast Bernard a decadent glance from beneath her lashes. "Chéri, I know you will keep him occupied for me."

Suddenly there were no other people in the hall for the dark champion and the voluptuous French girl. Her eyes traveled the length of him. "Does your lance always hit its mark?"

His eyes danced as he nodded solemnly. "Yes, it is an extension of my body." He heard her swift intake of breath.

"You rode in more than one bout . . . did that not tire you?" Her voice grew huskier by the minute.

"I can ride six times in succession without spending my strength, chérie."

Lisette licked her lips over him. "I admire endurance." Her legs had gone so weak, she wondered how she would climb the stairs. "My chamber is the east turret," she murmured, slipping away with unseemly haste.

Christian Hawksblood became Drakkar. With the alertness of a trained warrior, he allowed his senses to gauge the level of danger about him. He could read minds easily and knew Baron St. Lô had no objection to Lisette giving her body if it secured Hawksblood's sword. There was a high degree of envy directed at him from his opponents in the tournament, but he allowed it to wash over him without reacting to it. Drakkar had more physical and supernatural powers at his command than any mortal should be allowed to possess.

Lisette opened the chamber door the moment he scratched. Just the sight of him aroused her without his lifting a finger. Her hands were already on the fastenings of her gown, which curiously were all at the front. Beneath the gown she was naked.

Though the chamber was shadowed, lit only by the square candle by the carved bed, he saw that her body was lush. As his hands removed his linen shirt, her deft fingers unfastened the laces of his codpiece. His marble phallus sprang out at her and she filled her hands with his cods and stones, marveling at the size of him.

His powerful hands stroked down her body from her breasts to her thighs and she shuddered at the callused roughness of them on her soft skin. She drew him toward the pool of candlelight, then drew in a sharp breath at the look of him. His powerful body was tempting as original sin. With a moan she lifted her arms about his neck, then wrapped her legs about his torso. The sight of his hard-muscled body had made her so wet she impaled herself upon him. She cried out her pleasure. It was the tightest fit she'd ever known.

He braced his legs and stood impassively as Lisette thudded her body onto his. He understood perfectly that she could wait no longer. When she shuddered her release and collapsed upon him, he carried her to the bed and spread her upon its silken covers. Then he proceeded to play her body like an angel plays a harp, plucking strings she never knew she had. She climaxed again and felt deliciously sated. Her pride was piqued, however, for she knew with a certainty he had not yet spent.

He rolled with her until her body was sprawled on top of his. She raised up onto her knees on either side of his thighs and looked down at him in wonder. His face was fiercely feral. He resembled a raptor. A curl of delicious fear spiraled inside her belly. How many men had he killed? He looked as if he had been trained since childhood to kill. She flushed. He still wore his chausses with the codpiece removed. She hadn't been able to wait for him to fully undress.

His fingers touched her with fire as she sat gazing down into a face that looked carved from mahogany.

"What manner of man are you?" she breathed.

"A man with control," he said simply.

"How did you learn to control your body so completely, *mon amour*?"

His lips twitched with amusement. "Controlling the body is child's play. The emotions and the mind are slightly more difficult. Controlling others, however, took years of practice."

"What are you?" she whispered, half afraid.

"Sometimes an Arab, sometimes a Norman." His finger flew from her mons to her lips and his eyes slewed to the heavy door. A moment's focused concentration told him St. Lô approached. The door latch moved, but the bar prevented it from swinging open. Then a low knock came. Lisette gasped. He had felt the presence long before there was any sound. She pointed to a door that led out onto the battlements and reached for a robe. "Whoever it is, I'll get rid of him. Just give me a moment."

The cool evening breeze dried the sheen of sweat that glistened upon his dark skin. He gazed toward the sea where England lay beyond. The French and the English hated each other with a vengeance. The English thought all French unmanly fops who cared more for clothes than war. The French thought the English uncouth, uncultured, aleswilling louts.

In that moment Hawksblood experienced a revelation. His blood was half Anglo-Norman. He could not sell his sword to France. He would go to England to seek out the Earl of Warrick. Did not England's laws of primogeniture award the eldest son the title and the whole of the estate?

Christian took a step toward Lisette's turret chamber, then halted in his tracks. A picture of his "lady" shimmered so brightly before him, he felt he might reach out to touch her. He saw her eyes for the first time. They were liquid with tears. Green and gold flecks shone through the diamond-like drops that hovered on her lashes.

A fierce protectiveness rose up in him. He felt her pain,

her sensitivity, her vulnerability. The experience was new to him. Though he had vowed as a knight to protect womanhood, he had never met a female who stirred any emotion beyond lust.

He reached out and a teardrop fell upon his brown hand. He had apported it from midair by magic power. He tasted it and all desire for another melted away like snow in summer. He gathered taut his muscles, swung lithely over the crenellated battlements, then climbed down the castle wall. Without rope or other device the feat was almost impossible, but Drakkar's training made it as simple as climbing down a ladder.

Back in his pavilion, Christian lay supine upon his bed, his arms folded beneath his head. He tested his senses.

All seven of them.

He saw the faint glow of moonlight through the silken ceiling, casting all into shadow. The shape of the unlit bronze lamp contrasted with a matching incense burner. The outline of Salome upon her perch was fiercely proud even in her sleep. His glance roamed the tent, seeing all, missing no finest detail.

He could smell almond and frankincense from his own body. He could also smell the sandalwood incense burning low. It did not mask the faint ammonia of the gerfalcon's droppings. From outside he could smell the smoke of the campfires, the fat drippings from the roasted game, the odor of sour wine mingled with the cheap scent of the whores. He smelled the rich brown soil, the tethered horses, chestnut trees, and beyond all, the tang of the sea.

Christian could feel the cool night air upon his skin. Beneath his back and buttocks the linen sheet was rough-textured. His fingers felt the warmth of the amber in his silver amulets. His body heat made the metal almost hot.

He could faintly taste the saffron and fennel from the meal he'd taken at the castle. The bouquet of the rich red wine lingered upon his tongue. He could also taste the iodine and salt in the sea air. Most subtle of all was the taste of the teardrop, warm and softly scented. His body stirred. His mind controlled it immediately and moved on to his sense of hearing.

One by one he blocked out the raucous sounds of

drunken laughter, music, barking dogs, restless horses and identified the sounds of nature. A faint breeze rustled the leaves, the fires crackled, a nearby stream gurgled, a night heron's cry carried from miles away. Without strain, his acute hearing identified his own heartbeat, then that of his hunting hawk.

He moved on to his sixth sense. Intuition was acute awareness when all the other senses were heightened. It was developed easily enough through deprivation. When his mentors had blindfolded him for seven days, his other senses gradually heightened to compensate for his eyes, until finally he had learned to ride, then fight in combat, seeing with only his mind's eye.

His seventh sense was still developing. Only occasionally had he reached this perfect state. It required that he go inside, deeper and deeper to the core where the supreme power known as Godhead could be tapped into.

Christian knew he was about to experience one of his "visions." There was a bright flash behind his eyes, then vivid scenes crowded one upon another. He was on a coast among a fleet of ships. When he realized the place would best be viewed from above, he elevated high above the masts of the sailing vessels so he could see the activities of the men below him. Knowledge came to him immediately that what he saw was the French fleet. Before his vision faded, he knew the exact number of ships and the location where the fleet was gathering.

Hawksblood let go of his control and slept. His mind now freed of its rigid constraints raced like an untethered stallion across the desert sand. His mind envisioned the elusive object of his deepest desire, yet whimsically allowed him the use of only one of his senses. Maddeningly he could not smell, taste, or touch. And so Christian set about looking.

Really looking. And found her.

Her skin was translucent as if it had been dusted with powdered pearls. Her lashes were dark, tipped with gold, over hazel eyes that changed color from brown to gold to green. Her nose was small, yet the nostrils flared sensually. Her lips were not fashionably pursed or pouting, but full, lusty, and colored deepest rose. Her chin displayed a dimple, nowhere near as marked as the cleft in his own, but nevertheless it was a sign of willfulness.

Her throat curved beautifully, drawing the eye to lush breasts of alabaster. He could see tiny blue veins beneath the fine skin. Her breasts were crowned by buds of deepest rose, the color of her mouth. If he could touch her, he knew his hands could span her waist, and he longed to brush the backs of his fingers across the fine down upon her belly and soft thighs. From between those thighs her mons rose high, crowned by red-gold ringlets so tempting he would have sold his soul to part them and explore the secret path that led to the treasure within.

Her hair, like a golden mantle, shimmered with light and fire. He knew a need to bind himself in it, to breathe its fragrance and taste its texture. In his dream she turned from him and he glimpsed a witch-mark upon her buttock that matched the tiny black dot on her cheekbone.

He strained against the forces that prevented him from touching her. The barrier could not be breached. Then suddenly a madness gripped him. No force on earth could keep him from possessing her. A blinding, bursting explosion of willpower swept away all impediment.

He was transformed into the black stallion, relentlessly pursuing a cream-colored Arabian mare. Her eyes were large, almond-shaped, and liquid with fear. Her neck arched high, proudly displaying the long, silken mane that the wind swept back across her shapely flanks as she tried to flee.

He ran her to earth. She trembled before her savage captor. His teeth bit cruelly into her neck, then he ruthlessly mounted her and mated her. When she screamed with his wild thrusts, his seed gushed into her.

Christian's eyes flew open just in time to see a fountain of pearly drops arc from his body to fall upon the sheet. He flushed in the darkness and cursed. He hadn't disgraced himself in a nocturnal dream since he was a boy of ten. His vision was to blame. So much for control, he thought ruefully.

Brianna had a restless night. When she awoke she could not recall the dark shadows that had prevailed in her dreams and was thankful for it. Before she broke her fast, there was a page at the door informing her that Princess Isabel had decided to go hawking today. Brianna was relieved there would be no time to attend chapel.

"Yer bath's ready, my lamb."

"Adele, you are so very good to me, but I must hurry or Isabel will be in the devil's own temper," Brianna said, stepping into the tub. "Just grab a riding tunic from my wardrobe, any will do."

"She's still a child. 'Tis shameful she's allowed to tyrannize her elders," Adele sympathized.

"Jesu, don't call her a child within her hearing. She's fourteen and never tires of pointing out her mother wed King Edward when she was her age."

A young chambermaid came in with a tray of food. There were little varlet rolls, a pot of honey, and a jug of mead. When a timid knock came upon the door, Adele ushered in an imp-faced page with a note. He looked like he wanted to flee, but Adele bade him wait for an answer.

The note from Joan of Kent read: *"B. Please forgive me. I hope your punishment was not severe. Wear something ravishing. I have plans! J."*

Brianna closed her eyes. Joan was plotting another escapade before the consequences of yesterday's antics were over and done with. As she glanced at the page she saw him look guiltily toward her worktable. She pounced on him, grabbing his ear. His cry of exaggerated pain was pitiful. "You little imp of Satan. Why did you ruin my parchment?"

He babbled denials and lies. Wisely she knew she would get nothing from him this way. The life of a royal page was one of survival. Up at four, running and fetching until their little legs almost dropped off, with naught but cuffs and curses for reward. Then at ten years when they became squires, the real misery began.

Brianna let go of his ear and popped a sugared almond into his mouth. "Did someone else tell you to do this?"

The snub-nosed child nodded.

"Then I cannot hold you to blame, can I?" she asked sweetly.

He shook his head.

"What's your name?"

"Randal," he replied.

The name and the red curls were vaguely familiar. "Are you Elizabeth Grey's brother?"

He nodded warily.

"If anyone tells you to ruin my parchments again, you won't do it, will you?"

"It was Princess Isabel," he blurted, confirming her suspicions.

The minutes were galloping by and she knew she must finish dressing. Brianna shoved a bread roll into his hand and pushed him out the door. Adele selected taupe velvet, but Brianna quickly shook her head and pulled a pale lavender underdress and dark violet tunic from the wardrobe. Adele plaited the right side of her hair while Brianna did the left. She pulled on her stockings, anchored them with lace garters, then dragged on soft chamois riding boots. She scooped up a pair of violet gauntlets embroidered with gold thread, drained her cup of mead, kissed Adele on the cheek, and breathlessly ran along the corridor to Joan of Kent's chambers.

Joan's waiting lady, Glynis, was Welsh and her dark hair and swarthy skin contrasted sharply with Joan's coloring. She was a font of information about what went on at Windsor and she was so superstitious she was also a source of amusement.

Brianna was surprised that Joan's hair was unbound. "You cannot hunt like that."

"I'm hunting a different quarry," Joan said, laughing, but she snatched up a silver-mesh snood and Brianna helped her tuck her tresses inside it. Once again the two girls picked up their skirts and ran like hoydens to the State Apartments overlooking the terrace.

Princess Isabel's bedchamber and dressing room were strewn with clothes she had tossed aside with displeasure.

When she set eyes on Brianna's dark violet and Joan's blush pink, she seethed with envy. Her bedchamber maids and ladies-in-waiting were almost in tears. One held up an azure blue while another proffered a smart black velvet. Isabel was the only dark Plantagenet, with her mother's Flemish coloring. She was an attractive young woman whose sullen mouth marred her looks.

Joan winked at Brianna. "You will look lovely in the azure, Your Highness."

Brianna let her anger toward the young princess slip away. She agreed with Joan's choice with all her heart. "The color is so vivid, it will contrast with your dark hair, Your Highness."

Isabel immediately chose the black velvet. Joan suppressed a bubble of pleasure; the black would turn her complexion to mud. With studied innocence, Joan said, " 'Tis a pity the king forbids you to ride far afield. The morning sunshine cries out for a long gallop."

Isabel rounded on Joan. "Whatever do you mean? I go wherever I wish to go."

"Oh certes, Your Highness, I didn't mean to imply His Majesty has you on a leading string. All I meant was your brother, Prince Lionel, is allowed to ride all the way to Berkhamsted. It seems unfair when he's younger than you."

"Lionel is mad to become as proficient at bearing arms as the Prince of Wales. That's the reason he's forever riding to our brother's castle of Berkhamsted."

Lady Elizabeth Grey sighed. "All men believe success in arms is the one thing worth living for. My brother trained with a blunted sword when he turned seven."

Isabel said proudly, "My brother Edward started lessons with real weapons before he was ten."

Brianna pointed out, "Ah, but Prince Edward at ten was as physically mature as any sixteen-year-old."

"Yes," agreed Isabel, "that's the Plantagenet blood. My father is the most spectacular warrior in Christendom and Edward is champion of all tournaments at only sixteen."

"Men think of nothing but honing their fighting skills," lamented Elizabeth.

"Then it's up to us to give them something else to think about," Joan suggested.

Isabel's mouth went sulky. "Now that Edward has his own army, all the attractive young men are at Berkhamsted. Your brother Edmund is there, I believe."

Joan jumped on her words immediately. She suspected Isabel had a fancy for her disreputable young brother, the Earl of Kent. "Yes, my brother is with yours. Did you know he is secretly enamored of you, Your Highness? What a pity we cannot visit them." She sighed with exaggerated resignation.

May God forgive you for the lie, thought Brianna.

Isabel's ladies plaited her hair and fashioned a coronet of braids held in place by jeweled hairpins. She eyed Brianna's embroidered hunting gauntlets and selected an impractical pair for herself that was encrusted with pearls and moonstones.

By the time the ladies arrived in the courtyard, the grooms were standing patiently with their saddled horses. The falconers stood outside the mews, holding the ladies' birds of prey. Each hawk had jesses attached to its legs with two bells engraved with the owner's name. Falconry had its own rigid rules of etiquette. Only royalty was permitted to fly falcons, which were considered noble and ranked higher even than eagles.

Brianna owned a merlin, most of the other young ladies flew sparrow hawks, but Joan preferred a tiny kestrel because of her small size. Isabel carried a male falcon, called a tercel, on her wrist only as a status symbol. She was not skilled at the sport.

As the grooms mounted to accompany the princess and her ladies, Isabel said imperiously, "We ride to Berkhamsted!"

The grooms exchanged looks of alarm.

Brianna and Joan exchanged looks of triumph.

Before they had ridden two miles, the princess became angry because her falcon's talons had torn some of the pearls from her gauntlet. She handed her bird over to a groom and ordered the others do likewise. They would never cover the distance with hawks perched on their wrists.

When the party of ladies arrived at Berkhamsted, the guard on the watchtower signaled the man on the portcullis to raise it immediately. Ten females accompanied by their grooms were no threat to a castle of three hundred men. As they rode across the inner drawbridge into the bailey, the servants, squires, and soldiers around the barracks gaped openly at the fashionable young women.

The Prince of Wales' castellan approached with an insincere welcome. He wondered what the devil the young princess was thinking of to intrude upon this stronghold of men.

"I've come to surprise my brother. Where is he?"

The castellan, being one himself, knew how much men loved surprises. "Prince Edward is training with his men-at-arms, Your Highness. I beg you come to the hall and refresh yourself."

Isabel looked him up and down. "Yes, we shall certainly avail ourselves of Berkhamsted's hospitality *after* we've surprised Edward."

As they rode the length of the bailey, Brianna saw that it was almost like a village with hens and dogs. A vast smithy producing lance heads and arrowpoints stood next to a shed where the armorers were repairing weapons and armor. An outdoor cookhouse was roasting ten sheep on its spits. Isabel pinched her nose at the smell of mutton fat. Brianna licked her lips over the delicious aroma.

The ladies rode through the quintain yard, drawing every eye. They laughed with amusement as a young warrior was knocked senseless by the heavy sandbag that swung round relentlessly because he had looked at the ladies, forgetting to duck. Scores of young men were training in the tilt yard. It was a dangerous place to be amidst splintering lances and flying chargers' hooves.

A blond demi-god in chain mail, carrying a broadsword, descended purposefully upon them. Elizabeth Grey screamed. Joan sighed.

"There you are, Edward," cried Isabel.

"Bella, what the hellfire are you playing at?"

"We've ridden all the way from Windsor to surprise you."

"Well, you can turn around and ride back again," Edward said bluntly.

The heir to the throne had a lightning temper, but his sister was merely a nuisance. The young men with whom he'd been practicing swordplay gathered behind him, grinning openly at Brianna, Joan, and the other delectable females who had suddenly emerged through a sea of males.

Isabel's cheeks flamed. "How dare you welcome Lionel and send me packing? When Father learns of your shabby treatment he'll call you to task." She looked with distaste at the sweat and blood on him.

"When Father learns you've ridden farther than Windsor's forests he'll warm your arse!"

A trill of laughter escaped from Joan's lips. Edward's brow cleared. "I'd know that laugh anywhere." He came to stand by Joan of Kent's palfrey. They were cousins and had played together as children. "Little Jeanette, how are you?"

Though Joan was a year older than Prince Edward, his great height and physical maturity made him seem at least ten years her senior. From beneath her lashes she saw the beads of sweat glistening on his face, saw the blood-streaked dirt along the muscles of his bare arms. Suddenly all she could think of was what it would feel like to trace a finger over those muscles. She forgot to breathe. He was her golden god, always had been, always would be. With a dizzying effort she regained her composure and raised her lashes. Her eyes sparkled as they looked down into his. "Is it not part of a knight's training to learn respect for women? Think of us as an opportunity to teach chivalry."

"Little minx," he murmured. He strode back to Isabel and said grudgingly, "Well, I suppose we have to eat anyway. Allow me to extend the hospitality of Berkhamsted. You may stay for the midday meal."

Princess Isabel was all smiles now she'd achieved her objective. She would have thrown a tantrum had she realized it was Joan of Kent who had wooed him into a giving mood.

The castle chamberlain showed the princess to a private chamber. At the door she said, "I'll only need Elizabeth," and shut it in the other girls' faces.

Brianna, refusing to blush, asked the chamberlain to show them to a garderobe. There was no scented water, no facilities at all for gently bred ladies in this male stronghold.

Joan pulled on Brianna's sleeve. "Come or we'll miss all the fun of passing the towel."

In the hall their birds of prey sat on the perch provided for visitors' hawks. The grooms who had accompanied them had already gone into the dining hall, which was filling up quickly with the young men who made up the heir to the throne's army.

Joan pulled Brianna to the lavatory close to the entrance of the hall, which contained washstands with pitchers and basins. The men surrounding the two females immediately began to tease and flirt with them. Brianna of Bedford had many would-be suitors who took this opportunity to vie for her attention. She laughed with them all, taking care not to single out anyone.

Joan slipped in beside Edward. "May I have the soap, Your Highness?"

He looked down in horror. "Didn't my bloody chamberlain show you to a private room?"

"Yes, but Isabel wouldn't share it with us." She laughed up into his handsome face, unable to hide her admiration from him.

"She's such a spoiled little bitch," he complained.

"Perhaps she's paying us back for the wretched things we did to her when we were children. Do you remember?" she asked breathlessly.

His blue eyes crinkled. "We were true conspirators." He had always been so fond of Joan, or little Jeanette, as he called her. In proximity to her he suddenly recalled she had been responsible for his first erection at twelve.

Suddenly she touched his face. "You have a smear of blood, just here."

He lathered his face, rinsed it, then reached for the towel. Joan whisked it away with a whoop of laughter and tossed it to Brianna. He grabbed Joan, lifting her high in the air, digging his fingers into her ribs to tickle her as if she were a child. Suddenly her hair net fell off and her silvery-gilt hair came tumbling down over his hands. He set her feet to the ground and their laughter fled as they stood looking at each other with heightened awareness.

"Sweet," he murmured for her ears alone.

At table a tall salt cellar divided the diners by rank. Field churls, servants, squires, and the visiting grooms sat below the salt, while high officers of the household, prominent guests, and members of the nobility joined the Plantagenets above the salt. Five young nobles jostled for seats that would place them directly across from Brianna of Bedford and Joan of Kent.

The castle seneschal presided over the meal and its servers. Today he had to do more than keep track of the silver spoons and knives, he had to see that the ladies were served first, that the drinking cups were kept filled, that the food was served while it was still hot, while at the same time keeping the squires from impropriety. His fierce glare promised retribution to any who spat, wiped their nose, or picked their teeth. To their credit some of them even remembered not to gobble down everything in sight and saved something for the poor basket.

Princess Isabel sat between her brothers, Prince Edward and Prince Lionel, which Brianna thought was a pity. It made her look like a crow among peacocks. Her younger brother, Lionel, was a blond giant with a ruddy complexion. He was no scholar, could neither read nor write, but he had an easygoing personality. He was good-natured even when drunk, which was every night according to gossip.

From her seat, which flanked the head table, Brianna studied the heir to the throne. He was already kinglike in appearance and manner. As well as being the Prince of Wales, he was Earl of Chester, Duke of Cornwall, and when his father was abroad, he was Guardian of the Kingdom. Edward was very tall with high cheekbones and an aquiline nose, a little blunted at the tip like his father's, and he had the same all-seeing blue eyes. His vitality and golden hair lent him a brilliant aura and all seeing him knew he was marked by destiny to be a great leader of men.

Brianna bent toward Joan so she could whisper. "You were flirting with Edward. Have you set your cap for him?"

"Of course not. We are cousins. Flirting comes naturally to me."

The corners of Brianna's mouth went up. Joan was such a mixture of honesty and deception, there was never a dull moment with such an amusing friend. "Then why did you maneuver Isabel into riding to Berkhamsted?"

Joan ate with gusto. She licked her fingers daintily. "Open your eyes. The flower of England's nobility sits across from us. Surely you are not blind to the hot, hungry looks cast your way?"

Brianna glanced at the table opposite. Her eyes widened as she saw Sir John Chandos, William de Montecute, Robert de Beauchamp, Roger de Cheyne, and Michael de la Pole, all heirs to great earldoms, watching her with avid interest. She smiled shyly, unable to keep a blush from her cheeks. Any one of them looked ready to woo and win her. Her glance moved down the trestle table identifying sons of Neville and Percy, the two great Lords of the North. Sir John Holland was staring at Joan with open lust. "It will do no good to allow your fancy to fall where your heart leads. The king will choose our husbands."

Joan sighed. "You are so practical, Brianna. You are right, of course, but even the king cannot deprive us of our fantasies."

The young men across the hall were indulging a few fantasies of their own. The highborn royal wards were off-limits for dalliance, although their maids and serving women were fair game for bedding. Still, virgins who invaded a male bastion of three hundred strong might be ripe for plucking . . . or fucking!

Princess Isabel turned up her nose at the mutton and bade her serving squire fetch her venison. She refused the ale and demanded wine.

Lionel said, laughing, "Good girl, that leaves more for me."

Edward said bluntly, "Wine is reserved for the evening meal."

"Have you no minstrels or jongleurs? Whatever do you do for entertainment?"

"We prefer whores, Isabel," Lionel said, emptying his fourth tankard.

Edward kicked him in the shins. "Bella, my men are here to learn warfare. I myself am here to learn how to train and lead armies. We are striving for knighthood, not dalliance with fair demoiselles."

"Speak for yourself, brother," Lionel said, dropping his great paw onto Lady Elizabeth Grey's knee.

Edward fixed him with an ice-blue stare. "You and your men will escort Isabel back to Windsor this afternoon."

"Shit!" Lionel cursed, giving Isabel a look of disgust. Then he shrugged good-naturedly and turned all his attention to a giggling Lady Grey.

Prince Edward excused himself, then sent a page running to summon Robert de Beauchamp, who was the highest-ranking officer in his young brother's service. As Robert walked toward him, the Prince of Wales noted the similarity between Lionel and his lieutenant. Although Beauchamp was older, he was another exceedingly attractive blond giant with a laughing, open countenance.

"The Duke of Clarence will be escorting Princess Isabel and her ladies back to Windsor this afternoon. He looks up to you, Beauchamp. Try to set an example and for God's sake keep him from lifting the ladies' tunics. If he wants to come back to Berkhamsted next week, discourage him."

"Has he offended you, Your Highness?"

"Nay." Edward shook his head. "I can't help liking the young devil, but his drunkenness and lechery are demoralizing for the men. His appetites are insatiable. His mind is never off his gut or his dangling gut."

"He came to manhood early," Beauchamp excused, smiling.

Prince Edward gave him a scathing look. "There is more to manhood than drinking and fucking. In any case, I'll be moving the men to Windsor soon. They would benefit from some of your father's harsh training." He clapped him on the back, wondering why the great Earl of Warrick's son had chosen to be in his brother's service rather than his. Warrick, marshal of all the king's armies, was nicknamed the Mad Hound because of his fierce temper and fighting skills. Warrick's son obviously had a milder nature.

When Edward bade his siblings good-bye, he thawed somewhat toward his young sister. "Sweeting, don't look so down in the mouth. I'll be back at Windsor in a fortnight." His eyes were drawn to Joan of Kent. William de

Montecute and John Holland were both hovering to lift her into her saddle. Edward was not surprised. To him, she was the most deliciously feminine creature in all of England.

He helped Isabel to mount, then raised his voice so that little Jeanette could hear. "When I return, I promise to take you hawking. We'll make a merry day of it."

Lionel lifted Elizabeth Grey onto her palfrey, managing to touch her in several intimate places with his big hands.

Brianna jumped as she heard a man's voice close behind her. She spun about and had to look up.

"May I assist you to mount, demoiselle?" He dipped one knee and held his hands together so she could place her booted foot in them. Brianna stood mesmerized for a moment, held in thrall by the unusual color of his eyes. He stood patiently in what must have been an awkward position.

"Sorry," she murmured with a smile of thanks, noticing the other young nobles casting envious glances at the man who was aiding her to mount. For the next five miles she argued with herself whether Robert de Beauchamp's eyes were turquoise or aquamarine.

When the fingers of dawn spread up the sky, it revealed to the French that the foreign dog and his squires had folded their tent and vanished like thieves in the night. As they made their way to the coast, Hawksblood informed his companions of his decision to go to England. There had never been the slightest doubt in Ali's mind where Drakkar was heading. He had known he was on the path of Destiny just as surely as his lord knew, if he but looked deep enough to acknowledge it.

Paddy was less philosophical, but infinitely more practical. Transportation across the Channel would be a bit of a problem with six valuable horses and a mountain of baggage.

"I don't suppose there'll be any excursion boats," he said dryly. "Will I commandeer a vessel at sword point?"

Hawksblood replied, "The simple expedient of bribery should suffice from what I've learned of the French."

Paddy grinned at Ali. "That's your forte, boyo."

"You have learned a new word. Your mental powers never cease to amaze me," Ali mocked.

The Irishman, always needing the last word, quoted a Bedouin maxim: "The beauty of man lies in the eloquence of his tongue." Even Hawksblood was impressed with that one.

They rode into an inn yard, then Ali slipped away to the wharfs. He chose a vessel that regularly transported men and horses between Cherbourg and Calais. The amount of the bribe easily covered the risk of the extra twenty miles to Dover. They departed on the evening tide before darkness fell, but the big Norman and his squires aroused no curiosity in a port the size of Cherbourg.

Ali remained in the hold to watch over their precious mounts. Warhorses were bred with vicious tempers, but the singsong cadence of his voice could calm them instantly if they became restive. Paddy paced the deck, trying not to show his excitement at returning to Britain for the first time in fifteen years. He'd been aboard a ship that was wrecked near Greece. It seemed a lovely warm place to live until the Turks overran the place. That's where he'd learned his warrior skills, fighting the mad Turks. Eventually, he'd been captured and rotted in a Turkish prison until the Islamic warriors called Ottomans conquered all of Byzantium.

Christian, or Drakkar as he called himself then, was a Janissary in the corps d'elite of the Ottoman armies. When he freed Paddy from the Turkish prison, he owned him. Paddy's life or death depended on the young Janissary with the face of a fierce hawk and the body of a Norman warrior. Paddy suspected he had been kept alive because he amused his new master. He still did.

Christian stood frowning at a small animal in a cage so cramped it couldn't turn around. It had the brightest eyes he'd ever seen.

"What the hell is it?" he asked Paddy.

"Looks like a black-footed ferret to me. Shall I set it free?"

"If you don't, I will," Christian agreed.

"Mon Dieu! Tenez-vous-en! Cease!" bellowed the captain.

Paddy never took orders from anyone except Hawksblood. The instant he sprang the door of the cage, the ferret shot out, flashed across the deck, ran up the captain's thigh, and bit him on the balls. Paddy and Christian whooped with laughter.

Not so the Frenchman. Screaming a filthy oath, he grabbed the creature by the throat and flung it overboard. Christian stopped laughing and went to the rail to peer down into the pewter water. The black-footed, bright-eyed creature treaded water frantically, then disappeared beneath a swell. In a moment it surfaced, but its distance from the ship increased steadily.

Christian pulled off his boots and chain mail and dove into the sea. The ferret climbed to his shoulder, then fastened its claws into his long hair and held on for dear life. Paddy helped Christian back aboard as calmly as if Hawksblood had been for his daily dip.

The captain and crew were having fits. "You must be insane to risk your life for a rat catcher!"

Christian looked at him with scorn. "You must be insane to fear a six-inch scrap of fur."

Paddy helped him replace his mail, then his doublet, and the shivering ferret disappeared inside. The captain opened his mouth to speak, saw the savage ferocity on the dark face and thought better of it.

Paddy murmured, "He's affeared if he opens his gob again, ye'll set the little gnasher on him."

Christian's lip twitched as he moved aft. The sea had been unbelievably cold. As he felt the wet chausses cling to his body, he separated his mind from the physical discomfort, knowing the stiff sea breeze would soon dry his garments.

The sky darkened and one by one the stars appeared. Astronomy had been a favorite subject when he was eight. After initiation into the Mystic Order of the Golden Dawn he'd been expected to name the stars down to the fourth magnitude, and see those as faint as the sixth. His gaze passed over Rigel and Regulus, Alpha Centauri and Altair. They seemed like old friends to him. It was another hour before the moon rose. When it did, however, Hawksblood became aware of a faint reflection, leagues behind them, but gradually gaining.

He stood transfixed, concentrating, focusing his full attention. He penetrated the barriers of distance and darkness for a few split seconds, but that was enough to tell him it was a French cog, small but swift. Logic told him piracy was best done in daylight, so this was probably a raiding party on its way to the English coast.

He moved toward the prow and again focused all his attention. Eventually, he saw the faint outline of the stone fortress atop the chalk cliffs of Dover. Hawksblood spoke quietly to the captain, who shuttered the ship's lantern. Then he went to the navigator at the wheel, pointed out the cliffs, which were only just becoming visible, and swept his arm to the south, indicating the direction he desired. The navigator, uncertain in English waters, followed Hawksblood's instructions to the letter. Hawksblood spoke with such confidence that he generated confidence.

The vessel was able to drop anchor in a sandy cove long enough to discharge its cargo, then slip away into the darkness.

"Since Dover is the gateway to England, it is bound to be garrisoned." Christian kept his voice low, knowing how sounds were magnified by wind and water.

"There's a watch all along the coast. They use a system of signal fires," Paddy explained.

Hawksblood smiled grimly. "You alert the watch; I'll set the signal fire."

Ali did not feel slighted that the task of seeing to the extra horses and baggage fell to him. After a lifetime together, he and Drakkar could communicate without words.

Hawksblood tightened the girth on his destrier and rode slowly along the coastline. His eyes were fixed on a black dot out to sea that sailed ever closer. He waited silently over an hour for the cog to sail close enough to disgorge its raiders. Every instinct screamed to descend upon them like death on the wind, but he schooled himself to patience until the last mounted man spurred from the sands.

He boarded the cog stealthily, listening for the skeleton crew. His nose led him to the tar barrels. A ship's lantern did the rest. By the time the explosion came, he was safely ashore.

The fire lit up the sky, drawing Paddy and the soldiers from the garrison of Dover. They killed or captured every last raider, for the French had no retreat. The prisoners were herded into Dover Castle, where the Admiral of the Cinque Ports, Robert Morley, extended his personal thanks to Christian Hawksblood and offered hospitality.

"Too bad His Majesty wasn't here to witness this. He was here until yesterday recruiting ships to sail against France. I'm sending twenty of my best. He's gone back to Windsor for the annual tournament."

Christian was dismayed. Twenty ships seemed so few against the might of France. "Surely the tournament will be canceled now that war threatens?"

Admiral Morley hooted with laughter. "You don't know Edward Plantagenet. Scotland and France may be threatening war, his debt to the Bardi bankers is nine hundred thousand florins and that's all spent on past campaigns; now he's borrowing for the wars that are pending, but nothing will stand in the way of the king's tournaments."

Christian Hawksblood wondered what he was getting himself into. A poverty-stricken country with a debt-ridden king and court made his prospects seem bleak. He gritted his teeth. He had made his decision and he would stick with it for better or worse. With resolution, Hawksblood and company were on the road to Windsor the next morning.

King Edward entered his wife's luxurious bedchamber and bent to bestow a kiss on Philippa's lips. "Sweetheart, how are you feeling?" He pressed a gold casket into her hands and strode across the chamber to peer into the cradle at his newest daughter.

"Edward, you are too good to me. You shouldn't give me jewels," Philippa protested.

"You give me precious sons and daughters and I give you precious little in return."

"Edward, you lavish gifts upon me. All I ask is your love."

"You will always have that, sweetheart. Don't deny me the pleasure of giving you a few trinkets."

The queen's ladies sighed at the king's devotion. Still in his thirties, he was the handsomest man in all Christendom. Every heart in the room fluttered wildly. He had a smile and a wink for every pretty face, but he was totally devoted to Queen Philippa. He never seemed to notice that her body had thickened from constant childbearing and her face and hair were much faded.

"I want you to be rested for all the entertainments we'll have at the tournament. I've decided to build a great round tower. Come to the window, love, and I'll show you." He slipped a strong arm about her and pointed. "The Upper Ward has only rectangular towers, but the Edward III Tower must be round so that I can re-create King Arthur's legendary round table. I've decided to found an order of chivalry. Only the premier knights of the realm will be inducted. If we start the building now, it should be ready in time for next year's tournament. We'll get that beautiful stone from Bedfordshire. What d'you think?"

"I'll mention it to Lady Bedford. Have you thought any more about her betrothal?"

"I've had at least a dozen petition me for her hand, but Warrick has spoken for her so the matter is settled. Speaking of betrothals, I think your idea of a marriage between the Prince of Wales and Margaret of Brabant is excellent. We must keep our allies, or France will woo them away from us."

"Have you spoken to Edward about it?" Philippa asked.

"Not recently, but he's always known that Margaret's name was on the list put forward by the Council. I'll send for him."

"No need, Edward, he's already here. I knew the tournament would draw him like a lodestone."

"Shall I carry you down to the hall tonight, sweetheart, or I could sup here with you, if you like?"

"Nonsense. You enjoy the company and the entertainment, and your sons and Isabel will want to dine with you." She saw that her rooms caged him. He had too much vital energy to play lapdog. He was an indulgent father and the most courteous and loving husband a woman could ever hope for.

He helped her back to her couch and pressed her hands to his lips. "Thank you, Philippa. I have a hundred urgent things to attend to, but you and the children come first. Never forget that."

When he left the Queen's Tower, King Edward made his way from the Upper Ward all the way down to the residences of his military knights in the Lower Ward where Katherine de Montecute was lodged while her husband, the Earl of Salisbury, was fighting in France.

When she saw that the king had come openly to her apartments, her hand flew to her throat. "You have news of William, Your Majesty." She saw pain in his blue eyes and knew the news was not good. She dismissed her servants and searched his face with growing alarm. Her head veil slipped to the carpet through nerveless fingers.

Her beauty took his breath away. She was exquisitely fine-boned, her hair a rippling golden glory. "William has been taken prisoner," he said gently.

A cry escaped her lips, then the king's arms enfolded her, trying to take her hurt into himself. She sobbed against his powerful shoulder, her tears ruining the fine double-piled velvet of his surcoat.

"Hush, Katherine, I will do all in my power to obtain his release."

She pulled slightly away from him to raise tear-drenched eyes to his. Her lips trembled. "Truly?" She felt so guilty, she wanted to die. She saw no sign of guilt, however, in Edward's deep blue eyes.

"Katherine, he is my friend. I will pay whatever ransom Philip demands."

Relief swept through her. Relief that William was not dead; relief that Edward was ever chivalrous. Though they both deeply loved their spouses, this attraction between them had been instantaneous. The raging desire between them was uncontrollable. Neither of them had ever strayed from their marriage bed until they had beheld each other that fateful day almost a year ago.

When he felt her go limp, his arm slipped beneath her knees and he lifted her against his chest, cradling her. "I hunger for you, Katherine. I cannot live another hour without you."

Dear God, they had no conscience. Their carnal need for each other had destroyed it. Consumed by a hot, raging fire, the king carried her to the bed.

When Adele opened the door to an imperious knock, the king's own messenger handed her a note addressed to Lady Bedford.

Brianna broke the king's seal with her thumbnail and scanned the bold writing. It read: "Kindly attend me in the Presence Chamber at the hour of vespers. Edward Plantagenet."

"Yes, please inform His Majesty I am honored to attend him."

The first thing that came to mind was that Dame Marjorie had reported her. Brianna sank down upon a stool with watery knees. "Adele, will you come with me?"

"Of course I shall attend you, it is only proper that I do so. Perhaps he has chosen someone for you at long last."

Brianna's heart raced. "Oh, do you think it may be so?" She acknowledged to herself it was a possibility. Brianna was suddenly breathless. "By Our Lady, I don't think I'm ready for this."

"Of course you are, my lamb. Most ladies are betrothed at fifteen."

"Whatever shall I wear? I must look my best." Her mind raced as erratically as her pulse. She felt more excited than she could ever recall. "Something green, I think."

"Green is the color of true love," Adele said, smiling.

"Oh, please don't tease me, Adele. Green brings out the red highlights in my hair. We must hurry. I need time to go into the chapel for a special prayer."

Brianna sank to her knees before the statue of St. Agnes. Like every other girl, she had prayed on the night of January 20 when it was traditionally thought possible a young woman could receive a revelation of her future husband. She had seen no vision, of course, but fervently hoped St. Agnes would help her today. Brianna hesitated. Young women were taught not to expect too much of their husbands. Men's ways must be accepted, like stormy weather or the pain of childbirth. She decided not to ask for too much, lest Heaven think her greedy. "Please let him be honorable, brave, and strong." She crossed herself. "And if it isn't asking too much, let him be noble."

Her father had been an earl, and though she knew she couldn't look that high, she dreaded the scorn of Princess Isabel if she were given to a man who had no hope of a title.

She wore a seafoam green underdress with a jade velvet tunic, caught at the waist by a girdle of real gold set with cabochon emeralds. Brianna believed the green gems had magic power to keep her safe from evil spirits—even from the mischievous harm of goblins and bad fairies. Her world was liberally sprinkled with spirits, undines, and other ministers of the devil.

Adele's clothes both contrasted with and complemented those of Lady Bedford. She wore a tasteful gray surcoat over a soft yellow kirtle. A fashionable wimple covered her hair. Only young maidens like Brianna were expected to wear their hair down. To be considered beautiful, it had to be the length of the arms. Adele took great pride in Brianna's golden hair. When brushed out, as it was now, the tendrils fell to her ankles like a cloak of silk.

They were admitted by yeomen into the Guard Chamber, which contained a collection of arms and weapons from the time of Great King Henry. Beyond this was the king's Presence Chamber, which was smaller, but far more sumptuously furnished with carpets, tapestries, a pair of massive gilt throne chairs, and smaller, padded chairs throughout.

The king was not alone when they entered, but the group of men with whom he'd been speaking left through double doors at the far end of the chamber. Edward Plantagenet strode down the room to welcome them. His smile lit up the chamber. "Do come in, Lady Bedford."

When she would have gone down into a curtsy, he took her hands. "No, no, we won't stand on ceremony."

Brianna took a deep breath to introduce her aunt. "Your Majesty—"

"No, don't tell me . . . it's Adele, your mother's sister, I believe. I never forget a pretty face."

Adele blushed to the roots of her hair, as if she had never felt prettier in her life.

"Sit!" Edward ordered. "Both of you."

They hesitated only a moment before they obeyed.

"I think better on my feet. Pay no attention, ladies. I beg you take no offense."

By protocol, they were the ones who offended by sitting in the king's presence while he remained standing.

"I have plans to do some building here at Windsor. A great round tower at the east corner of the Upper Ward. I have a fancy for your beautiful stone from Bedfordshire."

Brianna couldn't believe her ears. Stone! This audience with King Edward was about stone! She let out a long breath. She didn't know if she felt relief or disappointment. Then she realized she felt both. "Your Majesty, I am deeply honored that you have chosen stone from my lands in Bedfordshire."

"Good! My steward will get in touch with your Bedfordshire castellan and work out a fair price."

"Ah no, Your Majesty, I wouldn't dream of accepting money for my stone."

"God's Splendor, what an innocent you are. It's high time you had a husband to look after your affairs. I assure you he wouldn't let me rape your land without charging me an arm and a leg!"

It was Brianna's turn to blush.

Edward thought, *God's Splendor, she's a beauty.* His eyes candidly admired her glorious hair and her upthrusting breasts. She was enough to make a corpse quicken. His face softened at her youth. His blue eyes crinkled into a smile. "The Earl of Warrick is without. He's asked for a private word with you. Don't be afraid. His bark is worse than his bite. He has something very special he wants to ask you." The king took Adele's hand and led her from the chamber.

Brianna's mind refused to function. She stared at the tall, barrel-chested warrior as if she were witless. As Warrick, the Mad Hound, descended upon her, every instinct told her to flee. Her legs, however, had stopped functioning along with her brain. Her eyes widened as she took in the battle scars on his face. Dimly, in the far recesses of her mind, she recalled he had been widowed for five years. She had assumed at his age he would remain in that state.

Dame Marjorie's words came back to haunt her. *I shall advise the queen to betroth you to an older man who will rule you with an iron hand.* Brianna swallowed with difficulty, her mouth suddenly as dry as a desert.

"Lady Bedford." His voice was harsh. *From years of giving orders that must be obeyed,* Brianna told herself.

"My Lord W-Warrick," she whispered. Her father had warned her to be careful for what she prayed in case her prayers were answered. Whatever had she asked of St. Agnes? Honorable, brave, and strong. He was certainly all of those, she thought wildly. Why hadn't she asked for someone young?

Because she had been without a family from such a tender age, it was the thing she longed for most. She had been an only child whose constant companion had been loneliness. Her dreams were filled with the laughter and noise of the many children she would share with a special knight whom she prayed would be a strong, yet indulgent father. Together, they would become loving and devoted parents. Therein lay happiness and security, banishing loneliness forever.

Her hopes for the young knight who would father her babies faded away dismally and was replaced by the bleak vision of the stern, old warrior breeding his last progeny upon her young body.

The Mad Hound spoke. Brianna tried to hear his words over the roaring inside her ears.

"I knew your father well. He was a worthy knight."

"Thank you," she managed.

"I don't think he would have any objections to uniting our two houses in marriage."

Jesu, she had asked for someone noble. None stood higher than the Earl of Warrick in all the land. "Nay, my lord, you do me too much honor . . . I am not worthy."

"That is for me to decide." His words silenced her. Then, as if he had spoken too harshly, he offered a compliment. "You will make a beautiful bride. I am well pleased. However, the decision is yours. You are gently bred and seem over-young to a man of my years."

Jesu, he must be forty, perhaps fifty, she thought wildly. They would have nothing in common. He would be no companion with whom she could share laughter and love. Her loneliness would last a lifetime.

Brianna clutched at the word "over-young." That would be her excuse. She raised her lashes and saw the look of pride and hope written on his craggy face. Her tongue could not form the words to refuse him. "You do me much honor," she said woodenly, then lowered her lashes, but not before she had glimpsed a flash of aquamarine eyes. The eyes, identical to another's, caused a sharp pain in her chest. As Warrick loomed over her, she felt as if a dark cloud had settled above her. The pain was heavy. She wondered if she might die of it.

She had never felt so miserable. "I—I will need time," she temporized, hoping she didn't sound as desperate as she felt. "I think a long courtship best, so the c-couple may get to know each other."

Warrick laughed. "I leave the courtship and the wooing to Robert, now that I know you are agreeable to a match with my son."

Suddenly the dark cloud departed and the sun came out. "Robert de Beauchamp . . . ." Brianna murmured with delight. She caught her breath, remembering the intense gaze of his aquamarine eyes. Her world was unfolding as it should after all!

She offered a quick prayer of thanks to St. Agnes. Jesu, she had treated the great Earl of Warrick wretchedly. To compensate, she gave him a brilliant smile and sank into a deep curtsy. "You do me much honor." This time she said it with all her heart.

He offered his hand to raise her to her feet. She was all soft, womanly compliance. A real man's woman. God's Splendor, if he were a young warrior again—

Adele was awaiting Brianna in the Guard Chamber. Her face was filled with anxiety. In her agitation she had shredded the hem of her surcoat. "Oh, my lamb, did Warrick have marriage in mind?"

Brianna's mood was light and carefree. "Yes, you were right. The king did choose someone for me at long last."

"Oh, Mary and Joseph, did you agree to the match?" Adele asked wretchedly.

"Of course I did. I never dreamed of setting my sights so high. I shall be a countess."

"Yes, but—"

"Of course, that is for the future. I shall have to wait until my husband, Robert de Beauchamp, succeeds to the title of Earl of Warrick."

"Robert de Beauchamp? Oh, my lamb, I thought you were being betrothed to Warrick!"

Brianna's laughter trilled out happily. "Adele, whatever gave you such a ridiculous notion?"

🐚 5 🐚

Joan of Kent's heart soared with excitement. She had succeeded in luring Edward, Prince of Wales, back to Windsor. She had known he would return for the tournament, but that was still a week away!

Now that he was here she must use every feminine wile to fix his interest. She had been obsessed with the heir to the throne for so long, she knew his daily routine, his habits. He arose before dawn, slipped in and out of the chapel before matins, and exercised one of his horses before breaking his fast.

As Prince Edward slipped into the royal pew, the tail of his eye was caught by a tiny figure. Her veiled head was bent in devout prayer, but when she raised her eyes heavenward, his pulse leaped. Joan crossed herself, then daintily made her way toward the vestry.

Edward crossed himself, then hurried after her. "Jeanette . . . Joan . . . I thought it was you. Whatever are you about at this hour?"

Her eyes widened in pretended surprise. "I didn't want anyone to see me. I cannot make up my mind what to do with my life. I am contemplating taking the veil, Your Highness."

He was aghast. The white head scarf, held in place by a

golden circlet to cover her silvery blond hair, gave her the look of an angel with a halo. He saw the glint of mischief in her eye and they threw back their heads and laughed aloud. Realizing they were still in church, they covered their mouths and slipped outside into the dawn.

"You are an irreverent little minx. What are you really doing here?"

"An assignation, perhaps," she teased, looking at him from beneath her lashes.

Anger and lust shot through him swiftly as an arrow. It was a potent combination. His strong hands seized her tiny waist and he dipped his head to take her mouth.

Joan's heart soared. He was acting as if he wanted to put his brand on her. The kiss left both of them dizzy. Edward's body was so big and so hard, it was everything she'd ever dreamed it would be.

Desire made his loins clench; hot blood pounded at his temples. He didn't want to let her go, but he was acutely aware they could be seen by anyone who might be about. "Come to the stables with me," he said thickly.

Hoyden she may be, but whore, never. The look of hauteur she gave him almost froze him.

"I didn't mean . . . I meant we could ride together. Jesu, that sounds worse." He ran a distracted hand through his golden locks.

She took pity on him. The teasing light came back into her eyes. "I know a place where you can take me in your arms without causing gossip."

"Where?" he demanded, angered that such a tiny wench could wreak havoc with his emotions.

"In the dance. I shall save one for you tonight, Your Highness."

She left him in such a pronounced state of arousal, he had difficulty walking. It showed no sign of easing as he made his way to the stables. He knew riding was out of the question until his erection decreased in size, so he made his way to the river, knowing an icy plunge was the other remedy for a swollen cock.

Back in her chamber, Joan looked at her reflection in her polished silver mirror. She touched her lips in wonder. She vowed to carry the feel of his kiss on her mouth until he did it again. Tonight! Joan had never felt so happy in her life.

Brianna painted late into the evening, humming and singing happily as she brush-stroked the heavy vellum with brilliant pigments. She could not resist sketching her future name, Brianna de Beauchamp, surrounded by hearts and flowers. A shiver of delight ran through her body when she thought of her betrothed and recalled the intensity of his turquoise eyes when they had gazed into hers at Berkhamsted.

Suddenly Brianna gasped aloud, "Turquoise . . . aquamarine!" She realized Robert de Beauchamp must be the knight of her dreams; the unusual shade of his eyes was identical! She let out her breath in a sigh of longing. Could this really be happening to her? Was she fortunate enough to become the bride of the irresistible phantom knight of her dreams? If it was so, she thanked St. Agnes with all her heart for sending the vision. She moved dreamily toward the bed and turned back the covers with impatient fingers. Would he come to her tonight? The sooner she was abed, the sooner the dream would unfold. When at last her excitement calmed enough to allow sleep to claim her, the first knight to enter her dream was Warrick. He loomed large and fierce as ever, but she was not afraid. "I am well pleased you are agreeable to a match with my son." The vision of Warrick faded and his son stepped forward.

Brianna's breath caught in her throat as the tall figure beckoned to her. As always, desire overwhelmed her. She went to him willingly, wanting him to touch her, to kiss her, to carry her off to a secret place. She was giddy with joy as their hands touched and she laughed up at him, gazing deeply into the compelling aquamarine eyes.

"You are mine at last . . . I have come to claim you." His voice was deep and thrilling; his eyes smoldered with desire. He was large and hard and powerful, everything she'd ever wanted in a man. His face was so fiercely proud she could not resist tracing her finger over the wide, bold planes. She touched his cheekbones, ran her finger along his strong jawline, then dipped it into the cleft of his chin. When she succumbed to the temptation of touching his lips, he bit her. A deep thrill ran all the way up her arm and straight into her breast as if she had been pierced by Cupid's arrow. Her sensual laughter floated all about them, teasing him, tempting him, begging him to take further liberties. His lips hovered above the beauty mark upon her slanting cheekbone. "Will you permit me to taste your witch-mark?"

Her mouth curved with pleasure and she lifted her face to receive his kiss of homage. His powerful arms swept about her, his palms cupped her bottom, and she felt one of his fingers touch her other beauty mark. "This is the one I want to taste."

She saw his white teeth flash in a bold grin. No one had ever spoken so wickedly and intimately to her before, yet she loved it. Her eyes sparkled with laughter as she met boldness with boldness. "I'll let you taste it on our wedding night."

"If you make me wait until then, I'll devour you," he vowed.

Brianna's voice turned husky. "If you make me wait longer for your kiss, I'll scream."

His mouth swooped down possessively, stopping a heartbeat from its goal for the pure pleasure of heightening her desire. Her lovely eyes flashed with an answering challenge as she opened her mouth to scream. The moment her lips parted his own closed about them in an act of total possession. His hot mouth branded her, claiming her as his own, now and forever. Brianna moaned in her sleep. The sound awakened her. Her eyes flew open. She was breathless. Her body tingled with her first arousal. The delicious dream lingered in her memory, its details so vivid she could still smell his male scent of sandalwood and almond. Her phantom knight was indeed Warrick's son. His powerful physique and aquamarine eyes had proclaimed him a De Beauchamp, but her lover had not the golden coloring of Robert. His face had been fierce and swarthy. He had the dark, dangerous, and compelling beauty of Lucifer.

The Banqueting Hall at Windsor was impressive. A great deal of money had been lavished upon it to make it warm, inviting, and comfortable, yet at the same time maintain that magnificent regal quality so revered by the Plantagenet kings.

The spacious hall, however, was not nearly so spectacular as the Plantagenets themselves as they sat upon the royal dais, laughing, talking, shouting, eating, drinking, and glittering.

The king had a magnificent wardrobe; both his clothes and his jewels were dazzling. Tonight he was resplendent in crimson velvet doublet embroidered with golden leopards and lilies. He wore a small gold crown at a jaunty angle. His golden beard, though clipped close, had a tendency to curl. He wore a heavy gold chain and collar studded with rubies. The hand that lifted the jewel-encrusted goblet had a ring on every finger.

Princess Isabel sat next to him tonight in the queen's ornately carved chair. She wore white satin, her wide sleeves edged in sable. Her tall coronet was set with large carnelians and she wore a bracelet and ring with the same reddish-yellow stones. She adored attention, especially her father's, and whenever he conversed with the Prince of Wales, seated on his other side, Isabel interrupted to distract him.

Prince Edward's favorite color was black. He had begun wearing it when he was a boy to make him look older. Then he fancied it brought him luck, so now he even used black in his heraldic devices. Tonight he was in black, doublepiled velvet imported from Lucca. On Edward the color was anything but somber. It emphasized his golden hair, the color of ripe wheat, his sun-bronzed skin, and his startling white teeth. He affected no crown, but the collar of his doublet was studded with diamonds, which glittered brilliantly with every movement of his proud head.

Prince Lionel had chosen blue, which played down his ruddy complexion. The heavy gold chain and pendant of cabochon sapphires would have seemed like a millstone on a normal-sized youth, but Lionel's wide shoulders and broad chest displayed the costly piece to perfection.

Prince John, who had been born in Ghent, was still a boy, but he already had a brilliant intellect coupled with elegant taste. Because his head was tawny as a lion's mane, he knew green suited him best. He wore a short cape, lined with red fox, fastened with an emerald clasp the size of a pigeon's egg.

As Brianna's gaze traveled down the dais, she watched Prince John remove his cape and place it around little Blanche of Lancaster's shoulders. He cast Lionel a look of contempt for the scurrilous song he was singing, then moved Blanche away from his inebriated brother, so that she was closer to her father, the great Earl of Lancaster. Brianna's soft heart was touched by the gesture. The two were betrothed and John of Gaunt was already protective of the ethereal little Blanche.

Because her brother, the Earl of Kent, had returned with Prince Edward, Joan dined with him and she had asked Brianna to sit with them. This meant a higher place of honor than Brianna usually occupied, because the brother and sister were royal. However, their father had been beheaded for treason when Joan was only two. He had not really been guilty of any crime, but he was unpopular because he maintained a riotous household and allowed his officers to plunder people wherever they went. As a result, Edmund was now very wealthy. He owned his own town house in London and it was every bit as riotous as his father's had been.

For years, Edmund had tried his best to seduce Brianna, but she had rebuffed him so often, it had become a joke between them. He finally realized virgins weren't much fun and he now did his plowing in other fields and treated Brianna like another sister.

Brianna hadn't yet told Joan about her amazing good fortune. Actually, she wouldn't believe it until Robert de Beauchamp approached her and began his wooing. She was amazed that Joan hadn't guessed something was different about her. She was wearing a new gown of amber taffeta, and again she wore her golden girdle studded with emeralds, which had brought her good luck earlier. A bubble of excitement was building inside her until she felt it might burst. She laughed at everything Edmund said, and though she had taken no wine, she felt giddy. The music coming from the glitterns and lutes of the strolling musicians was so captivating she tapped her feet to the rhythm.

She glanced across the Banqueting Hall to the table reserved for the king's highest nobles. The Earl and Countess of Pembroke were at the top of the table, next to the lovely Countess of Salisbury. The Earl of Warrick was deep in conversation with the Earl of Northampton, and on Warrick's right hand, sat his son, Robert de Beauchamp. He was watching her! Jesu, how long had his gaze rested upon her? She lowered her lashes, then took a sip of wine to cool her warm cheeks. It had the opposite effect. She recalled her dream of last night, the details of which were now slightly blurred. The knight in her dreams had the same powerful physique, the same aquamarine eyes, and without doubt would likely have the same potent mouth that teased and kissed until she was mindless. Her warm cheeks began to burn with hot blushes. How strange that she had dreamed of Robert with jet-black hair. Still, that was the nature of dreams, a lady had no control over the images that danced about her head in the dead of night.

Suddenly, Brianna felt very shy. She was thankful the jongleurs would entertain them during the last course of dinner. Then Godenal, the king's minstrel, would perform one of the great heroic epics. Brianna loved to listen to these legends. They inspired her to set them down on parchment in ornamental script and paint brilliant scenes to illustrate them. She glanced at her friend Joan, and noticed that she was every bit as excited and animated as Brianna herself was tonight. Joan wore a new gown of shimmering peach sendal, edged in costly ermine, and had threaded loops of pearls through her hair. Brianna fancied that she too hugged a delicious secret to herself.

Joan met and held Edward's meaningful glances throughout the meal. The intense interest she read in his face made her feel especially beautiful. When she became utterly breathless, she lowered her lashes demurely and laughed provocatively at whatever her brother said. Her glance was soon drawn back, however, to those dark sapphire eyes that promised their relationship was about to become much more exciting.

Prince Edward was impatient for the meal to be finished so the social mingling and dancing could begin. He was fascinated by the effect Jeanette was having on him. While studying warfare, he had learned strategy. He did not intend to sit another hour gazing at her from afar, while Godenal performed a lengthy epic. Edward smiled at his sister. "You look lovely tonight, Bella. When the dancing begins I know you will be deluged with partners, but save the first one for Father so you don't injure his pride."

Isabel was looking forward to dancing with the king in her mother's place. They would draw every eye and it would give her a chance to show off her new finery.

Edward lowered his voice. "Oh Lord, here comes Godenal. If he gets started on Roland or Charlemagne there won't be time for dancing tonight."

Isabel pulled the king's sleeve urgently. "Father, I'm so looking forward to opening the dance with you, do we have to listen to Godenal tonight?"

"Sweetheart, everyone loves these epic ballads and romances. He is a master storyteller. He can move the entire hall to tears."

"Tears of boredom," Isabel said petulantly. "You don't want to dance with me," she accused.

King Edward patted his daughter's hand. The young were so impatient and impetuous. He beckoned Godenal to the dais, had a private word with him, then removed a ring. Ironically, the reward for not performing was more costly than the one for performing.

While the trestle tables were moved against the walls to make room for the dancing, the courtiers repaired to the gallery. As Brianna walked with Joan, she could contain her news no longer. "The king has chosen someone for me," she said breathlessly.

"Oh, Brianna, who?"

"Robert de Beauchamp."

"Warrick's son? Ah, Brianna, you will be the handsomest couple at Court. All will envy you. The maids are mad for him."

"I can't believe my good luck." Brianna whirled about as she heard a voice ask, "May I join you, demoiselle?"

She looked up into the blond giant's face. Surely he was the most attractive young man she had ever seen. Suddenly she was tongue-tied and her feet seemed rooted to the spot. Joan, however, smoothed the path for her friend. "I hear the musicians. The hall must be ready for dancing."

As they walked the length of the gallery, Brianna imagined every eye was trained upon her and her tall escort. Her heart swelled with pride. As Adele joined them, she suddenly found her tongue. "May I introduce Robert de Beauchamp?" The name sounded heavenly. "This is my aunt Adele."

He bent over Adele's hand, gallantly bringing it to his lips. His eyes were teasing. "She is far too young to be a chaperone." He captured Adele's heart on the spot. "Have I your permission to ask our lady for a dance?"

Adele would have given him permission for anything at that moment, but then, so would Brianna.

Isabel was being swung about the room by the king and after a few moments alone, it was acceptable for other couples to join in the dancing.

Prince Edward walked a circuitous path around the hall toward Joan of Kent. William de Montecute, however, walked a direct path and arrived at her side first. She was acutely aware of Edward's every move. She bestowed a smile upon Montecute and allowed him to lead her onto the floor. This morning she had learned that Edward became angered when he thought she had an assignation. Jealousy was a spur she could make use of. "I'm sorry about your father, William."

"Goddamn French. I can't wait to cross the Channel. All-out war is the only answer. Before we go though, I'd like you to take my suit seriously. Joan, you know you have captured my heart. There is no one but you. I think of you night and day."

Joan was unmoved by flattery and protestations of undying love. It was the fashion for a young man to declare he was a lady's slave, when in truth what he really wanted was just the opposite.

"What you think of, night and day, is the glory of war."

He grinned at her. "When I have won my spurs, I shall woo you and win you. I won't take no for an answer," he vowed passionately.

Prince Edward positioned himself so that when the music ended, he was directly in their path. "Well, cousin, will you partner me?" Edward asked casually.

"If you cannot find a partner, I shall have to take pity on you, Your Highness," Joan teased.

As they moved away, Edward said, "Montecute seemed most earnest in his attentions. Does he mean anything to you?"

"I told him I was sorry about his father." She made a little moue with her mouth. "Are you jealous?"

"Has he kissed you?" Edward demanded, the muscle in his jaw tightening.

Joan looked up at him from beneath her lashes. "He's tried," she admitted, wondering if he would again put his brand on her. Suddenly she saw that was exactly what he was about to do. She stiffened. "Edward, everyone is looking at us."

"I'm sorry, Jeanette, but you're driving me mad. I want to be with you . . . talk to you, where there's no one to stare at us."

"That's impossible, Your Highness."

"Nothing is impossible if I put my mind to it. It just requires a little strategy."

"You make dalliance sound like a military maneuver."

He wanted to crush her in his arms. She was so small, so delectable. God's Splendor, he couldn't think coherently when she was this close. He raised his head and glanced about the hall. "I'll dance with Isabel and you dance with your brother, then have him take you into the gallery."

Robert de Beauchamp bowed before Brianna. "Do you care to dance, demoiselle?"

"Oh yes, my lord, I love to dance." She feared she sounded too eager. As they moved onto the floor, she kept her lashes lowered. Finally, she found the courage to look up at him. "Oh, you have a gash on your neck!" she blurted.

"A scratch. Scars are badges of honor, my lady."

Brianna had never thought of scars in that way. Men saw things in a different light from women. Perhaps scars did show courage in a warrior. She remembered Warrick's battle scars and shuddered.

"I'm more at home in the field than in the dance, my lady," he explained. He was far too large to dance gracefully. He was a little clumsy, but suddenly she found that a most endearing quality.

"Please call me Brianna." Jesu, she sounded too eager again.

"Only if you agree to call me Robert."

" 'My lady' and 'my lord' are so formal." Now she was stating the obvious!

"Brianna, I would like to be your champion in the tournament. Will you give me your scarf or sleeve to wear?"

"Oh yes, Robert, I would be honored."

As the measure came to a close, Prince Lionel clapped Robert on the back. "Beauchamp, come and sit with us. You hate to dance as much as I do." Lionel's eyes traveled from Brianna's mouth, down to her breasts, then up again. "She's a tempting morsel, Robert, but the king's wards are off limits for bed sport."

Brianna blushed hotly.

"Prince Lionel, Lady Bedford and I are to be betrothed soon, I hope," Robert said repressively.

"Ah, you lucky dog! Then she won't be off limits for bed sport." He laughed at his own wit.

Beauchamp placed a protective arm about Brianna and drew her away from the prince. "Excuse me, Your Highness, I must return Lady Bedford, then I shall be happy to join you."

Brianna was thrilled that Robert was chivalrously shielding her from Prince Lionel. "He is so coarse," she murmured, embarrassed.

"I am in his service, my lady. He is a generous liege lord to me. I hope to become steward of his household."

"Loyalty is an admirable quality, my lord." Brianna could have bitten off her tongue for criticizing the royal prince. They were back to formalities.

"My lady . . . Brianna, I hope you are not angry because I said we were to be betrothed, when I haven't yet asked you."

"No, no, I'm not angry," she assured him.

"I may arrange it then?" he pressed.

"Yes, my lord . . . Robert . . . if you wish it."

Beauchamp bowed over her hand and left her with Adele.

"He's going to arrange the betrothal," Brianna told Adele breathlessly.

"After only one dance? He must be head over heels!"

Oh no, that's me, thought Brianna.

Joan strolled along the gallery on Edmund of Kent's arm. At the far end he spied Prince Edward and Princess Isabel. "This meeting is no accident," he accused; "admit it was deliberately planned!"

Joan was about to vehemently deny his accusation when she realized of what he accused her.

"Princess Isabel talked you into bringing me out here, you little devil!"

"If you don't wish to be alone with her, take her straight back to the Banqueting Hall to dance." Joan had to bite her lip to keep from laughing aloud.

"I'm happy I amuse you. How the devil will I escape from Isabel? I have an assignation with a lady at ten."

"You wouldn't waste your time with a lady," Joan teased.

"Edmund, I've been looking everywhere for you," Isabel said happily.

"And I for you, Your Highness. You promised to save me a dance."

"And when did I do that, sir?" she simpered.

"When the two of us were private in the stables at Berkhamsted," he said outrageously.

"Edmund, you are so wicked." She let go of her brother's arm and took hold of Edmund's.

The Prince of Wales winked at the Earl of Kent. "Just a moment, Bella. I don't think I should let you go with this wild man."

Isabel's mouth turned sulky. "Edward, please, just one dance?"

The Earl of Kent placed his hand over his heart. "One dance, I swear on my honor as a gentleman!"

As Edward watched the pair walk down the gallery toward the Banqueting Hall, he captured Joan's hand and pulled her through the gallery doors. They slipped upstairs to the solar, which was deserted at this hour. It was used most in daylight hours, when its long windows let in the sunshine. No candles burned, but the moonlight flooded in, touching Joan's hair and gown with its pale, ethereal light.

"You are so unearthly fair," Edward murmured, tracing a finger along the soft white ermine at her shoulder.

Joan placed her palms against his broad chest and stroked the hard muscles. The heat from his body spread into her hands and she felt his heart thudding, hard and strong.

Edward groaned. He threaded his fingers into her hair and cupped her face as if he were holding a chalice. Slowly, he lifted it to his lips. "I've waited three hours to do this." The curve of his lips fit hers perfectly, moving with a slow, deliberate thoroughness. The pressure of his mouth increased and his thumbs moved up to brush their lips where they fused, then parted them so he could plunge inside her.

Joan gasped as a thrill ran down her entire body and his sleek tongue probed deep, mastering her.

His powerful arms slid about her body and lifted her to fit his. His thighs were solid as marble and his phallus, which rose up against her soft belly, was rigid with his need.

She arched against him and slid her arms about his strong neck. His hands went beneath her buttocks to support her and the feel of him was so intense, she tore her mouth away so she could cry out her pleasure.

"Sweet, sweet," Edward murmured against her throat. "Jeanette, I cannot let you go from me tonight. I want to make love to you until dawn."

"No, Edward, we cannot. I must remain virgin or I will be worthless to your father."

He let her feet slip back to the carpet. "You'd wed another?" he demanded incredulously.

"The king will betroth me and there is naught I can do!"

The king, at this moment, was pressing Katherine de Montecute to dance. The Countess of Salisbury thought it would occasion gossip. He used the Countess of Pembroke to persuade her. "William will expect me to take good care of her, isn't that so, Lady Pembroke? Come dance with me, Katherine, I have some news that will hearten you."

"Edward, you have no shame," she whispered.

"Katherine, where you are concerned, I have not." He

squeezed her hand intimately. "I do have news, though. Your husband is in Paris. He's a guest at the French Court until his ransom is arranged."

"He's a prisoner, not a guest, Edward!"

"Katherine, he has no doubt dined as sumptuously as we have tonight and at this moment is very likely enjoying some delicious French tart."

She laughed at his witticism.

"That's better. No tears, beloved. Life's too short. When this dance is over, I want you to come with me to the solar. Before I go up to the queen, I want to say good night to you in private."

Prince Edward and Joan drew apart quickly as the door swung open. The cresset lamps at the entrance revealed the king and the Countess of Salisbury.

"Father!" Edward said in surprise.

"Edward? Is that you?" The king took a lamp from its bracket and lifted it high so that it illuminated the occupants of the solar. The two Plantagenets stared at each other in silence. Neither pair of brilliant blue eyes showed the slightest hint of guilt.

❧ 6 ❧

The king said, "We have much to discuss. Has your mother told you our plans?"

"No. I haven't seen her yet."

"Good, we will go together." The king turned to Katherine de Montecute. "I want you to stop worrying about William. I will get him home safely."

She curtsied. "Good night, Your Majesty."

Joan's nimble mind searched frantically for something plausible to say. "I was searching for my brother. Good night, Sire."

The two tall men left the solar and walked toward the Queen's Tower, each occupied by his own private thoughts.

Philippa welcomed them with pleasure and dismissed

her ladies as her husband and eldest son bent to kiss her, inquiring after her good health.

Prince Edward immediately took the initiative. "I've been giving some thought to marriage. The last time you broached the subject, I showed little interest."

"Your mother favors an alliance with Margaret of Brabant—"

"Nay, I fancy an English bride," Edward cut in.

"Edward, you must marry someone royal. There is no one suitable in England," Philippa pointed out.

"Joan of Kent is royal," he said firmly.

The king's suspicions were confirmed.

"You are cousins," Philippa said, her eyes hardening.

"The Pope will grant us a dispensation." Edward waved his hand, dismissing the objection.

Philippa allowed her distaste to show. "Your father chose me to forge a strong alliance with Hainault and Flanders. The King of England's sons must follow his example."

"My brother John is betrothed to Blanche of Lancaster," Edward argued.

"Blanche is heiress to the Lancaster fortune. Joan's brother inherited the Kent fortune and lands. She has little money of her own," the king said bluntly.

Prince Edward was not foolish enough to insist money didn't matter. It did.

"Lack of money isn't my objection to Joan," Edward's mother said. "Her father was beheaded for treason."

Prince Edward spoke up, "I've learned enough history to know he was innocent of that heinous crime. Mortimer executed him to save his own neck."

They never spoke of the king's mother, Queen Isabella, and her paramour, Mortimer, who murdered King Edward II.

"The Kents were tainted by the scandal. I don't believe Parliament would agree to Joan of Kent becoming the next Queen of England," Philippa said with finality.

Prince Edward held his tongue. Obviously the less he said about his little Jeanette, the better.

"The Council would certainly agree to a match with Margaret of Brabant. We can only conquer France if we keep our allies loyal. Edward, if you have no objection, I'll start negotiations for a union with Brabant," his father suggested.

Prince Edward was shrewd. At one time Parliament had proposed he marry a daughter of the French king, Philip of Valois. That had fallen through when King Edward claimed the throne of France. Next had come the daughter of the Count of Flanders, but his father had a well-known tendency to be arrogantly overdemanding and he was never open and aboveboard in his dealings with foreigners. Edward suspected his negotiations with Brabant would bear little fruit. If things did start to move forward, he would simply be uncooperative. "You will do as you think best." He changed the subject. "How many ships have the western ports pledged?"

"Your mother's good knight, Walter Manny, is bringing me seventy vessels, all over a hundred tons. I've made him Admiral of the Fleet north of the Thames."

"Thank you, Edward." Sir Walter Manny had accompanied Philippa from Hainault almost eighteen years ago.

"Come, we don't want to exhaust your mother with our incessant discussion of war. We'll talk alone."

The king accompanied Edward to his own tower. The prince dismissed his servants and poured his father a cup of wine.

"I'm sorry about Joan. Is she pressing you for marriage?"

Edward stiffened. "Of course not."

"Princes cannot marry their mistresses," his father commiserated.

"She's not my mistress! I find her enchanting . . . you wouldn't understand," Edward said repressively.

"Not understand the desires of the flesh? Edward, you must be jesting. Let me tell you a story. Last year when the Scots invaded and I beat them back and managed to capture the Earl of Moray, I received a message that Wark Castle was besieged. My friend, William de Montecute, was fighting in France and his countess was courageously holding out against the Scots with only a handful of knights. It was no more than my duty to help my friend's wife. Wark sits on the south bank of the Tweed and we soon routed the Scots and sent them fleeing back across the border.

"The Countess of Salisbury lowered the drawbridge and came out to welcome the king who had just saved her. I had never seen Katherine de Montecute before. Her beauty was blinding. It hit me like a thunderbolt. She wore a tightly fitted jacket that showed off her tiny waist. I remember her surcoat had lovely trailing sleeves, but most of all I remember her glorious hair, shimmering in golden waves. When we looked into each other's eyes, a raging desire took possession of me, but I could not be unfaithful to your mother. I burn for Katherine, but I am a chivalrous knight and must not besmirch her good name."

For the first time Edward saw the king as a man, rather than a father. "You have succeeded in protecting the Countess of Salisbury's good name. There has never, ever been a whisper about her." He held his father's eyes. "Nevertheless, you are lying."

The king drained his wine, then finally nodded. "I am still consumed with fire whenever I touch her. To me she is a goddess. My passion consumes my guilt. I do not allow it to interfere with my duty or my deep and abiding love for Philippa." He gripped Edward's shoulder with a powerful hand. "Joan is a delectable little hoyden. Take her, by all means, but find a way to protect her good name."

As Christian Hawksblood traveled from the coast to Windsor, he was most impressed by what he saw. Instead of an impoverished country, he saw that England thrived. The crops were abundant, the verdant fields were crowded with milky herds, the hills were dotted with fine sheep, and the rivers swarmed with fish. The laughing peasants who tilled the fields were well fed, their children rosy-cheeked. Workshops in every town and village were producing bows and arrows, blacksmiths hammered out war weapons, and saddleries were making harnesses for warhorses. England was a beehive of activity from carpenters to tentmakers. Prosperity was everywhere.

When he arrived at Windsor and saw the lavish lifestyle of the king and court, Hawksblood was stunned. He lost no time seeking out a private meeting with the Earl of Warrick. He sent a note asking the earl to meet with him regarding a private matter and signed his name, Christian

Hawksblood. Bearding the lion in his den, Christian made his way across the Lower Ward to where the military knights were housed.

He had hated Warrick for many years. As a boy, he had visualized confronting him, then cleaving him in two with his broadsword. When he became a youth, his plan for revenge grew more subtle. By then he had been trained to isolate, capsulate, and bury deep problems that could not be immediately solved. To be managed, emotions must first be controlled, then set aside until the time was ripe.

He wondered briefly how long it would take to learn if Guy de Beauchamp was his father. He had mastered patience. He cared not if it took a lifetime.

Hawksblood knew immediately.

And so did Warrick.

The aquamarine eyes staring back at him were his own.

Slowly, Warrick circled him, openly curious at what he had spawned.

Hawksblood took a massive chair by the fireplace.

Warrick took its mate. Still they did not speak. The very air crackled with tension.

So this was the Norman warrior from whose seed he had sprung! Scarred, hardened, fierce; a body and a will of iron. He had inherited more than his sire's long limbs.

Warrick stared at the dark, hawklike face, stamped with the pride of an Arabian prince. Wild, cruel, fearless, enigmatic; all these things, yet by God's Splendor, he was a *man*.

Finally, Warrick spoke. "Your mother had an ironic sense of humor; she named you Christian."

"Did you know of me?" The words came like steeltipped arrows, direct and to the heart of the matter.

"If I had known of you, you would have been brought up at Warrick. Ten years ago I met a Hospitaler Knight from the east who had heard of a youth in their secret order who was rumored to be my son. "I didn't believe it. I didn't want to believe it. I didn't think she would deceive me! Yet, over the years, I wondered."

Reluctantly, he admitted Warrick could be speaking the truth. Though his mother had insisted Warrick did not know, he had never believed her. She made excuses for

Warrick's desertion because she had lost her heart to the Norman.

"I decided not to investigate. If it was true, you were receiving the finest training in the world, and I knew you would come when you were ready. If it was false . . . my hope would have been destroyed."

The words were private—from the heart. Hawksblood knew the gnarled warrior was not in the habit of sharing confidences.

"This is thirsty work." He poured them ale and offered a leather jack to Hawksblood.

When he first entered the room, he would not have drunk with Warrick. Now he took the ale. Silence stretched between them. Hawksblood was a most private man. Secrecy had been an integral part of his life since birth. He had seldom spoken of himself. Finally, he broke the silence.

"I lived in the palace until I was almost seven. Though it was a closely guarded secret, I knew the princess was my mother. When her marriage was arranged, my life was in danger. She smuggled me to Jerusalem and gave me into the care of the Hospitaler Knights." He paused, remembering, then continued. "She told me your name that night. I was initiated into a Mystic Order. When I was ten, I was trained as a warrior by Norman knights."

That told him everything. And nothing.

"Was the Mystic Order the Golden Dawn, secret order of the Knights Templar?" Warrick asked, fascinated.

"The Mystic Order survives because of its secrecy," he said flatly.

"How did you get the name Hawksblood?"

The man before him actually sounded as if he cared. "I had to go alone, without weapons, into the Rub 'al-Khali, the Empty Quarter."

Warrick nodded, "The special haunt of djinns, demons, and other evil spirits."

"I survived by killing and eating hawks."

"How?" Warrick asked skeptically.

Christian showed him his hands. It was such a simple gesture, there was truth in it. Warrick knew he would always be able to survive with his bare hands. So this was his firstborn. His *legitimate* son. His princess had agreed to a Christian marriage ceremony. Warrick felt no guilt that he had deceived his English lady into thinking herself a true wife. It had never harmed her in any way. But now he experienced a deep pang of guilt that Robert thought himself his heir when he was actually only his bastard.

"You are entitled to the name Hawksblood. You are also entitled to the name Beauchamp." It was a statement. He did not ask if he would use it. Hawksblood was glad. He did not yet know. Probably he would use it, if it served his purpose.

"Did you never see your mother again?"

"When I was sixteen I became a Janissary so that I could see her upon occasion. Her father, Ottoman, and her husband were dead, so there was less danger. Her two brothers divided their father's domains and founded the corps d'elite of the Ottoman armies. Most Janissaries are Christian."

Even Warrick was impressed that his son had been selected as a Janissary. They had reputedly never lost a battle. They were the conquerors of all Byzantine. "Why did you leave?"

Again, silence stretched between them. If he told him, it would expose his Achilles' heel.

So be it.

"Because we enslaved those we captured."

Silence filled the chamber. This time it was Warrick who feared to reveal vulnerability.

"How is Princess Sharon?" *My Rose of Sharon,* his heart whispered.

"She was well. She was being courted again."

"Courted?" Warrick bellowed like an enraged bull.

"She is exceptionally beautiful," Hawksblood said with relish, rubbing salt into the wound now that he had discovered it.

"How long ago?"

"I left Arabia over three years ago, selling my sword to the highest bidder until I arrived in France. I had to choose sides in the coming war. I chose England."

Warrick nodded with satisfaction. "You're here in time for the tournament."

Hawksblood raised his voice for the first time. "Tournament? Christ Almighty, is that all anyone can think of? Philip of Valois has gathered over a hundred and fifty ships!"

"Rumors . . . unconfirmed."

"Confirmed! I've seen them," Hawksblood said flatly.

Warrick's face blanched. His aquamarine eyes glittered dangerously. "Come with me."

They might not love each other, but the two warriors felt a healthy measure of respect.

Both the king's Guard Chamber and Presence Chamber were empty.

"Where's the king?" demanded Warrick of one of his squires.

"He has gone out to the park to inspect the lists for the tourney, my lord."

"Tell him I have news. Tell him it's urgent!"

The squire took off at a run, a healthy measure of fear of Warrick showing on his face.

Christian looked about the opulent chamber. "I expected it to be more Spartan. I heard the king is in debt to the Bardi for almost a million, and that for past campaigns."

"He is." Warrick grinned. "King Edward is an optimist. If a campaign fails, he doesn't worry his guts to fiddlestrings, he just moves on to the next."

"How can he live so lavishly?"

"He borrows. He could easily raise taxes, but he won't. That's why he's so popular. He takes only the tenth he is entitled to, but it's never enough, so he borrows large amounts from many sources. You'll be able to judge him for yourself, when he gets here."

Hawksblood wondered if the king would answer a summons from Warrick. Perhaps he was a puppet king. He didn't have to wonder long. Two men strode into the chamber with purpose. The king was dressed in the latest French fashion of tight hose and short doublet that came only to the hips. The colors were brilliant azure and gold. Save for the golden beard, the second man was identical. Only when they drew close was a difference in age apparent. It was obvious the young man in black could only be the Prince of Wales.

The king's all-seeing blue eyes raked over Christian, then his voice boomed out, "By the Rood, you can't deny this one, Warrick, despite his dark visage."

"Nay, Sire, I don't deny him. This is my elder son, Christian Hawksblood de Beauchamp."

The blue Plantagenet eyes scrutinized him keenly. "Beauchamp." He nodded. "This is my eldest, Edward, Prince of Wales."

Hawksblood bowed his head. "Your Majesty, Your Highness."

The two young men measured each other openly, frankly assessing what they saw. They had almost identical builds: the same height, the same long limbs, the same athletic body in superb physical condition. Each liked what he saw.

"Your news?" the king asked Warrick.

"My son's news. He's just arrived from France."

"Philip has amassed a fleet of perhaps a hundred and forty large ships. As well, there are numerous smaller vessels from Normandy and Breton."

A fierce light of conquest came into the king's eyes. "You saw this? You know where his fleet is anchored?"

Hawksblood nodded. "It is off the coast of Helvoetsluys."

"God damn Valois! He is using the coastal waters of Flanders. Flanders is supposed to be my ally!"

"Let's blow them out of the water," Prince Edward urged. "You said Walter Manny was sending seventy ships."

"The Thames fleet has twenty-five ships," Warrick offered.

"Admiral Morley is sending a score from the Cinque Ports," the king added. "That gives us a hundred and fifteen."

"They've already taken three of our best, the *Edward,* the *Rose,* and the *Katherine.* Let's make sure those are the last ships they ever take!" Prince Edward urged his father. He had never yet taken part in a campaign, though it seemed he had been training all his life to fight the French.

The king looked at Warrick. "Will you oversee this operation?"

Warrick's eyes met those of his son. Hawksblood nodded. No words were needed. Each thought privately it would be an ideal test of the other's courage, honor, ethics, and ability.

The king's voice was rich, his laugh spontaneous. "We'll do it! The tournament will have to wait until we get back. God damn Valois for inconveniencing us."

"I heard a rumor that Philip has hired Genoese bowmen to sit in the watch turrets of the ships," Hawksblood warned. "The Genoese are the best arbalests in the world. I've fought against them."

Prince Edward, the king, and Warrick exchanged glances, then began to laugh.

A frown creased Hawksblood's brow.

The king waved his arm. "Show him! Go on! Warrick and I will go to the map room and settle on a port of departure. We can't use Dover or Sandwich. Word would get to Philip too fast. We need a port with a lot of estuaries that will hide most of the fleet as it gathers."

Hawksblood assessed Edward III shrewdly. He was extravagant, ostentatious, and likely vainglorious, but he was brave and decisive. This was no puppet king. This was a conqueror!

Prince Edward led the way to a meadow where about two hundred men were taking target practice. At first glance, Christian thought the bows primitive. Did they hope to succeed against Genoese crossbows, engineered for accuracy?

"Do you have no crossbows?" he asked Edward.

"We do. But we believe longbows are superior."

Christian picked one up. It was above six feet in length and lightweight. The arrows were steel-tipped; the feathers from the common gray goose of England.

The prince spoke with a couple of men who selected weapons from an arms wagon. One chose a longbow, the other a crossbow. "Watch this," Edward said.

The men aligned themselves. The crossbowman went down on one knee to brace his heavy weapon. He fitted in his arrow, wound it taut, then released it. The man beside him stood tall and fired off three in the same space of time.

Edward and Christian loped down the field to examine the butt. All the arrows had accurately hit the target, but the missiles of death from the longbow had pierced clean through the butt, halfway up their shafts.

"Christus! These longbows propel a violent power. I want to master this skill."

Edward grinned. "These are foot soldiers, common yeomen or Welsh. Noble knights wouldn't be caught dead with a longbow."

Aquamarine eyes met deep blue and held. "You are an expert with this weapon."

"I am," Prince Edward conceded. They were so much alike. Each had a burning desire to excel. At everything.

The next three hours melted away as Hawksblood was caught up in the challenge of mastering a new skill. Edward, equally enthusiastic, taught him the finer points. Soon, they had set up a target in another meadow on the far side of the Thames and were determined to hit their marks clear across the wide river.

By this time Ali and Paddy had tracked Hawksblood down. They had stabled the horses with the Beauchamp mounts and had found space for themselves in the barracks, but they were unsure about their lord. Would he reside in the Beauchamp wing or would he prefer they set up his campaign tent?

Prince Edward spoke up. "There are vacant rooms close by my apartments. My cousin, Edmund of Kent, has bought his own town house in London. Come, I'll show you."

At that moment a small figure climbing on the weapons wagon caught his eye. He swooped down on the intruder in five long strides. "What the hell are you doing here?" he demanded of an imp-faced page, clutching a longbow. He cuffed him across the head. "Don't you realize you could be killed?"

The boy's face lit up at the danger he was in. "Your Highness, I've a note from the princess." He fished a filthy hand into his livery and produced a grubby note.

Edward groaned. He knew what it was about without reading it. "I promised to take my sister hawking, I can't think why." He looked down at the page boy. "Tell her too many pressing things need my attention at the moment." Joan insinuated herself into his thoughts and suddenly he remembered why he had told Isabel he would take her hawking. "Hold a moment," he told the page. He looked at Christian with speculation. "It will take a few days' preparation for our . . . French lesson. Can we squeeze in a morning's hawking?"

Christian was bemused. These Plantagenets were determined to mix pleasure with business.

"Inform Isabel I'll take her tomorrow. Early. I won't hang about. Now get the hell away from these archers and stay away." The prince picked up a steel helmet with a missing nose-guard and tossed it to the lad. "And if you can't stay away, wear this!"

The imp of Satan pulled off his cap, crammed the helmet over his red curls, and grinned like a lunatic. He was happy as a fart. Prince Edward was his idol.

The accommodation was far better than Hawksblood had expected in a castle that housed almost a thousand nobles, military men, clergy, and servants. He left his squires to unpack his belongings and plenish his two rooms while he and the prince rejoined the king and Warrick.

"We've decided on the Port of Ipswich. I've sent messengers off to Admiral Morley and Walter Manny informing them Warrick will direct this operation. All the vessels will have their own crews. How many fighting men do you reckon?"

"Say, fifty extra men on each ship for boarding parties," Warrick decided.

"Don't forget my Welsh bowmen," Prince Edward interjected. "They have to pick off those Genoese." The men all looked at Hawksblood.

He laughed and shook his head. "I don't believe the Genoese arbalests will stand a chance."

"You'd better swear fealty to me if you're coming with us," the king demanded.

Prince Edward laughed. "He's already sworn fealty to me, Father. He's my man, though I've no objection to his giving you his oath."

For the second time in an hour, Christian placed his hands between those of a Plantagenet. His father's name was of use sooner than expected. "I, Christian Hawksblood de Beauchamp, swear by my faith to obey, defend, and serve thee entirely as my sovereign against every man, without deception." Though he did not give his oath lightly, he was jaded enough to believe few men acted without deception. There were three motives for everything: what a man told others, what he told himself, and the real motive.

"News spreads like wildfire. By the time we sit down in the hall tonight, all in the castle will be buzzing like hornets with a stick up their nest. Edward, you will be inundated with overeager youths anxious to win their spurs. Choose wisely."

"News of my Arabian son here will cause a few eyebrows to raise and a few tongues to wag. I'd best find Robert and apprise him of the truth before the rumors start."

It was too late, of course. Robert de Beauchamp had already learned his father's bastard was at Windsor—and a foreign bastard to boot! A dozen friends had apprised him of the Arabian Knight, speaking of him with both awe and admiration. Apparently he was older, experienced in warfare and already knighted. Robert, fearing this paragon would cast him in the shadows, conceived a personal dislike before he ever met his unwanted half brother. If the foreign bastard coveted the title or one acre of Warrick land, he'd best watch his back!

7

There were two efficient networks to relay information at Windsor. One was male-dominated, the other female. The men's grapevine began at the top with the king, and worked its way down through the nobles, squires, servants, and finally to the pages at the bottom of the pecking order. The women's grapevine grew vice versa, from the page boys to the maids, on to the married women, up to the ladies-in-waiting, then finally to the noble ladies themselves. The result of this was that the women received their information long after the men, and the results were highly embroidered distortions of the facts.

The maids' tongues were busy with news of the new arrival, complete with all the juicy details. He was an Arabian Knight on a secret mission. He was a mercenary, a spy, or an assassin. Perhaps all three. Arabs were notorious whoremasters, allowed four wives and a harem filled with concubines. This particular Arab was so darkly handsome, he had more than his allotted share of women. He had left a trail of brokenhearted females across three continents. At this point in the telling, the servant girls' voices dropped to a shocked whisper. The bathhouse maids had seen him naked. The weapon between his legs was a black, lethal obscenity! Most were repelled, a few were attracted; all were wildly curious.

In all fairness, Christian had the advantage when he came face-to-face with his half brother. He knew Warrick had another son; whereas Robert could not have known until today. Under the circumstances, the fair-headed young giant acknowledged him with considerable grace.

A granite-faced Warrick simply apprised him of the hard facts. "This is my son, Christian, conceived in Arabia before I married your mother."

Robert held out his arm with a welcoming smile. Christian knew it was to test his strength. Robert was warm, good-natured, and easygoing.

On the surface.

Beneath were hidden depths with undercurrents. When the two clasped arms, Robert was shocked to learn the Arabian's strength was greater than his own. The smile faded, but the mask stayed in place.

Christian knew his brother would be difficult to read, though not impossible. Robert de Beauchamp was opaque rather than transparent. Christian knew immediately Robert had already learned of him before this meeting, because all his thoughts, good or bad, were carefully concealed. Christian noted the badge on Robert's sleeve. "You are the Duke of Clarence's man. I've not met Prince Lionel yet."

"He'll be in the hall tonight. Lionel and I have much in common, our size and a father with a warrior's reputation that can be daunting. Now it seems we both have older brothers who outshine us." He grinned to show he felt no bitterness.

"That remains to be seen," Christian said, returning the grin.

"I suppose the brotherly thing to do is offer you one of my rooms."

"I thank you, but that is not necessary. I have accommodation." He nodded to both men. "I'll see you in the hall."

Robert's eyes narrowed as he watched Christian depart. Now that he had come face-to-face with the usurper, seen the respect in his father's eyes, learned the bastard's strength was greater than his own, the seeds of hatred took root.

"Perhaps we'll see him in the hall tonight," Joan said to Brianna. "I wonder who he is? The name Hawksblood doesn't sound familiar."

"It sounds dangerous," Brianna warned her friend, knowing that friend's propensity for mischief.

"Oh Lord, yes." Joan shivered.

Brianna shuddered. She had chosen to wear a turquoise tunic over a jade sarcenet with diaphanous sleeves. Again she wore the emerald-studded girdle. "You don't think Robert will think these colors too bold?"

"You look stunning. I never dreamed those two colors would look so striking together. Has he kissed you yet?" Joan asked eagerly.

"Of course not!" Brianna said in a shocked voice.

"He will tonight. Your emeralds will be lucky for you."

"Joan, you are so wicked," said Brianna, but she laughed and her eyes sparkled brighter than her jewels.

In the hall, Princess Isabel beckoned them imperiously. "Edward is taking me hawking tomorrow. I will need you both an hour early."

Joan had seen no trace of Edward all day, though she had watched for him. She was wise to Isabel's tricks though, and knew she would exclude Joan and Brianna from the hawking if she could.

Queen Philippa had come to the Banqueting Hall tonight and the king gave her his undivided attention. They shared a silver porringer, laughing and talking throughout the entire meal.

Princess Isabel's mouth was sulky because she wasn't the

center of attention tonight. Neither Prince Edward nor
Prince Lionel was on the dais, both choosing instead to sit
with their men.

Prince John of Gaunt coolly ignored his sister so that she
would not engage him in conversation. Though he was only
a boy, he was Isabel's intellectual superior.

Joan felt a pang of disappointment at not being able to
flirt with Edward, but was soon distracted when she spied
Robert Beauchamp beside Prince Lionel. Joan nudged Brianna. "He's looking at you."

Brianna whispered, "I don't think he is. He's looking at
someone behind us."

Joan watched more closely, then her gaze traveled over
the other diners. "As a matter of fact, everyone's looking
behind us. I wonder why? Oh, you don't suppose it could
be the Arabian?"

Brianna hardly heard her. She was watching Robert. His
eyes were narrowed. He drank cup for cup with Prince
Lionel. Robert nearly always laughed. Tonight he did not.

Queen Philippa had her own minstrel this evening who
sang some lovely ballads in Flemish. Because she did not
wish to sit too long, she retired early, taking the king with
her.

When Joan and Brianna stood up, they looked down the
hall behind them. There was a crowd of men gathered
about the prince in deep conversation so they moved off
into the gallery.

It wasn't long before Robert de Beauchamp sought Brianna.

"Good even, my lord," she managed shyly.

Joan decided to help the courtship along. "Brianna was
just about to show me her parchments that the queen has
put on display right here in the gallery."

"Oh, please, no." Brianna suddenly found her voice.

"Don't be so modest. I'm sure Robert would love to see
how talented you are."

Brianna marveled at Joan's easy manner. She had no
difficulty calling him Robert. The leather-bound parchments had been placed on a reading stand beneath the
gallery's stained-glass oriel window. They told the legend of
King Arthur and his Knights of the Round Table. She had

illuminated all the capital letters in gold and accompanying
the script were delicately painted illustrations of his sword,
Excalibur, Merlin the Wizard, and Queen Guinevere.

As Robert de Beauchamp looked at the parchments, a
frown came between his brows. "You write?" he asked Brianna. His tone of voice was accusatory.

Joan immediately realized her mistake. "Ah, I take it you
do not, my lord."

He laughed derisively. "Writing is unmanly. 'Tis a task
for clerks and priests."

Brianna felt a sharp stab of disappointment that she
could not conceal. When he saw the look of dismay on her
lovely face, he said hurriedly, "I have no objection to your
little pastime, if it amuses you."

Brianna bit her tongue. She must not get off on the
wrong foot with her future husband or she would have no
husband at all. She glanced up at him and was alarmed at
the look of purest black hatred, but it was so fleeting she
thought she might have imagined it. She turned to see who
or what had provoked such emotion. Suddenly a hush fell
all about her. Time slowed down so that everything seemed
to take on a dreamlike quality.

Two men approached, but she did not even glance at
Prince Edward. Her eyes were drawn to the dark man at his
side. Though she tried, Brianna found she could not take
her eyes from him. He wore a crimson silk jupon with the
spread wings of a black hawk rising in full flight. His dark
face was exceedingly masculine, his compelling eyes were
brilliant splinters of aquamarine.

All Brianna's senses were heightened. She smelled her
own freesia perfume mixing with the man's body scent of
sandalwood. Her own colors of jade, turquoise, and emerald were suddenly brilliant, as if she were bathed in sunlight.

Christian was stunned. It was *she*!

His eyes widened at the breath-stopping beauty of her.
His nostrils flared at her provocative woman's scent. His
body quickened at the memory of her naked flesh cloaked
in her golden, ankle-length hair. The impact upon all his
senses was staggering and it slowly dawned upon him that
this was all predestined.

The man and the woman stood transfixed, gazing at each other as if they were the only two people in the gallery. The pupils of his eyes dilated until they turned black.

Brianna felt strange. Her heartbeat slowed, her very blood seemed to thicken. She forgot to breathe. Her hand went to her throat in a fluttering gesture of supplication.

Robert de Beauchamp's voice broke the spell. "This is my brother, Christian Hawksblood . . . Lady Brianna Bedford."

"*My* lady," the dark warrior said, his look so intense and possessive, she shrank back against De Beauchamp. He had clearly placed the emphasis on the word "my" rather than "lady."

Now that she had broken her glance from his, Brianna did not dare look at him again. She glanced about nervously. Everyone seemed to be acting normally, in a perfectly ordinary manner. Yet she knew what had happened between herself and the dark stranger was *extraordinary*.

Prince Edward introduced Christian to his cousin, Joan of Kent, and only then did he take his fierce gaze from her.

Brianna breathed again.

Joan, never at a loss for words, said, "So, you are the Arabian Knight who has set Windsor all agog. I had no idea the Earl of Warrick had another son."

"Neither did he, my lady," came the amused rejoinder. Everyone laughed. His voice was rich, deep, faintly accented. Yet Brianna noticed he did not place the emphasis on "my" when he called Joan "my lady."

Christian Hawksblood glanced down at the parchments on the reading stand. "These are very beautiful. They remind me of the treasured manuscripts I have seen in Baghdad."

"Baghdad!" Robert scoffed.

Prince Edward said, "Baghdad was a great center of culture and learning when Europeans couldn't even write their own names! Are these yours, Lady Bedford?"

"Yes, Your Highness," Brianna said, her cheeks flushed. Jesu, why did the subject of writing have to come up when Robert held it in such contempt?

Joan couldn't leave it there. She simply could not resist.

"Do you share your brother's views that writing is un-manly?"

Hawksblood looked amused. "Hardly. I have translated Persian and Sanskrit to Arabic."

"Perhaps you would have made a good priest," Robert said in jest.

"I venture he would excel at anything he undertook," Prince Edward stated with undisguised admiration for his newfound friend.

"Then let us see if you excel at dancing, my lord," Joan said prettily, taking Christian's arm.

Inside, Robert de Beauchamp was seething. He vented his ill-humor the moment his foreign bastard of a brother left the group. "Your friend, Joan of Kent, is a little slut," he muttered.

Prince Edward's eyes blazed. Always quick-tempered, his hand shot out and struck Robert in the face. "You are as foul-mouthed as my brother Lionel." Edward took Brianna's hand. "Come, Lady Bedford."

Brianna was mortified! She was caught in a cleft stick, damned whichever side she took. She had no choice but to obey the Prince of Wales, yet loyalty to her future be-trothed was a duty. Why did men have to act so . . . male? In truth she did not feel charitable toward Robert de Beauchamp after what he'd said about Joan. It was most unchivalrous! He was in a nasty mood tonight and she knew the reason was Christian Hawksblood. A tiny bud of pity blossomed in her heart. Poor Robert had fared badly in comparison with his magnetic brother.

As soon as the prince and Brianna entered the hall, Christian Hawksblood and Joan danced toward them and stopped. Hawksblood knew Edward and Joan could not wait another moment to be in each other's arms.

The prince smiled his gratitude, opened his arms, and Joan went into them. It was done smoothly and quickly.

Brianna found herself face-to-face with the dark Arabian once again. His proud head bowed slightly. "*My* lady."

Her heartbeat quickened, her pulse raced, her cheeks grew warm. He was the ultimate all-powerful male, and the most arrogant man she had ever encountered. "I am not *your* lady!" She raised her chin in defiance. A voice inside her cried out, *This is the irresistible knight who dominates your dreams!* Brianna firmly silenced the voice, refusing to listen.

He was almost overcome with lust. Visions of her always had a profound physical effect upon him, but her flesh-and-blood presence almost undid him. He had to clench his hands to prevent himself from touching a finger to the tiny cleft in her chin. It provoked his imagination. She had other clefts he lusted to dip his fingers into. Her head was high, her golden hair swirled about her in a crackling mass. He had never seen such a glorious array. The women of Arabia, Greece, and Byzantium were all black-haired. He saw himself lying naked upon a bed while she trailed her gilt tresses over all of him. He caught her beautiful cries of passion with his mouth. It was a glimpse into the future. "I have seen you many times, demoiselle."

"Where?" she scorned.

"In my visions."

Brianna was immune to men's empty flattery. "In your dreams, of course! How original."

"In my visions and in my dreams also," he conceded. "You have a witch-mark on your—" He saw her stiffen.

Jesu, how can this be? How can we have had the same dream? The roses in her cheeks bloomed scarlet as she recalled he had wanted to taste the beauty mark on her derriere.

"How dare you?" she whispered.

"We will dance," he declared.

"We will *not*," she replied.

"Why not?" he demanded, his eyes devouring her face.

"I . . . I am going to be married to your brother, Robert."

"I think not," he said firmly.

"If he sees me with you it will anger him."

"Then he, and you, had best get used to it, *my* lady."

Her scalp prickled with fear. Her emeralds had not brought her luck tonight. She knew every curious eye in the hall was on the Arabian Knight and therefore at this moment on her. She wanted no gossip, no rumors that she was his latest conquest. "Good night, sir!" She almost flung away from him, but knowing that would raise eyebrows, she walked quietly back to the gallery.

Brianna was relieved when she spotted Robert's blond head towering above everyone else's, at the far end. She lifted her skirts so she could walk more quickly and was soon at his side. "I'm sorry. I returned as soon as I could."

He drained his cup of ale. "Come, let's get out of here," he said curtly.

Brianna hesitated, but she understood he felt humiliation at being struck by the prince. They went outside into the darkness. The night breeze cooled her warm cheeks. When she fell in step beside him, he reached out to take her hand. Brianna searched her mind for something to say, but she could not speak of Joan, she could not speak of Prince Edward, and she could not speak of Robert's brother. She wanted to comfort him, not anger him, so she remained silent as they walked through the Upper Ward.

When Robert stopped walking, Brianna was dimly aware they had reached the Clarence Tower. He took out a key and unlocked the heavy studded door. Then he took her hand again. "Come up with me," he murmured.

"I cannot. These are Prince Lionel's apartments," she protested.

"It's all right. He's not here. He won't mind," he urged.

"Robert, I am unchaperoned."

"Christ!" he swore. "Please?" His hand tightened. "Brianna, I need you!"

She hesitated and the moment she did so, he swung her up into his arms and carried her upstairs. Cresset lamps burned low, casting enormous shadows. He was so big, she knew it was futile to struggle, yet she did so, vigorously. She was not truly afraid. He had always been good-natured and easygoing on the surface. But she put his behavior down to too much drink and this made her feel nervous.

He finally complied with her demands to be put down when they reached an upper chamber, but the moment Brianna's feet touched the floor, his mouth was on hers in an unrestrained kiss. He tasted of strong ale. He smelled of male perspiration. Neither was offensive, but they were far from romantic. The pressure of his mouth increased so that she was forced to open her lips and allow his tongue to thrust inside. Brianna was still not afraid, but she was angry. Her hand groped at his face and by accident her finger slid into his eye. He took his mouth from hers so he could curse, then he took his hands from her so he could cover his eye. She tried to dart away from him, but he took her hand to prevent her. "Brianna, don't be afraid of me. We are almost betrothed . . . surely you won't deny me a kiss?" he coaxed.

"I shouldn't be here alone with you," she protested.

"I need you, Brianna." He drew her closer to his hard body. "Can't I coax you to a giving mood? We are going on a mission to France, perhaps within days. I hoped you would be generous to me. Let me get you a drink. A little verbena mixed into your wine will make you crave my kisses."

Brianna was shocked at his suggestion of a potion. Is that what he and Prince Lionel drank? "No more wine. You've . . . we've had too much." She tried not to show her disgust.

His fingers threaded through her hair. "You gave me permission to court you. Don't struggle, Brianna. I won't force you against your will."

"I'm sorry, Robert. I . . . I have little experience. I've never dallied with a man . . ."

"Hush, sweeting, I know you are virgin. You saved that virginity for your future husband. And that is me, so I am the one who will take it." Brianna knew he was leading to dangerous ground. He said he wouldn't force her, but he had been drinking and was clearly in an amorous mood. Physically, he could easily overpower her and she knew she must extract herself from this intimate situation.

His fingers lifted her chin and he said softly, "You are such a lovely, warm woman. If I don't return from France you will be sorry you were cold to me."

Was he afraid? She would have let him hold her, if he had gone about the business differently. She would have been more than willing to comfort him with a sweet kiss and a tender caress, but she was afraid he would press her for more. "Robert, I really must say good night."

His voice became husky and very intimate. "Why did you come up here with me? To tease?"

She took a steadying breath. "I left the hall with you because I knew you were troubled. I thought you might talk to me about what it is that is threatening you."

He wanted to throttle her. She was nothing but a cockteaser. The last thing he had in mind was talk. However, if he expected to woo and win her, he could see he would have to cool his carnal appetite until they were safely wed.

"It was no doubt a shock to learn you had a brother, but the shock will have worn off by morning."

"I am my father's rightful heir and will be Earl of Warrick someday. The fact that my bastard brother has insinuated himself into the royal circle doesn't interest me in the least!"

He protested so vehemently, Brianna realized he felt threatened in the extreme. Her heart softened toward him. She stood on tiptoe, kissed his cheek, then quickly headed for the door.

He stared after her, then filled the chamber with a crescendo of filthy oaths. He heard something that silenced him. It sounded like Prince Lionel had returned and from the giggling on the stairs, he had brought a female with him. A modicum of his good nature returned to Robert. Perhaps the evening could be salvaged after all.

Prince Edward's gaze drank in Joan's delicate loveliness as they moved sedately about the floor under the watchful eyes of the Court. "Jeanette, did you speak of us to Christian Hawksblood?"

"Of course not, Your Highness. We spoke of my brother, Edmund."

"Am I so transparent then, that he could see my hunger for you?"

Joan thrilled at his admission. "All he had to do was look at *my* face. It gives me away every time I glance at you."

"Then we must both learn control," he warned.

Joan looked up at him, unable to hide the hurt in her eyes.

He squeezed her hands. "Sweet, not control our feelings, only control the way we look at each other in public. I have a duty to protect your name."

Joan smiled up at him. "And in private, Your Highness?" she teased.

"Would to God we could be private," he lamented, while his quick mind discarded one strategy after another.

"We could meet in the garden by the fountain," she suggested eagerly.

"Too many windows look down upon the gardens. Meet me up on the battlements of my own tower."

"What about the guards?" she asked breathlessly.

"Trust me to handle the guards, sweetheart," he responded.

"I would trust you with my life," she whispered.

Edward left immediately; Joan tarried a few minutes. She looked about quickly for a means of escape as William de Montecute approached her. She saw Christian Hawksblood nearby talking with Prince Edward's men.

He raised his eyes in her direction almost as if he read her thoughts. She beckoned him with a glance and miraculously he arrived at her side a moment before De Montecute.

"May I have this dance, my lady?" De Montecute looked at her with calf's eyes.

"I am sorry, my lord. My brother wishes to see me and has sent Sir Christian to escort me."

Hawksblood led her from the hall. "You have an agile mind, a facile tongue, and a love of intrigue, Lady Kent. You would make a brilliant spy."

"Oh, is that what you are?"

He threw back his head and laughed. "Is that what rumor says?"

She noted that he answered her question with another question.

"I fancy I am taking you to your cousin, rather than your brother," he said shrewdly.

Joan's silvery laughter floated out across the Ward. "How did you guess?"

"Did rumor not also say I am psychic?"

Brianna heard Joan's unmistakable laugh as she walked quietly back to her chambers. She saw her friend across the Ward in deep conversation with the dark, dangerous knight who was fast making his mark on all their lives. Suddenly, she felt most aggrieved with Joan. It would serve her right if she too ended up with a rampant male on her hands. Then see if she could save herself as Brianna had done. But perhaps Joan would not want to save herself! Why was the thought unendurable? Would he not be a good match for Joan? The answer came back a resounding *no*! He was *her* knight . . . the knight of her dreams and she wanted him for herself! The moment the thought came into her head she tried to erase it. How could she be so wicked? She had just come from the arms of her betrothed. How could she even think of his brother?

🦢 *8* 🦢

Atop the Prince of Wales Tower, Joan ran into Edward's waiting arms. He enfolded her possessively so she was pressed against his hard warmth. Her ear came just up to his heart and she thrilled at its strong, heavy beat as she breathed in the heady essence of him. His closeness made her shiver with longing.

Edward immediately took off his cloak, wrapped it about her small figure, then slipped his hands inside to gather her close again. It seemed so much more intimate with his hands reaching beneath the garment to caress her body. It aroused them both to an aching longing. When he kissed the corners of her mouth, Joan parted her lips, inviting him to explore the warm, dark cave of her mouth. The sweetness he tasted there drove him to explore other treasures.

His arms slipped into the wide armholes of her tunic to unfasten the front of her silken underdress, then his hands cupped her small, perfect breasts tipped with their tiny delicate buds.

Joan gasped with pleasure as Edward's sensitive fingers first stroked her, then toyed with her nipples until they thrust out like tiny spears. Her gasps turned to cries as he freed her breasts from the confines of her bodice and bent his head to touch the tip of his tongue to them. He raised his head and smiled into her eyes. "You are sweeter than honeyed wine. Little Jeanette, I'll never have enough of you." He covered her breasts and pulled her to him, leaning his back against the crenellated stones.

She leaned into him, feeling his solid body against the softness of her own. Her mons tingled deliciously as she pressed it against a ridge of saddle muscle on his thigh. His shaft throbbed against her soft belly.

He groaned. "Oh, God in Heaven, if I don't stop now, I won't be able to."

Joan was dizzy with desire. Her need for Edward was already far beyond her control. She clutched at him to steady herself. The hard slabs of muscle beneath her hands set her imagination afire. She longed to feel and touch and taste him without the impediment of his clothes. When he had played with her breasts, every touch had penetrated to the core of her heart, then radiated downward, stabbing into her belly, pulsing between her legs.

He began tenderly stroking her hair to calm her, to quiet her. "My little love. Forgive me for arousing you, without being able to carry you to my bed, but I must put your well-being before my needs. I must find us a private place where we may safely spend a few hours together."

"Perhaps tomorrow we can find a private glade in the forest away from the hawking party," she whispered. They made a secret plan to meet at a place where they had played as children.

Edward kissed her good night, keeping an iron control on his lust. "Go! Go from me now while there is still time. I'll follow you discreetly and keep in the shadows to see that you are safe."

Joan had no will of her own. She would obey him no matter what he demanded of her.

Brianna sat at her desk long past midnight. She found that the concentration required to script a legend blocked out her troubles. She invariably felt better after an hour or two of writing. A sense of well-being came to her when she created something that would bring pleasure. When she put the legends into her own words, she tried to evoke her readers' emotions, either making them laugh or cry.

She was working on a book of saints and patiently retold

the story of St. George and the Dragon that young Randal had ruined. She made the capital *T*'s into magnificently ornamented swords. All the great warriors of history had treated their swords with reverence and given them names as if they were human. Roland's was named Durendal and Charlemagne's had been Joyeuse. King Edward's favorite broadsword was named Invincible.

As she cleaned her quills and brushes she found herself wondering about the dark knight with the hawk's face and the hawk's name. He was most likely a warrior who would have names for his weapons. How strange that he was a De Beauchamp! If she wed Robert, the Arabian would be her brother-within-the-law. She shuddered. Her old nurse would have said a goose had walked over her grave. Brianna shook herself mentally. If she wasn't careful, she would lose her tranquil mood and slip back into her earlier depression.

She had been so disappointed in Robert tonight. Her head had been filled with romantic notions. She had breathlessly anticipated each delicate step along the road of courtship that led to love and fulfillment. Somehow she felt cheated of the looks, the sighs, the hand-holding, and the long talks where they explored each other's likes and dislikes, dreams and hopes. Surely a first kiss should be tentative, delicate, not an onslaught! She felt as if Robert had left out too many stages of the wooing, jumping ahead to total intimacy. An intimacy she was not ready for. Both his actions and his attitude had left her feeling somewhat violated. Suddenly, he was no longer her knight in shining armor nor her *gentil parfait* knight.

Then she began to rationalize. He was a flesh and blood man, training for warfare. He had no time for reading romantic epics. Men and women were brought up in two entirely different worlds. His lust tonight had been brought on by anxiety about the coming confrontation with the French. The arrival of an older brother with such striking looks, who was already knighted, made him fear loss of face. It was a human-enough emotion.

Perhaps the fault lay with her. Her ideas were silly and romantic and probably very unrealistic. She must learn to be more of a woman.

When Robert de Beauchamp opened the door, Prince Lionel fell into the room. With all he had imbibed, the stairs proved too much for his rubbery legs. He was accompanied by Lady Elizabeth Grey, who was none too steady on her own pretty legs.

"Can't manage, Rob. As usual, you'll have to help me."

Robert hauled him to his feet, wrapped Lionel's arm about his broad shoulders so that he took most of his weight, and led him to the massive curtained bed.

Lionel fell upon it, laughing like a clown. "Lift her on the bed for me, Rob. Can't manage her myself."

Elizabeth was so tipsy that when Robert picked her up, she mistook him for the prince.

"Get her some of my special wine," Lionel said with an owlish wink.

"By the look of things, she's already had a bellyful," Robert said, laughing.

"Not yet she hasn't, Rob, but she's going to get a bellyful," Lionel said with a leer, patting his cock. A crease came between his brows. "Limp as a bloody lamprey," Lionel muttered.

Robert watched Elizabeth closely for the effects of the verbena and calamint, as she sat on the wide bed and sipped from the goblet. It had always had a marked effect on the serving wenches and he was most curious to learn how it affected a virgin. He didn't have to wait long.

Lionel fumbled with his codpiece, finally managing to get it unlaced. "Shit, why can't I get it up?"

Robert knew it was his extreme youth, combined with the heavy drinking. The insatiable urge was there, but his ability to perform was nonexistent tonight.

Lionel's good nature returned. "Can't manage, Rob. As usual, you'll have to help me."

Robert grinned as he stripped off his chausses and climbed onto the wide bed.

Elizabeth's giggles turned to tears. Even though she was intoxicated and inflamed with the verbena and calamint, she knew she shouldn't be on this bed with these two men.

Robert pushed her back and mounted her.

"Christ, when I watch you fuck, Rob, it excites me more than doing it myself!"

* * *

Brianna's candle burned so low, it almost extinguished itself by the time she blew it out and climbed into bed. Her dreams began with fragments of sights, sounds, and words from the day just lived out.

"Hasn't he made love to you yet?" Her friend mocked her chastity, but then Joan had a vast experience with many different men. Brianna's dream changed. She was holding hands with Robert. She reached up to touch his wheat-colored hair. He smiled into her eyes and bent to whisper a little romantic nonsense. Suddenly, the chamber door flew open to admit the dark, dangerous warrior who claimed to be brother to her betrothed. They could not be brothers; they were opposite in every way. One fair, the other swarthy; one good, the other evil; one kind, the other cruel. He advanced upon them with his drawn broadsword.

Hawksblood pierced Brianna with his pale, ice-blue gaze. "Name my sword and I will spare him."

"Its name is Mortalité!" she cried.

Hawksblood began to laugh as he advanced upon her. "I only promised to spare *him*."

She fell down before him. He raised his sword on high. Then it plunged down into her. It was not his sword, however, that entered her body. It was his male center. He had taken her virginity!

Brianna awoke with a scream upon her lips. Her eyes flew open to see Adele standing in the doorway. "Oh, it cannot be morning," Brianna protested.

"You must hurry if you don't wish to earn Princess Isabel's wrath," Adele urged.

Christian Hawksblood, astride an Arabian with Salome upon his wrist, surveyed the scene before him and thought it was like a magnificent hunting tapestry he'd seen upon a palace wall. Then the tapestry sprang to life, engaging all his senses.

The princess, with nine young ladies in attendance, was resplendent this morning. She was adorned in royal purple, her palfrey draped with a silver cloth beneath its saddle.

Hawksblood's eyes sought his lady immediately. She wore crimson from head to foot. Her glorious hair was plaited and bound tightly with ribbons, her tabard had wide sleeves with slits up each side to ease her movements in mounting and riding. Even her boots were crimson leather and around her neck hung an ivory hunting horn, chased with gold.

Prince Edward's hunter was glossy black, his saddlecloth black silk with the dragon of Wales embroidered in gold. His boots and chausses were black, his doublet, deep forest green. As well as the prince's gentlemen, grooms, squires, falconers, and servants were in attendance, all wearing their own liveries.

The hoods on the hunting birds were as splendid as the finery of their owners, all embroidered, bejeweled, and brightly plumed. Above the shouts and laughter, Hawksblood heard the winding of the horns, the bells on the harness of the princess's palfrey, the piercing shrieks of the falcons and hawks, and the neighing and stamping of the impatient horses as they milled about the pack of baying retrievers.

Christian Hawksblood stood out from the others, as he intended. He wore a sleeveless shirt of Saracen chain mail so fine it was the envy of every warrior. It was polished so highly, it dazzled the eye. Beaten silver bracelets adorned with uncut amber were clasped about his biceps, and his long black hair was drawn tightly back and fastened with a silver clasp, emphasizing his sharp, slanting cheekbones. His weapon belt held an ax, a spear, and a long, curved scimitar. He wore one plain black leather gauntlet. His black kidskin boots came up to his thighs. In contrast, his squire, Paddy, wore sober Lincoln green, like the other squires in Prince Edward's household.

Princess Isabel stared with hauteur at the foreigner. "Edward, he breaks the rules. He carries a gerfalcon. Only royalty has the right to fly such a bird!"

"Christian's mother is an Arabian princess." Edward hid his amusement as his sister's attitude did an about-face. The light of speculation kindled in her eyes and she walked her palfrey toward the newcomer. "I am delighted you are joining us this morning. Any friend of Edward's is a friend of mine."

"Thank you, Your Highness." Though Hawksblood's

bow was deferential, his air was superior. He piqued her pride, yet at the same time piqued her interest.

"Where the devil is Elizabeth Grey?" Isabel demanded of Joan of Kent.

"I don't know, Your Highness, she doesn't confide in me," Joan replied. To Brianna she whispered, "She's her bloody friend!"

The princess eyed Brianna's crimson with a sulky mouth. "Lady Bedford, go and find her. You may catch us up." She lifted her silver hunting horn. "Joan, you go with her."

Prince Edward took a firm hold of his sister's bridle. "Obviously Elizabeth doesn't wish to hawk, but Brianna and Joan do. Let's be off, ladies."

Joan sent him a secret smile of thanks and in return Edward winked at her.

Brianna kept her lashes lowered to avoid eye contact with Christian Hawksblood, but as they headed out through Windsor's park she found him at her side.

"You haunted my dreams last night, *my* lady."

Her lashes flew up and her cheeks became crimson as her ribbons as she recalled her dream of *him*. Logic told her their dreams could not be the same, yet he seemed so intense and compelling, he defied logic. What was this strange power he had over her? With effort, she concentrated upon her horse and her merlin, perched upon her wrist.

Christian removed his falcon's hood. "This is Salome, my *other* lady."

Brianna glanced angrily at his bird, ready to make a disparaging remark, but the sheer beauty of the raptor prevented her. Her plumage shone with the subtle hues of almost indescribable colors. Her head had the proudest curve she had ever seen.

As they neared the river, a heron arose from the water and half a dozen falcons, tercels, goshawks, and lanners were cast into the air. Christian rose in his stirrups to cast Salome. Brianna caught her breath as the bird flew straight up, then began her dive, speeding past the other hawks in just seconds. She struck the heron with a balled-up foot, then grasped it with her sharp talons and sped back to her master. After Christian put the offering in his saddlebag, he praised her lavishly and rewarded her with a morsel fished from his weapon belt.

"Why is she superior to our birds?" She fully expected him to proudly boast of the way he had trained her.

"She was captured along the Persian Gulf in the wild. She did not need to be taught to hunt."

To her dismay, Brianna found him fascinating. She looked about for Joan, but saw her disappearing through the trees with Prince Edward. Up ahead, Isabel was causing a scene. Her tercel had flown to the top of a hundred-foot oak and would not return. It had caught a fish crow and was devouring it. Isabel was in the midst of browbeating a falconer, a groom, a squire, and two servants. The falconer swung a lure and whistled a three-note call over and over. The bird ignored it. The princess threw a tantrum.

As Hawksblood approached, the princess appealed to him. "The servants are useless, could you help me, sir knight?"

He frowned. "It is a fallacy that only a starving bird will hunt. As you see, a starving bird fills its craw." He rode to the far side of the oak for an unimpeded view of the hawk. Brianna followed him, yet stayed a distance back to keep her merlin unruffled. She wondered what the princess expected him to do, climb the damn tree? She observed him closely as he quietly walked his horse beneath the branches and held out his free arm.

Hawksblood stilled to gather his power, then projected his entire focus upon the raptor. It took two full minutes of silence before he managed to merge with the creature long enough to subdue its will. It flew to his wrist like a tame dove.

Princess Isabel was fulsome with her praise, yet demanded over and over to know how he had done it.

"It was just chance, Your Highness. The bird simply decided to return at that moment."

Brianna knew this was not true. Even Isabel rejected this possibility. Finally the princess pressed so persistently for an explanation, he said, "Your falcon is a male; mine female. It was Salome who lured him down." The mystery was solved for Isabel, but Brianna suspected the dark Arabian had more to do with the bird's behavior than his falcon had. When he handed the hunting bird back to the princess, Brianna noticed that though it had landed upon his bare wrist, it left no mark with its razor-sharp talons. Then she noticed that though he was a warrior, he had no scars. At least none on his face or magnificent bared arms. That was unusual. Every man she knew, old or young, displayed scars as badges of courage.

While Christian Hawksblood was occupied with Princess Isabel, Brianna took the opportunity to spur her horse and catch up with the other ladies. She felt slightly alarmed that a part of her wanted to stay at his side, engage him in conversation and watch his every move. It was almost as if he exuded some nameless power over her.

She successfully eluded him, but his squire stayed close to her. When they entered the forest the squire rode just ahead of her, as if he were guarding her path. When he held aside some low branches that could have badly scratched her face, she felt grateful for his attention. At least his squire was comfortably ordinary with his commonplace looks and livery.

The hawking was good on this fine morning. The hunters bagged heron, partridge, and many other game birds as well as hares and coneys. Brianna caught up with Joan and then Prince Edward showed them both how to cast their birds more effectively and how to thread the jesses through their fingers to keep their hawks more secure while they rode through the forest.

When the sun was almost above them, they rode into a clearing that was suitable for their alfresco meal. The grooms took charge of their mounts, the falconers collected their birds, while the servants and the prince's gentlemen laid out the tablecloths and food. Though there were only ten ladies hawking, the entire party, counting all their retainers, numbered over fifty.

When Princess Isabel arrived she made certain she was the center of attention. "Christian de Beauchamp saved my life!" she announced dramatically. "A wild boar almost gored my horse. He killed it with his bare hands." She launched into a blow-by-blow reenactment, but when the hero came into the clearing, he looked no worse for wear. When he sat down on the ground between Brianna and

Paddy, Isabel's mouth became sulky. "I shall ruin my gown if I sit upon the grass. Lady Bedford, please go and fetch the saddlecloth from my palfrey."

Brianna, quite accustomed to Isabel's demands went off toward the horses. She was shocked when she saw the size of the boar slung across Hawksblood's saddle, and though he had many weapons with him, there was neither blood nor wound-marks on the carcass. When she returned with the cloth of silver, Isabel occupied the spot she had vacated. Brianna felt relieved and sat down on the other side of Paddy.

Everyone was enjoying jacks of ale, cider, or mead. Everyone that is, except the princess. "Surely there is wine? Edward, whatever were you thinking of?" she complained.

"Bella, hawking is thirsty work. Wine doesn't quench the thirst half so well as cider. Try the mead. No one else is complaining," Edward said pointedly.

"Perhaps there is wine in my saddlebags, or mayhap one of the grooms brought some. Lady Bedford, please go and ask them."

It was quite obvious to Christian Hawksblood that the princess was determined to ruin Brianna's lunch. It only seemed fair for him to ruin Isabel's.

When Brianna returned empty-handed, she caught sight of Hawksblood's face. It was rapt with focused attention. His eyes glittered aquamarine as they stared at the princess.

Paddy handed Brianna a jack of mead. It was delicious; sweeter than honey. Isabel, however, thought differently. "Ugh! This mead is bitter. It must be rancid!" Her eyes narrowed. "Did someone put something in mine to spoil it? Here, Lady Bedford, taste this."

Brianna sipped the mead and handed it back. "I think it's delicious, Your Highness."

Isabel tried it again. It was so bitter on her tongue, she spat it out. "Faugh! You must be mad."

Brianna alternately watched Christian Hawksblood and Princess Isabel. Each time she selected an item of food, it tasted dreadful to her. For once, Brianna did not think Isabel was doing it to be difficult. She looked exactly as if everything she tasted was bitter as gall. Hawksblood had such a look of satisfaction on his dark face, Brianna suspected he had actually spoiled Isabel's luncheon. She engaged Paddy in conversation. "Do you believe in the power of magic?"

"I'm Irish, Lady Bedford. Magic and casting spells are as real to me as the wind and the rain."

"What of Arabians, Paddy?"

"Cock's bones, they make us Irish look like amateurs."

On an impulse, she asked, "Does Hawksblood have a name for his sword?"

"That he does, lady. His broadsword is Mortalité in name and in truth."

Brianna caught her breath. It was the same as her dream. She had known it would be so!

"He has another sword named Maelstrom." Paddy's humor got the better of him. He leaned closer as if imparting a confidence. "He has a secret weapon. A curved scimitar we all refer to as Killbride."

Brianna recoiled. She needed no one to tell her he was a dangerous devil. Her instincts did that.

" 'Twas meant to amuse you, lady," Paddy half-apologized.

She felt foolish and laughed with him. He was brimful of Irish blarney. "In truth, I don't envy his bride. He just might kill her with fear."

Christian and Edward moved apart from the ladies and stood laughing together. Princess Isabel decided she'd had enough of the great outdoors and declared everyone was to return to Windsor Castle. Most of the ladies trooped after her and the servants began to pack up the remnants of the meal. Brianna and Joan walked toward their horses. "Do you find Christian Hawksblood strange?" Brianna asked.

"Well, he certainly looks different from the other men today," Joan agreed.

"I wasn't exactly referring to his looks. I can't really explain what I mean, I just have a feeling he has strange powers."

"Perhaps he has cast a spell upon you," Joan teased.

Brianna lifted her chin. "He doesn't attract me, he repels me!"

"He is most chivalrous, Brianna. Last night he rescued

me from William de Montecute and escorted me safely home, whether I wished to be safe or not."

"I saw you walking with him. Joan, I think we should both be more careful about being alone with men."

"Oh ho! You were alone with Robert de Beauchamp and his wooing overstepped the boundaries! Isn't love exciting?" Joan asked breathlessly.

Brianna smiled ruefully at Joan's enthusiasm. She certainly didn't find it exciting, but then again she didn't think she had quite fallen in love yet. The girls were riding alone. Isabel and the rest of her ladies were long gone. The forest path narrowed, then forked. Brianna rode ahead of Joan, but when she turned to speak to her companion, Joan seemed to have disappeared. She called her friend's name, but there was no reply, only a faint echo of her own voice.

The forest seemed strangely still and quiet as Brianna listened for the sounds of any members of the hawking party. Only an eerie silence met her ears. She touched her heels to her mare so it would quicken its pace. Nothing looked familiar as she cantered along and she began to suspect she was becoming hopelessly lost. A little bubble of panic arose in her breast as the woods seemed to become more dense.

What if a wild animal scented her horse? To be alone in the forest was foolish and unsafe. The silence made her more nervous than the cracking of twigs and the rustle of leaves would have done. Perhaps the uncanny stillness indicated a storm was brewing. She reached for her hunting horn. A sharp blast or two would soon alert someone. She looked down in dismay to see that her ivory and gold horn was missing. How could she have been so careless?"

Suddenly, she heard another horse approaching. Her knees felt weak with relief. Then she stiffened. Coming toward her through the dense trees was Christian Hawksblood. Slung around his neck was a crimson silk cord holding her ivory horn. He lifted his head like a predator scenting its prey. His dark, hawklike visage compelled her to flee.

Brianna tried to turn her mare so she could flee, but the wretched animal ignored her. It trotted to Christian Hawksblood like a trained pony at a fair. She had been brought up on tales of wolf men, humans turned to beasts who attacked lone travelers, Draco who carried off children to subterranean realms, and imps who hugged you to suffocation. She did not think the Arabian any of these, but she suspected him of being a sorcerer who practiced black magic. He could certainly charm animals and though she knew it seemed impossible, she suspected him of making her lose her way in the forest so she would encounter him!

Christian Hawksblood saw the fear in her eyes and knew he must dispel it. He knew if he was to make this woman his own, he must make use of every encounter. There was a ritual to everything in life and there were at least twelve steps in a courtship or seduction that led to intimacy. Before physical intimacy could be enjoyed, he knew he must forge an emotional connection. The emotion need not be love. It could be jealousy, fear, or hatred, but it was much more pleasant if the emotion was joy or infatuation. Hawksblood had experienced the first step to intimacy long before he ever met her. He had seen her face, seen her body, and was instantly, hopelessly attracted.

For Brianna the first two stages had merged into one the moment they met. Their eye-to-eye encounter had been prolonged, something that was taboo between strangers. When a man stared at a woman, it was an act of aggression. In his case it had been even more than that. He had marked her as his! She had resisted, of course. She had sent him a freezing look, then lowered her eyes and kept her gaze from his. Two clear signals that he should stop! But he had no intention of stopping and pressed on toward intimacy. He wanted her too much to pay the least heed to her negative signals.

They were now in the third degree of intimacy, voice-to-voice. Up until now, it had been a very public contact, yet

he had overstepped the bounds by making intimate state-
ments. He had called her *his* lady. He had tried to make
her dance with him so that the fourth degree of intimacy,
touching hands, could be shared. She had refused him,
eluded him, and shown her anger because he had shocked
her. By calling her *his* lady, he had instantly made their
relationship sexual and propelled her further toward intimacy than she wanted to be.

Hawksblood was encouraged. Anger was a powerful
emotion. Today he was determined to achieve the fourth
level of intimacy at the very least, perhaps even more.

Brianna's chin went up and her eyes met his angrily.
When she spoke, she showed her anger by her accusing
tone. "I am lost!"

He smiled into her eyes and shook his head. "You are
found."

She had given her merlin to the falconer, but his still
perched upon his wrist. Brianna reasoned he could not do
much to her with only one free hand. "You have an uncanny way with animals." Again, it sounded like an accusation.

He pretended it was a compliment. "Thank you. You
enjoyed the hawking today. Hunting is the closest women
are allowed to come to martial pleasure."

"Martial *pleasure*? There is no such thing in my vocabu-
lary. War and killing cannot be pleasurable unless you are
twisted and evil!"

"Your king would differ," he said dryly. "Surely you are
not hypocrite enough to deny you enjoyed today's sport?"

"I do enjoy hawking, but not hunting. I find it cruel." She
challenged him with every haughty word.

He decided to bring her down a little from her high
perch. "You enjoy hawking rather than hunting because
you yourself do not have to do the actual killing, so you
think it absolves you. It does not. When you cast a hawk it
is just as much an instrument of death as an arrow or a
spear."

"Think what you will, sir." She was damned if she would
call this bastard "my lord." "I do not enjoy shedding
blood!"

"Perhaps," he conceded. "Yet you do it and wear red so that the blood won't show."

Ohmigod, that is exactly what I do, Brianna thought. *How can he know these things when I didn't know myself until he pointed them out to me?*

"I know, because sometimes in battle I wear red so my enemy won't know I bleed."

Her eyes widened in alarm. "You read my mind!"

"I did, *my* lady," he acknowledged.

Brianna had had enough. She raised her riding crop to strike him. His face became fierce, his eyes chips of aquamarine. Brianna froze and could not slash him even though she felt the urge to do so. *He has the power to stay my hand!* she thought wildly. "I am not *your* lady, and will never be *your* lady," she panted.

"Never is a long, long time."

"Exactly! Not in this lifetime, nor the next!"

Christian laughed. "You speak as if you were an immortal, Lady Bedford, yet I suspect you know very little of such things."

Brianna thought, *There is no such thing as an immortal,* but she looked at him more closely. "I am to be betrothed to Warrick's son," she said flatly.

"I am Warrick's son."

"You are his bastard!" she flared, then caught her breath at her own daring.

"Ah, now we come to it. The Lady of Bedford has too much pride to look kindly upon a bastard."

Why did he enjoy playing provocateur? "That is not true," she flared.

"Heaven be praised," he mocked solemnly, "then there is still hope for me."

Suddenly, Brianna began to laugh. "You are a damn devil, Christian Hawksblood! 'Tis a game you play to amuse yourself. You enjoy goading me just to provoke me."

When she laughed she was all woman. Her sensuality was potent and arousing. He pictured her beneath him in bed, laughing up at him. Once she was his he'd straddle her for hours for the pure pleasure of looking down at her delicious mouth as it curved with laughter and love. In that

moment he decided he wouldn't release her today until he
had tasted that provocative mouth.

"You are as bad as Princess Isabel, tormenting me for
the sport of it."

"Untrue," he protested, unable to hide the light of humor in his eyes. "I punished her for running you ragged at
lunchtime."

Her eyes widened. "I was sure you had a hand in it. Do
you really have such powers, sir?"

Christian grimaced. "A magician's trick, like mind reading."

"What sort of trick?" Brianna was half-fascinated, half-
afraid.

"Hypnotism. There was nothing wrong with her food. I
just controlled her mind for a moment so that she thought
everything tasted bitter."

Brianna crossed herself. "You are a demon," she whispered.

Hawksblood laughed again. His teeth flashed white
against his dark skin. "There is nothing demonic about it.
'Tis a simple matter of possessing a strong mind, a strong
will. Come, I will take you back to the castle before you
suspect me of casting an enchanted spell upon you."

She rode by his side, half-believing he was capable of
doing such a thing. He had simply held out his hand and
the falcon had flown to him. Could he have the same power
over a woman? Could he have the same power over her?

Gradually, her surroundings became more familiar and
Brianna knew she was close to Windsor's great parklands.
"I can find my own way from here. Give me back my horn,
please."

His face was still, unreadable, yet his words were plain
enough. "I do not dismiss so easily."

Her chin went up, her eyes snapped in vexation.

"I'll give back your hunting horn in exchange for a
favor."

"A favor? You must be mad!" She flushed warmly.

"Ho, did you have a kiss in mind, Brianna?"

How could she deny it when the devil could read her
mind?

"I meant a favor to wear in the tournament."

"Robert will wear my favor; I promised."

"Give me the crimson ribbon from your hair. No one but you and I will know the champion honors you."

She laughed in his face. His bold words amused her in spite of herself. "You have a fine conceit, you foreign devil. What makes you think you will be champion of the tourney?"

"I have set my mind on it, chérie."

"Just as you have set your mind on my ribbon. I suppose if I don't give it to you of my own free will, you will set upon me and take it." Her hands began to unravel her plaits.

His heart soared at the teasing quality he detected in her voice. She was close to flirting with him. His eyes danced with amusement. "I threatened no such thing, Brianna."

She cast him a glance from beneath her lashes. "You don't need to threaten. Your power forces me to obey you."

As she unbound her magnificent hair, it held him in thrall. If only she but knew it, her power over him was infinite. She held the ribbon out to him. He lifted the silken cord over his head and held out the ivory horn. They were not close enough to make the exchange. She felt herself being drawn to him against her will. Her palfrey took three dainty steps toward the Arabian stallion until their stirrups touched. When she reached for her hunting horn, their hands brushed. She jumped as if she had been burned.

"You too felt the fire," he murmured.

Brianna put up her chin in denial, took the horn, and placed the red ribbon upon his palm.

"If our fingers burn each other, imagine the conflagration when our mouths touch."

His outrageous words sent her senses reeling. Her eyes were irresistibly drawn to his sensual lips as her imagination took flight.

Slowly, Christian Hawksblood dipped his dark head with a sure purpose in mind. His mouth then took total possession of hers. He did not touch her with anything save his lips, yet Brianna felt herself imprisoned, unable to escape, not wanting to escape. Tiny rivulets of molten gold ran along her veins, spreading heat to every part of her body. She closed her eyes and leaned into the kiss to enjoy the pure rapture of it. This was how he'd kissed her in her dreams! The kiss was glorious, filled with magic. She wanted it to last forever. His mouth claimed her as *his,* just exactly as a lover's mouth should claim *his* lady's.

"Your mouth was made for love," he said softly against her lips. The sound of his deep voice broke the spell she had fallen under. She opened her eyes, gazed with shock into his for a heart-stopping moment, then she wheeled away from him and dug in her spurs. She managed to remove herself from his odious presence, yet she could not rid her thoughts of him. He stayed as close as her shadow, intruding each and every hour that was left of the day, then on into the night.

Joan of Kent and Edward of Wales had their prearranged assignation. They lingered in the forest until everyone headed back to Windsor, then they rode to the pool, three miles through the bluebell woods, where they had swum as children.

Edward was there before her. Joan's heart fluttered wildly at the sight of him. He was the handsomest prince in Christendom and she was determined to steal his heart. Edward fastened her mare's reins to a tree, then came to her stirrup and lifted his arms to her. She gazed down at him, wanting to capture this moment in time to savor it forever. The sun caught his golden hair. His teeth gleamed white in his tanned face. His deep blue eyes flashed like sapphires. Her heart overflowed with her love for him. She went down into his strong arms in a flurry of seafoam petticoats. Breathlessly she whispered, "I wore green so the grass stains wouldn't show."

Edward groaned as her words ignited his desire. He had only intended to be alone with her so they could talk and laugh and yes, kiss and touch, but now they were alone together in this enchanted place that evoked such happy, carefree memories, his desire for her blotted out everything else.

The shaded pool was private, quiet, and temptingly intimate. He carried her into the tall grass by the pool's edge, then sank to his knees, still holding her. "Jeanette, have you any idea how I feel about you? You have captured my heart for all time."

Joan's arms tightened about his neck and she lifted her lips for his kiss. He brushed his mouth against her lips softly, gently. There were things he wanted to tell her and he knew that once their mouths fused in deep possession, it would be too late for words. "Jeanette, I want to marry you. I spoke to the king about us."

She drew back so she could look up at him, shock and dismay mixed with happiness and love on her heart-shaped face. "Edward, you should not have said anything! They will never let us wed. My poor father was labeled traitor and you know you must make a political marriage."

Edward ground his teeth in frustration. "So my parents informed me in no uncertain terms. But I don't want a political marriage, I want you. All I can hope is that their plans come to naught, as usual."

"Edward, it is enough that you want me. I ask for nothing more. I love you so much. I've always loved you, and I always will! Let's not spoil our time alone thinking of what cannot be. We have today, this minute. No one can ever take it from us."

They clung desperately for a moment, then his mouth claimed hers in a heart-wrenching kiss that deepened to desperation. They hungered to join their bodies, their hearts, their very souls, until they became one.

"Let's go swimming as we did when we were children," Joan begged breathlessly. It seemed the natural thing to do. Each began to undress without embarrassment. Edward stripped off his doublet while Joan removed her tunic and boots and stood before him in her diaphanous petticoat, revealing yet concealing the creamy skin and womanly curves of her small, perfect body. "Let me help you with your boots. Princes need help undressing, I understand," she said mischievously.

Edward propped his back against a tree and lifted his foot, amused that such a tiny creature thought she could aid a six-foot man. She managed to remove the first one without incident. As she bent to her task, Edward's gaze was fastened to her breasts as they almost spilled from her bodice. The other boot proved more stubborn. She pulled with all her might, then suddenly it gave way and she sprawled backward into the grass, giggling like a little girl.

Edward was on top of her in a heartbeat. He pulled down her chemise so he could claim her delicate breasts. She lay before him naked to the waist, all pink and cream loveliness. Her small hand could not resist the naked chest above her, covered with damp golden curls. When her fingers tangled in the crisp pelt, she cried out with joy at the splendor of him.

His mouth crushed hers and they gloried in the taste of each other. His hands went to her plaits to unbraid them. Her silver-gilt hair was a lure to him. He needed to bind it about his throat, needed to see and feel it between their naked bodies.

"Leave it bound up while we swim," Joan gasped.

Little innocent, Edward thought, *doesn't she know I don't want to swim? Doesn't she know I want to make love to her?* "Let me have the pleasure of seeing it down."

Giving Edward pleasure was Joan's fervent desire. She helped him take it down, then sat very still as he spread it all about her. She drew in a tremulous breath as he removed her chemise, then lifted her legs so he could take off her stockings. Her garters were a froth of lace and pearls high on her thighs, and between the garters sat a tiny mop of silver-gilt ringlets.

Everything about her was so deliciously feminine, it cried out to his overt masculinity. When Edward buried his face in the fragrant curls, Joan was both amazed and thrilled. He pressed a burning kiss upon her mons, then sat up to gaze his fill of her. He knelt before her and drew her small buttocks up onto his thighs. Then he opened her legs and parted the pale curls with his fingers. Edward cupped her with the palm of his hand between her legs, then he slid his middle finger up inside her. She was so impossibly small and tight, and he was so unbelievably large and swollen at the moment, he doubted he would be able to breach her, at least not without hurting her brutally.

The tiny muscles of her sheath gripped his finger convulsively and she gasped out her pleasure as she experienced a contraction. "Oooh, it feels lovely, Edward." Her hand tried to reach the bulge at his groin. "I want to see you, too."

"No, sweetheart. I'm too big for you."

"I don't care!" she cried passionately. "I want this. I've wanted you forever, Edward!"

With trembling hands he pulled her into his lap and began to dress her. "I want you unbearably, my love, but you must trust me in this. We need to spend the entire night together to consummate our love properly. We need a private apartment with a soft bed. I'll arrange it . . . soon, soon," he swore.

Joan was in paradise to think she had so much power over her godlike prince. "Oh, Edward, I love you so much. I want you to be the first."

"The first and the last," he growled. Then he finished dressing her with tender, loving hands. When he was done he kissed her again, tasting her sweetness. "Precious, precious," he murmured against her throat. He lifted her before him on his horse and led Joan's mare by its bridle. When they came in sight of Windsor, Edward's strong hands lifted her into her own saddle. Then he touched his fingers to his lips and galloped toward the castle.

Joan stared after him a long time. She was happier than she had been for many years. Prince Edward loved her. Only love could have made him brave enough and foolish enough to tell the king and queen he wanted Joan of Kent for his wife.

🐦 10 🐦

Prince Edward made his selection of young nobles who would accompany him on the French mission and sent to Berkhamsted for a hundred men-at-arms and a hundred Welsh archers.

The Earl of Warrick's best were trained at Windsor. He decided to take most of them, four hundred men-at-arms and two hundred archers. Another five hundred came from Lancaster's Savoy Palace, a few miles down the Thames.

The king gathered two thousand men from the royal strongholds of Woodstock, Havering, and Kenington. The remaining three thousand would be provided by the garrisons at Rochester and Colchester, which were close to the Port of Ipswich, where the fleet was gathering.

Prince Edward thought his brother Lionel, should be allowed to join them, but his father said, "Your mother begged me to leave him in England."

"Surely you don't want him to become a weakling?" demanded Edward.

"I promised your mother he wouldn't see action until he turned fifteen."

"Age has nothing to do with it. He is strong as an ox and taller and broader than either of us."

"Has he asked you to plead his case?" asked the king.

"No, but he'll be furious when he learns he is to be left behind," Prince Edward pointed out.

Prince Lionel was not the only one to be furious. His lieutenant, Robert de Beauchamp, was livid. "Christ Almighty, that's ridiculous. It's no doubt the Prince of Wales' doing. He wants all the glory for himself!" Robert could still feel the humiliating slap in the face from Edward. "I'll go and speak to my father. Warrick might be able to change the king's mind."

But when Robert spoke to his father and he learned that Christian Hawksblood was going, while he was not, a bitter hatred began to fester within him. Arguments availed him nothing. Warrick judged a man by his ability to obey orders.

When Robert returned to Prince Lionel, he commiserated with him while the young giant railed and cursed. Lionel was an extremely physical youth who vented his spleen by smashing an oak refectory table before he began to feel better.

Robert's rage turned inward and the seeds of revenge began to take root. "Now that I've had time to reflect upon it, Your Highness, the king is probably wise not to allow both of you to fight. You are second in line to the throne of England and if aught befalls Edward, you will be the heir apparent. I think you should be given the Scepter and named prince regent while your father and brother go on this campaign." Robert knew Lionel was Queen Philippa's favorite son. "Why don't you speak with your mother? She has a way of persuading the Council to carry out her wishes."

Prince Lionel was placated. It might be enjoyable to peacock about as King of England; to be flattered and fawned upon, and receive the adulation of the fairer sex.

Robert de Beauchamp, however, was not placated. Jealousy, humiliation, and hatred spawned a need for vengeance.

As they traveled to Ipswich, the king, Warrick, and Prince Edward had many opportunities to talk with Christian Hawksblood and observe his actions. Among a throng of six thousand men there were always minor ailments, injuries, and quarrels. Hawksblood had obviously had medical training and his squires were extremely knowledgeable about horses.

Warrick noticed that the men under young Edward's standard were well disciplined, even though most of them had seen no military action. Their morale was high because Edward and Christian set the tone. Warrick decided to put his son in charge of two hundred men. He was a natural leader, had much experience in battle, and was the only one who knew exactly where the French fleet gathered.

Prince Edward's squire, Sir John Chandos, was older than the prince, just as Paddy and Ali were older than Hawksblood, and the five men spent much time in each other's company. This was the Prince of Wales' first military maneuver and the other four men made a silent pact to protect him.

The night before they sailed, Christian knew the thoughts that crowded in Edward's head. He had no fear of facing the enemy; his only fears and hopes were that he would acquit himself well in the eyes of his father and the eyes of his own men. They sat talking in Hawksblood's tent. Ali had oiled their muscles with almond and frankincense while Paddy and John Chandos selected and polished the armor that would be donned before they embarked.

Edward said, "It will be a disaster without horses if we make land before we encounter the French fleet. I've trained all my life to fight upon a destrier."

"It is not horses that win battles, it is men. Before and after fighting are difficult times, but once you engage in battle you are filled with a divine power that transcends fear, doubt, fatigue, defeat. A calm descends so you are able to focus all thought, energy, and strength. It is a feeling of omnipotence. You see all in such a crystal-clear light that every hazard is avoided. Everything is stripped down to its simplest terms: fight or run, win or lose, live or die."

Edward said quietly, "My father, the king, always believes in victory and he is able to make others believe it. That is his strength."

"It is a gift from the gods," Christian said. "I, too, am firmly convinced we will be victorious. I believe battles are won before they are ever fought." Edward nodded, for they shared the conviction.

When Edward left, Paddy succumed to doubts and misgivings that clogged the very air men breathed before a military campaign. "Chandos questioned me about Helvoetsluys, asking how long since we were in Flanders. I didn't let on we'd never set foot there."

Christian gripped his shoulder to suffuse him with confidence. "Cast out all doubt, Paddy. The French fleet is exactly where I said it was."

Ali censured Paddy. "He has been taught to totally trust his instincts, to never, ever, doubt himself. It is his life's sacred secret."

Paddy shook his head. " 'Tis an Eastern philosophy, sometimes incomprehensible to me, Ali-Babba."

"Nay, Paddy's Pig, it was a secret order of Knights Templars who taught him the mystic rites; they just happened to live in the East. I suspect most of them had Irish blood."

"Jasus, now I've really got the wind up! Anybody with any brains knows the Irish are a bunch of shiftless, lying con men."

"The expression 'con men' is derived from Connaught men, I have no doubt."

Paddy began to laugh, and his mirth banished the darklings. It was an intrinsic trait of his cursed Irish blood to be melancholy and introspective. He fought the urge to drink himself into oblivion whenever he faced death. Only the fact that he feared Hawksblood's contempt more than he feared death kept him sober.

Christian Hawksblood lay abed thinking. He was impressed by the English vessels he'd seen. The larger ships were mounted with bronze cannon with long-spouted barrels. The admirals had brought a good supply of shells and gunpowder, which carried the disadvantage of blowing a whole ship to kingdom come if it received a direct hit.

Christian began the meditation that preceded his visions. He was amazed at the detail he saw. His instincts told him the French had been alerted, for they were at this moment busy with plans to defend the great harbor of Sluys. They were forming their ships into four lines of defense. In the center of the first line rode the three magnificent English vessels they'd captured in coastal forays. The ships were linked together by metal chains so it would be impossible for the enemy to retake them.

Christian projected his vision ahead to the time when the French scouts spotted the English fleet. He saw the watch turrets crawling with Genoese arbalests. The vision was identical to his previous one, so he was able to sleep untroubled.

They embarked at dawn, but before he went aboard, Hawksblood sought Warrick, who commanded the entire operation. "Will you trust me to lead the way?"

Warrick searched the dark face for any trace of treachery. He saw none. "I will. We stand or fall together."

Christian hesitated. Warrick was a plain, no-nonsense military leader who looked as if he would put no faith in visions. "The French have placed the *Edward,* the *Rose,* and the *Katherine* in the front line because they believe we will try to retake them, but they have chained them to their own ships and they must be destroyed. They have blocked Sluys so we cannot enter the harbor, but the fools don't realize the entire French fleet is a sitting duck. It is your operation to direct, not mine, but if I were in charge, Welsh bowmen would be on the deck of every English vessel to take out the Genoese arbalests."

There was absolutely no precedent for a sea battle being fought with bows and arrows. Bowmen on deck would hamper the gunners who manned the cannons. Moreover, Admiral Morley had sworn an oath to the king to retake the English vessels.

Warrick rubbed his nose, wanting to ask how his son came by his information. He made a decision not to question him. He crammed his helmet over his graying head and turned to shout his orders.

Christian and Edward clasped arms before they boarded the ships they would command, then Hawksblood's ship weighed anchor and sailed out into the northern Straits of Dover.

Robert de Beauchamp sought out Brianna and found her returning from her daily lesson with Dame Marjorie. She knew his pride must be smarting at having been left behind while his father and half brother were in the front lines of the action. Her heart filled with pity. "Robert, I'm so sorry you are stuck here in England. It seems so unjust."

He laughed and waved a negligent hand. "Prince Lionel was disappointed, but he was left behind for political reasons and since I'm in his service, it is my duty to remain here, not only to guard him, but the queen and you ladies as well."

He seemed puffed up with hollow pride. She shouldn't have said anything. It was his way of rejecting her pity. "Then yours is the more important responsibility," she complimented him.

"If either the king or the Prince of Wales is killed, then Prince Lionel becomes heir to the throne."

Brianna inwardly recoiled from his blunt words. Dear God, is that what he hopes for? Disloyalty and guilt swept over her for her unkind thoughts of Robert. He wanted no such thing! He was merely facing facts. She supposed it was his responsibility to be prepared for any eventuality.

"I see that the foundations for the new Round Tower are dug. I spoke with the king about the stone he wants from Bedfordshire. He asked me to oversee its transport."

Brianna was surprised that Robert had taken this upon himself without first discussing it with her. After all they weren't yet betrothed.

"I thought it would give me the opportunity to visit Bedford and inspect it for myself. The king thought you might like to go home for a visit and I could escort you."

The suggestion that she return to her home took the sting from his high-handedness. Her father had died in the king's service, fighting the Scots, when she was twelve and she had made her home at Windsor ever since. The king had appointed a castellan to run Bedford Castle and its holdings and her moneys were collected and kept for her by the Treasury.

When she married, she expected to live part of each year at Bedford and part of the year at her husband's castle. Since she was an heiress, wealthy enough to be taken into royal wardship, she had taken it for granted her groom would own castles. She knew a woman's property went to her husband when she married, but hoped he would be generous enough to pass her property to their children, if God so blessed her.

"Oh, Robert, that would be wonderful! I haven't seen it for five years, though it's only about fifty miles north. I'll ask Queen Philippa's permission to leave Court."

Robert caught her hand and drew her close. "It will give us a chance to get to know each other more intimately."

She blushed at his words and glanced up at him to reassure herself that she had nothing to fear from this good-natured, blond giant who was always laughing. He took her by surprise, covering her mouth with his. Brianna did not pull away until his kiss deepened and he began to ravage her mouth. "Robert!" she gasped, "you go too fast."

At that moment, Lady Elizabeth Grey rounded the corner and almost collided with them. A look of horror came into Elizabeth's face. Her hands flew to her cheeks, which had turned a flaming red. Then she turned on her heel and ran as if the devil were after her.

"Oh Lord, if she spreads this abroad, I'll be called on the carpet by Dame Marjorie, and if the queen learns we've been kissing in public, she may not let me come to Bedford with you."

"Elizabeth Grey will keep her mouth shut. She has no room to talk about anyone else's behavior."

Brianna cast him a puzzled glance. Why in the world did he insist first Joan and now Elizabeth was immoral? Joan

might be flirtatious, but the red-haired Elizabeth wasn't
even that. She supposed he recalled her nervous giggling
when Prince Lionel had singled her out for his uncouth
attentions. Brianna felt relief when she saw Adele hurrying
toward her. She enjoyed Robert's company more when
they were not alone together.

Both King Edward and Warrick had misgivings when
their vessel approached the Flemish coast and they saw no
sign of ships. It was only when they came up to the massive
harbor of Helvoetsluys they glimpsed the forest of masts.
"By the Chalice," swore Warrick, "my son was right
about everything." He gave the signal for the English bowmen to topple the Genoese from their turrets, and they
proceeded to clear the decks with their steel-tipped arrows
in preparation for the boarders.

Christian Hawksblood swore an Arabic oath beneath his
breath. By firing only a few of the French ships, the entire
fleet could have been destroyed, but the vainglorious fools
preferred hand-to-hand fighting rather than see the three
captured English vessels go up in flames.

The grappling irons were thrown and, swords in hand,
King Edward's warriors swarmed from their own decks to
board the French ships. Hawksblood and his two squires
fought with sword in one hand and long-knife in the other,
dispatching twice as many as the others about them. He
saw the king and Warrick taking the leaders prisoner. He
cursed again, believing all should die rather than be ransomed to fight another day.

Christian spotted Prince Edward and fought his way to
his side. They grinned at each other, unable to speak and
be heard over the deafening pandemonium.

For the next two hours they fought shoulder to shoulder
with their squires at their backs, and at one point went to
the aid of Edmund of Kent. When the battle was about
finished and they had won the day, Hawksblood stood
transfixed as he watched Warrick order ropes slung over
the rigging. Then his father gave the order to hang the
French leaders from their own yardarms. Now Christian
knew why his enemies called him the Mad Hound.

When the unharmed English vessels were unchained, a

great cheer arose from the throats of the English. Admiral Morley and the queen's knight-errant, Sir Walter Manny, sailed the ships out of the harbor and the king boarded the *Edward* and stood on the forecastle to acknowledge the hero-worship of his men.

Warrick caught sight of his son and saluted him with his sword. Christian Hawksblood's feelings for Warrick were slowly undergoing a metamorphosis. His father had put total trust in him to lead them to the French. The sole basis for that trust could only have been the fact that he was his son. He had seen Warrick in action, leading over six thousand men-at-arms, as well as indirectly commanding another four thousand sailors. He now had total respect for Warrick's leadership and courage. However, he reserved judgment on him as a husband and father.

Hawksblood admired the audacity of retaking their own ships. It was tantamount to thumbing their noses at the French. He bowed his head to his sire in very genuine respect for his leadership. When the gains and losses of the day were tallied, it was estimated that the French must have lost over twenty thousand men, while the English losses were between two and three thousand.

Hawksblood and Ali were kept busy staunching, binding, and sewing wounds on the journey back to England. Hawksblood knew that wounds taken at sea seldom festered, and in fact healed faster. Probably it had something to do with the salt air.

The coast was lined with English waiting to cheer them on their return. It was decided to sail the three recaptured vessels up the Thames estuary, right into the Port of London, and anchor at Tower Wharf. Word of their great victory had spread so that the banks of the great river were packed with what appeared to be the whole populace.

King Edward was well satisfied with the success of the sea campaign. It would give him time to build up his army for the invasion of France. After the battle, King Philip had sent his envoy to offer a one-year truce, but King Edward had demanded the release of his friend William de Montecute before he would parley. He had no intention of waiting a whole year before he invaded France, but perhaps he could deceive the French king long enough to get De Montecute home to Katherine.

The king was both pleased and relieved that the Prince of Wales had emerged unscathed from his first military campaign. He now had no worries that Prince Edward would follow in his own footsteps and make a magnificent warrior king, when the time came. He embraced his son warmly. "You are truly my son in every way, Edward. I am more proud of you than of any other achievement."

"You set such a glorious example, Father. I swear I will never shame you in battle. Christian de Beauchamp fought with a long-knife as well as his sword. I think he should train some of our men-at-arms to fight two-fisted."

"Warrick and I are indeed blessed when it comes to our sons. I'll have a word with him. I believe the men of Cornwall are good with knives. We'll give Hawksblood some men to train, never fear."

When the ships docked at Tower Wharf the entire Court, as well as most of the citizens of London, came out to give their men a heroes' welcome. Queen Philippa, Princess Isabel, Princess Joanna, and all their ladies, adorned in their finery, lined the wharf. Prince Lionel and his household, on Robert de Beauchamp's advice, were turned out in their finest polished armor and plumed helmets, to pay homage to the victors. Both understood they must never reveal the resentment they harbored against the king, the prince, and Warrick.

King Edward greeted Queen Philippa, Princess Isabel, and Princess Joanna with kisses. John of Gaunt, feeling himself too old for kisses, saluted his father and brother with his sword, then pressed his brother Edward with dozens of questions about the fighting.

The queen had brought all the children to London from Windsor on the royal barge, even the new baby, so the citizens cheered themselves hoarse. Princess Isabel and her ladies followed the queen's lead and congratulated the noble heroes with kisses. She kissed her brother, the Prince of Wales, his squire, who was already a knight, Sir John Chandos, then she moved on down the line anticipating touching her lips to Edmund, Earl of Kent.

Joan began with her brother, kissing him and lightly

touching the wound on his forehead. "You were far too handsome anyway, Edmund."

He laughed with her. "I don't think the damn thing's deep enough to leave a scar." Joan glanced up at the approaching princess. "Jesu, if it does, she will eat you alive!"

When Joan stood before Prince Edward, he was almost blinded by her loveliness. She wore pale peach trimmed with white swansdown, reminding him of the delicious icing upon a cake. She looked absolutely edible! After the blood and gore of the naval battle, her sweetness would cleanse him, her pretty laughter would erase the echoing screams of death from his ears. When their hands touched, Joan slipped him a note and their hearts soared with joy that they were young and alive and in love.

Brianna kissed Prince Edward upon the cheek, but she was determined that Christian Hawksblood would receive no such familiarity. When she stood before him, she lowered her lashes and held out her hand as she had done with the others.

He raised it to his lips, then very deliberately bit the end of her finger. Her lashes swept up and she met his gaze, but a strange feeling came over her as she looked into his eyes. *Are they sapphire or turquoise?* she asked herself, utterly mesmerized.

"Aquamarine," Christian informed her with a grin.

She immediately saw that his face was unscarred. Still he bore no mark of battle. *He was an irresistible force.* Against her will she felt herself being drawn to him. She went up on tiptoe making a moue with her lips. She intended to spit on him. His glare, fiercer than any hawk's, challenged her. Moreover, it promised retribution if she offered him the insult. She set her will against his, refusing to let his overpower hers. He had bitten her finger, albeit gently, and she would pay him back in kind.

In a flash, Brianna fastened her teeth onto his earlobe and bit down sharply until she drew blood. Her action told him immediately that she was not indifferent to him. It also aroused him. He felt his hot blood throb in his earlobe and beat wildly in his throat. Brianna of Bedford's effect on him was thrilling and he knew without doubt he had the same effect upon her.

Perhaps now he would be scarred, she thought with satisfaction as she whirled away to lose herself in the crowd. The metallic, salty taste of his blood, however, stayed with her long after she escaped his presence.

King Edward decided to return to Windsor by barge with his queen and their royal children. He held up his arms for silence. "We offer thanks to God for our great victory. We shall have a thanksgiving service in Windsor's chapel tonight. Next week on the feast of St. Swithin's we shall hold our tournament. Of necessity, it will only be a small affair this year, but I promise we will make up for it next year when my new Round Tower is built. I am going to establish an Order of Chivalry that will be the highest in Christendom and we will celebrate it with the most magnificent tournament this or any country has ever held!"

The cheering crowds drowned out King Edward's words, but the tall king did not tire of waving along all the miles of the Thames that took him back to his beloved Windsor.

❧ 11 ❧

It was past the hour of midnight before the king dared to seek Katherine de Montecute's chamber. She had lit the candles and turned down the bed, but she had not retired. She knew he would come. She wore a diaphanous chamber robe of azure, his favorite color. She brushed her dark gold hair for an hour so that it would crackle and cling of its own volition.

Katherine's worries had tripled while King Edward had sailed toward France. That country already held one man she loved. Next she had feared for her son, and then for her lover. She had been giving much thought to the future. If something happened to her husband, the Earl of Salisbury, that title would pass to her son. In spite of the earl being the king's friend, William had never profited from it. They only had Wark Castle, a formidable, stark fortress near the Scottish border. Tonight, she intended to press the king for an heiress for her son, William. Instinctively, she knew she would get more from Edward before he slaked his thirst for her. Her royal lover was capable of bestowing favors with a lavish hand.

"Katherine, you are more beautiful than a goddess." He went down before her on his knees in homage to her loveliness.

"Edward, thank you for keeping my son safe for me. If he too had been captured, I think I would have lost my sanity."

"I almost decided to leave him here in England to spare you anxiety, Katherine, but he is a young warrior, entitled to earn his spurs."

"I know he is a man grown, Edward. I want him to make a good marriage, one that will befit the future Earl of Salisbury." She ran her fingers through his thick hair and pressed his face between her warm breasts.

He unfastened the ribbons of her robe so that his mouth and hands had full access to her voluptuous globes. His voice thickened as he began to nuzzle and kiss her ripe body. "Let me love you, Katherine. We will decide this later. Never fear, I will reward the De Montecutes with a worthy bride."

Katherine covered her breasts with her hands, preventing him from suckling her. "Edward, I want to get this out of the way so that I can give my full attention to welcoming you home, as a hero should be welcomed."

He searched her face and rose to his full height, desire beating in his temples. "Who do you have in mind, beloved?"

"Blanche of Lancaster?" she asked with great cunning, knowing full well that child and her fortune were being reserved for one of the king's sons.

"I cannot promise you Blanche, my love. She is royal and her father has the right to demand a royal husband for her. Katherine my love, ask me for any but her."

Katherine sighed heavily, allowing the silence to stretch between them.

The king's heart constricted, fearing he could not please her.

Finally she took pity on him and broke the silence. "Well, I believe William is much taken with Joan of Kent.

He would be well pleased with Joan, I have no doubt, and if her son is well pleased, can a mother be other than well pleased also?"

Edward swept Katherine into his arms and carried her to the bed. "Joan of Kent it shall be!" he declared magnanimously.

Katherine's arms slipped about his neck and she lifted her parted lips for his kiss. "Thank you, darling. You can announce it at the tournament."

Edward felt a qualm about his son's infatuation with Joan, but if she were married, it would remove the temptation to make her his wife. Once Edward lay down beside Katherine, thoughts of everyone, save the two of them, were blotted from his consciousness.

If he had known the depth of emotion Edward and Joan felt for one another, however, he would have had more than one qualm. In the Banqueting Hall they had tried to pay attention to what others said to them, tried to listen to the epic tale of valor that Godenal had composed in honor of the Plantagenet victory, but they could not. Neither knew what was said to them, neither even knew what they ate. Both were obsessed by the object of their desire. Their eyes met a thousand times. They tore their gaze from each other, only to find it drawn back again and again.

Prince Edward carried Joan's note like a lovesick swain. He had read it so many times, he knew it by heart: *"My Prince, Words cannot tell you how proud I am of your great victory at Sluys. My heart is bursting with pride and love for you. I want to cry from the highest turret of Windsor that you are my champion! I long to embroider your beloved name upon my sleeve for all the world to see. You are my Perfect Gentle Knight. I ache to be in your arms again. Yours forever, Jeanette."*

It was agony to have only one dance together, but it was long enough for Edward to pass her a love letter and to touch her for a few minutes. The result of being in proximity, however, only able to touch hands, took its toll. Joan was left with a longing that made her heart ache. Edward's hunger raged until he was in an agony of need.

Joan waited until she was in her bedchamber before she read Edward's words: *"My little Jeanette, I thank you with all*

*my heart for your love note. From now on I shall write to you
each day. We cannot go on this way, never being alone together. I intend to buy a house in London, as your brother has
done. I shall entrust Christian Hawksblood with my letters for
you and ask you to do the same. I burn for you, but ask you to
be patient until our haven is ready. I kiss your lips, I kiss your
heart, but save the other kiss for lower until you are safely in
my arms. E."*

Joan touched her lips to the letter and slipped it beneath
her pillow. "Glynis, I want you to make me a spell."

The dark Welsh girl drew close. "What kind of spell, my
lady?" With the ancient knowledge of her pagan ancestors
she was completely aware that Joan was in love. It was the
object of her affections that disturbed Glynis. She knew
Joan's path would not be smooth. The road to her goal was
long and littered with stumbling blocks. Glynis sighed. Her
charge was so sweet, childlike, and uncomplicated, she
thought that if she wished hard enough for something, she
would get her wish. Joan had no idea that wishes could turn
to curses.

"A love spell," Joan confessed. "Glynis, I am in love and
I want to be loved in return. Cast me a spell that will make
me irresistible!"

"Take off your clothes. The nude body adds to the power
of your invocation and the spell you project." Glynis gathered green candles, herbs, and an incense burner. With a
long taper she lit the green candles, then set aloes and
incense to smolder. "Repeat after me," Glynis intoned, and
Joan began the incantation:

> "I am possessed by burning love.
> Let this man yearn for me, desire me.
> Let his desire burn for me.
> Let my love come forth from the spirit and
>   be transmitted to him.
> Let him desire me as nothing has been
>   desired before.
> Fill him with love for me!"

The following day Joan was inundated by young men
who asked for a favor to wear in the tournament. She gave

scarves to John Holland, Michael de la Pole, Roger de Cheyne, and William de Montecute.

De Montecute refused the scarf. "Lady Kent . . . Joan, I beg you give me something more personal. I ask a token that represents a pledge between us."

"What sort of pledge?" she asked, amused.

"A pledge of love. Give me a stocking, Joan. Something personal you have worn against your body."

Suddenly she was not quite as amused. "William, you shock me! You should not be saying these things to me," she rebuked.

William became more intense than ever. "Soon I hope I will have the right. Joan, you must know you are irresistible to me."

The word "irresistible" echoed back to the love spell she had cast. Jesu, she hadn't been specific enough. She should have invoked Edward's name especially! "I'm sorry, William. Take the scarf or ask another lady for her favor."

He had to be satisfied for the moment. He took Joan's scarf, pressed it to his lips, inhaled its fragrance, then tucked it into his doublet.

For Prince Edward she had a sleeve. Inside, she had embroidered their entwined initials. She had it tucked inside her bodice in case of a chance encounter. Joan spotted Brianna coming from the Queen's tower and called for her to wait. Brianna was wearing buttercup yellow, which made her look as if she walked in sunshine. "Let's play truants and go to the lists to watch them practice," Joan suggested.

"We shouldn't, but I cannot resist you," Brianna agreed.

"Mmm, no one can resist me today, it seems."

"Have you bestowed your favor upon anyone yet?"

"I've handed out four identical pink scarves," Joan said with a giggle.

"Any combatant courageous enough to fly the color pink must indeed be smitten," Brianna said, laughing.

"I have a sleeve tucked away for my special champion," Joan said, patting her bodice.

"And that champion is?" Brianna inquired.

"I haven't decided yet," Joan said lightly. "Have you given Robert your favor?"

"Not yet," Brianna replied, "but he asked me and I promised."

In the field beyond the lists, the pavilions of the contenders were being set up. The tents held armor, weapons, changes of clothing, wooden bathing tubs, medical supplies, saddles, harnesses, cots, and stools. Each contestant had his own squires and pages whose main duties were to help him don armor, replace broken lances, assuage thirst, bind wounds, and offer unfailing encouragement.

When challengers came from far afield, they might even have to sleep in their pavilions if the castle was filled. This tournament, however, would be relatively small with contenders coming only from the surrounding counties. But no matter how small, a tournament was a lodestone attracting merchants, peddlers, jongleurs, bards, and a ragtag assortment of scoundrels who lived by their wits.

In an adjoining meadow merchants were setting up stalls to display their goods imported from near and far, so that by the day of the tournament, Windsor would take on the atmosphere of a fair. Horses, tapestries, Syrian silks, Persian rugs, Venetian glass as well as things like home-brewed beer would be on sale.

Brianna stopped feeling guilty about their truancy when she saw Princess Isabel and her other ladies watching the jousters practice. In fact, most of the female population of Windsor was here, be they scullery maid or countess. Those who worked in the kitchens knew today was their only chance for a bit of leisure, for tomorrow they would be working sixteen hours a day preparing festive food.

Some men were erecting a canopy above the lodges where the queen and the noble ladies would sit to watch the jousting. A jongleur on horseback was practicing tossing a sword high into the air then catching it.

Sir John Chandos had set up Edward's pavilion next to Christian Hawksblood's. Joan and Brianna recognized them immediately. One was red and purple, topped by a gold minaret, while the other was black silk, flying a golden dragon of Wales pennon.

Brianna blinked in disbelief as she saw Adele and Glynis emerge from the Arabian tent. Close on their heels came Paddy and Ali. When Adele saw Brianna, she quickly explained before she was questioned. "Paddy is from my own county in Ireland."

Glynis added, "We were curious about Drakkar's pavilion."

"Drakkar?" Brianna asked vaguely.

Ali bowed to her. "Drakkar is Lord Christian's Arabian name, my lady."

"Lord Christian?" she mocked with raised eyebrows.

"Actually, it's Prince," Paddy asserted in an offended tone. "Prince Drakkar!"

"How romantic!" Joan cried, as if she believed every word.

Brianna pulled her friend away just in time to prevent the foursome from seeing her burst out laughing.

Joan joined in her friend's laughter. "His squires are very droll."

"I really like Paddy," Brianna whispered wickedly, "he's so full of shit!" Again they went off into peals of laughter.

Hawksblood had been up since four in the morning. He was training a company of Cornish fighters in warfare with the long-knife. He wanted to make them proficient in night attacks under cover of darkness, where the need for stealth and silence must be practiced over and over.

Later in the morning he had directed his squires to set up his pavilion next to Prince Edward's. He promised to pass Edward's letter on to Joan of Kent and told him he'd help his squire, Chandos, to select the armor and lances he'd need for the tournament, so that Edward could go into London to house-hunt. Christian decided he had an hour to spare to train Gnasher to obey his signals. He stopped by one of the kitchens to get some scraps of meat, then with the ferret riding on his shoulder, headed toward the lists.

Young Randal Grey spotted the little animal from a great distance and was drawn by curiosity. "Is that a tame ferret?"

"Half-tame," Christian replied.

"Can I hold him?" Randal asked eagerly.

"Sometimes he bites," Christian warned.

"I don't mind," the redheaded imp assured.

Christian hid his amusement. "Here's a piece of meat. Hold it out and see if he'll come to you. No! Not between your fingers, his teeth are like needles. Hold it on the flat of your hand."

When the ferret took the meat and pried his fingers apart searching for more, Randal was delighted. "Can I have him?" he begged.

"No. The little Gnasher is one of my secret weapons," Christian explained.

"Why do you call him Gnasher?" Randal asked.

"I'll show you." Christian pointed his finger at an unsuspecting Paddy and ordered, "Gnash!"

The black-footed ferret streaked across the grass, ran up Paddy's leg, and would have bitten him on the balls, if he hadn't been protected by the leather cup he wore. However, the surprise attack took Paddy so unaware, Randal fell down laughing at the Irishman's antics.

When the Gnasher returned to Christian, he scratched it behind the ear. "Don't you have a pet?"

Randal shook his head, then a faraway look came into his eyes. "My dad gave me a little dog once, but my mother made me get rid of it. I miss him. He's dead."

Christian knew Randal was not speaking of the dog, but of his father. He knew the pain a child suffered when he was separated from a loving parent at too tender an age. "How would you like to be in charge of Gnasher here during the tournament? We'll keep him in the tent and you can bring him food and water. If I'm in need of my secret weapon, I'll call on you for his services."

"Thank you, Sir Christian." Randal's grin almost split his face in half.

"Has anyone spoken for you for squire's training?"

The mop of red curls shook and for a moment Randal looked utterly forlorn. "I was hoping Prince Edward—" His voice tapered off to silence.

Hawksblood fixed him with a fierce glare of scrutiny. "I'll have a word with him," he muttered.

Randal thought he might die of happiness.

Prince Lionel and the men of his household had been practicing with their lances since sunup. Robert de Beauchamp manipulated him by giving him encouragement. "I'd like to see you champion this year, Your Highness. I think you can defeat Prince Edward."

Lionel wiped the sweat from his dripping brow. "My father, brother, and I fought as a team last year and we were victorious."

"I'd like to see the House of Clarence challenge the House of Wales. You've grown a lot since last year. You are heavier, taller, and your reach is the longest at Windsor. I myself have a long reach, but you've got me beat, I believe."

"Do you think we can do it?" Lionel asked slyly.

"Queen Philippa's knight, Walter Manny, is here. Why don't you ask him to be our thrid man? He's a seasoned veteran."

"Goddamn, I'll do better than that. I'll get my mother to ask him." He glanced over toward the palisade, a wooden barrier running the length of the lists, to enjoy the crowd of females gathered to watch their practice. "Don't look now, but your bastard brother watches us."

Robert grinned. "Let's give him a little demonstration."

Lionel grinned back. "Hugh! Richard! Let's show the ladies how we thrust a lance."

The two young men galloped a hundred yards down the lists. "Which one do you want?" Hugh asked.

"What the hell's the difference? We'll both eat dirt! Why the hellfire don't those two goddamn giants joust against each other?" grumbled Richard.

"De Beauchamp is too proud to sprawl in the dirt and too wise to unhorse Prince Lionel," Hugh said shrewdly. "I'll take the Ox." It was a name the prince's men used behind his back because of his thick skull.

Hawksblood watched the performance with a practiced eye. For a big man, Lionel couched and charged well enough, but when it came to the strike, he relied upon his size and weight to carry his opponent from the saddle, rather than skill. Both lances were splintered with the heavy impact, but it was the smaller man who was flung to the dirt.

Squires ran out to clear the broken lances from the lists, while Robert de Beauchamp and Richard positioned themselves, with lances couched. A tournament marshal dropped the white baton, but Robert began his charge before the baton fell, giving him a head start and a longer gallop. Momentum alone would be enough to unhorse his opponent. Robert's lance splintered with an earsplitting crack, but its impact had been enough to unseat his challenger.

If De Beauchamp had thought to impress his brother, he had not succeeded. Hawksblood shook his head. How would they fare in battle if they had not mastered the lance?

Christian sensed rather than saw Brianna. He turned his dark head to watch her approach. His body quickened at the sight of her. Whatever she chose to wear always made her look more beautiful than the last time he'd seen her. The color yellow had mystic properties. Today, she looked like the Egyptian goddess Isis.

He smiled inwardly at their last encounter. She did not realize it, of course, but when she bit him, it had moved them many steps closer to intimacy. In truth, biting was actually a form of foreplay.

Hawksblood remembered Edward's letter when he saw Joan with Brianna. Suddenly, Joan broke away from her friend and ran to him. She was about to ask the prince's whereabouts, but when he pressed the letter into her hand, she realized Edward had written because he would not be able to see her. Joan slipped the folded sleeve from her bodice and pressed it into Christian's hand. "Will you give him this favor, my lord."

"I will, demoiselle," he pledged, seeing exactly why Prince Edward was besotted with the angelic-looking creature.

Brianna watched the exchange with dismay, disappointment, chagrin, regret, disenchantment—all these and more! She felt pique that Joan was irresistible. She felt anger that Christian Hawksblood gave Joan a love note when he had led her to believe that his heart belonged to her, Brianna. A voice inside her head clearly said, *That's not anger, that's jealousy!*

Aloud she said, "Rubbish!" She caught sight of Robert and waved gaily. He left Prince Lionel and galloped over to meet her. He took off his helm and ran his hand through his blond, unruly locks. As she gazed up at him she thought he presented a handsome picture astride the great charger. When he grinned down at her, he looked so boyish, she told herself she was lucky to have him. "Queen Philippa gave me leave to go home to Bedford," she said breathlessly, "providing I take Adele and a couple of serving woman for propriety."

"That's wonderful, Brianna. We'll leave the day after the tournament. The king is most impatient to begin the building. Did you bring me a favor to wear in the lists?"

"No, I . . ." She hesitated only a moment, then on impulse she unthreaded the ribbon that attached one of the yellow sleeves she was wearing. "Here, take this."

He touched it to his lips and winked down at her. She was left standing there with one bare arm.

Joan of Kent rejoined her and Robert. "What an impulsive thing to do, Brianna."

"You never seem to suffer from your impulsive behavior," she said coolly, hoping with all her heart that Christian Hawksblood had witnessed her generosity to Robert. She felt the pull of his gaze but fought valiantly against looking his way. She was a willful woman; he a mere man. She'd be damned if she'd allow him to overpower her!

"Brianna, can we announce the formal betrothal at the tournament banquet?" Robert asked.

Brianna hesitated, looked at Joan, then almost defiantly she looked up at Robert. "Yes, have the papers drawn up, my lord."

❧ *12* ❧

Joan of Kent was forced to school her impatience to read Prince Edward's letter. The only place she would have any privacy was in her own chamber and she didn't return there until after the evening meal. She had missed Edward in the Banqueting Hall and had left early to avoid spending the evening with William de Montecute.

When she broke the wax seal and began to read, her heartbeat quickened at his words.

My little love,

I miss you as if it were a thousand years since I held you in my arms. At the forest pool we made memories I will cherish for a lifetime. I am looking at a house in London, close by the river near your brother's residence. Our time spent together must not ruin your reputation. We must be discreet, though my body and even my heart and soul cry out for indiscretion! Forever yours,

Edward.

Joan kissed his signature, then pressed the letter to her heart. Being in love was the most thrilling thing that had ever happened to her. Everything in the universe paled beside this all-consuming emotion! She vowed to do her utmost to keep their love a secret since that was what Edward wanted. Actually she was proud of herself for concealing it from her dearest friend. Brianna was wise and so very astute, she was amazed she hadn't already guessed her secret.

Joan fell into mischief so easily and she relied upon Brianna's strong and courageous character to extract her from trouble. Brianna also advised her when she was unsure of herself. But regarding Prince Edward, she was absolutely sure their love was meant to be.

Joan searched among all her lovely things until she found what she was looking for. It was a silver filigreed casket with a cunning little lock. She placed Edward's letters inside, scattered a few rose petals on top, then popped it beside her pillow. Since she couldn't yet share a bed with Edward, she would share it with his "essence."

Excitement for the tournament was building inside of her. She had watched her beloved joust many times, for Edward had been a champion since the age of thirteen, but this would be the first time he would carry her favor and become her very own champion!

Because it was to be just a small tournament, the king set aside two of the rigid, ancient chivalric rules. The first forbade a man of lower rank challenging a superior. The king and Prince Edward were so confident of their jousting skills, they agreed to accept all challengers. The second rule stated jousts be ridden according to rank, starting with the king. It was not pride alone that prompted the Plantagenets to save the best till last, but an innate sense of pageantry and showmanship.

Earl Henry of Lancaster was chosen field marshal of the tournament. It was both an honor and a grave responsibility bestowed only upon one who embodied the highest ideals of knighthood.

The colors chosen for the spectacle were gold and azure and the silk standards that marked the length of the field sported golden leopards and fleur-de-lis upon backgrounds of brilliant azure.

Christian Hawksblood was impressed by the costliness of the prizes that could be won. He had taken part in many tournaments whose prizes paled in comparison with those offered by this Plantagenet king of England. Whoever defeated an opponent received a dagger bearing the sovereign's coat of arms. Any man emerging victorious from three jousts received a broadsword whose haft was encrusted with semiprecious tourmalines, amethysts, or carnelians.

The Prince of Wales offered the day's most magnificent prize. It was a golden chalice whose bowl was clasped in the claws of the dragon of Wales. The piece had great value as well as beauty and naturally every contestant had designs upon it, if only in his wildest dreams.

The king, as always, would have a pile of crown-filled purses to toss to any challenger who pleased the crowds. As well as the prizes offered by the royal family, there were the usual horses and armor at stake and in addition there were private wagers between contestants for a valuable hawk, hound, weapon, or saddle.

Christian Hawksblood was surprised that he did not receive many challenges. Surely any man with red blood in his veins would like to pit himself against an untried newcomer in the hope of emerging victorious. He had no idea how intimidating his dark visage was to the fair-skinned English youths.

Godfrey de Harcourt, a French knight who had offered

his services to England because the French king had seized his estates, challenged Hawksblood. He had heard of the Arabian's reputation and wished to try his luck.

Christian did not challenge his brother, Robert; he had no wish to humiliate him before that vast assembly. However, as the day of the tournament drew nigh, Robert issued his own challenge to his foreign bastard of a brother. Christian schooled himself in patience, hoping a third challenger would come forward since he fancied winning one of the jeweled broadswords. On the eve of the tournament, however, when he received no more challenges, he approached his friend Prince Edward with the intent of issuing his own challenge. He coveted a black Berber Edward owned and sought him out in his pavilion.

Edward groaned, "God's teeth, Christian, have mercy and don't challenge me."

Christian saw that his friend was indeed serious. His glance swept over Edward, looking for an injury. "Is aught amiss?"

Edward threaded his fingers through his fair hair in agitation. "Tell him," he bade John Chandos, his squire.

"The prince has received two dozen challenges. Half a dozen is most men's limit. We are in a bit of a dilemma. If a challenge is refused it might make him appear a coward."

"Since I have received so few, and you so many, I have a suggestion, Your Highness, if you will be open-minded," Christian said.

John Chandos put down the black breastplate he had been polishing and gave his attention to Hawksblood.

"You and I are the same size and we both possess sable armor. I'll relieve you of half your challengers. None will know the difference."

"I couldn't," Edward protested, his sense of honor coming to the fore.

"You could," Chandos pointed out, "if you would!"

The three men laughed at the audacity of the scheme, then the prince's squire thought better of it. "Even twelve would be an impossible feat."

"Yes, if we rode in one bout after another. But if we alternate, resting between each joust, I have no doubt whatsoever we could take on all comers," Christian urged.

"John, I could certainly manage a dozen," Edward asserted, then lapsed into laughter again and shook his head. "Nay, I could not be so deceitful. It goes against the grain, but thanks for the generous offer, friend."

Their tents stood side by side, so when young Randal couldn't find Hawksblood, he entered Prince Edward's pavilion with another young page in tow. Randal dipped his head and spoke up. "Sire, the king sends this page with a message for you." He turned to Hawksblood. "I have one for you, m'lord, from Warrick."

The men took the notes, dismissed the pages, then both groaned aloud and said at the same time, "A challenge from my father!" Suddenly they looked at each other with renewed speculation.

Edward said, "I have no qualms at unseating him because he's king, only because he's my father."

"There is no pleasure in my making Warrick eat dust, either," agreed Christian.

"We could switch fathers," Edward suggested, with a glimmer of hope. "Last year we jousted in teams. It was a larger tournament of course. Lionel, Father, and myself were all on the same team. We disguised ourselves as Cossacks, from Muscovy, in great fur hats."

"If you perpetuated a hoax upon the spectators last year, why do you cavil at our disguise?" asked Christian.

"Let's do it! We shall have to confess all at the climax of the tourney, of course."

"If your honor demands it," Christian reluctantly agreed. "John, ask my squires to attend us, this will take some planning and coordinating."

A holiday air surrounded the whole of Windsor. Excitement gripped all. The dogs were noisier, the children more mischievous, the adults laughed more and scolded less. Windsor was busy as a human beehive.

A huge canopy was erected over the stands where Queen Philippa, the princesses, and their noble ladies would sit. The queen's household, however, had swelled to one hundred and sixty females, so some of them would have to sit in the sun.

Windsor Castle overflowed with visitors from the other

royal residences of Berkhamsted, the Savoy Palace, Woodstock, and Havering. Crowds from London thronged into the town of Windsor the day before the tournament, happy enough to sleep under a hedgerow or upon a churchyard's tombstone.

Hawkers made a fortune selling cups of ale, steaming black peas, and hot cross buns. Jugglers, minstrels, and jackanapes entertained the spectators, hoping for farthings from indulgent merrymakers with well-lined pockets.

Whores were thick as fleas on a dog, but saucy servant girls and milkmaids gave them a run for their customers by flirting prettily with any man they thought connected with the Royal Court.

The early morning sunshine sat patiently upon Brianna's windowsill, waiting to flood inside her chamber when Adele drew back the drapes. Brianna was doubly excited, for today was the tournament and then the betrothal, and tomorrow she would journey back to her own castle of Bedford with her betrothed. For a moment she felt subdued and noticed the sun had gone behind a cloud. Her betrothal would be announced at tonight's banquet, sealing her future. She was still so unsure about Robert de Beauchamp, but she realized all maidens must experience these selfsame doubts. She should be ashamed of herself. Robert was handsome, young, strong, noble, ambitious, and physically attracted to her. What more could she possibly ask? An answer to her private thoughts came stealing to her, but she pushed it away firmly and arose to drink in the fresh crisp air of morning.

As Adele opened her wardrobe, Brianna caught a glimpse of the buttercup-yellow gown she had worn yesterday. Its missing sleeve would flutter bravely from Robert's helm or lance. Her thoughts went immediately to the scarlet ribbon Christian Hawksblood had demanded from her and she wondered if he would wear it or the delicately embroidered sleeve Joan had pressed into his hands so prettily. She crushed down the stab of envy. Joan was her dearest friend and if she was attracted to the Arabian Knight, what in the world did it matter to her?

It mattered. It mattered.

As Adele spread the new amethyst sarcenet across the

bed, Brianna caught her breath at its loveliness. Her aunt had sewn her one of the fashionable tight-fitting jackets in deep purple velvet that would show the curves of her figure in the most daring way imaginable. When Brianna donned the new outfit, her pulses sped up with pleasure at the picture reflected in her polished silver mirror. The tight sleeveless jacket pushed up her breasts so that they swelled above the heart-shaped neckline.

Brianna wet her lips. "Perhaps I shouldn't," she murmured.

"Nonsense," Adele declared, pulling through the amethyst sleeves of the undergown so that they would trail and flutter. "Joan is wearing one and it is much more elaborate than yours. Glynis showed me yesterday. 'Tis embroidered all over with silver threads and beads. The pair of you will put the royal princesses to shame."

"Then how can I resist?" Brianna asked, laughing, as she reached for her cloak.

"No, don't take that cloak, my lamb, I've a surprise for you. I remembered your mother's favorite was packed away in one of the trunks we brought from Bedford." With flowing pride, Adele brought forth the soft gray velvet, lined with vivid heliotrope. "It personified your mother, Brianna. Exquisitely tasteful on the outside, shockingly flamboyant on the inside! It would make her very happy if she knew you wore it the day of your betrothal."

Brianna reached out to stroke the gray velvet with the scent of violets still clinging to its soft folds. She swallowed the lump in her throat. "Carry it for me, Adele? I want to take parchment and charcoal so I can sketch one of the jousts."

Brianna's mother had died a few months after giving birth to her second child, who was stillborn. People said Brianna was far too young when it happened to remember her mother, but she did remember. She remembered vividly! Her mother had been gifted with second sight. Some whispered she was a witch; an accusation that sent her mother off into peals of rich, ripe laughter. It was the laughter Brianna remembered whenever she daydreamed about her beloved mother.

As she and Adele made their way through the throng in

the Upper Ward, Joan cried her name joyously as if she was her savior. In a way she was, for poor Joan had been selected to help Princess Isabel dress for the tournament. "My brother, Edmund, will never forgive me for the white lies I've told about him since dawn."

"Isabel is rather like a dog with a bone where Edmund is concerned," commiserated Brianna.

"A bitch, you mean! When she saw my silver jacket, her palm itched to slap my face, but the fear that I would complain to Edmund stayed her hand. I swore Edmund would wear her favor."

"Perhaps we'll see him at the lists and you can remind him."

"At this hour? He'll still be snoring in a Dowgate brothel," Joan said with a giggle.

"You shouldn't know of such things," Brianna whispered.

"I don't, damn it!" Joan complained, and their laughter spilled out.

In reality, they did not expect to be in the company of any young men today. Knights and those men aspiring to that heady status took their jousting seriously. They would not spare one thought for the gentler sex until the mock battles were waged and won. Tonight's banquet would be soon enough to leave their men's world behind.

"I'm freezing," Joan said with a shiver. "When I saw the sunshine, I didn't think I'd need a cloak."

"Here, put mine on," said Brianna, taking it from Adele.

"I'll go back and fetch one for you," Glynis said. "I need one myself."

Joan ran her hand over the soft velvet. "I've never seen you wear this. It's lovely!"

"It belonged to my mother," Brianna explained. When they arrived at the stands they were ablaze with the brilliant colors the women had chosen. The contests taking place here were every bit as combative as the ones in the lists.

Queen Philippa was dazzling today in gold brocade. She was wearing the very latest fashion, a steeple headdress with a diaphanous azure scarf that fell to her brocade slippers. Young Princess Joanna was arrayed in an identical costume and sat basking in the fulsome compliments bestowed upon mother and daughter for such a clever device.

Joan whispered to Brianna, "Isabel looks as if she's been sucking persimmons."

"Whyever did she choose such a hideous color?" Brianna asked, blinking in disbelief at the disturbing shade of bile green.

"Because I told her it was Edmund's favorite, of course!"

"You are so wicked," Brianna said with glee. How could she stay angry with Joan when she was so endearing? No wonder Christian Hawksblood was attracted to her. How could he help it?

The loges had been erected so that the spectators had an unimpeded view of the lists that were a hundred feet long and fifty feet wide. Some of the chattering and laughter ceased as the heralds in their royal livery, carrying golden trumpets, paraded down the lists toward the mass of tents and pavilions, crying, "Let the jousters make ready!"

Following the heralds rode the field marshal, the lesser marshals in charge of the contests, and then the sergeants who would keep order, all wearing brilliant bliauts. Behind all, a jongleur on horseback tossed a sword high and caught it. The field marshal raised his white baton. "Bring in the jousters!"

The ladies in the loges and the spectators thronging the palisades held their collective breath, then let it out on a great cheer as the competing jousters rode onto the field, two by two. Brianna thought she had never seen such a brave display in her life. She hoped she would be able to capture the brilliant spectacle on parchment.

The colors of the knights' silk jupons covering their armor were brilliant crimson, cobalt, peacock, jade, ocher, silver, and sable. Each sported a device such as a lion, eagle, leopard, or dragon. Their horses were draped in matching caparisons that fluttered in waves as the breeze caught the silk.

The king, in azure and gold, rode beside Prince Edward, accoutered in black. The golden dragon of Wales with its tongue of flame looked ready to consume all in its path. Behind these two rode Lionel, Duke of Clarence, in startling cobalt blue. The young giant's fair hair fell to his shoulders and beside him rode his lieutenant, Robert de Beauchamp, his equal in size, wearing aquamarine to match his eyes.

Next came two warriors whose knighthoods had been won by fire and sword, Warrick and the queen's own knight, Sir Walter Manny. Their colors of green and silver, respectively, complemented each other.

Christian Hawksblood rode onto the field with Joan's brother, Edmund of Kent. Far from spending the night in a brothel, Edmund had been practicing for three days and looked fresh, young, and very eager, in rich murrey. Beside him, astride a white charger, Christian Hawksblood wore a simple white jupon with a red cross, the symbol of a Templar. Behind them rode twenty-six more pairs of riders, totaling sixty in all.

As the knights rode past the ladies, they danced and curveted their horses, amidst a shower of tossed flowers, ribbons, and gloves. Brianna saw that her buttercup-yellow sleeve floated from the tip of Robert de Beauchamps lance, but not before her glance had stolen to Christian Hawksblood to see if he carried her crimson ribbon.

He did. *The bold devil!* She was secretly pleased that he sported her favor rather than Joan's sleeve. It was a secret they shared and for one moment she hoped he would become champion. Then her glance was caught by the king and the Prince of Wales and she realized the odds were against it. "Joan, Prince Edward is carrying your sleeve!"

Joan's quick mind came to her rescue. "So many ladies offered him sleeves, he decided it was best to wear his cousin's to avoid favoritism."

Brianna watched Joan's face to see if she was disappointed that Christian Hawksblood had not kept the sleeve for himself, but Joan looked happy as a lark.

❧ *13* ❧

Once the field was clear, Henry of Lancaster, the field marshal, returned. "Take your stations!"

An azure and gold–clad herald cried, "Let him come to joust who wishes to do battle!"

From opposite ends of the field, two trumpets answered each other. Pursuivants stepped forward to announce the contestants. It was traditional for each to boast of his own jouster's skill and to revile the challenger. The more foul the insult, the greater the laughter from the crowds.

The inside of Prince Edward's tent was organized chaos as the three squires removed Hawksblood's armor, then dressed him in sable to match Edward's. A slight altercation broke out between Paddy and John Chandos about shields.

"Prince Edward prefers the round shield, it is less cumbersome while in the saddle."

"Prince Drakkar prefers the teardrop. Once you are on the ground, its sharp edges and point make it an offensive weapon."

John Chandos was about to overrule the Irish squire, when Edward spoke up. "I defer to Hawksblood's experience."

Ali, who was in charge of their mounts, lined up two white chargers and two black, each identically accoutered with black harness, saddle, and caparisoned in sable silk, boasting the golden dragon of Wales. Inside Christian's pavilion was a stack of forty fifteen-foot ashwood lances with lozenge-shaped heads of Castile steel. Armor and weapons sat in piles, ready to be snatched up on a moment's notice.

In one corner, Randal sat talking softly to Gnasher, who was curled up on his shoulder. To be on the safe side, Christian had secured him on a long, silver leash.

The marshal's list had been made up at the last possible minute to keep it current. They had shaken their heads over the number of times Prince Edward's name appeared and alternated it as best they could. In the morning he was scheduled to ride in the third, fifth, seventh, and so on, up to and including the twenty-fifth joust. The fourth contest pitted Hawksblood against De Harcourt. This meant his changing into silver armor, then changing back to sable the moment it was over.

"We'll have to polish off the first dozen in short order if we are to be effective throughout the afternoon," Christian warned before the prince left the tent. The two men looked into each other's eyes, grinned, then Edward lowered his visor and strode out to do battle.

The pursuivant had been instructed to announce him only as the Black Prince. It was a name they had chosen together, which could in truth be applied to both. "Sir John Holland challenging the Black Prince!"

A hush fell over the crowd as it waited to see if the Black Prince was indeed the Prince of Wales. When the sable-clad rider became visible, a great cheer broke from the spectators and rolled across the field like a wave upon the shore. For one moment, Joan was paralyzed by fear. Her throat closed so tightly, she could not cheer.

Prince Edward, with single-minded determination, hit Holand's shield dead center. The grinding shock of the splintered lance forced Holland from the saddle. He fell so hard, his squires had to rush onto the field to carry him off.

Everyone in the stands surged to their feet, crying their joy at the top of their lungs. Joan's fear turned instantly to joy. Her glance fell upon her embroidered sleeve, which he had attached to his scabbard ring, and her heart almost burst with pride.

Glynis pushed through to her mistress carrying the peony-colored mantle that matched Joan's underdress.

"Hurry, Glynis, you're missing the fun." Joan handed Brianna's cloak to Adele and slipped on her own.

"Sir Godfrey de Harcourt challenges Christian Hawksblood de Beauchamp," cried the pursuivant. The majority expected the fierce-looking Arabian to defeat the Frenchman. Hawksblood simply angled his shield so his opponent's lance glanced off it. At the same moment his own lance impacted De Harcourt's shield so solidly the Frenchman dropped like a stone. Hawksblood's lance had not even shattered. He tossed it to his waiting squire, Ali, and fell upon his opponent with such speed, Harcourt could not gain his feet. Christian pressed his powerful thigh across the Frenchman's throat. He rendered his challenger helpless without drawing his sword. The crowd roared its appreciation of such agile strength. Even the king tossed him a purse.

Brianna forced herself to breathe normally. Her breath had stopped when she saw her crimson ribbon fluttering atop Hawksblood's helm. She blushed deeply, hoping none guessed the favor was hers.

Next came the Black Prince against John de Vere, Earl of Oxford. Edward dispatched him to the dust while Paddy rapidly removed Hawksblood's silver hauberk and replaced it with sable.

Joan's heart was in her mouth when she heard, "Edmund, Earl of Kent, challenged by Prince Lionel, Duke of Clarence."

Brianna took hold of Joan's hand. "You fear for him?"

Joan replied, "Lionel is a giant and a bully, while Edmund is so slim."

"He will acquit himself well, Joan. He has twice Lionel's intelligence." Their attention was drawn to Princess Isabel. She came to her feet with an avid look upon her face. She was licking her lips over this match. When the jousters impacted, Lionel leaned his great weight into his lance and it was inevitable that the lightweight Edmund left his saddle. Kent, however, anticipated the move and aimed to the side while Lionel was off-balance. Clarence too was unhorsed.

Isabel screamed, "Kill him!"

Queen Philippa tried to hush her, thinking she rooted for her brother.

Edmund had his sword drawn by the time he gained his feet. Lionel the Ox was clumsy as his nickname. He lumbered to his feet and advanced upon the smaller man, thinking to defeat him by brute force. In a trice, Edmund caught his sword and sent it spinning away, leaving him weaponless. Lionel conceded in one second flat, wishing to God they were fighting in teams as they had the previous year.

The king and queen were both disappointed in their

son's defeat, but Isabel snatched a purse from her father and flung it down to the young Earl of Kent. He lifted his visor and touched his fingers to his lips in a gallant gesture to the princess, and the crowd burst into applause.

The few hard-bitten knights who had the temerity to challenge Warrick regretted the impulse when the warrior made mincemeat of them.

The Black Prince rode out time after time, taking up the challenges issued to him by the earls of Pembroke, Northampton, Lincoln, and Hereford. He set down his opponents one by one, either by lance or by sword. By this time all the knights had lost their fine silk jupons, as well as their favors from the ladies. Even their mount's caparisons hung in shreds.

The entire throng was agog that their prince fought and won joust after joust. It was a feat unmatched in history. Both Christian and Edward were thankful for the coolness of the morning, knowing by afternoon the day would heat up considerably.

Pondering Hawksblood's victory, Brianna had been struck by a disquieting thought. What if the brothers Beauchamp fought a joust? Who would she cheer on to victory? She would champion Robert, of course; it was her duty to do so, yet she silently prayed they would not joust together. She shivered and Adele wrapped her in the gray velvet cloak.

She felt as if her mother's arms had stolen about her. The Black Prince was again upon the field. Surely he was the most gallant prince in all Christendom to meet so many challenges. Suddenly, Brianna went still. The knight in the sable armor who rode down the field so relentlessly was not Edward. It was the Arabian, Hawksblood! She could see him as clearly as if he rode without armor. She turned to Joan, expecting her to know the identity of the Black Prince, but quickly realized Joan had no idea when she said, "Edward's strength must surely be spent. This time he will go down."

Brianna's glance again flew to the jouster clad in sable mail. "Nay! None will defeat him!" She watched in fascination as Christian couched his lance and spurred down the lists as deadly accurate as the Angel of Death felled his chosen victim. Hawksblood danced a violent ballet that was perfection. Brianna could not understand why it was not clear to everyone that this was the Arabian.

"Edward, Edward, Edward," they chanted, and the king was on his feet, waving the great banner of England.

The sergeants removed a few unruly Londoners from the front ranks and everyone sat back to enjoy the next contest. Joan clasped Brianna's hand as she heard, "William de Montecute challenges Robert de Beauchamp."

Robert looked enormous as he charged down the field. The Countess of Salisbury screamed as her son was flung from his saddle. De Beauchamp withdrew his sword and beat down his opponent without dismounting, as was his right, but Brianna could not dispel the thought that it was unchivalrous.

The excited crowd applauded the win, however, and she joined them. Joan whispered, "Montecute is always so full of himself, I'm glad Robert defeated him."

The final joust of the morning was announced and who else would it be but the Black Prince? Brianna watched intently. This time, however, she knew it was Prince Edward beneath the sable armor. How strange it was to be able to tell them apart as if they were day and night. Suddenly the sun blazed forth and she slipped the warm cloak from her shoulders. The moment the mantle fell away, her clear perception disappeared. Had her imagination played a trick on her? She glanced down at the gray velvet and wondered. Her mother had the gift of second sight. When Brianna had been wearing her cloak, she too had seen things other people seemed unaware of.

The royal stewards made their way into the loges with refreshments for the queen and her ladies. The king departed for his own pavilion. He was on the afternoon program and eager to join the lists.

Paddy and John Chandos ate heartily, sharing their food with Randal and the Gnasher. Christian and Edward, however, did not eat. So they would not become dehydrated, they drank water brewed with rosemary and agrimony to keep them alert. Ali massaged the muscles of both men with almond oil and myrrh. The prince was most impressed by the Arabian squire's talents.

"Would you consider becoming my personal leech?" Edward asked.

Ali shook his head. "Alas, Your Highness, I was there when Drakkar was born and I shall be there when he dies, Allah be willing."

Edward and Christian exchanged an amused glance, yet beneath the surface, both men were moved at such selfless devotion.

An infirmary tent had been set up with Master John Bray, the king's physician, in charge. It was rapidly filling with casualties suffering cracked ribs, broken collarbones, dislocated shoulders, and concussions. Minor wounds, cuts, and abrasions were attended by squires in the jousters' own tents.

Prince Edward began to pace in anticipation of the afternoon's challenges. Christian stretched himself on the pavilion floor and appeared to doze. "How is he able to do that?" Edward asked Ali.

"Long years of discipline. First you must separate the three states of being: the mental, the physical, and the emotional, then it is simply a matter of deep breathing."

But the moment the heralds sounded their trumpets, Hawksblood was on his feet ready to have Paddy don his hauberk. This time, both wore silver, for Edward was jousting as Hawksblood, riding against Warrick, then Christian and Robert de Beauchamp would do battle.

Brianna clasped her hands tightly as Warrick's name and that of Hawksblood were announced. *Don't let either of them get hurt,* she prayed.

Prince Edward knew he would have to unseat Warrick with his lance if he hoped to win, for if the seasoned warrior had him on the ground, then came at him with his powerful sword arm, he doubted the outcome.

Brianna surged to her feet as the pair collided with an ear-splitting crash that splintered both lances and sent the combatants flying from their saddles. Fortunately for Edward, he had not landed as heavily as Warrick and he was able to gain his feet first. Warrick, however, was able to swing his great broadsword from a kneeling position. When it struck Edward's shield, however, the protective guard flew from the tip of the sword and Warrick stopped fighting immediately. It was a thing that happened often, usually resulting in a bloody accident, but Warrick was well disciplined in swordplay. When Prince Edward saw Warrick put up his sword, he did likewise and the contest was considered a draw. Christian couldn't have been more pleased with the outcome.

In the next joust, Prince Lionel challenged Lord Stanley, Earl of Cheshire. They were easy to tell apart, for Cheshire's lance boasted a blue and white banner with three stags' heads. Lionel missed his opponent's shield by a mile and embedded his lance point in Stanley's dappled gray charger. As the horse went down, the crowd gasped then groaned as they watched it thrash in agony. Stanley, concerned only for his mount, went down in defeat to Lionel, who totally ignored the frenzied animal. The crowd began to boo.

King Edward threw off his leg guards and sprinted onto the field. Without concern for his own safety, he quickly assessed the horse at close range. He withdrew his dagger and severed the horse's main neck artery. It gave only one more kick, heaved a shuddering sigh, then lay in red ruin.

The crowd's boos changed to cheers. They knew their king's deeds were invariably brave as well as honorable. The animal was covered with the glorious flag of England and dragged from the field.

Prince John of Gaunt's voice carried to Joan and Brianna. "By the Cross, that was clumsily done! Lionel has covered us with shame!"

His sister Isabel turned upon him. "A little blood and gore enliven a tournament. Stanley can well afford the loss of a charger."

Prince John gave her a look that would have withered someone more sensitive.

In his tent, pitched next to Prince Lionel's, Robert de Beauchamp inwardly seethed. The great clumsy Ox had not only been easily defeated by his older brother this morning, but had also gone down to defeat in the joust with the Earl of Kent. Now, for Christ's sake, he had killed a bloody horse! Robert ground his teeth in chagrin. How the hell could Lionel aspire to kingship? The brainless swine would ruin all Robert's fine plans for the future if he didn't have a care.

Robert tried to focus on his own impending joust with his foreign bastard of a brother. He had been waiting for this moment all day. He knew he needed to vent his spleen, and what better target than the Arabian? The two jousters presently in the lists had removed their thigh guards in emulation of the king. As Robert's squire held his horse so that he could mount, he saw that none of the men had kept them on. In a vainglorious gesture, he ordered his squire to unstrap his guards. It would give him considerably more freedom, especially on the ground, so his main objective was to separate Hawksblood from his charger.

Robert couched his lance, moved his shield across his body, and allowed his hatred full rein.

Brianna wanted to leave. The last thing she wanted to witness was this encounter between the dissimilar brothers. But of course she could not; she was rooted to the spot. Turf flew from their chargers' hooves as they began their inevitable head-on clash. In a blur she saw the yellow streaming from Robert's helm and the crimson ribbon fluttering from Christian's scabbard ring. It sounded as if the thud of the hooves beat upon her eardrums. She had no idea that it was her own heart that pounded.

Joan shouted encouragement. Brianna heard not the words, but knew which De Beauchamp Joan championed. The question was, which De Beauchamp did Brianna champion? She wanted neither to lose; she wanted both to win. She sucked in a breath, trying to distance herself from this contest. It was up to them; it had nothing to do with her! *It had everything to do with her.*

Christian Hawksblood's arm became one with his lance. Through the slitted helm he saw every detail with crystal clarity, every movement in slow, fluid motion. Man and horse merged into one powerful entity. Hawksblood was a big man, but his half brother was both taller and heavier. Robert relied upon his brawn in all encounters. Hawksblood knew if he lured him off-balance, the sheer force of his weight would take him down. Christian shifted to his left so that Robert must overreach. 'Twas so subtly done, Robert expected his hated opponent to go down with the impact of the lance. Instead it slid harmlessly to the right, dragging him with it, while his brother's lance hit him such a true and solid blow, it smote him from his saddle.

Hawksblood had couched, charged, and recovered as he had done thousands upon thousands of times. Robert was on his feet instantly, unable to check his fury. He did not expect Hawksblood to dismount; chivalry was the last thing he anticipated. Robert felt a surge of glee, for Hawksblood wore protective leg guards that would hamper him. Christian's armor, however, was so well articulated, he could turn a somersault if the need arose. He unsheathed his broadsword, deftly blocking every slash and thrust Robert executed.

In Hawksblood's experience it was the coolest head that prevailed, and he knew Robert was hotly mad. Christian saw the guard had come off the tip of Robert's sword, if it had ever been there in the first place, and he knew his half brother was gripped by bloodlust. Robert plunged the sword with a mighty downward thrust. Hawksblood lowered his shield to protect his loins. Robert's wide blade slid down the length of the teardrop shield and pierced his own ungirded thigh! He rolled to the ground, biting his lips so he would not cry out at the searing pain. Robert's squires as well as Warrick's rushed onto the field.

Randal, wanting to view the last two jousts of the day in which both Hawksblood and the Black Prince were scheduled to ride, stood at the barriers with the little ferret curled upon his shoulder. Since they were now the best of friends, he judged the silver leash unnecessary.

The crowd was in such an uproar, Gnasher decided to attack. He streaked across the lists, scented Christian, scented his enemy's blood, flashed up De Beauchamp's leg, and tried to sink in his teeth. Only the fact that Robert wore a protective codpiece saved his manhood. Gnasher, tenacious as a terrier, found the wound and bit down to the bone. Robert screamed in agony, the startled squires laughed in spite of themselves, and the Gnasher fled back to an abashed Randal.

Christian Hawksblood could not linger on the field. He had agreed to joust against the King of England in Edward's place, and had to immediately change into sable armor. Amusement tugged at the corners of Christian's mouth for the brother who had intended to draw blood and had succeeded, albeit his own.

Back in the pavilion, when he was ready, the two friends faced each other in their black helms and hauberks. "Don't humiliate him too sorely," Edward appealed.

"God's teeth, I'll be lucky if I can hold him to a draw. Your father has a passion for tournaments because his long arms and legs make him a champion!"

As he had expected to, Hawksblood hit the ground. In fifteen jousts it was the first time he had been unseated. However, King Edward had not been able to stay in the saddle either, and now the two men were enjoying the contest of wits and broadswords. The king was both thrilled and confounded that his son's skills equaled his own.

Hawksblood was impressed by the king's stamina as the fight went on and on. Finally the royal foot slipped on a patch of blood and he went down in defeat. Hawksblood wanted to protest that he had not won fairly, but speaking would have revealed his identity.

The crowd went wild. The Black Prince was their champion. More, he was their god at this moment. The throng along the palisades, the ladies in the loges, and the crowds who could not even get close enough for a glimpse, chanted his name in unison.

"Edward! Edward! Edward!"

The prince hurried to his pavilion to get Christian so they could share the glory, but Hawksblood had disappeared along with his squires. Edward took off his helm to run a frustrated hand through his flaxen hair. John Chandos handed him a note.

Today you became a legend. Never seek to destroy their faith in you.

The Black Prince stepped out onto the field to acknowledge the tumult.

🐝 *14* 🐝

Brianna was in a quandary. She made her way toward the pavilions to find out how Robert fared. Would it be unseemly for a lady to enter the infirmary tent? She heard a familiar laugh behind her and turned to find the king. "Your Majesty, I came to inquire about Robert's wound, but I can see I'll only be in the way."

"Rubbish!" He took her arm. He could never resist charming a beautiful woman. "If you are with me, none will dare deny you. I've come to visit all the tournament casualties."

The king's physician, Master John Bray, was busy setting broken limbs. Warrick and Hawksblood stood beside Robert, who lay upon planks supported by sawhorses.

The king boomed, "Here's a poor maiden fearing your demise."

Brianna inwardly shrank as all eyes turned upon her. She could clearly see that Robert was seething, and the look he gave her would have consigned her to the devil, if he had his way.

"Have no fear, *my* lady, I myself will stitch him back together." Hawksblood's glance locked with hers for a moment. She knew he read her thoughts. The Arabian knew she was there for duty's sake, not love's.

The last thing Robert de Beauchamp wanted was his foreign bastard of a brother's hands on him, yet he did not have the guts to protest for fear of seeming a coward. "Get her out of here," he said through stiff lips.

King Edward was enjoying himself. "You're in no condition to travel to Bedford tomorrow. Hawksblood, will you go in your brother's stead to fetch my stone for the tower?"

"It will be my pleasure, Sire."

Brianna flushed. The bold devil was looking at her when he spoke of his pleasure. "I shan't go now," she said, swallowing her disappointment.

"Nonsense!" the king contradicted. "You've been looking forward to it. My tournament won't be responsible for disappointing you. You'll be safe enough in Sir Christian's hands."

Holy Mother, can he put thoughts into the king's head, words into the king's mouth? She flashed Hawksblood an accusing look, but he was busy scrubbing his hands while Ali threaded a needle. He was completely aware of her, however. "Perhaps Lady Bedford will feel more comfortable if Lady Joan of Kent accompanies her," he suggested smoothly.

"Splendid idea," concluded the king.

Mary and Joseph, did the dark devil have designs on both of them?

Her glance sought out Robert's. "You won't be attending the banquet—"

"I'll be there!" Robert cut in, unable to hide his fury.

Warrick and the king exchanged amused glances. "We won't have the betrothal ceremony tonight, but we'll announce it. I've another to announce as well. The ceremony can take place when you are restored to full manhood." Only the king could have gotten away with such an outrageous remark. Brianna picked up her skirts and fled.

King Edward sobered for a moment. "I'm going to need this man to fight in France shortly. See that the leg is good as new," he bade Hawksblood before he moved on to the next casualty.

When Brianna arrived at her chamber, she found Adele about to unpack her traveling trunk. "Leave it. We are still to go to Bedford tomorrow."

"Robert shouldn't travel with a wounded leg! The king should get someone else to fetch his stone."

"He has. Christian de Beauchamp has been ordered to escort us and see to the stone. Oh, Adele, I never should have gone to inquire about Robert's wound. I should have sent Randal."

"Things usually have a way of working themselves out for the best. I, for one, am delighted that we are still going home. Aren't you, my lamb?"

"Well yes, no. That is, I'm longing to see Bedford, but I was supposed to go with Robert," Brianna said lamely.

"Perhaps Fate has conspired to foil the intimacy of traveling together before the wedding. Personally, I think it was putting you both in the way of temptation. Now you'll be safe."

Brianna looked at her in disbelief. Did Adele truly think her safe in Hawksblood's hands? "Robert is extremely angry with me."

"Not with you, lamb. He's angry that he accidentally wounded himself. What about the betrothal ceremony?"

"His Majesty said he would announce it tonight at the banquet, but we won't have the actual ceremony until Robert is recovered."

"Perhaps he and Warrick haven't drawn up the papers yet. In any case, you must look your very best tonight. Let me help you off with your dress and I'll pour you some rosewater."

Two hours later when Brianna entered the Banqueting Hall, she did indeed look her very best. The pale amethyst sarcenet and purple velvet jacket made her hair look like spun gold. Warrick was at her side so quickly she realized he must have been watching for her. The old warrior gallantly took her fingertips, rested them upon his arm, and escorted her to her seat at the table.

He placed her between his two sons, then took his own seat beside Robert. Brianna knew Robert must have been half-carried into the hall and was thankful she had not been a witness to it. His fair skin had a pallor that made his eyes seem brilliant. Christian de Beauchamp was on his feet instantly in deference until she was seated. He too wore purple, but its shade was so dark, it looked almost black. Brianna felt like a bone between two dogs.

The atmosphere was highly charged tonight from the events that had taken place during the day. Tonight, the king had given up his carved chair to the Black Prince, who occupied the place of honor. Princess Isabel for once was content to bask in her brother's glorious light. His black silk tunic made his flaxen hair appear to have a nimbus of light about it like a halo. And why not? Hadn't the gods smiled upon him this day?

The Plantagenet court was a brilliant one when it celebrated, its courtiers extremely noisy and festive, sporting costly furs and sparkling jewels. The wine flowed rich and dark into goblets, while stewards staggered beneath platters created especially for the banquet.

Swans with gilded beaks, sitting upon blue silk, vied with herons and peacocks for the center of the table. Crisped and larded stags, cut into quarters and flavored with pepper sauce, were carried in, followed by boars' heads stuffed with apples and herbs. Beef, mutton, and pork were among the meats served in the first course, while pages stood by with a second course of piping hot roast teal, mallard, and wood duck.

Brianna shared a silver porringer with Robert de Beauchamp, showing they were pledged. He sat beside her, making no effort at polite conversation. His eyes were stormy. A tempest also raged inside Brianna, battering her composure, scattering her thoughts like feathers in the wind. Was he in pain? Did he want her to talk or remain silent? Did he prefer beef to venison? Should she eat the game or leave it for Robert?

Brianna realized she was sitting with her future family. She had wanted to be part of a family for so long, she should be overjoyed. Instead, she felt bereft. Hawksblood's dark presence overwhelmed her. His maleness was blatant, primal. His barely leashed energy was a tangible thing. He dominated the space about him. She imagined she could feel the heat from his powerful body and smell his man-scented skin.

"Each time I see you, you are more beautiful," Christian murmured softly. The deep timbre of his voice did strange things to her composure. She did not dare look at him, but lowered her eyes to her lap. From the corner of her eye she saw with horror that a long tress of her hair fell across Hawksblood's thigh. Against his dark purple, it shone like gold. She watched in dismay as his fingers threaded through it possessively.

"Your hair is glorious, Brianna. You put every other lady at Court in the shade."

She wanted to snatch it away from him and slap his face, but such a tempestuous action would expose to Robert what he was doing and there was already contention between them, so she did her best to ignore him. The vexing devil knew she would not make a scene and she feared he would spend the entire evening whispering in her ear, wooing her with outrageous compliments.

"I am looking forward to escorting you to Bedford tomorrow. Unwittingly the king has given us the opportunity to be together."

Brianna suspected Christian Hawksblood had contrived the whole thing, yet surely his powers could not have dominion over everything? Nay, it was as he had said, he simply had a stronger will than others.

Brianna lifted her goblet and drained the wine to prevent herself from screaming. She should have kept Adele at her side as a buffer between her and this dangerously dominant Arabian Knight. Her glance darted about until it found Adele. She was sitting next to Glynis, who was with Joan and Edmund of Kent. Joan caught her eye and waved. Brianna waved back, but to add to her chagrin, her hand trembled visibly. She took a deep breath to calm herself and felt the wine she had drunk blossom into a bloodred rose inside her chest.

Suddenly everything seemed ridiculously funny. Robert de Beauchamp was angry at the entire world when he had no one to blame but himself. Anyone who stabbed himself by mistake was a figure of fun akin to a buffoon. She glanced at Warrick. He lifted his goblet to salute her and gave her a conspiratorial wink. Brianna caught back a giggle. So, he too thought the situation amusing!

She turned so that she looked Robert full in the face. She did not laugh; instead she gave him a breath-stopping smile and was rewarded by a slight softening of his fierce glare.

The king and queen had invited a jongleur renowned for his great epics who could move his audience to tears or wild excitement. He took all the speaking parts of the drama, mingling prose and verse, breaking into arias without ever losing the meter. Tonight he was performing *Tristan and Isolde,* and from the first word he uttered, Brianna was entranced, totally caught up in the great romance.

As the bard finished his tragic tale, the audience gave a collective sigh. Brianna brushed away a tear, drank from her cup, and set it down on the board.

There were not many dry eyes among the ladies, and the men applauded with lusty enthusiasm. Brianna again reached out her hand, but she saw that Christian Hawksblood held her goblet to his lips. Then she realized it was not her goblet, but *his*. She drew in a quick breath. Realization washed over her like spring rain. Just as Isolde had done at the great feast, she had inadvertently drunk from the same loving cup as the dark warrior. She was utterly convinced he had lured her to it by placing his cup ready to her hand. She had drunk the magic potion and he had enchanted her! She could feel it flowing through her veins, warming her blood, stealing her senses. She cast him a look of horror. In reply, he lifted the goblet in salute and drained it. *What could she do?* she thought wildly.

Nothing. She could do naught.

The deed was done!

When the tumultuous applause died down, the king got to his feet and raised his arms. They hushed to hear his words.

"We have much to celebrate this day: our glorious naval victory over the French and our victorious battles that have yet to be fought! Yet there is more. The minstrel's epic has filled the hall with an aura of romance, and justly so. Tonight it is our very great pleasure to announce two betrothals that will soon take place.

"I am bestowing the hand of Lady Brianna of Bedford upon Robert de Beauchamp. None stands higher in my esteem than the House of Warrick." The king grinned. "It is said that love heals all wounds." Good-natured laughter rolled about the hall at the reference to Robert's injury.

Brianna's cheeks were flushed. Shyly, she stole a glance at Robert. He too was flushed, as if with victory. He was so fair, so brawny, so strong. Yet she sensed weakness. The weakness must be in character, in lack of self-control, for it was assuredly no physical weakness.

She stole a glance to her right. There was no weakness in that one. No softness either, she guessed. He would pursue a goal relentlessly, by any means, until he achieved his desire. He was darkly beautiful, magnetic, compelling. For the first time she admitted the attraction. Of course she was drawn against her will, bewitched by the powerful knight.

She tossed back her golden hair, impatient with herself.

It mattered not. The king had announced her betrothal. Her future was sealed.

Again, the king was speaking and Brianna tried to hear his words as her pulses raced erratically.

"As you all know, my oldest and dearest friend, the Earl of Salisbury, is a guest of Philip of France. I am presently negotiating his release, but in the meantime, I honor his son, William de Montecute, by betrothing him to Lady Joan, the fair maid of Kent."

The delicate color drained from Joan's face, leaving her white as parchment. *No! No!* a voice screamed inside her brain, yet she smiled tremulously and cast down her lashes to hide the pain that must be visible in her eyes.

Prince Edward did not betray his feelings by word or glance, yet when he set down his silver goblet, it was crushed like an eggshell. His eyes met those of Christian Hawksblood. Their gazes held until Edward felt a measure of calm. He was a tactician. He would find a way to thwart this betrothal.

Hawksblood knew exactly what his friend felt. Their situations were identical. Tonight they could do little. Tomorrow . . . ah, tomorrow they must both seize the moment!

Brianna heard Joan's name with disbelief. What a sly little minx her friend could be at times. She hadn't breathed a word to Brianna. She had hinted at a secret infatuation, but had always pretended to dread Montecute's attention.

Brianna looked across the room to where Joan sat with her brother. She smiled angelically, yet a discerning Brianna noticed her friend was pale unto death. Could it possibly be that Joan was just as surprised and shocked as she was when the king made the announcement? Brianna forgot her own dilemma as her heart went out to her friend.

Tonight there was to be no dancing since the hall held too many to clear the tables. In any case most of the men had spent their legs' strength in the joust and were content to laugh and drink or at most to mingle and collect the ransoms from the losers.

Brianna wanted to rush over to Joan, but she could not leave Robert's side until all who wished to offer congratulations came forward. She was enormously relieved when

Hawksblood removed his dominant presence from her side. After a few minutes she dared to search him out with her eyes and saw him in earnest conversation with Prince Edward. The pair conspired well.

The two Black Princes had exchanged places throughout the tournament. Was she the only one with knowledge of their conspiracy?

Brianna's wandering thoughts were brought abruptly back as Queen Philippa graciously stopped to offer Robert congratulations. He tried to struggle to his feet, but the queen stopped him. "Lady Bedford is a special favorite of mine," she told Robert. "She has a God-given talent as well as grace and beauty. You are a most fortunate young man."

"Thank you, Your Majesty," Robert said stiffly.

Lionel followed his mother. He was well into his cups, as were half the people at the banquet by now. "Too bad you bloodied your weapon in the lists." He leered at Brianna. "You should have waited until tonight. Perhaps I could help you out in your duty to your betrothed."

Robert's eyes glittered. He laughed shortly and replied, "No thanks, Your Highness, but perhaps you could teach me how to spear a horse sometime."

Lionel roared. "Tit for tat, Rob."

At this moment, Joan, too, wished she could sink into the earth. When the king had announced her upcoming betrothal, she had almost fainted from the shock. She had grabbed her brother's hand beneath the table in dismay.

"Sweetheart, 'tis a good match. He is heir to the Earldom of Salisbury and the Montecutes are high in the king's favor."

Joan felt suffocated. She sucked in a breath as her hand flew to her heart. It felt as if it were being torn asunder. What Edmund said was true enough, and though she had known a husband would be found for her shortly, she resented being used as a sop to Katherine de Montecute because her husband had been taken in France.

Joan did not dare seek out Edward with her eyes. She could not bear to read what would be written in his face, whether it be anger, pity, or regret. She must accept her lot, but she wished herself a thousand miles from this Banqueting Hall.

William de Montecute possessed himself of her hand
and every few minutes pressed it meaningfully. When
Queen Philippa congratulated him, she did not use the
same words she had said to Robert de Beauchamp. Philippa felt greatly relieved that Joan was safely betrothed
and her son Edward out of her pretty clutches. Joan's tiny
figure was too perfect to a woman who had borne nine
children and was already caught with her tenth.

"Congratulations, William. You must start your family
right away. When I was Lady Kent's age, I had already
produced two and a half."

Lionel, still following his mother, leered at Joan. "You'd
better get started. Push the goblets aside and lay her back
on the table."

De Montecute flushed, but did not dare to offer Prince
Lionel insult. Joan, however, had no such scruples. She
turned to William and said sweetly, "The Queen meant two
and a half-wit."

Lionel roared his appreciation. God's balls, he'd be willing to bet Joan was a hot little piece in bed.

Christian Hawksblood politely congratulated William de
Montecute, successfully masking the pity he felt for the
besotted young man. When he raised Lady Kent's fingers
to his lips, he secretly slipped a note into her small hand.
Her eyes flew to his, but his steadfast gaze told her nothing.
As she clutched the tiny paper, however, it brought a measure of comfort to her aching heart.

Brianna's glance was again drawn to Joan. She watched
her friend give Christian Hawksblood an almost pleading
look. She saw the dark knight use the excuse of kissing
Joan's hand to pass her a note. What did he write? Poetry?
Avowals? Times and places of assignations? If there was
any truth in the maids' gossip, he had left a long line of
broken hearts that stretched from England to Arabia. His
power over women was legendary. He had the skill to mesmerize, bewitch, enchant. On the way to Bedford she would
have to be on her guard.

Edmund of Kent approached. "Lady Brianna, you have
broken my heart. That the fairest lady in Windsor prefers a
De Beauchamp to a Plantagenet is inconceivable."

Robert put up with the banter, smug in the knowledge

that Brianna had rebuffed Edmund long ago. However, when Edmund decided to rub salt in his wound, Robert's temper began to boil.

"Congratulations on winning in the lists of love, it must go a long way to compensating you for badly botching the other joust."

Robert hailed his squire. "I've had enough! Get me the hell out of here," he growled. Brianna arose with him. "Are you trying to make me a laughingstock? I don't need to lean upon a female!"

Brianna bit her lip. "I pray your pain eases, Robert. I bid you farewell until I return from Bedford."

"You shouldn't be going," he said coldly.

"I'm sorry, but the king says I must."

"You should learn the art of deception, lady. A pretended illness would easily thwart the king's orders."

She quietly followed as Robert, leaning heavily on his squire, hobbled from the hall. When they arrived at the Beauchamp wing, she bade him a gentle good night and started off toward her own chamber. *You should learn the art of deception, lady.* His incredible words rang in her brain. Mayhap she would do just that! Brianna changed directions and returned to the Banqueting Hall.

Edmund of Kent was the first to see her. "Sorry about De Beauchamp. Was it something I said?" He grinned down at her.

"Edmund, you are mischievous as Joan. Take me to her, I haven't congratulated the lucky groom-to-be."

"Little Jeanette doesn't feel very mischievous tonight, I'm afraid. Try to give her a little moral support, sweetheart."

"Are you saying she knew nothing about it?" Brianna asked, outraged for her friend.

"She was stunned as a bird flown into a wall."

Edmund and Brianna approached the betrothed couple at the same time as the king. Ever chivalrous, he swept her a bow when she curtsied to him and insisted she speak to the couple before he did.

"Robert asked me to convey my congratulations, William. Joan, would you and Glynis accompany me on my visit to Bedford? I know it's short notice, we are leaving tomorrow."

Joan's face lit up. "I should love it above all things." Joan tried not to seem to be clutching at straws.

Montecute stiffened. "You may not go," he informed Joan.

The king cocked an amused eyebrow. "It was I who suggested Lady Kent accompany Lady Bedford. The betrothal papers haven't been signed yet. Patience, William."

De Montecute flushed. "I . . . I beg your pardon, Sire. I didn't mean to suggest it would be improper."

The king winked at the two beautiful young women who lit up his Court. "Of course you didn't. What could be improper about two friends enjoying a breath of freedom before they must be shackled in the bonds of matrimony?"

❧ 15 ❧

Joan and Glynis busied themselves packing for the journey to Bedford. It was like a godsend to Joan. She not only wished to escape from the possessive De Montecute, she wished to avoid Prince Edward. She loved him so much, it would be too painful to encounter him in the dining hall or even glimpse him across the Ward. She hadn't even been able to bring herself to read his note, fearing it was a letter of good-bye. She had tucked it next to her heart, hoping it would ease the raw pain, but it had not.

"I should never have asked you for the spell to make me irresistible, Glynis. William de Montecute went straight to the king and how could he refuse when the Earl of Salisbury was taken prisoner fighting for King Edward in France?"

"My lady, I know you have little affection for William, but he is besotted with you, and that is no bad thing, especially in a husband. You must marry well, and someday William will make you Countess of Salisbury."

Joan sighed. It was useless to rail against her fate. The king held supreme power. She shuddered. Her father had been executed for stepping out of line. She could not risk falling from favor. When their trunks were packed, Joan undressed slowly, then bade Glynis good night. When she was alone, she took out the paper with resignation, held it to the light of the candles, and read:

I am more angry at this moment than I have ever been in my life! You have been promised to William de Montecute for selfish reasons of my father, which I will relate to you in private.
You are my precious love and so you shall remain. Because we must avoid each other, Christian Hawksblood will act as go-between. You may put complete trust in him. E.

Her eyes read again and again the words: "You are my precious love and so you shall remain." A tear slipped down her cheek before she blew out the candle. She climbed into bed, clutching the letter. She would not put it in the casket with the others just yet.

Brianna tossed and turned all night long. The day of the tournament had held so much excitement, culminating in the announcement of her betrothal, that she found it impossible to relax and give herself up to sleep. Try as she might, Brianna could not dispel a feeling of guilt over leaving Robert de Beauchamp alone to recover from his wound. Because she could not yet give him her love, she knew she should at least give him her loyalty, and deserting her betrothed in his time of need seemed disloyal in the extreme.

Brianna fell asleep an hour before dawn and the romantic epic of *Tristan and Isolde* colored her dreams. She dreamed that she accidentally shared a loving cup with Christian Hawksblood and became instantly, hopelessly enchanted by the magnetic Arabian. When he looked deeply into her eyes and pulled her into his powerful embrace, she went willingly, unable to resist the lure of him. When they touched, their mouths tasted of the potent wine they had drunk, intoxicating her to the point where she had no mind or will of her own. His kisses were shockingly sensual, drugging her so that she craved his mouth, his hands, his body.

Her husband, Robert, caught them together in her bower and mortally wounded Christian with a poisoned dart. Brianna cried out that she did not want to live without him.

"Approach me then," whispered Christian, "for I feel death coming upon me, and I should like to breathe my last in your arms."

When she embraced him, he withdrew his sword from its sheath and plunged it into her heart. Its name was Killbride! Brianna awoke with a cry upon her lips, but when she realized it had all been a dream, she laughed from relief. How ridiculously fanciful she had become of late.

When she stood before her mirror to braid her hair for riding, she noticed how the clothes Adele had chosen enhanced her coloring. The apricot undergown covered by the amber velvet tunic turned her hair to pure gold. Brianna straightened her shoulders and resolved to enjoy this visit to her home. It had come as an unexpected gift and she was suddenly determined that nothing would mar it.

There was a low knock upon the chamber door and Adele opened it to find Hawksblood's squire, Paddy. "I've come for your trunks, ma'am."

"You may call me Adele," Brianna heard her say, but her next words were said low, as was Paddy's reply, and Brianna suspected they were on the brink of a flirtation.

At the same moment Ali was collecting Joan of Kent's baggage. The Welsh maid, Glynis, was a female very much to his taste. In her own way she was as alien as he among these Anglo-Normans who ruled England. She also had an air of mysticism about her that called to his senses.

Joan was nowhere near ready, so she told Glynis to go on ahead with the trunks and she would do her own hair. She wore a cream underdress of jaconet and over it a tunic of coral velvet. She grabbed her brush and parted her platinum hair down the back, then bound each half with coral ribbons, looping her hair so it only fell to her shoulders. Then she knotted the ends of the ribbons firmly. She pulled on her kid riding boots, scooped up the casket containing Edward's precious letters, and hurried down to the Lower Ward. In her haste, she forgot to retrieve Edward's last note from beneath the bedcovers.

Within half an hour of Lady Kent's departure, a plump

chambermaid handed the letter over to Robert de Beauchamp. A few coins exchanged hands and the girl slipped away unnoticed.

A frown creased the brow of Warrick's son as he read the intimate note. He suspected his bastard brother was having a clandestine affair with the fair maid of Kent and had bribed the servant to bring him evidence. This love note, however, was from Prince Edward, who obviously was at odds with the king over Joan's betrothal to De Montecute! The prince was clearly enjoying a sexual liaison with Joan and his bastard brother was acting as go-between.

Robert winced as he moved his wounded leg to a more comfortable position while he pondered the information he had uncovered. Dissention in the royal ranks could always be used to advantage. Secret information was ammunition. He believed it could be used to Prince Lionel's advantage. Now that he considered the matter, Prince Edward likely wasn't the only one furious at the betrothal. Sir John Holland was ever dangling after the little strumpet. He grimaced. John Holland was one of the most ambitious young cockerels at court. It would pay to make an ally of such an ambitious man. He would send him a note inviting him to dine privately with Prince Lionel and himself.

Hawksblood was taking a score of heavy carts to Bedford that were usually used to carry war weapons. Each wagon had two men trained in driving oxen teams. As well, the company of Cornish soldiers now under his command were riding out with him.

The ladies' trunks were loaded upon one of the carts and the royal grooms led out the ladies' palfreys. As Lady Bedford mounted her white mare, Papillon, she noticed with amusement that both waiting ladies were helped into their saddles by Hawksblood's attentive squires. The horses curvetted restlessly as the entire party awaited Lady Kent.

Christian Hawksblood gave the signal to start the ox carts and they rumbled beneath the turreted gate out onto Thames Street and headed north. Brianna cast a glance in Hawksblood's direction, imagining his impatience at being kept waiting. No sign of annoyance was visible. He looked at ease in the saddle, as if he were prepared to wait an eternity if necessary.

At last Joan arrived. Christian Hawksblood gallantly dismounted and came to her immediately. He placed his powerful hands at her waist and lifted her upon her cream palfrey as if she were thistledown. Joan rewarded him with one of her angelic smiles and Brianna told herself Joan was naturally sweet-natured and had no idea of her devastating effect on men.

The party of mailed knights followed the ox carts at a leisurely pace, through the Thames Valley, across the river past Eton College, traveling north toward the ancient town of Amersham, with its lovely medieval High Street. It had taken half a day to reach this point, and Hawksblood decided to stop in a meadow on the far outskirts for the midday meal. There was a shallow stream and the carters fed and watered their oxen while Hawksblood's men unloaded a victual wagon and handed out bread, cold meat pasties, cheese, and ale.

Adele and Glynis looked at each other with dismay. Adele said, "I never thought to bring anything."

Brianna said, "I assumed we'd enjoy the hospitality at one of the royal residences."

Glynis said, "Perhaps the men will share with us. You ask, Joan. I never met a knight who could refuse you aught you asked for."

Brianna lifted her chin and tossed her long braids back over her shoulders. "I'd rather manage without food than go begging to him!"

Her companions were startled at her vehemence.

Ali came over to help them dismount. "Ladies, if you will sit in the shade of the beech trees, a special lunch has been prepared."

"Oh, how lovely," Joan exclaimed. Three followed him eagerly, one reluctantly. Ali was a squire who observed every nicety. He presented them with scented water and hand towels as soon as they sat down upon the greensward. Then he opened a hamper, spread a linen cloth, and laid out game birds, wedges of cheese, cold artichokes, and tiny spiced crab apples. He handed them small silver goblets, then retired a short distance so his presence did not intrude upon their privacy.

Hawksblood approached the ladies carrying a wineskin. First he came to Brianna to fill her goblet. A vivid picture of sharing wine with him came full-blown into her memory. She recoiled from him immediately. "I will not share your wine!"

He stared at her intensely for a full minute. Under the circumstances her words sounded ridiculous. "You must drink something, my lady," he said softly.

She jumped up, clutching the silver cup. "I shall drink water," she declared, and headed toward the stream. The ladies were embarrassed at Brianna's uncharacteristic behavior and graciously held up their cups for the proffered wine. After a few minutes Christian followed Brianna, determined to breach the barrier she was trying to erect between them.

"My lady—" he began firmly.

She whirled about. "Leave me alone," she cried, putting out her hand to ward him off as if he were an evil spirit.

She was being totally unreasonable. He had not done or said anything to warrant this behavior. He decided to goad her into spitting out whatever was stuck in her craw. "I realize it is a female's nature to be perverse, but I expect common courtesy when you address me. I will not tolerate being spoken to like some lackey."

Green and gold flecks glittered in her eyes. "I know what you are trying to do, you devil!"

"Enlighten me, my lady."

"You are trying to cast a spell upon me so that I'll fall under your control, but it won't work. You cannot hypnotize nor mesmerize me into doing your bidding!"

His dark eyebrows rose and a corner of his mouth lifted in amusement. "Can I not, lady?" he asked enigmatically. His voice surrounded her like dark velvet, challenging, luring, seducing.

She looked like an enchantress from some mythic tale with the sunlight turning her hair to finespun gold.

"Be on your guard against me every moment of the day and every second of the long night, lest I possess your very soul," he teased.

Spoken aloud, in the bright light of day, the words seemed no more than ridiculous nonsense, but Brianna knew that deep down, beneath the banter, lay a kernel of truth. He did possess a power that was supernatural. Christian Hawksblood was not as other men. She wondered briefly if there were such things as immortals. She turned her back upon him and felt him withdraw.

Brianna lingered by the stream as long as she dared, then slowly made her way back to the beech trees. When she reached the others, she saw that they were feeding a fey little creature with four black feet. Brianna was immediately diverted. "Why, it's a ferret! I never saw one so tame before." She laughed at its bold antics as it stood on its hind legs to take a piece of meat from Glynis, then pulled her fingers apart, searching for more.

Brianna bent down and held out the silver cup of water. The bright-eyed ferret came to her immediately and lapped up the water just like a cat. Then it began to bob up and down and chatter to her, performing what looked like a weasel dance.

"Whatever does it want?" Brianna asked, laughing at its antics.

"It wants to play with you," said a deep voice at her elbow. She stood up and whirled about. The look on Hawksblood's face told her clearly he, too, wanted to play with her. She blushed. "Is it yours?" she asked quickly to cover the disquieting effect his closeness had upon her.

"Aye, we've formed a close attachment to each other. Gnasher has fallen victim to my charm," he mocked.

"No doubt you have cast an evil spell upon the poor little creature," she said repressively.

"No doubt," he mocked.

Christian wanted a private word with Joan. She looked forlorn today and exceedingly fragile. He walked beside her toward her palfrey, towering at her side. "Are you weary, my lady?"

"A little," she admitted, her voice sounding lost.

"It's slow traveling with ox carts, but we don't have too much farther to go today." He watched her face carefully, wanting to see the radiant smile when it came.

"You are most kind to trouble about me, Christian. Where will we stay?" she asked indifferently.

He set his hands to her tiny waist to lift her into the saddle. "Berkhamsted," he replied.

Joan's eyes widened with hope.

"Edward awaits you there," he said low.

Joan threw her arms about his neck and kissed him on the cheek. Her smile was radiant indeed, almost like the sun emerging from the clouds.

Brianna checked her steps as she saw the intimate by-play. A searing jealousy ran along her veins like green fire. Joan hadn't the brains she was born with. Brianna, in that moment, could have throttled her.

Paddy aided Brianna to mount, then picked up the ferret and moved on to Adele. The two chattered happily together and when Paddy mounted his own animal, he stayed at Adele's side.

Brianna was out of charity with everyone. It did nothing to soothe her irritability when she saw Ali fall in beside Glynis. She had no choice but to ride alongside Joan. Suddenly she couldn't believe her ears. Her friend was actually singing! Something inside Brianna snapped. She opened her mouth and the words came tumbling out in a torrent. "Joan, it's high time someone took you to task about your behavior. You flirt with every man who comes near you. It makes you look like a shameless hussy!"

Joan, jolted from her lovely reverie about Prince Edward, stared at Brianna blankly. "Whatever do you mean?"

"Don't pretend that angelic innocence with me, it's a bloody act! You can't keep your hands off that damned Arabian, but at least you should have enough sensibility to do your kissing in private."

"Why, Brianna, you're jealous."

"Jealous? That's preposterous! I'm betrothed."

"So am I," replied Joan, "but that doesn't stop me from loving another. Brianna, are you in love with Christian?"

"You must be mad! Haven't you ever heard the gossip about him? He seduces women as casually as he would pluck peaches from a tree. Flirting with him is asking for trouble."

"I have never flirted with him, Brianna," Joan insisted.

"You don't even know you are doing it. You act like a strumpet!"

"And you are acting as petulantly as Princess Isabel. It seems to me you think both De Beauchamp brothers your own personal property. Look to your own morals!" Joan replied.

The two girls stared at each other furiously. Then Joan spurred her palfrey to catch up with Glynis, Adele, and their attentive squires, leaving Brianna to her own devices.

She was oblivious to the beauty all about her. Usually she viewed nature reverently with an artist's eye, appreciating the shimmering greenness, the silver birches, the red rowan trees. With every mile she felt worse. She felt wretched that she had exchanged angry words with her dearest friend. Anger blazed up in her. Anger at herself and at the dark, dangerous Hawksblood. He obviously would like to have his way with both of them, and Joan was too innocent to suspect him!

The light was fading from the day before the wagons, the ladies, and their mail-clad escort arrived in Berkhamsted's bailey.

Paddy immediately unloaded Brianna's and Adele's trunks from a wagon and Lady Bedford led the way into the castle. "I had no idea we were coming to Berkhamsted," she remarked to the squire.

Paddy replied, "We came here for more wagons, my lady."

"Oh, I see," said Brianna. "Ah, here comes that dreadful chamberlain. I hope he provides us with decent chambers this time. I don't suppose he will be as high-handed without Princess Isabel's urging."

As it happened, Prince Edward had given his chamberlain very specific instructions regarding his guests' chambers. Adele was put in her own room beside Lady Bedford's. When Paddy put down Adele's trunk, he asked her to sit with him in the hall. She dimpled and told him she would try her best. When she went in to attend to her lady, Brianna said, "I'm not fit company, Adele. I think I shall dine in my chamber tonight."

"After a bath and an early night, you'll be right as rain, my lamb."

Brianna doubted it. She had behaved peevishly to Joan and now felt pangs of guilt. "When you order my bath, be sure to order one for yourself, Adele. I'll be perfectly happy left to my own devices. I'll probably do some sketching while the scenes from the tournament are still vivid in my imagination." She hung the amber tunic in her wardrobe and awaited her bath. Afterward she put the apricot under-dress back on and stood gazing out into the twilight, trying to sort out her feelings.

When Adele brought her a dinner tray, she remarked, "That strange chamberlain put Lady Kent in another wing. But perhaps it's just as well; you and she didn't seem to be getting along too well today."

Adele's words added to Brianna's misery. When she didn't enlighten Adele about what had gone wrong, Adele said, "Glynis and I are going to the hall together. Joan asked for a tray in her chamber too. Perhaps it's best you avoid each other tonight." When Brianna kept silent, Adele bade her good night and departed.

Brianna sighed and took up her sketch pad. She began to draw one of the horses she had seen in the tournament. Its coat had outshone the plumage of a peacock. She was usually good at capturing the image of fine horseflesh. The head should be lean, the eye gray like a falcon's, the breast large and square. It should be round of thigh and tight of rump. She looked at her sketch in dismay. "The horse that looks like a dog!" she said with disgust.

Brianna's thoughts darted about but kept coming back to Joan. She sketched on absently, unmindful of what her fingers created. Suddenly she looked at her pad in dismay. Staring back at her from the paper was the face of Christian Hawksblood. She threw down the charcoal and impatiently washed its black traces from her fingertips. Sighing heavily, she resumed her place at the long window.

The door to Joan of Kent's chamber opened quietly and Prince Edward stepped into the room. He wore a black pelisson embroidered with the dragon of Wales. With a cry of joy, Joan flew into his open arms and he enfolded her. She was so petite, she stood only as high as his heart. She pressed her cheek to his breastbone and felt the strong, steady beat beneath. "Your Highness, how did you get here before us?"

"Sweetheart, don't call me 'Your Highness.' It sets up a barrier between us, and God knows there are already too many of those."

"Oh, Edward, I feared I would never be able to see you alone again."

"From now on I will make it my first priority, Jeanette."

He felt her tremble. "I . . . I don't want to wed William de Montecute."

He dropped a kiss on her pretty hair and placing a finger beneath her chin, lifted it so he could look into her eyes. He saw them liquid with unshed tears. "My little love, you shall not marry him," Edward said emphatically.

"But the king—"

"The king is Katherine de Montecute's lover, he can refuse her naught. Trust me to find a way for us, sweeting."

Joan was shocked into silence. It was thought by the whole Court that King Edward was completely faithful to Queen Philippa. She was already having another child!

"He is discreet and careful of Katherine's reputation," Edward explained as if he read her thoughts. "I have bought a house in London where we can enjoy time together in privacy." His words drew a parallel between her and Katherine.

Joan's tremble turned to a shiver. The prince's words told her plainly that he intended to become her lover. His fingers began to unthread the coral ribbons from her hair.

"I've waited so long for this. At last we have all night together." His voice was husky with desire. "Will you let me love you?"

"Yes," she cried passionately. "No matter what the future brings, they'll never be able to take this night away from us."

Edward sat down in a massive padded armchair and pulld her into his lap. His lips kissed the tears from her lashes then brushed across her pink mouth, savoring the sweet taste of her. "Lord God, you're like honeyed wine." His kiss deepened and she clung to him, never wanting them to be parted again.

His building desire made his hands clumsy as he tried to

remove her tunic, so she helped him with the lacing and sat on his knees in her diaphanous underdress. "Jeanette, you're delicate as a flower, how can you love such a clumsy brute as I?"

"Edward, you are no brute, you are my *gentil parfait* knight."

"I want to undress you. Where will I start?"

Suddenly he seemed so youthful and in that moment Joan became all woman. She drew up her skirts, exposing her stockings held in place by exquisite, pearl-embroidered garters. It was Edward's turn to tremble as he inched the stockings from her legs. Then his hand stole back up inside her skirt to caress her silky-soft thighs.

Joan's mouth parted as she gasped at the pleasure his touch brought her and his mouth covered hers, delving deeply, as he explored the scented alcove. His hand sought her other scented alcove as his tongue touched hers, and with a little cry she opened to his questing fingers. Edward traced the delicate folds, then slipped a finger into her cleft, seeking the jewel hidden in her woman's center.

She drew in her breath in a rush, feeling the heat of his hand and feeling an even greater heat from his loins beneath her buttocks. Suddenly she realized Edward was naked beneath his long robe and she could wait no longer to look upon his splendid male beauty.

A wild thrill went through him as Joan's hands reached out to part the robe and push it from his shoulders. Instantly he shrugged it from his body so that his nakedness was revealed from throat to thigh. Her small hands smoothed over the great slabs of muscle in his chest, turning his male nipples to diamonds.

She sighed with the overpowering love she felt for this prince. "You are my golden god," she whispered.

Edward groaned with disbelief at his great good fortune. That such an exquisitely beautiful creature loved him was no less than a miracle; a gift from the gods. Her skin was like silk and he needed her naked in his lap, needed to hear the love sounds that would come from her pretty throat as his hands moved her against his hard body.

Finally the love play was no longer enough for Edward.

He needed to lie with her: beside her, beneath her, above her.

Inside her.

He got to his feet, cradling her high against his heart. His rampant shaft rose up to touch her bottom and her pale, platinum hair fell over his arm like rippling moonlight.

Brianna knew what she must do. She would never be able to sleep until she had made her peace with Joan. She didn't bother with a robe. She still wore her apricot underdress and didn't think anyone would be about at this hour. She walked softly down the stone passageway where Adele had indicated Joan's chamber. Perhaps Joan was already asleep. She turned the handle slowly and the heavy door opened a crack.

What Brianna heard gave her pause. She heard the swish of cloth as if a robe fell to the floor. At the same time she heard a gasp, a sigh, a kiss. She heard the unmistakable, sensual sounds of love. A sword of jealousy lanced deep into her heart. Joan was playing wanton with Christian Hawksblood de Beauchamp, Brianna's own Arabian Knight!

She felt totally betrayed. She swung open the door in outrage, then her eyes widened at the blindingly intimate scene before her.

❧ 16 ❧

"Brianna!" Joan gasped.

With a hand over her mouth, Brianna turned and fled.

Edward's arms tightened about his beloved. "Let her go. I'm sure we can trust her with our secret."

"I'm glad she knows. I don't know how I kept it from her this long. Perhaps I should go to her, Edward. She looked so shocked, I think she needs me."

He laughed deep in his throat. "My need is greater, little Jeanette. We will explain together. Tomorrow will be soon enough." As Edward walked to the bed, Joan hid her blushes against his throat.

Brianna rushed headlong down the darkened passageway of Berkhamsted, her thoughts in the most indecent disarray. She did not see the tall, dark figure in the shadows. She almost ran into him as he stepped into her path.

Hawksblood gripped her shoulders to steady her. "What is amiss, lady?"

"I . . . I went to Joan's chamber . . . His Highness is with her . . . she . . . they—"

"You did not know of their secret liaison?" he asked incredulously.

Brianna shook her head. Her pallor alarmed him. "Come," he said with command, and ushered her into his chamber. As if she had no will of her own at that moment, she allowed him to take her into a room and sit her down in a chair. "When I heard a man, I thought it was—"

He finished her sentence for her. "You thought it was me," he said ironically. "Have I not made it plain, *you* are my woman?"

She looked at him in panic. The candles made his dark shadow loom gigantic up the wall. The great four-poster bed dominated the chamber. He saw the fear in her face and dropped down upon one knee. He took her cold hands into his and spoke calmly, quietly.

"Have no fear of me, Brianna. I will not claim you until you are ready," he pledged. The candles bathed her in their soft glow. The apricot underdress clung to her lush breasts, her golden hair fell in waves to the carpet. In that moment he knew he lied. By the Splendor of God he *would* claim her if she resisted him overlong.

Her fear of Hawksblood receded, allowing her thoughts to return to Joan. "I am so afraid for her. Joan has a talent for getting herself into trouble. They will never allow Prince Edward to marry her."

"Never is a long time," he said mysteriously. "However, they are aware they cannot marry, aware they cannot even be seen together; hence the clandestine arrangements."

"But it is wrong. She cannot give herself to one man when she is betrothed to another!"

"Apparently she can. Brianna, love has its own mystic power. It will not be denied."

"You mean royalty has its own power that will not be denied," she flared.

He opened her palm and gazed at it intently. "It is commendable that you wish to protect her, but Edward has had a deep affection for Joan since they were children, and she for him."

"She will be hurt!" Brianna cried.

"Yes, she will be hurt," he said quietly. "When you open your heart to love, it makes you vulnerable. It takes courage, but love's rewards are so glorious, some believe it worth the price of pain."

She knew his words were directed at her. "It takes more courage to choose between right and wrong, to do the honorable thing," she insisted.

"One day you will see there is no dishonor in love." His finger traced a line upon her palm. "You believe your head rules your heart. You are wrong. It does not."

She snatched her hand from his. "You think yourself clever. You think to plant seeds that will give you power over me."

"I shall plant my seed in you, Brianna, never doubt it!" he vowed.

She gasped at his carnal words. It was tempting the devil to be alone in his chamber with him. She jumped to her feet. "Let me go!" she cried.

He indicated the door with a lift of his hand. "You are not my prisoner, lady. You are entirely free."

Desperately, Brianna fled his dark, compelling presence. Free? She didn't believe for one minute she was free. Not entirely.

Christian longed for Brianna to stay with him this night, but the time was not quite ripe, so he did the next best thing. He called up a vision of her. This Brianna, brimming with love and laughter, was warm and willing. Her face was upturned to him like a flower to the sun. He dipped his head to possess her mouth and thrilled to his very bones at her generous response. She was delightfully playful and mischievous—insatiably curious and deliciously uninhibited.

She pulled the covers from him and knelt at his side to explore, to touch, to experiment, and yes, to tease and taunt and torment him! She threaded her fingers in the black curls covering his chest and set the tip of her tongue to his male nipples. When they spiked, she took them between sharp white teeth, threatening to bite him, then going beyond pretense to the actual act.

He yelped, grabbed her with mock roughness, and pretended to be fierce with her. She loved it. She pulled his hair, then ran her fingernails over his rib cage and down across his flat belly where the black hair narrowed to a fine line ending at his navel, then starting again directly beneath it, before it formed a thick sable thatch covering his groin. He groaned as she dipped her tongue into his navel, licking delicately like a kitten, then she lifted a long golden tress of her hair and began to tickle the pulsing head of his shaft until he begged for mercy.

"Behave yourself," he admonished, wanting her to do no such thing. Immediately, she lay down beside him like a sacrificial virgin and covered her nakedness with her golden hair. He came up on one elbow to drink in her loveliness, but when he raised his hand to sweep the silken mass from her she cried out, "No, you can't use your hands!"

"Change the rules, will you?" he growled, enjoying any and every game she wanted to play. He began by blowing softly, soon disturbing the curls that covered the mounds of her breasts. Her pink nipples ruched and poked up through her gilt tresses. Christian bent to taste them with the tip of his tongue, but was overcome with the need to suck the whole luscious crown into his mouth with a hunger akin to starvation. He moved her tresses aside with his nose, breathing in her intoxicating feminine scent until he was dizzy.

He blew gently upon her rounded mons. His warm breath titillated and aroused her so that she arched up with the pleasuring. The moment she did so, he buried his face in her loveliness. His tongue searched among the tight curls until it found her pink cleft, then he stroked her over and over until she felt swollen with love.

"What a lovely thing to do to me," she whispered, wanting more of him, wanting all of him. Brianna began to arch into his mouth, inviting him to plunge deeper. She wrapped her legs about his neck, crying almost incoherently with her need, "More, Christian, please, please."

His powerful hands held her hips, his long fingers splayed out around her bottom, then his tongue pierced her all the way until suddenly he felt her barrier break and tasted blood upon his tongue. Christian panted, "My God, I just took your virginity!" He was so deeply into the fantasy it had taken on the dimensions of reality. As his sensual vision of Brianna dissolved, he vowed that when the actual time came the hymenal ritual would be completed in a more traditional manner.

Before the gray light of dawn crept up the sky, Edward eased himself from the great bed with the utmost care. Joan was sleeping and he would not disturb her for the double crown of England and France.

He made his way to Hawksblood's chamber and slipped inside without knocking. Even in his sleep, Christian sensed he was not alone. His sword was in his hand before his eyes opened. "It's Edward," the prince said into the dimness. "You won't be able to leave today."

Christian knew how difficult it must be for the prince to part with Joan. "I should go," Christian pointed out.

"I realize that," Edward conceded, "but Jeanette won't be able to ride today."

Hawksblood stood up and pulled on his chausses. "The men will benefit from a little martial combat. I'll tell the carters not to harness the oxen."

"Lady Bedford walked in on us last night."

"Brianna only wants to protect Joan," Hawksblood assured him.

Edward nodded. "I'll see you in the quintain yard."

"Take your time. After breakfast will be soon enough, Sire." Christian added quietly, "Lock your door."

*　*　*

Edward turned the key in the lock, knowing he would never be that careless again. He moved toward the bed, then stood transfixed at the picture of his sleeping beauty. She looked so small and young in the big bed. She was the image of a princess from a fairy tale with her silvery hair spread across the pillows and cascading to the carpet. Her lashes lay in crescents upon her cheeks and he imagined dark smudges of fatigue beneath them. He slipped in beside her very gently, not wanting to disturb her, yet unable to resist her fatal allure. She smiled and murmured, "Edward."

"Hush, love, go back to sleep," he said softly as he curved his big body about her protectively.

Joan of Kent did not join Brianna until afternoon. The men of Berkhamsted were engaged in military practice and only an occasional servant came into the herb garden where Brianna sat sketching.

"Are you very angry with me?" Joan asked in a small voice.

Brianna shook her head. "Last night I came to apologize for being beastly to you."

"Are you very shocked?"

"If you had confided in me, I would have warned you against allowing Prince Edward to take advantage of you."

Joan's laughter floated out over the sage and saffron. "Brianna, it has taken me forever to persuade Edward to take advantage of me."

Brianna patted the bench beside her. "Come and sit." Then she said gently, "The king is negotiating for Margaret of Brabant. Edward will not offer you marriage, Joan."

"Oh, Brianna, I don't care about any of that; Edward and I love each other. I don't want his crown, I want his heart."

Joan was so endearingly, sweetly naive. Whatever would she do if she conceived? "What if—"

"Brianna," Joan begged, "please be happy for me." Joan's eyes were soft with love now, but before long she might cry a river of tears. Brianna smiled. She could not bring herself to spoil Joan's happiness.

* * *

In the late afternoon the Black Prince and Christian Hawksblood finally laid aside their swords and shields.

"Are you trying to cripple me?" Edward asked in half-jest.

"No, I'm trying to exhaust you." Christian looked about to see who listened. "I want you to *sleep* tonight, Your Highness."

Prince Edward grinned. "Point taken, Hawksblood."

All four ladies dined in the hall. Their host, Prince Edward, tried to give them equal attention and luckily it was only Hawksblood and his squires who noticed the intense looks he cast at Lady Kent every few moments. And fortunately it was only Brianna and Glynis who noticed Joan's dreamy euphoria.

To protect Joan's reputation, the ladies retired from the hall together. Then Hawksblood kept Edward talking at table a full half-hour before he gave up trying to have an intelligent conversation. "Go to her for God's sake, before you drown in need."

Bedford lay twenty-five miles to the north of Berkhamsted and it would take the ox carts from dawn until dusk to cover the distance.

Brianna was far more amenable to engaging Hawksblood in conversation today. He had traveled the world extensively and the ladies were fascinated to hear of the customs in foreign lands. He couldn't resist needling Brianna about her imminent betrothal. "Since you ladies will soon be wed, would you like me to describe how we go about it in Arabia?"

"Oh yes," Adele enthused, blissfully unaware of the undercurrents.

Hiding his amusement, he said, "A man of my ancestry is allowed countless slaves and concubines, but only four wives."

Adele gasped, Brianna bristled. Aquamarine eyes held hers as he said, "When an Arab falls in love, he loses all reason!"

Joan gave him her rapt attention.

"My bride would sit upon a golden mat studded with rubies and sapphires. I would shower her with a thousand pearls from the Arabian Gulf. Each guest would be presented with a ball of musk containing a slip of paper promising a racehorse, an estate, or perhaps a slave girl."

"Surely no country has so much wealth?" Adele asked.

"Ah, you forget," said Brianna sweetly, "Prince Drakkar is Arabian royalty." She cast him a sideways glance. "At what part of the ceremony do you present her with your scimitar, Killbride? Or is that done in private?"

Hawksblood fixed Paddy with a searing look of accusation.

Teats of Fatima, thought Paddy, *he'll have my balls for this one!*

By the time the landmarks of Bedford came into view, it was evening. Brianna felt such a wave of nostalgia at the outline of the Chilterns rising before her, a lump came into her throat. The grass-covered chalk slopes that rose and fell so gently offered magnificent, panoramic views of the unspoiled glories of nature.

Compared with Windsor and Berkhamsted, Bedford Castle was small and Brianna suddenly wondered if it could accommodate such a large party of carters and men-at-arms. She needn't have worried, for Hawksblood bade the men set up tents in a meadow close by the castle. He and his squires escorted the ladies under the portcullis and into the bailey, but once he had turned them over to her household chamberlain, Sir James Burke, he returned to his men.

Mr. Burke welcomed her with open arms. He had come with her mother and Adele from Ireland when they were little more than children. He insisted that Brianna have her mother's chamber and of course Adele took her old room, which evoked happy memories for her. Curled on the end of her bed was an old striped tomcat she had named Clancy. He opened his eyes wide at the sight of her and she could have sworn his greeting sounded exactly like "Adele?" When she kissed him, Clancy closed his eyes and began to purr.

Joan and Glynis were given adjoining chambers with views of the poetic beauty of the Chilterns. Two maids scurried about, plenishing the chambers while Mr. Burke took himself off to the kitchens to make sure the cook did not skimp on anything for the newly returned mistress of Bedford.

Next morning, Brianna arose early so she could ramble through the gardens on her own. The magnificent rhododendrons were in full bloom, setting off the mellowed Bedfordshire stone of the castle, but she wondered what had happened to all the flowers. Even the pretty quarry garden had been converted from flowers to herbs.

On her way to the solar, she encountered Mr. Burke and invited him into the light-filled room where her mother had spent so many hours. He sat across from Brianna, marveling at the beautiful young woman who had replaced the girl who had left five years before. She was lovelier even than her mother had been. Her hair was brighter than newly minted coins.

"Mr. Burke, where have all the flowers gone? I remember Mother used to fill the rooms with them."

"I'm sorry about the flowers, my lady. I had to economize more and more over the years. We now have a flourishing kitchen garden that feeds the people of the castle."

"I always assumed there was lots of money, Mr. Burke. You know I don't administer my own estate. The money goes to the crown to be administered on my behalf."

"Yes, my lady, and I receive a percentage of what Bedford produces to run the household, but it has diminished steadily every year. I'm sorry the place doesn't flourish as it did when your father was alive."

"Our stone doesn't fetch in the revenue it used to?"

"I don't know, my lady. Your father appointed his own man, Sir Neville Wiggs, as castellan. I was your mother's man. I am only in charge of the household."

"Oh, I see," Brianna said. "What about the people in our villages?"

"Truth to tell, the peasants have a meager existence. They have a hard enough time keeping their bellies filled, so they don't produce much in the fields."

"I'm to be married soon, Mr. Burke, to the son of the Earl of Warrick. Perhaps things will change for the better when Bedford is administered by the De Beauchamps."

"Ah, lady, I am happy the king has chosen such a noble family for you."

"Thank you, Mr. Burke. This solar brings back such poignant memories of my mother. I'd love to talk with you about her."

"This is where she did most of her painting and sometimes she'd sit up half the night writing her legends." He looked at her keenly, wondering what she remembered or what she'd overheard. "She had the second sight, you know. Sometimes she had mystic visions."

"What were they about, Mr. Burke?"

"Anything and everything. She knew you were going to be a girl-child right from the beginning."

"They were likely disappointed that I wasn't a boy."

"Nay, lass, I believe she somehow knew if she ever conceived a son, it would be the death of her. She never told your father, of course. Theirs was a true love match. She adapted well to Bedfordshire and the people loved her."

Brianna was filled with a bittersweet sadness for what might have been. If only her parents had lived, what a happy family they would have been. It was what she wanted more than anything in the world. She wanted Bedford to prosper and she wanted to fill it with her own children. Perhaps the castle would never flourish until it enclosed a happy family within its mellowed stones.

"Your mother even foretold the decline of this proud old place. But after she had you, she told me she had a vision of the man who would be your destiny and she told me he would be Bedford's salvation."

Brianna was wildly curious about the man her mother had seen, yet she hesitated asking Mr. Burke for details. "More than anything in the world I want Bedford to prosper. I hope her prophecy comes to pass."

"She said that Bedford would suffer a worm at its core, but the great noble who bestowed his love upon you would root out the rot, before your children were conceived."

Brianna held her breath. "Did she mention the man's coloring? Was he fair?"

"Nay, lass, she always referred to him as the Dark Knight."

Brianna let out her breath slowly, a sense of destiny beginning to enfold her. If she listened to her heart, it told her Christian de Beauchamp was that destiny. If she listened to her head, it told her she was pledged to Robert de Beauchamp for better or for worse.

Adele took Joan and Glynis on a tour of Bedford and its villages while Brianna was content to examine all the things that had belonged to her mother. Her chamber still held some of her clothes, layered with woodruff, and carefully stored in a heavy trunk. Her sketches and paints were stacked in an alcove of the solar. There were so many, Brianna was immersed for hours in the pleasure of discovery.

Some of the sketches were on parchment that had turned brown with age, but the colors her mother had used to illustrate some of her legends were as brilliant as if they had been done yesterday. Brianna came across several drawings of a mail-clad knight. The man had an aura of dark mystery about him, as well as a decidedly dangerous quality. If Brianna had not known it was impossible, she would have sworn her mother had used Hawksblood for her model.

She took one over to the large oriel window to examine the dark features more closely and there below in the bailey, talking earnestly with Mr. Burke, was the man himself. It was as if she had conjured him. Both men's faces were grave, as if they discussed a subject that was deadly serious. She wondered what Hawksblood spoke of to *her* Mr. Burke.

She wondered how far along with the stone cutting they were and how many days she would be allowed to remain in this pleasant haven. Brianna decided to join them and inquire immediately.

"How much stone has been cut?" she asked tentatively.

"None," Hawksblood replied almost curtly.

Obviously, he wasn't about to offer her an explanation, so she demanded with great hauteur, "Why not?"

"I have other priorities," he replied flatly.

"Such as?" she inquired sweetly.

He frowned, impatient at her questions. "Hunting for one thing. The accounts for another." He turned from her and again addressed Burke. "More later, on the matter we discussed," and turned on his heel.

As Brianna's mouth fell open, she heard Mr. Burke say, "Thank you, my lord, you have saved the day."

Mr. Burke hurried to explain. "He has been so generous and helpful, I don't know how I would have managed without him. He and his men have been hunting since first light. Now I have enough game, rabbits, and venison to feed all the men who came with you, as well as everyone in the castle, for a fortnight."

Brianna was only slightly mollified. As she and her chamberlain walked back into the castle, she said, "The hunting might be appreciated, but how dare he scrutinize the accounts?"

"Oh, I think he has the right, Lady Brianna, as the king's representative and as Warrick's. I, for one, welcome an audit. I know my accounting is scrupulous, but I have long suspected irregularities in the castellan's books."

"Sir Neville Wiggs?" she demanded. "What irregularities do you suspect?"

"Suspicions are not enough, my lady. Let us leave the matter in the capable hands of Sir Christian."

So, he already had Mr. Burke eating out of his hand. Sooner or later he controlled everyone so they were eager to do his bidding.

Brianna joined the other ladies for dinner and was surprised when she saw that every seat was filled, both by the men of Bedford, and the men who had traveled with Hawksblood.

Joan and Glynis chatted on about the things Adele had shown them that day, but Brianna listened with only half a mind. Her attention was elsewhere on undercurrents that seemed to flow about the hall.

Sir Neville Wiggs and his men sat on one side, while Burke, Hawksblood, and his squires sat opposite. The carters and Hawksblood's men-at-arms mixed freely with the servants and grooms of Bedford Castle, but Wiggs and his men held themselves aloof and Brianna could see they were surly with suppressed anger. Her glance traveled to Hawksblood, who once again was in deep conversation with Mr. Burke. They did not look exactly angry, but they were certainly serious.

As she watched him, she couldn't help but notice he was the most dominant man in the hall. He had an air of supreme confidence and command, as if he were in his own castle and was master over every stick and stone, every man jack within its crenellated walls. No matter where he went, he was treated with deference, even by the Plantagenets, and Brianna concluded that this was because of his secret power.

When the meal was over, the men began to cast dice and the ladies retired to the solar, where Adele showed off her talent with the lute and the Irish harp. She had a lovely soft voice and as Brianna listened it evoked memories of her mother and her childhood.

By the time she retired to her chamber, she was in a strange, reflective mood. She half undressed, then she felt the irresistible lure of the old trunk that held her mother's things. She sat on the floor and slowly lifted the heavy lid. A smell like new-mown hay drifted up from the layers of clothing as Brianna took out a night rail. It was made of Irish lace in a shade of unbleached ecru, finely spun as a spider's web. She lifted the candle to examine the lace more closely and saw it was done in an ancient Celtic pattern, very similar to the ribbon painting she designed as borders for her parchments. The symbols and animals had mystic properties with no beginning, no end, but rather they were seamless and intertwined.

Brianna knew she must try it on. She stood before the silver polished mirror, took off every stitch, then drew the night rail over her nakedness. It opened all the way down the front and fastened with love knots. The moment the lace fell about her body, she felt different. She certainly looked different. The flesh-colored garment was designed to flatter and enhance the female form. It was low-necked, clinging to her breasts provocatively. The sleeves trailed, covering her hands, the skirt billowed open when she moved to reveal her legs and what lay between.

Inside, she was bubbling with suppressed happiness and excitement. She looked into the mirror, marveling at the change in herself, and looked straight into a pair of aquamarine eyes. She could not look away. She did not wish to look away. She smiled into his eyes. The knowledge came to her that he often watched her. Especially when she was naked. In spite of herself, she was thrilled to her very core.

He was in a trance. Suddenly, she realized she had the power to watch him. What a fool she had been not to do so, when simply looking at him brought her so much pleasure. As she focused on her task, her eyes widened, her pupils dilated as her mind expanded.

The eyes in the mirror transformed into a face. Then as she concentrated, the face transformed into a body. Brianna had never seen a man naked before. She was supremely grateful the Arabian Knight was the first. The sheer symmetry of the powerful, lithe male body would set the standard for all men as far as she was concerned. He looked as if he had been sculpted from bronze.

Her gaze caressed every rippling muscle as it gleamed in the candlelight. She breathed deeply and smelled the almond-scented oil he had rubbed on his body. Her glance traveled lower, somehow knowing exactly how he would be made. The corners of her mouth lifted as she saw his thick male center jutting boldly from its dark nest. His thighs were not white, they were as swarthy and olive-skinned as his face and chest.

Suddenly she stiffened. God's mercy, what was the black object marring the inside of his long, muscled thigh? All was shadowed. Brianna focused, clearing her mind of every other thought in the universe. Was it a scar? Yes and no. Was it a burn? Perhaps. For the space of one heartbeat it came into focus and she saw that it was shaped like a scimitar. In the next heartbeat the vision was gone and she again saw herself reflected in the silver mirror.

Excitement blossomed like a bloodred rose inside her breast. She knew he awaited her! She smiled a secret smile. How delicious to keep him waiting. His magnetism was too strong to resist him for long, thank God, so Brianna threw a cloak over the finespun night rail and slipped up to the castle ramparts.

The deep shadows adored lovers. They knew exactly
where to find each other, drawn together like the moon
and a lunar tide. They stood close without touching while
they looked into each other's souls. Beneath his sable cloak
he was naked bronze, beneath hers she was fine-spun lace.
They moved together in unison. Each felt the shocking jolt
of primal lightning as heat leaped between them and the
night exploded.

His powerful hands swept inside her cloak, molding his
palms about her voluptuous breasts. Her taut nipples thrust
through the lacy holes of the bodice and as his thumbs
grazed over them, they instantly became swollen. His hungry mouth found a pulse point in her throat and his lips
began their journey to every other pulse point on her body.

His lovemaking was like a firestorm, turning her
splendidly uninhibited. His body was big, burning, and demanding. His powerful hands were impatient as he undid
the love knots and pulled apart her gown. Then it was all
hot sliding friction as naked bronze met silken skin. As
their mouths fused together in hunger, his hands pushed
both her cloak and her lacy gown from her fevered body
and gathered her inside his mantle.

The moment her mother's night rail fell from Brianna's
body, she came to her senses. She was not on the castle
ramparts with her forbidden lover, she was standing naked
before her mirror. Had she left this room to behave wantonly? She grabbed the night rail and pulled it on quickly to
cover her shame.

The moment it fell about her limbs, her feelings of
shame vanished. Her eyes became smoky with the smell
and taste of the man she had just left. She felt languorous
with the sensuality he had aroused in her.

Her fingers traced across the pulse beat in her throat,
then up across her lips where his demanding mouth had
traveled. She was filled with the memory of the sight of
him, the feel of him. Again she pictured the proudly jutting
manroot, but again she saw the great black scimitar, marring the inside of his thigh. What was it? She concentrated
and focused. Then she felt the overwhelming, agonizing
pain of it. It seared through her body into her brain. It was
unendurable. Brianna screamed and fell to the floor, un-

conscious. As she sank to the carpet, the garment parted, leaving her naked beauty bathed in moonlight.

At dawn, she opened her eyes and sat up. When she did so, the lacy night rail slipped from her shoulders to the carpet and she stared at it for long moments, recalling the shadowed images of the night just passed. What was real and what imagined? She frowned. Had it been a dream? A fantasy? A trance? A vision? Yes, it had been all these things, yet she feared it had been more.

Brianna was beginning to recognize an overwhelming desire for Christian Hawksblood though until last night she had denied it to herself. Her friend Joan was having a blissful liaison with Edward, throwing all caution to the wind. Was it so wrong to follow your heart? Why should she resist such an overwhelming temptation? She believed her mother would have been woman enough to indulge her desire.

One thing was certain. The strange episode was somehow connected with the lace garment. Her mother had visions and Brianna knew she had experienced one of them when she donned the Celtic robe with its mystic properties.

It had all been so very real, yet, thank God, that was impossible. Christian Hawksblood slept in his tent in the meadow. She took up fresh clothes and poured water from the jug to wash. Her lips trembled as she noticed traces of almond oil upon her skin. Surely hallucinations did not leave physical evidence behind.

She dressed quickly and went to find her chamberlain. "Mr. Burke, is Christian Hawksblood still quartered with his men in the meadow?"

"No, my lady," he said, beaming. "He's in the Chiltern Tower."

Brianna blushed hotly at the possible implications.

"I took the liberty of plenishing the chamber for your betrothed last night."

Brianna stared at him in disbelief. "My *what*, Mr. Burke?"

"Your betrothed." He searched her face uncertainly. "You said you were betrothed to Warrick's son. Is this not he?"

"Hawksblood is Warrick's bastard son! I am betrothed to

Robert de Beauchamp, Warrick's legal son and heir. My betrothed was wounded in the tournament at Windsor and so the king asked Hawksblood to fetch the stone."

"Forgive me, my lady. He has taken such a paternal interest in Bedford's welfare, I assumed he would be the new master here."

"Just because he hunted to feed the horde he brought with him doesn't give him the right to act as if he owns the place!"

"It is not just the hunting, Lady Brianna."

"Now I understand why you thought he had the right to examine the accounts."

"He has the king's authority for that," Mr. Burke said quietly.

"Where is he?" Brianna demanded, barely able to hold onto her temper.

"He has gone to a monastery in the Chiltern Hills."

"God-a-mighty, he is the least monkish man of my acquaintance!"

"He thinks the best way to restore Bedford's fortune is wool. The Cistercian monks breed the best sheep in England. Their wool is of superior quality, so he has gone to buy some."

"Mr. Burke, you tell me I have no money one day, and the next you tell me Hawksblood is wasting what little I have on sheep!"

"Ah no, lady. It is his own money he is lavishing on Bedford."

She was brought up short. She knew little about him, but what money could a landless mercenary, who sold his sword for his livelihood, have?

A small voice told her, *He intends to have your land.*

"When he returns, tell him I wish to see him. He was sent here to get stone. It seems he has spent his time on everything but that task."

"It is Bedford's salvation that he has, my lady. He has such practical ideas. At this moment his men are building dovecotes and his Irish squire has gone to buy beehives. Tomorrow he has offered to help the villagers make rabbit and coney warrens so the peasants will have meat all year round."

His words took the wind out of her sails. Gratitude replaced the anger she had felt. How selfless of him to help the people of Bedford. It should have been Robert's responsibility to set things right and make Bedford flourish. She wondered what he would have done. A small voice said, *He would have taken the stone to Windsor and set an exorbitant price for it. No, no, he would not! Why do you always think badly of Robert?* she asked herself.

Brianna tried to rekindle her anger against Hawksblood. It wasn't difficult! Why couldn't he have discussed these matters with her? Because he was a bloody male, that's why, and she a "mere" female. The fact that Bedford was hers made little difference to him. He was a law unto himself. He was such an arrogant swine, he would set the universe right if it suited his purpose. The small voice said, *He has the power. He is an immortal.*

"Nonsense!" she said firmly.

Mr. Burke looked bewildered. Though he loved Brianna deeply, she was a stubborn little wench. Fiery, too, just as her mother had been. He smiled to himself. She could call Hawksblood names like "bastard" until the cows came home, but that didn't alter the fact that the pair of them were made for each other. She simply hadn't admitted it yet, but she knew all right. Knew it in her very bones.

At that moment, Joan came across them. "I've been looking everywhere for you, Brianna. You are becoming a positive recluse. Adele is taking us to the wishing pool in the enchanted forest. Please come with us."

Joan was as excited as a child and her enthusiasm was infectious. "Of course I shall come. I'd love to see it again myself, but it's just a crystal pool in Elstow Forest. It's not really enchanted and there is no guarantee that wishes made there will come true."

"Brianna, you have no romance in your soul."

"Do I not?" Brianna asked, laughing. "You would be astounded at how fanciful some of my thoughts have become lately."

"Good! I want you to promise you will suspend your disbelief for one afternoon."

"I promise."

"Come then, Adele and Glynis have gone to the stables to get our palfreys saddled."

The spot where the crystal-clear pool lay beneath the oak trees of the forest was most enchanting, if not exactly enchanted. The sunshine filtering through the leafy canopy danced upon the water, making pretty patterns of light and shadow. In the spring these woods were filled with bluebells and their heady fragrance, but now the pool was edged by forget-me-knots and marsh marigolds. Stretching beneath the trees were lacy ferns, while the far edge of the pool was covered by water lilies and watercress. The air above them was filled with birdsong. The thrushes and blackbirds flew from branch to branch, while the kingfishers skimmed low over the water to catch the iridescent dragonflies.

Each of them had brought coins to throw into the wishing pool and without hesitation Joan went first, drenching her slippers and the hem of her gown with the springwater. Brianna felt a lump in her throat as she watched Joan. She knew she was making wishes about herself and Prince Edward that could never come true. "It's not really a wishing pool," she cautioned.

"You promised!" Joan reminded her.

"I'm sorry. Actually the last wish I made here did come true. I wished that I would return to Bedford."

Now it was Adele's turn to swallow hard and keep the tears at bay. She remembered the afternoon as if it were yesterday when the orphaned Brianna had been ordered to Windsor by writ of the king.

Glynis, with her head on one side as if she were listening for the earth's pulse beat, said, "The atmosphere here is unusual. I can sense deep emotional vibrations, as if this has been the sight of much happiness and much sorrow and . . . something else. Passion, I believe. Great passion."

Adele said, "There've always been legends about the place. One folk tale said pagan rites were celebrated here, even pagan sacrifices. Another fable said a young woman drowned herself when her lover spurned her."

Joan shivered. "How morbid. It's beautiful here." She asked Glynis, "What about the happiness, and don't forget the passion?"

Glynis replied, "It has definitely been a trysting place for lovers."

"How lovely," Joan said dreamily, remembering another pool in another forest.

Adele laughed. "Legend says that if a female bathes naked in the crystal pool, she will see the face of her future husband."

Brianna protested, "I never heard such a legend!"

Adele's eyes sparkled. "You were just a child. As if we would repeat such things to you."

Joan giggled gleefully. "You did it, didn't you?"

Adele blushed. "My sister and I did. It was before she was married to your father, of course."

"Oh, tell us what happened, Adele," Joan urged.

"I saw no face, but Rhianna insisted she saw the face of Sir Brian."

"Oh," Joan cried, "your name, Brianna, is a combination of Rhianna and Brian, how utterly romantic!"

As Adele and Glynis moved to the water's edge, Joan whispered, "I bet Adele is making a wish about Paddy and Glynis is thinking of Ali."

"Paddy and Ali? Those two damned reprobates. I think of them as Vermin and Pestilence!"

"The Irishman being Vermin, of course," Joan teased, and her laughter floated out across the crystal pool. Brianna was last to throw in her coin. As the surface rippled, a dark face appeared. Her heart leaped joyfully in her breast. Had she wished to see the face of the Arabian Knight? Brianna believed she had wished it deep down in her heart. Her emotions were in turmoil. Why couldn't she be satisfied with Robert de Beauchamp? A whispered answer floated back to her. *The heart wants what the heart wants.*

As the ladies rode back to the castle they were all fast friends again, as they had been before the misunderstanding between Joan and Brianna. "Your parents were so lucky to marry for love," Joan said wistfully.

Brianna asked softly, "What does it feel like to be in love?"

"Heaven . . . and hell," Joan replied with a sigh of longing. "His face is ever before you. He fills every waking thought and comes each night in your dreams. The desire to be together is so strong it cannot be denied. Love is so good and so powerful it transcends all barriers. You know it will be hell to be separated, but it would only be unbearable if you had no love memories to cherish." Joan flushed. "I know you think me foolish to love Edward, but I will take whatever is given me. He has made me a woman and I have no regrets."

In that moment Brianna did not think her friend foolish, she thought her most courageous.

It wasn't far back to the castle, so they had lots of time before the evening meal.

As they reached the top of the stairs, Adele gasped in alarm as she saw the black-footed ferret streak toward Clancy. The old tomcat paused from washing his face, lifted his paw, and batted the ferret on the nose. Gnasher sat back quickly on his haunches, then crouched submissively before the dominant cat who had ruled this territory for a decade. Adele laughed with relief.

Brianna said, "Attitude is everything. Old Clancy probably only has half his teeth left, but the ferret doesn't know that."

Adele swooped the tabby into her arms. "I'm going to change into something more elegant before I go to the hall."

Joan winked at Brianna, for here was more evidence that Adele wanted to attract the Irish squire. "Let's all wear something special," Joan suggested, and immediately Glynis agreed with her.

"What will you wear, Brianna?" Joan asked as they all entered her chamber. Adele bent to pick up the lace garment from the floor where it had lain since morning. "What lovely material, what is it?" Joan asked curiously.

"It belonged to my mother; it's a night rail," Brianna said, hoping her cheeks did not flame into color.

"How lovely," said Joan, fingering the delicate folds. "This was her chamber; are there any more of her things?"

"Yes, there's a whole trunkful."

"Oh, can we look at them?" Joan begged.

"Of course," said Brianna, dropping to her knees before the heavy trunk and lifting its lid. The other ladies knelt beside her and she handed out the garments one at a time.

"Just look at the brilliant color of this gown!" exclaimed Joan. "What would you call it?"

"Aquamarine?" Adele suggested.

"Turquoise?" Glynis said.

"Peacock!" Brianna decided.

"Oh yes, peacock," Joan agreed. "But it's cut in the latest French style with tight bodice and full skirt, how can that be?"

Brianna shrugged. "When it comes to fashion, there's nothing new under the sun. If you hang on to your clothes long enough, they always seem to come back in style."

"Brianna, you must wear this tonight. Only think how your emerald-studded girdle will set it off!"

Brianna hesitated. How would she ever be able to walk into the hall and face Hawksblood? Then common sense prevailed. Last night's episode had been a fantastic dream. She must banish it from her thoughts. She decided that she would wear the gown to give her confidence. Her mother had been a countess who presided over her own hall with the regal air of a queen. Tonight she, too, would preside over her own hall.

"Glynis, come and help me find something that won't put me in the shade," Joan urged, and the two of them went off to her chamber.

"Would you like me to help you dress?"

"No, Adele, go and get ready yourself. Perhaps you can help me put up my hair later, if you have time."

As Brianna admired her reflection in the oval mirror, the corners of her mouth lifted in a secret smile. She knew she had never looked lovelier. She had never felt more alive either. The anticipation of seeing Christian in the hall left her breathless. She knew with a knowledge as old as Eve that their coming together was inevitable.

Fated.

Mated!

Wearing her mother's peacock gown altered all Brianna's perceptions. What had been distant was now very close. What had been feared was now desired. What had been impossible was now attainable. How simple it was to separate pretense from truth. The pretense was her indifference. At last she admitted that she had all the symptoms of love that Joan described, and more. Could she possibly allow her friend to be more of a woman than she herself was?

Christian Hawksblood had taken an interest in Bedford because he cared deeply about her. He had made it plain that he desired her intensely. Had told her he intended to claim her as *his* lady. She made up her mind to grasp the happiness that was offered her. Before she married Robert, perhaps unhappily, she would sample rapture in the arms of the man she had begun to love. No one could take away her memories!

How easy it was to separate fantasy from reality. Last night was a dream. Tonight would be real. They would come together in the flesh, drawn by their hunger and need for each other. In the peacock gown she had the power to realize she had chosen him long ago, at the beginning of time!

When the ladies entered the dining hall, the first person they encountered was Hawksblood. Brianna smiled into Christian's eyes. "Good evening, *my* lord." The emphasis was unmistakably upon the word *my*!

⨳ *18* ⨳

It was as if the world and everyone in it fell away for long moments while the couple caressed each other with their eyes. Finally, she offered him her hand and he carried it to his lips as if it were precious to him. His warm breath teased her skin. "Will you sit beside me, my lady?"

"With the greatest pleasure, my lord."

The desire he felt was almost blinding.

Joan's eyebrows elevated as she looked at Adele, and took a seat farther down the table from the dallying couple. Anyone seeing them could tell they had a claim upon each other.

Paddy and Ali came immediately to the sides of Adele and Glynis to hold their chairs and the seven people sat down cozily as if they had always dined together. As

Hawksblood held her chair for her, Brianna placed her hand upon his arm to steady herself and the moment she touched him, she needed steadying. Her brows went up, slanting the witch-mark on her cheekbone. "Why do you wear mail to the table?"

He pulled up the sleeve of his linen chainse to reveal the powerful, muscular arm. "I wear no mail, lady."

Brianna caught her breath on a shiver. She was reeling from the nearness of him. She swept down her lashes to hide the wild desire she felt at the intensity of his dark look. Then she raised them halfway to give him a glimpse of it. He smiled slowly, wickedly, dangerously.

His eyes lingered on her hair, which had been braided and looped with peacock ribbon. He anticipated that it would give him as much pleasure to take it down as it would to undress her, then he contemplated which he would do first. He began to fill and harden. He almost controlled it, then decided to enjoy the pleasure of arousal.

Everything about him fascinated her. His coloring was in complete contrast with the golden Plantagenets and the blond knights of England. Physically he was perfect and without scar. Almost, she amended, wildly curious about the black scimitar on his inside thigh. His past and his origins fascinated her also. He was an enigma, but she smiled inwardly, knowing she possessed the key to his mystery. *I'm in love! Why should I keep resisting him when it's the last thing in the world I want to do? Christian Hawksblood de Beauchamp is the one with whom I want to spend my life! It's preordained.*

Tonight, even the food upon Brianna's trencher tasted like ambrosia. Then she realized that Christian had supplied it. "I am in your debt for providing this delicious venison, as are all in Bedford Castle. How shall I repay you?" She asked the provocative question deliberately.

His eyes were splinters of aquamarine. They crinkled in amusement, promising her he would show her how to repay him. They were so close, their thoughts were shared without words. "Taste the boar. She gave me the devil of a chase, then threatened to gore me." The teasing light in his eyes implied she offered the same sort of challenge. He cut off a succulent chunk and held it to her lips.

Brianna took it with sharp white teeth, then licked her lips over the zesty morsel. "How fortunate that you managed to subdue your quarry. Do you always?"

"Usually. I enjoy the chase and I enjoy the kill." Again Brianna shivered, and Hawksblood was aware of every tremor. "I've decided to make some changes here that I should apprise you of," he said on a more serious note.

Brianna's eyes laughed up into his. "I wondered when you would get around to seeking my permission."

His intense look robbed her of breath. "I seek an endless number of things from you, lady, but none of them is *permission*!"

"Domination and submission is a game that holds little appeal for me," she warned provocatively.

His smile flashed out. "That is because you have not yet experienced being dominated by me."

"And never will," she assured him.

"You shall, you shall," he promised in a low voice.

Her throat went dry. Brianna gathered what wits he left her. "You spoke of changes?"

He experienced a surge of male satisfaction when she took a verbal step backward. "I've made Sir James Burke the new castellan of Bedford."

She gasped. "Won't Sir Neville Wiggs be angry?"

"Furious," he conceded with a grin.

"Have you asked him to step down?" she asked, wide-eyed.

His brow rose. "Asked him? Hardly! I've ordered him to turn over his keys and accounts to Burke."

"Will he obey you?"

A bark of laughter escaped him. "Implicitly. He'll soon be too busy to be Bedford's castellan. I've recruited him and his knights for the king's army. Like the rest of us, Wiggs is about to go to war."

Her shoulders drooped, her hand went to her throat. "How can you speak so eagerly of war?"

He shrugged and grinned. "It is what I have trained for all my life."

Her eyes searched his. Her teasing banter fled. "I am filled with apprehension for you, Christian," she whispered.

His eyes softened. "Sweet. Fear not, I shall return victorious."

Brianna blushed, realizing she had let him see she cared. "Mr. Burke is a perfect choice. I approve wholeheartedly."

Hawksblood experienced another surge of male power as she retreated to safer ground. "That is because you are as intelligent as you are beautiful."

She cast him a tempting sidewise glance. "You think flattery will gain you aught?"

"Words are powerfully seductive. They can bring a woman to rapture."

Her cheeks held a delicate tint. "I know naught of rapture," she said primly.

The look he gave her was smoldering. A muscle hardened at his jaw. "You had better bloody well not."

Her insides went weak at his possessive tone.

Joan saw the intimate progression as the pair parried and thrust in their verbal game of courtship. She realized Brianna was on the brink of the precipice with the edge crumbling beneath her feet.

"I would love to visit the stone quarries. Are they finished cutting yet?"

Two pairs of eyes stared at Joan blankly for a moment before they realized there were others about to observe what they did and said.

"We start cutting tomorrow, Lady Kent."

"Oh, may we come and observe?" Joan asked prettily, and the other ladies looked at him hopefully.

"It is really no place for ladies."

"Of course we shall visit the quarries. I am mistress here," Brianna said firmly.

The ladies exchanged amused glances. It was unlike Brianna to assert her authority.

Hawksblood murmured outrageously, "Mistress . . . the word conjures such forbidden fantasies. I'm weak at the thought."

Devil! Would the blush ever leave her cheeks? She dared not look into those mesmerizing eyes another moment. She lowered her lashes so that all she saw were his hands upon his goblet. It was a mistake. His hands were so attractively powerful, her throat ached for their touch. He had such an animal strength she almost screamed to be touched by him. She was well snared. She'd scream if he touched her; scream if he did not!

Brianna reached for her own goblet to cool her throat. Bedford had no wine, only October ale for the men and cider for the ladies, but she found it a potent brew tonight. She felt alternately giddy and dizzy, yet she knew it was not cider alone that stole her senses.

He selected a pear tart, then carried the first spoonful to her lips. She allowed him to feed her, then licked the spoon lustily. It was Christian's turn to shudder. Her lashes flew up so her eyes could meet his, but his gaze was riveted upon her mouth with such blazing desire she closed her eyes against his raw male sexuality.

The servers began to clear the tables and it was the signal for those in the hall to stretch their legs and regroup for conversation or dice. The men and women at the head table were loathe to part company. Adele had been telling Joan and Glynis and Hawksblood's squires what it had been like here in the old days. Joan took up a beribboned lute and passed it to Brianna's aunt. "Adele has promised to sing as she did when you were a little girl."

"How lovely. I remember the special times when Adele and my mother sang the old Irish ballads. Those were such happy days for Bedford," Brianna recalled.

"Rhianna had a far more striking voice than I," Adele said modestly. "A happy hall should always have music. I will sing if Brianna too will entertain her guests."

Everyone applauded this suggestion and gave their attention to Adele. She had a lovely soft, gentle voice. The notes fell sweetly as she accompanied herself on the lute. When she sang, her plain features were transformed to beauty. Brianna was surprised to see the hint of a tear in Paddy's eye as he listened to the plaintive Irish ballad. With their applause, they persuaded her to sing again and again, until at last she laughed firmly and insisted it was Brianna's turn.

Brianna arose and went to the corner where the Celtic harp stood. She pulled up a stool and drew the carved instrument against her shoulder. Everyone save Adele was astounded. Brianna's voice was full and rich. Unsuited to plaintive ballads, it was perfect for the rousing song she chose. It was a song often used for battle to fire the blood and lead men on to victory. Her voice was like rich, dark wine. If Adele's songs appealed to the soul, Brianna's appealed to the body, arousing it physically, potently.

In her peacock gown with a nimbus of candleglow about her golden head, she looked and sounded exactly like the countess had when she presided over this hall. Brianna made no secret of whom she sang to. Christian Hawksblood sat enthralled. Looking at her and listening to her told him she would be generous and reckless and wonderful in his bed. She was a woman fit for a prince.

Drakkar smiled. His world was unfolding exactly as it should.

When Brianna finished, the applause was thunderous. Everyone in the hall had ceased what they were doing to give their mistress their undivided attention. It was almost as if the countess had appeared to them in a vision. It was a sign, an omen, that Bedford's fortunes were on the rise.

Brianna lingered in the hall until the hour was advanced. She could not bear to part with Christian Hawksblood's company. At last, with a sigh, she arose and the ladies went up to their chambers.

Alone, she stood before the mirror, dazzled by her reflection. The gown had transformed her both physically and emotionally. She felt fully alive . . . the girl had been replaced by a woman. She closed her eyes to savor the feeling. She hugged herself and beneath her hands the silk of the peacock gown felt so sensual to the touch she was reluctant to remove it. When she opened her eyes to steal a last glimpse of herself, she looked into aquamarine eyes! Ah God, it was happening again.

"You are *my* woman."

She whirled to face him.

Christian Hawksblood was no vision but a very real flesh-and-blood man. She should protest. She should order him from her chamber. She should remonstrate with him for his boldness, demurring to be alone with him. Brianna knew all the things she should do.

She did none of them.

"I knew you would come," she said simply.

There were still a few steps to intimacy that had not yet been taken, but both knew they would be taken this night. Without hesitation, Hawksblood reached out for a peacock ribbon and his long fingers undid the bow, then threaded through her hair to unplait it. He had anticipated the feel of the golden silk mass spilling over his hands since the first moment he had seen it, but he had been unprepared for the physical impact it had upon him.

He was aroused the moment he entangled his fingers in it. He felt the jolt hit the center of his chest, lance deeply into his belly, then slither along his manroot until he was big and hot and hard. He felt his self-control melting away; that same control he'd worked a lifetime to develop.

He reached for the other plait. Hawksblood had learned in his training that hand-to-head contact was a major step toward trust and forging an emotional bond. An injury to the head usually caused instant death, and to duck away was a survival reaction. Brianna did not duck away. She stayed absolutely still, allowing him to do whatever he wished with her glorious hair.

"It feels like I have waited a lifetime to learn its texture" —he lifted it to his face—"and its fragrance." She smelled of spice and flowers and woman. The next step to intimacy was mouth to mouth.

Brianna licked her full bottom lip in anticipation of the kiss. The sight of the tip of her tongue undid him. His mouth covered hers and he took possession of the full underlip and tongue, drawing them into his own mouth as if he would devour her.

Brianna kissed him back, thoroughly, wantonly, as he took advantage of their full embrace. His powerful fingers splayed through her hair, holding the back of her head so she was a prisoner for his ravishing. The taste of her was everything he had dreamed and more. He allowed all of his senses full rein so that he saw and heard and smelled and tasted and felt all of her womanly essence, so rich and ripe and succulent.

Brianna's hands slid up his chest, relishing the solid muscle beneath them. She had no thought to push him away. Rather, she celebrated finally laying her hands upon his magnificent body.

When at last he took his mouth from hers, she put her arms behind his neck and touched her lips to the pulse beat in his throat. Lifting her arms made her breasts slide up his chest in such a provocative manner, his desire was savage, hungry. His hands went to her waist and he lifted her against him slowly, pleasurably.

She laughed down into his face, trusting him, tempting him. Her golden hair fell in masses upon his chest as his mouth lifted to first lick the tiny black witch-mark, then worship her mouth, learning the shape of her curved lips, mastering her teasing tongue. Then slowly, blissfully, he allowed her body to slide down his until her toes touched the carpet. He would repeat the exercise when they were both naked, so they could experience the wild, hot slide of love-slick skin against skin.

His passion grew so that even his face hardened and when Brianna's fingertips feathered up his jaw to his saber-sharp cheekbones, he felt his blood beating in his brain, his throat, even the soles of his feet. It did not beat in his male center; it pounded savagely, it throbbed deeply, it surged demandingly in the most stunning arousal he had ever experienced.

Christian wanted Brianna to enjoy every nuance of arousal along with him. He wanted her to feel desire in every silken inch of skin she possessed. He wanted her passion to run the gamut from purest heaven to exquisite hell. His lips began to whisper love sounds against her temple, then moved down to her ear where his words became shockingly erotic. Against her throat, his whispers became enticing, then as his fingers unfastened her peacock gown, baring her shoulders; his whispering mouth tantalized her skin until it felt like hot silk.

Brianna's breathing deepened so that her breasts seemed to rise toward his seeking mouth. The crests ruched as his whispering breath teased the taut peaks and his powerful hands cupped her full breasts, weighing, caressing, playing, and finally worshiping them as precious love objects.

Brianna wanted to scream with excitement when she thought of her bare breasts touching his naked chest. Her greedy fingers unfastened his linen chainse and peeled it from his torso. When he crushed her soft breasts against the swarthy expanse of muscle covered by its black pelt, she did scream with pure, unadulterated lust. Brianna was panting, almost incoherent with her rising desire.

Christian smiled, knowing she needed an outlet. "It's all right to bite me, my love," he whispered, and the temptation was so overwhelming, she bit his shoulder, leaving crescent teethmarks across the flesh of his breastbone.

All the barriers to privacy had been passed. Both naked from the waist up, they indulged in endless foreplay until she was clinging to him and they were entwined in her hair as if they had been bound together by golden thread.

Christian bent his head so that he could dip his tongue into her navel and at the same time his hands slid up her legs, raising the hem of her peacock gown all the way up to her golden mons. His palms covered her bottom cheeks and he urged her against his rigid thighs. He knew she would gasp with pleasure and so he lifted his mouth to possess hers.

With a delicious gasp she opened to the demanding pressure of his lips, welcoming the probing sleek tongue deeply inside her. She rubbed her woman's center against his swollen phallus, feeling the heat of him through his chausses. Suddenly she wanted him to take her so that she could possess him utterly, totally. She wanted him inside her body, deep inside, where it was hot and dark and wet. She wanted him to plunge his sword into her tight sheath. She wanted him to come home.

The gown was a terrible impediment between them and she was frantic to free herself of the sensual peacock fabric. With a cry she shoved it down from her waist until finally it fell to the floor and she stepped away from it.

The moment she did so, a wave of awareness swept over her. What in the name of God was she doing? She was completely exposed and vulnerable to his possessive hands and seeking mouth! What madness had induced her to allow him to undress her? She desperately tried to cover her nakedness with her hair. In a blinding flash of comprehension, Brianna realized it was the peacock gown that had changed all her perceptions, all her emotions, and all her inhibitions. It had been the same at the tournament when she had donned her mother's gray velvet cloak. She saw

Christian Hawksblood through the vision of someone with second sight. Her mother's mystic power had come to her through the clothes she had worn.

"Stop! Hawksblood, I cannot do this thing!" she cried.

He did not remove his hands from her body, rather he tightened his hold upon her. "We are both committed; we cannot turn back," he said hoarsely.

"Nay, it was the gown, don't you see?" she cried desperately. "When I wear my mother's garments, I am insatiably attracted to you. When I take them off, I return to my senses. I return to being Brianna."

"My love, that is the most ridiculous thing I have ever heard. You have always been Brianna; will always be Brianna. You are you, forever!"

His words were solid common sense. How could she refute them? It was not her mother's power that had lured her to this wickedness, it was Christian Hawksblood's power. It was Drakkar's dark, compelling power. "You have lured me to let you have your way with me. You control my mind, my body, and no doubt wish to control my soul!" Her eyes were wide with fear and shame for their carnal behavior. "How can you make me do these things? Leave me at once! It is wrong! Wrong!" A vision of Robert's golden beauty came to her and she was covered with guilt.

Hawksblood took hold of her naked shoulders in a brutal grip and shook her. "Stop it!" he commanded savagely. "Stop it, now!"

Naked beneath his powerful hands and his blazing wrath, she was totally vulnerable and helpless.

"It has nothing to do with your mother. It has absolutely nothing to do with some mythic power you attribute to me. It involves you and you alone, Brianna. You have chosen me of your own free will. Face it! Be woman enough to admit you want me."

It was a revelation. His eyes held hers, forcing her to face the truth. Drakkar de Beauchamp was a compelling force to be reckoned with. Brianna wanted him. She wanted him exactly as he was. The truth was that she loved him, had always loved him, would always love him. As if the silken mass of hair were too heavy for her, her head fell back, exposing the curve of her throat with its tempting, enticing vulnerability.

One arm swept beneath her knees as he lifted her high against his chest and carried her to the bed. "We are about to become more intimate than any lovers since the dawn of time. We will start by talking."

Christian knew how much control this would take on his part. He decided to keep on his chausses for the moment, for her sake and his. He set her down upon the bed to really look at her. She was so lovely, she was a pleasurable assault upon the senses. One side of her golden hair spilled from the bed to the carpet like a molten waterfall. The other side followed the ripe curves of her body, all the way down to her feet. It both concealed and revealed the melon-ripe breasts and the exquisitely high mound of Venus crowned by curls of golden fire.

He lifted her foot and placed a kiss upon her high instep. Brianna's toes curled deliciously. She wanted to enjoy the sensations he aroused in her, but she was filled with apprehension about what he would do next.

Christian knew her thoughts. "Trust me for this loving." His voice was a husky, intimate murmur. "I know you are a maid. I will not fall upon you and ravish you, love. That can come later, after you have learned to ravish me. Love play is a sport where both must enjoy the arousal and the fulfill- ment, or the pleasure is greatly diminished."

He lifted a tress of her hair, breathed deeply of its fra- grance, then watched as it curled possessively about his fingers. "I must dispel this notion that I possess magic power. I do not, Brianna," he murmured. "At a very early age I was given over to the care of the Hospitaler Knights of St. John. When I was old enough, I was initiated into the Mystic Order of the Golden Dawn, men who were mostly Knights Templar gone underground when the order was forbidden. I was taught to harness the power that every human possesses. Through constant training and practice I was taught to enhance, magnify, and control the power within that is lost to so many because it is never used.

"It is a simple exercise of mind over matter. The brain should control the body and the emotions rather than the other way about. It is priceless training for knighthood. In battle it allows you to focus on the victory rather than the pain. When the mind is totally focused, the perception of time slows to permit you to see clearly and perceive your enemy's every move. When you have learned control, it benefits every other aspect of your life. Do you imagine I could be here like this unless I had supreme control of myself?"

Brianna smiled a secret smile. She wanted to shatter his control and would before too many moons had waned. It was extremely erotic to lie naked before him while they conversed. Brianna's murmur was as husky as his. "What of your visions?"

"Everyone is capable of visions. It is simply a matter of developing your sixth sense. You are beginning to experience them, my love." It was not a question. She silently acknowledged that this was true. "In the tournament you wore sable armor and jousted for Prince Edward."

Christian's eyes widened. Brianna was beginning to perceive that which was hidden. "You will make an apt pupil. I will teach you every nuance of lovemaking, then we will go on from there."

Brianna swept her tongue across lips gone suddenly dry and Christian had to put an iron clamp on his rising desire.

"What of that day in the forest? Your magic made the princess's food bitter."

He smiled patiently and shook his head. "Not magic power, merely a magician's trick. My mind is much stronger than hers. By the power of suggestion her food tasted bitter. It was not actually bitter. I cannot alter the very taste or smell of things—only their perception."

"Is your mind stronger than mine?" she asked breathlessly.

"Sometimes yes, oftimes, no. If it were otherwise, you would have warmed my bed from the first night I saw you."

Her cheeks tinted delicately and he stretched out a finger to touch the tiny black dot upon her cheekbone. "One night you turned from me in my vision and I glimpsed the twin to this witch-mark."

Her blush deepened. "Beauty mark," she corrected.

He shook his head. "I know you for witch, beloved."

His words pleased her. Perhaps she was. She had assuredly conjured his vision when she was curious about the strange object on his thigh. Brianna sat firmly upon her witch-mark, knowing it tempted him or he would not have spoken of it. Their eyes met in amusement as they discerned each other's thoughts.

"Perhaps it is time I revealed all, as you so generously have done."

Brianna caught her breath as he stood to remove his chausses. She stared at him in fascinated horror. The shaft of his male weapon was engorged to a great length and thickness, jutting from its sable forest. Beneath, on the inside of his thigh, stretched the black scimitar. Quietly, patiently, he allowed her to look her fill.

Finally she spoke. "Which weapon do your squires refer to as Killbride?"

He threw back his head and his deep laughter rolled out over her. "Those two devils love to amuse themselves at my expense. At Windsor the servant wenches are forever creeping into my chamber, hoping to catch a glimpse of the black obscenity between my legs."

Brianna could not help herself. She reached out a tentative finger to touch the mysterious object. The skin was raised in a thick welt along the blade, thicker at the handle and she shuddered as she remembered the pain connected with it. "What is it?"

"It is a brand. An initiation rite before I was knighted into the Mystic Order."

Silence stretched between them.

"Tell me," she urged, softly.

"After the hot iron was removed, they rubbed black sand into the raw burn. Then I was left alone in the desert to survive or die."

"The pain was unendurable," she whispered.

"That's how I learned to move beyond pain. The lesson was invaluable."

Brianna avoided looking at his other weapon.

Christian's mouth curved in understanding. "It doesn't repel you?" he asked.

"No," she replied quickly.

"And this?" he asked, indicating his male sex.

"I . . . I'm not sure. I'm ignorant of such things."

His heart sang that it was so. "I think perhaps it is time to move beyond talking. I cannot tell you of love, I can only show you."

❧ 19 ❧

Brianna drew back as he came upon the bed full-length and stretched his swarthy limbs beside hers. "Yield to me, love."

She hesitated for perhaps three heartbeats, then she opened her arms and offered herself to him.

Christian enfolded her in his powerful embrace and took her down to the bed. His mouth covered hers hotly, boldly and she opened to his hungry demands, allowing him to plunder her honeyed mouth. When Christian felt he would drown in need, his kiss turned sensual. He knew he must awaken Brianna's sexuality. When his mouth elicited low moans and her body shivered with liquid tremors, he would proceed. He hoped it would take at least a hundred kisses.

The shadowed chamber was filled with the sensuous sounds of rustling bedcovers, the whisper of sleek skin against skin, the gasp and moan of mouth upon mouth, the slide of rough hands through silken hair, the vibration of hot breath upon fiery flesh. Erotic sounds, intimate sounds, love sounds.

When Brianna's mouth was love-swollen from too many kisses, Christian's lips traveled a slow, burning path down her throat to her breasts. The act was so private, Brianna was shocked. Christian soon melted away every vestige of reserve as he licked and gently bit, then sucked her areolas into his hungry mouth.

Brianna was amazed at the sensations she experienced, all so new, but blissful in the extreme. She felt as if threads of fire went from her breasts, down through her belly, then lower, turning her woman's center to searing flames that threatened to consume her senses, her very reason. Slowly, surely she began to long, to lust for something. She knew not what, but it was so compelling, she felt she would die if she did not get it.

She looked down at his dark face to watch his mouth worship her body. Her fingertips touched his lips where they were joined and she began to whisper his name over and over like a supplicant. "Christian, Christian, Christian."

He knew she was not ready for that which she begged. Each stage of intimacy had tightened the bonds between them. Their face-to-face kisses and caresses had imprinted his powerful identity upon her, but he had put neither hand nor mouth to her woman's center and coitus could not be enjoyed to its fullest until all the traditional foreplay had been completed.

He pressed her back, spread her glorious hair upon the pillows, and gently drew her hand to cup her breast. He took the fingers of her other hand and drew it lower toward her mons.

Her eyes followed where his hand led and she saw the red-gold curls that looked exactly like flames. Their entwined fingers touched her together. "Oooh!" she cried as if she had been burned. Christian's manroot jumped against her thigh and she imagined it a velvet-tipped iron spear. He would render her vulnerable, she would yield, then he would conquer her with this formidable weapon! Could she bear such an assault? The answer came back yes, a million times yes! He was all man; she fervently hoped she could be all woman.

He unclasped her hand. "Place your fingertips on the back of my hand so you know what I do. If you don't like it, you can stay my hand. If you receive pleasure, your touch will urge me to proceed."

She was startled that he would allow her even a semblance of control and rested the pads of her fingers where he bade. His square, warm palm cupped her and he threaded his fingers through her golden curls, over and over. The sensation was almost drugging. Then he brought his broad thumb up across her pink cleft and she arched up into his hand joyously. The pressure of his thumb increased, opening the cleft to allow his thumb to breach her defenses. What he did to her felt so deliciously erotic, she abandoned touching his hand. She wanted no control. As he had suggested earlier, she would *trust him for this loving*.

As the pads of his fingertips sought out her tiny jewel, he hung over her watching her mouth. When her lips opened with breathless desire, he took possession of her mouth and the tip of his tongue matched the slow, rhythmic caress of his fingers.

"Do you like this, Brianna?" he murmured against her lips.

"I love it," she whispered breathlessly, allowing her thighs to fall open so he could go deeper.

Christian wanted everything from her and for her. He knew it would be all pleasure if he brought her to climax with his hand. He knew it would be pure bliss if he brought her to her first joy with his mouth, but some deep primal urge told him their bodies must be joined deeply, totally. The pleasure must be mingled with pain as nature had intended. That way they would be bonded forever.

He slowed his fingers and his tongue to draw out her arousal to its farthest limits. When she was on the edge of madness, he would take her.

She lay in a sensual, wanton sprawl, almost incoherent with need, her hair a wild, disheveled tangle. When he moved between her thighs, he hung above her allowing the head of his shaft to trace its teasing touch across her thighs and belly. As if by magic he positioned the velvet tip so that it rested upon her jewel, then he cried, "Now!"

He plunged down, sliding across her bud, slipping down her cleft, then burying himself in her tight velvet sheath.

Brianna's scream shattered the night. She contracted so tightly upon his long, thick phallus, it was momentarily as painful for him as it was for her.

He brushed his lips across her eyelids murmuring honeyed love words. "Beautiful . . . delicate . . . exquisite . . ."

He held absolutely still, allowing her to become used to the fullness that stretched her so tautly. She too held absolutely still, then they became aware that they pulsated against each other intimately. It was no more than a flutter at first, but as her body gradually accepted his bold invasion, the pulsations became heavy, strong throbs.

Brianna's body was generous as he had known it would be and suddenly she was welcoming him in an undulating rhythm that made him think of rippling hot silk. What had been forbidden was now accomplished.

Christian felt triumphant as he began to move with potent, powerful thrusts. He wished it could last forever, but in his wisdom he knew he must not prolong it for Brianna. Too much would take her from Heaven into hell. Her liquid tremors began just as he felt his seed start. He cried out. Lord God how she made him quiver! She had been splendidly uninhibited for her first time.

He collapsed onto her, spent and satiated as never before. She smiled into the darkness, welcoming his great weight. She felt as if she had drained him of his strength and power, and his essence would remain with her forever.

As Christian Hawksblood lay upon his beloved to catch his breath, he felt himself being renewed. Vitality, strength, and power swept over him in wave after wave. The experience was similar to what he felt in battle. When the fighting ceased and the day was won, he was momentarily drained. Then the exhilaration of victory swept over him, filling him with glorious omnipotence.

He gathered her in his arms and cradled her against his heart. "Sweet . . . wild . . . temptress. You were magnificent. You came through the mystic initiation of pain and blood like a goddess. You have all of my heart, Brianna."

She knew what had happened this night in this bed had been cataclysmic. Suddenly it was all too intense for her and softly she began to cry, bathing his heart with her tears.

In that moment, Prince Drakkar, Christian Hawksblood de Beauchamp, vowed never to hurt her again. He would protect her with his life, honor her with his body, cherish her with his heart, and love her with his soul.

In the dead of night, Brianna half-roused from a deep sleep and cried out in alarm at her unfamiliar surroundings. Christian was there to gather her in his arms and take her down in the bed, secure, tucked against his side. It was such a warm, safe haven, she fell asleep with her lips against the dark powerful column of his throat.

When she again came up through the warm veils of

sleep, she was alone in the big bed. A cry of protest escaped her lips as her hand sought the cooling sheets beside her.

"Christian." The name she uttered brought her to full consciousness. Ah God, another erotic dream? Her body told her otherwise. Her breasts were still swollen from his mouth and between her legs ached where his fullness had stretched her more than one time.

Her cheeks burned with her blushes as her eyes fell upon the bedsheets. The spots of bright blood told their own tale of the hymenal rites he had performed upon her body. Brianna was aghast at what she had done. It was wrong! She was betrothed to another! He had lured her against her will to give him that which should have been preserved for her future husband.

She stripped the linen sheets from the bed before anyone discovered her shameful secret, and set the bundle beside the chamber door. Then she carefully bathed, firmly denying the sensual feelings the hot water evoked in her newly initiated body.

She had just finished dressing when Adele came into her chamber. "My lamb, I'm certain sure that pale peach gown is unsuitable for a visit to the stone quarry, but I understand why you wish to look ravishing."

Brianna ignored Adele's choice of words. "I'm not going."

"But you promised Joan and Glynis. They'll be that disappointed. Whatever is so important here to keep you from the excursion?"

"I . . . I thought I'd change the beds," Brianna said lamely.

"Then we'll do it together. You take the sheets to the wash house and I'll get fresh linen from the drying cupboard. By that time Joan should be ready to go. I know she is eager for it."

Brianna decided an argument would only attract attention to herself. Doing the work of a chambermaid was a strange enough occupation. She gathered up the sheets with their telltale evidence and stopped by Joan's chamber where she proceeded to strip the beds.

Joan's laughter trilled out. "You are a most dedicated

chatelaine, Brianna. Are you going to serve our breakfast too?"

Brianna's sense of humor returned. "No, I'm not. Get you down to the hall and I'll join you in a few minutes." Perhaps she could think of somewhere else she could take them today. But when the ladies sat down to break their fast, they were set on visiting the famous Bedford stone quarries.

They could hear the stone being cut before they reached the rim of the gorge. Chisels rang upon the slabs of stone as they were hit with heavy wooden mallets in such a way as to separate the stone into massive square blocks. The labor of quarrying Bedford stone was hard, heavy work. Ox carts were lined up on the quarry floor and each massive square stone took two hefty men to lift it to a wagon bed of straw. The men worked stripped to the waist, their bodies covered with the sweat and dust of their labors.

Brianna was startled to see that Hawksblood worked shoulder to shoulder with the quarry men. His tall physique and dark skin contrasted sharply with the other men. Brianna drew in her breath as she saw the sweat glisten upon his mahogany skin. He was a magnificent male specimen. No other words could do him justice.

She marveled that those were the same muscular arms that had held her all night, that thick column of throat was where she had rested her lips and the rippling muscles of his chest covered by its black pelt was where she had pressed her cheek as she clung to him in her passion.

As she watched him, she admitted to herself that she had indeed chosen him of her own free will, and a thrill ran down the entire length of her spine as she acknowledged that she would choose him again tonight, to warm her bed and intoxicate her blood!

He chose that moment to glance up at her. Their eyes locked across the space between them as they remembered every intimate detail of their mating. His ardent gaze told her clearly that she filled his consciousness. The intensity of his stare informed her that they would again be sharing their bed and their bodies. Brianna went weak with the hunger he aroused in her. She tried to break the mesmerizing gaze, for surely all who watched them must know them for lovers.

When Christian saw how it was with *his* lady, and that she could not deny him even if she had wanted, he gifted her with a brilliant smile that made her heart turn over in her breast.

Brianna had brought her sketch pad so she could capture some scenes of Bedford stone being quarried, but later at the castle, when she assessed them, she saw that the magnificent, lithe body of Christian Hawksblood dominated every sketch.

That night, none sat late in the hall. Brianna's companions, with Joan as ringleader, conspired so that Christian and Brianna could spend the evening hours together as well as those of the night. It was impossible to conceal the way they felt about each other and Joan knew all they would ever be allowed henceforth was stolen moments. While they were in Bedford, the king, Prince Edward, and Warrick were off recruiting for the war in France. The minute the king had a sizable army, he would be off across the Channel.

Brianna lit the candles, then undressed slowly and slipped on her velvet bed-robe, scented with violets. She picked up her brush and absently began to stroke her hair. Would he be bold enough to come again? Would she be woman enough to welcome him?

"Let me do that." His deep voice enveloped her in dark, rich velvet. How did he appear from nowhere out of the night? She caught her breath as he drew nigh and towered above her. He held out a strong, callused hand and obediently she placed the brush in it. A pulse beat erratically in her throat as he sank to his knees beside her and raised his hand. Her heart began to palpitate and her breathing made her upthrust breasts rise and fall before his intense gaze.

Each stroke of the brush aroused her. It was unbelievably erotic for the dark warrior to brush her hair as if he were her body servant. Deliberately she let the robe fall slightly away from her body. Would it tempt him to touch her? In truth she craved that he lay hands upon her, and soon.

Still on his knees before her, he slipped his hands beneath the robe. The roughness of his callused fingers made her shudder as he stroked the silken flesh of her breasts, making them swell and become heavy upon his palms. Then he slipped his hands beneath her armpits and lifted her from the stool so that she knelt face-to-face with him. Even on their knees, he was still much taller and she had to lift her mouth for his kiss.

As she lifted her arms, her robe opened and he quickly slipped it from her shoulders and enfolded her nakedness against his hard body. Taking her with him, he lay back upon the floor and held her at arm's length so he could look up at her and at the same time have her hair cascade upon his chest in golden pools.

"You enthrall me. I never believed aught could be as lovely as my visions, but I was wrong. Tell me you feel the same, Brianna. Tell me that last night you were not simply caught up in the flicker of the candlelight. Tell me that you love me."

"God help me, I believe I do," she whispered, her eyes and her voice smoky with desire.

He set about her arousal with deliberate cunning. Her own sexuality was so new to her, she was by degrees enchanted, enamored, enthralled, enraptured, entwined, engrossed, ensnared, enchained, and finally engulfed by the driving force that was Christian Hawksblood.

When she was on the edge of mindlessness, begging him to fullfil all the fantasies his rampant manroot had promised, he demanded, "Swear to me you will renounce your betrothal to my brother." His fingertips caressed her woman's cleft with drugging strokes until she felt she would drown in her need to have him anchored deep inside her, thrusting until the night exploded.

"Yes, yes, I swear," she promised raggedly, and in that moment she meant the vow with all her heart.

Their mating was so fierce, Brianna feared she might not survive it, but all too soon she was screaming her pleasure, then mourning his withdrawal.

Again Christian experienced a surge of renewed vigor after he lay upon her totally spent. He gave thanks that it was so. No woman had ever affected him in this way before.

Brianna cast him a playful glance as he lifted her and

carried her to the bed. She was suddenly in a mood to test her power over her warrior lover. Could she take him to the edge of mindlessness where he would swear any vow if only she would give him that for which he begged? She smiled a secret smile and set about her diabolical foreplay.

He had taught her well. Taught her the value of feathered fingertip caresses; taught her the effect of sleek tongue sliding into hidden clefts, then licking and suckling until he cried for mercy. She had weapons he had no defense against, like her silken hair drifting upon his hard body until it screamed for release. Like nipples that grazed his flesh, teased his lips, and scalded the head of his phallus as she rubbed each little jewel across the tiny opening on his cock tip.

"Brianna, enough torture, I'll spill," he gasped. He rose up and tried to drag her beneath him, but she pushed him back upon the bed and slowly mounted him, then proceeded to draw out the torture just a little longer.

He gazed up at her with love shining from his eyes. "You are beautiful in your passion, as I knew you would be."

His words were her undoing. She slipped down into his arms and his deep kiss brought her to instant fulfillment. "Swear you will always love me as you do at this moment." She smiled ironically, for once again it was Christian who demanded vows from her kiss-swollen lips.

Much later as her Arabian Knight slept, Brianna crept from the bed with the compelling need to capture his likeness. Even relaxed in sleep, his long, muscular limbs looked hard as iron. She sketched every detail of the black scimitar, curving along the inside of his thigh. In the candleglow, his magnificent torso was all flame and shadow and she knew it would take every ounce of her skill to do him justice. She carefully put the sketches away with some she had made of Gnasher, then unable to be apart from him one moment longer, crept back beneath the covers into their warm love cocoon. Possessive arms reached out to enfold her against his heart.

Again, he left her before dawn. Later, Brianna wondered if he had had a premonition that Warrick was about to descend upon them.

The hall, the courtyard, and the surrounding fields were

filled with men. The earl had been to his castle of Warrick, forty miles west, to fetch all his knights and fighting men, as well as those at the nearby royal residence of Kenilworth. He told Hawksblood that Prince Edward had gone east to fetch the men garrisoned at Castle Hedingham and Colchester, while the king himself had traveled south to gather the fighting men from Odiham, Winchester, and Arundel.

Hawksblood found his father in fine fettle. They grinned at each other as they looked over the army he had gathered. It seemed every man in England was ready to follow their ambitious king to France to pluck the crown from the usurper and place it where it rightfully belonged.

"I'm turning the men of Warrick over to your command." Hawksblood knew this was no test. Warrick had seen him in battle and knew his worth. His father expected him to hone their fighting skills and then be responsible for the men of Warrick when they went to France.

"I'll put them to work hauling stone today. We'll leave for Windsor at dawn."

Hawksblood spent the day getting to know the men of Warrick. He was pleasantly surprised that the demesne boasted a thousand fighting men. It was only forty miles from Bedford and he decided he would have both in the not too distant future.

Brianna was concerned how Bedford would feed such a horde, but the "Mad Hound" earl had trained his men to live off the land. She was relieved that none came to the hall that night, not even Hawksblood.

Brianna and Joan spent the long evening together. Now they were not just best friends, but allies in love. They shared their secret hopes and fears about their lovers, promising each other everything would somehow work out happily, and in this way they banished the terrifying specter of imminent war.

As Brianna sought her own chamber, Mr. Burke handed her a note. Her heart constricted. Surely Hawksblood wouldn't compromise her with a furtive visit? A sigh escaped her lips as she avidly scanned his words.

Precious Lady:
I will not approach you until we are safely back at Windsor,
but I shall hold you to your vow.

There was no signature, only a curved scimitar.

🐚 *20* 🐚

On the ride back to Windsor, Paddy had been assigned to look after the ladies' comforts. He was glad that Adele had decided to leave Clancy behind. She loved the cat enough to want what was best for him and decided he would be happiest left on his own territory. Paddy no longer had a rival for Adele's affections.

On the road they were joined by a small army Prince Edward had gathered from Hedingham, Colchester, and Berkhamsted. He told Warrick and Hawksblood that the king had summoned his earls from the north, from Wales, and from Ireland. They knew without being told that Edward III would embark on his great offensive the moment the vast army was gathered. The king's towering ambition coupled with his excessive energy and recklessness could see them under sail in a fortnight.

Prince Edward found it impossible to be alone with Joan and had to content himself with a hastily scribbled note.

Sweetest Jeanette:
Though I long to hold you to my heart, conditions make it
impossible. I will arrange for you to visit your brother on
Fish Street in London and send a message by young Randal
Gray. I count the hours. E.

Every mile that brought Brianna closer to Windsor, brought her closer to Robert de Beauchamp. She was dreading the confrontation. How could she repudiate him? What words could she offer in explanation? To tell him she loved his bastard brother would not only be cruel, it would be reckless, like throwing oil onto fire. Somehow she would have to find the words. She had promised Christian she would not go through with the betrothal. She realized it would be the most difficult thing she had ever had to do, but resolutely decided to break it off as soon as possible.

Brianna bathed away the dust of the road, chose a sober-colored tunic of blue, and went in search of Robert. She was shocked to learn from his servants that he was not yet recovered from his wound. She found him in his chamber, reclining on a couch with his leg propped up with a pillow.

His face lit up at the sight of her. "Brianna! God, how I've missed your lovely face."

She saw with dismay that he could not arise, but held out his arms to her. Most self-consciously she approached his couch, allowed him a kiss upon her cheek, then stiffly withdrew to a seat a short distance apart. "Robert, you are not yet recovered," she said with compassion.

"Recovered?" he said bitterly, "I'll never be recovered!"

"Whatever do you mean? Has the wound not healed?" Brianna could not dispel a feeling of impending doom.

"It would have healed long ago if that accursed animal hadn't bitten me. The king's physician, John Bray, says the thigh bone is infected and I'll be left with a limp."

"What animal are you talking about?" Brianna was puzzled.

"When I lay wounded at the tournament, a weasel or some such vermin ran up my leg and bit me on the wound. If I ever find out who owns the vicious, filthy creature, I'll put my sword through his belly."

A weasel was a ferret. It could only have been Hawksblood's pet, Gnasher! Its very name condemned it. Guilt washed over her. "There must be something we can do to make the leg whole again," she cried desperately. It was unthinkable that a brawny young warrior like Robert de Beauchamp would have his military ambitions ended so cruelly.

"You don't fancy being saddled with a cripple, do you, Brianna?" he asked bitterly. "Go ahead, withdraw from the betrothal. A beautiful young woman like you will want a whole man."

"Stop it, Robert! How can you think so badly of me?" she demanded. She had been trained to duty and obedience all her life. She knew she could not and would not repudiate a man because of a physical disability. She felt the jaws of the trap closing in about her.

He moved clumsily because of his leg, but he managed to draw close enough to grip her hand. "Swear to me you will not cast me aside because of this."

"I . . . I swear, Robert," Brianna said helplessly.

Some of the desperation left him. His hold upon her hand became less brutal as he raised it to his lips. "We are pledged," he said with finality, and Brianna could not summon the callousness to repudiate his claim.

Brianna had only been gone a short time when Neville Wiggs asked to see Robert. He intended to get his story in first.

"I am Sir Neville Wiggs, the rightful castellan of Bedford. Your brother took an instant dislike to me and removed me from my post. I think he overstepped his authority. Since you are betrothed to Lady Bedford, I believe you would be best served if you reinstated me."

Wiggs resembled an Airedale with frizzy brown hair and beard. At the moment a very angry Airedale.

"Of what did my brother accuse you?" asked Robert, scenting another strong ally.

"He said the accounts did not tally, but Sir James Burke was in charge of the bookkeeping," he lied.

Robert's icy eyes examined him shrewdly, before his mouth curved into a satisfied smile. "I think we understand each other. My *bastard* brother had better watch his back in the coming conflict. Make yourself useful to me and I will reinstate you as castellan when I marry Lady Bedford."

Brianna was caught between two strong men. She had listened to her heart and it had led her to wantonness and infidelity. She had tumbled into love with Christian Hawksblood, when she had no right to. His brother had a prior claim upon her. If she set Robert aside, the scandal would be horrific in view of his lameness. Christian was by far the stronger of the two. He would easily recover from her loss. On the other hand, Robert would be doubly pitied by all for the rest of his days.

Brianna felt she had no free choice in the matter. Fate

had decided for her. She was fast in a web of her own making. When she told Hawksblood, his fury would know no bounds. He was a man who would not be thwarted. He might make such a terrible scene that scandal could explode about them.

Another thought struck her. He had the power to bend her to his will, despite his denials. Christian Hawksblood was not like other men. It would be best to avoid a confrontation. Though it smacked of cowardice, she decided it would be better to put her dilemma down on paper and show him clearly that she was honor-bound to Robert de Beauchamp.

She tore up her first three attempts. They were cries from a broken heart, guaranteed to make a hot-blooded knight rescue the torn damsel in distress. When she had laid out the facts in an unemotional manner, telling him her decision was final, she dispatched it with young Randal before she could change her mind.

Within minutes of reading Brianna's letter, Christian forced his way into her chamber, not caring a damn about the impropriety. "You vowed to me that you would renounce your betrothal to Robert. I will not allow you to break that vow!"

His dark face was so fierce she took a step back from him to catch her breath. "Christian, he is crippled! I cannot be so cruel and callous. Everything is changed because of his leg. Please listen to me, Christian. I love you with all my heart, but I am pledged to your brother and cannot in conscience break that pledge."

"You would ruin both our lives from a misplaced sense of pity?" His outrage knew no bounds. He closed the gap between them, then with powerful hands lifted her by the waist until her eyes were level with his. "Do you honestly believe I will let you go to another?"

"Christian, please be reasonable," she begged. "The king wants this betrothal, your father wants it. There is naught you can do!" It was a cry from the heart for him to concede. She saw his face harden against her pleas.

His glittering eyes held hers as if he would bend her against her will, then he set her back on her feet and removed his hands. "You will see what I can do and what I cannot do, Brianna." His words hung in the air long after he departed. Her throat ached with unhappiness at the wound she had given him. Brianna spent the next three days on an emotional rack, dreading his retaliation. None came. Neither did she once catch a glimpse of that dark face filled with pride.

The minute Warrick saw the condition of his son, he summoned Hawksblood and his Arabian squire, Ali. Both had received extensive medical training at Córdoba and in the East, which Warrick knew from firsthand experience was superior to Master Bray's knowledge.

At first, Robert refused to let his bastard brother examine him, until Hawksblood goaded him into it.

"I am responsible," Hawksblood insisted. "Don't be a stubborn fool; let me see the leg."

"Don't dare claim responsibility because you wounded me in the joust. Your sword never touched me," Robert said arrogantly.

"I claim responsibility because my ferret inflicted a bite upon your self-inflicted wound."

Robert almost choked. "You set it on me deliberately. I'll poison the rat!"

"I'd keep my distance if I were you, unless you'd care to lose a testicle. Gnasher collects them."

Robert blanched as he realized how close he'd come to castration. Reluctantly, he stripped down his chausses to reveal the wound's angry red inflammation.

Hawksblood and Ali conferred, then agreed that a poultice of woundwart would dry up the flux of the humors, then in a couple of days when the inflammation disappeared, the juice of loosestrife would quickly close the lips of the wound.

"We'll have you on your feet in no time," Hawksblood assured him. "You won't miss out on France."

Silently Christian wondered if Robert was malingering. The wound wasn't as bad as he'd imagined and certainly not enough to keep a strong man on his back. Surely his brother wasn't a coward? Christian dismissed the thought. He must not let his feelings for Brianna prejudice his every thought of Robert. When his brother learned the fighting men of Warrick were under Christian's command, it would likely be the spur necessary to get him on his feet again.

When the king returned to Windsor, over two thousand fighting men followed in his wake. The meadows as far as the eye could see were filled with tents and Dame Marjorie Daw lectured the young ladies of Windsor about the dangers of roaming outside the walls of the castle.

The king set his builders to work on the new Round Tower the same day he arrived back. The thought of beating the French into submission spurred him on as if he had the energy of ten men. It was long after dark before he read the pile of dispatches that had accumulated in his absence.

Prince Edward was closeted with his father, acting as a sounding board for the king's ideas, helping to decide which matters would be put before the Council, and which would be kept secret.

"Shit!" The king threw down an official missive from the King of France.

Edward picked up the parchment with its dangling seals and lifted a golden eyebrow in his father's direction.

"Philip offers to release William de Montecute in exchange for the release of the Earl of Moray."

"That exchange is impossible, Father. Holding Moray prisoner is the only thing that keeps the Scots from marching across the border."

"I know it! If one Scot barbarian steps across my English border, Moray gets the death sentence. I want surety that Scotland won't invade while I'm conquering France!"

"Father, since you've brought up the war, I would like your sacred word on something."

King Edward looked at the son he had created in his own image. A king made promises with one breath and broke them with the next. He knew, however, that the Black Prince would hold him to anything he pledged. "What is it you ask of me, Edward?"

"When we fight, I ask that you put me from the forefront of your mind. I will look to my own safety. Do not come to my aid if I fall in battle. All I ask is a chance to win my spurs."

For a moment the king looked bleak, then he realized he

must not shame his son before his men. Though he was only sixteen, he was all man, thank God. He would become the greatest knight in Christendom, and he would do it without the aid of his father! "I give you my word, Edward," the king pledged, firmly gripping his son's shoulder. He let his hand drop, then grinned. "You'd better live a charmed life. If aught befalls you, your mother will have my guts for garters."

"I'm Plantagenet," the prince said simply, sounding for all the world like a golden god.

King Edward vowed silently to have a private word with Christian Hawksblood. Though he had promised not to hover over him, the prince must have an invincible sword at his back!

It was midnight before the king climbed the dark stairs to Katherine de Montecute's chamber. He was disappointed to find her fully dressed, with all the lights ablaze. "You should be abed, love," he chastised, wanting nothing more than her beautiful, pliant body beneath his.

"Ah yes, all the world must defer to the king's pleasure."

He sighed. The last thing he wanted was a lover's quarrel. He should have gone straight to Philippa if he wanted peace and quiet. He admitted that he did not. He wanted Katherine's passion in bed and knew he would have to accept Katherine's passion in all other things to get it.

"You have received a communiqué from France about William's ransom!"

"Come to bed, my sweet, while I reveal all."

"Your wit does not amuse me, Sire. I insist on business before pleasure, for all too often I cannot move you beyond pleasure."

"Cruel Katherine," he said wistfully, lifting a dark gold strand of hair to his cheek. "How do you know I've received a communiqué?"

"I have spoken with the French ambassador."

A wave of jealousy swept over him. By Christ's holy wounds, he was willing to share her with her husband, but the thought of her trading her favors for information was like a knife in his heart. "I will share with you whatever information I receive about William. Trust me, Katherine."

She placed her hands upon his broad chest in supplication. "I do trust you, Edward. I know you will exchange the Earl of Moray for your dearest friend."

Edward groaned as his hands cupped her lovely shoulders. "Sweetheart, so long as I hold Moray, we are safe from a Scots' invasion."

She drew away from him as if she could not bear his touch. "So, you refuse me the only thing I've ever asked of you?"

"Sweet Kat, you find it easy enough to refuse what I ask."

"I have given you my love; I have given you my body! When have I ever refused?"

His hands found the fastenings of her gown. "You are refusing me now," he whispered hotly.

She took his hand and drew it to the breast he had just bared. "I'll give you anything . . . everything. I know how to be generous."

Edward groaned once again as he picked her up and carried her to her bed. Before dawn arrived the king had to be generous in return. He promised to exchange the Scots' Earl of Moray for William, Earl of Salisbury.

Messengers rode back and forth hourly between Windsor and the coast where ships were gathering at every port to transport Edward's army. Horses, weapons, and ammunition were taken to the east coast from every county in England. The Welsh longbowmen were issued a uniform of green jacket, brown chausses, and a deerskin quiver case to hold their goose-feathered arrows. Knights were expected to furnish their own full armor for themselves, their squires, and their warhorses, while the common fighting men were issued a helmet, a hard leather hauberk and shield, a knife, and a sword made of finest Sheffield steel. Hundreds of wagons had to be transported to France to carry weapons, cannon, fodder, medical supplies, and hopefully the spoils of war they would gather.

The very air of Windsor had an urgency about it. The stonemasons worked from dawn to dusk in an effort to complete the Edward III Round Tower. Wives hoped their babes would be born before their husbands rode off to war, and many an aspiring knight pressed a maiden to surrender to Cupid's arrow as well as his own, before he went off to risk his life.

Young William de Montecute took every opportunity to slip away from the incessant arms practice to visit Joan. She avoided him as often as she could, for he kept insisting their betrothal take place before he embarked for France. But each evening as she sat with him under the watchful eye of his mother, the Countess of Salisbury, she thought longingly of her golden prince and prayed that she would receive her brother's invitation to Fish Street.

Joan hurried along to Brianna's chambers, breathless with excitement. "My summons to Fish Street has finally arrived! William and his mother have had me trapped. They are insisting on the betrothal ceremony and have even drawn up the contracts."

"I've been under the same pressure from Robert. I finally agreed to abide by whenever the king decides. Warrick drew up our contracts long ago," Brianna said hopelessly.

"Come with me, Brianna. It will be a temporary escape for you."

"When are you going?"

"I'm going now!" cried Joan. "Give me time to change into one of Edward's favorite gowns, then come along to my chamber and we will slip down the river stairs and go by water to London."

When Joan left, Adele said practically, "You had better pack a night rail and your toilet articles."

"Oh, do you think Joan will spend the night?" asked Brianna as she pulled a violet tunic over her lavender underdress.

"My lamb, once Edward gets her to himself, you don't imagine he'll unlock the chamber door before tomorrow, do you?"

Brianna blushed. "I hadn't thought," she murmured. When she arrived at Joan's chambers, she was surprised to find Lady Elizabeth Grey. She had come to ask a favor of Glynis, who often dispensed herbal love potions and spells. When Brianna entered the room, the other girls fell silent. She noticed the look of panic on Elizabeth's face and then she saw that she had been crying. "Elizabeth, whatever's amiss?" Brianna asked with concern.

"I'm . . . I'm with child," Elizabeth blurted. "I want Glynis to give me something to bring down my courses."

"Oh, Elizabeth, no!" Brianna's heart wrung with pity for Lady Grey.

Glynis said, "I do know of something, but it's very dangerous. I know a maid who died after she dosed herself."

"I don't care, I don't care! I'd rather be dead than face a terrible scandal. If Princess Isabel learns my secret, she'll spread it all over Windsor."

Brianna had a very good idea who was the author of Elizabeth's misery. If she was right, marriage was of course out of the question. "Is Prince Lionel responsible?"

Elizabeth nodded miserably, blushing furiously before Lady Bedford and Lady Kent.

Joan's soft heart melted. "Don't be shamed, Lizzie, none of us are virgins here," she confessed. Joan thought that might cheer her up, but Elizabeth burst into tears again. "Oh, Glynis, please help her," Joan pleaded.

Glynis looked from Joan to Brianna and back again. "You two be off. I'll take care of Lady Grey. 'Tis a private matter between her and me, and you must both forget what you have heard here today."

After the ladies left, Glynis took out her herbal chest and mixed bayberries into a syrup made from figs. "You'd better stay here with me, Lady Grey. Your pains will be fearful for the next few hours."

"Thank you, Glynis," she said with fervor, swallowing the not unpleasant mixture. She sat down and nervously fingered the links on her silver girdle. "Prince Lionel isn't the father," Elizabeth blurted.

"In that case, my lady, perhaps the gentleman can be persuaded to marry you."

Elizabeth shook her head. "He's betrothed to Lady Bedford. Robert de Beauchamp made me pregnant."

"Judas, never let Brianna hear a hint of this. It would ruin her life!"

Elizabeth couldn't respond because at that moment she was taken with a cramp that almost cut her in half.

Joan and Brianna were unusually silent on the wherry ride down the river to London. Each was lost in her own thoughts. Finally Brianna murmured, "But for the grace of God, either one of us could be in Elizabeth Grey's predicament right now."

"Oh, Brianna, Edward will look after me," Joan said innocently.

Brianna sighed. It had just been forcibly brought home to her that it was up to a woman to look after herself, and from now on she swore she would never behave wantonly again. Her brow creased. She wished Joan was a more sensible girl. She was a little hoyden, far too mischievous and affectionate for her own good.

The two girls, each carrying a small overnight bag, climbed the water stairs and hurried along Fish Street to the tall stone house belonging to Edmund of Kent. He was awaiting their arrival and gave his sister a brotherly embrace. Then with a twinkle in his eye, he embraced Brianna. She gave him a playful slap when he tried to kiss her lips instead of her proffered cheek.

"You can't condemn a man for trying, especially when he'll be riding into battle soon." His glance swept her from head to toe. Her skin was more translucent than the pearls she wore. "De Beauchamp is a lucky bastard."

Brianna's color heightened.

Edmund led them through to the back of the house into the small yard. "I want you to meet my new next-door neighbor."

Joan's eyes widened with joy as she realized Prince Edward must own the adjoining property.

Edmund escorted them to the back door and turned them over to John Chandos, the prince's squire. He took Joan's bag and pointed down a corridor. "I believe you will enjoy the view from the front rooms, Lady Kent."

Joan flew down the hallway, all save her beloved prince vanished from the world. Chandos stood awkwardly beside

Brianna, quite at a loss how he would entertain Lady Bedford.

She knew she must put him at his ease. "Pray, John, don't worry about me. I have brought my sketch pad. All I need is a chamber with a view of the river."

The squire, more at ease with a sword in his hand, tried not to let his relief show on his face. He led her up a narrow staircase, then along to a bedchamber at the front of the stone house, overlooking the Thames. "We are fortunate to enjoy the services of one of the best cooks in London. The smells coming from the kitchen will make your mouth water."

"It smells like treacle tart," Brianna said hopefully.

"I'll bring you some and whatever else I can steal." He blushed endearingly. "Cook has developed a soft spot for me."

With a cry of joy, Joan ran across the room into Edward's waiting arms. He swung her into the air, marveling again at how unbelievably dainty and feminine she was. She wore palest seafoam green, edged in ermine, her platinum tresses threaded with seed pearls. Her eyes sparkled with love and laughter and the knowledge that this rendezvous was secret and forbidden. "Edward, I feared you had abandoned me," she said breathlessly, not believing for one moment that he had.

"My little Jeanette, my thoughts seldom stray from you, even when they should be elsewhere."

She threw her arms about his neck and kissed the blunted end of his aquiline nose. "I love you."

"And I adore you, my angel. It seems an eternity since we loved."

Brianna sat by the window sketching the traffic on the busy river and the colorful people who walked below on Fish Street. As the light began to fade, she thumbed through her sketchbook assessing her work, and she came upon a drawing she had made of Christian Hawksblood. Her heart contracted painfully as her mind winged back to the first time she had seen him, then relived every look, every word, every touch that had passed between them.

She stared out at the lights on the river with unseeing eyes. Why was it that duty was always unpalatable, while daydreams were perfection? Her senses became saturated with his essence. The door opened and he filled the frame with his overpowering presence. By all the saints in Heaven, why hadn't she realized he would be here with the Black Prince?

Brianna jumped up so quickly, the stool overturned. Christian strode across the chamber and took her shoulders in his powerful hands. His dark face was fierce, his eyes aquamarine chips.

She closed her eyes against his raw male magnetism. He was such a dominant force to be reckoned with, she trembled at the thought of defying him. But defy him she must. "We lost our heads in Bedford. I should never have given myself to you when your brother had a prior claim. Now that he has a lame leg, I cannot be heartless enough to reject him."

"Ah, you are quite capable of being heartless, Brianna. You are *my* lady, *my* woman. You have belonged to me, body and soul, since the dawn of time."

"Stop it, Hawksblood! I belong to Robert de Beauchamp. Your father has drawn up the contracts and our betrothal is inevitable."

His hands gripped her painfully. His face was fiercer than any hawk's. "Know this, lady: You will never belong to Robert de Beauchamp, not in this life or the next. There is a blood bond between us. We are one!"

"Christian." It was a cry from the heart. "I will never regret what we shared. If they cut my heart from me when I die, it will be filled with my love for you. But I am drowning in guilt over Robert. He will be crippled for the rest of his life. I must do my duty!"

"Your first duty is to me," he ground out. "I have chosen you, and only you, to be the mother of my children."

"Christian, that can never be," she said sadly.

He thrust his powerful arm beneath her knees and swept her up in his arms. "By Christ, I'll take you to bed now and plant my babe in your belly."

"Put me down . . . stop this at once!" she cried, but he strode swiftly from the room and swept up the staircase and into a chamber that contained a very large bed. She doubled her fists and smote them against the hard muscles of his chest. He ignored her struggles completely. He put his lips to her ear, whispering all the words of love for which she'd been starving the last three days. "Yield to me, love, yield to me now."

Suddenly she was filled with dread. This might be the last time they would ever be together. He was going off to France to fight a war. How would she bear the separation? How would she bear the heavy guilt of refusing him her love if he was killed in battle? His words were fast melting her resolve of chastity. It would be an act of cruelty to deny him. She stopped struggling and slipped her arms about his neck.

He sank down on the bed and crushed her in his embrace. When she lifted her trembling mouth from his, he said, "I don't want you to merely submit to me, Brianna, I want you to take joy in it."

Suddenly, she wanted exactly what he wanted.

Brianna ran a provocative tongue over her lips and Christian set his mouth on hers capturing the pink tip before she could withdraw it. Though the afternoon sun was still high, they both decided it was bedtime. Brianna kicked off her slippers as Christian's hand stole beneath her skirts to pull off her lacy stockings. Her garters came off with them and Christian stared at what he held, totally bemused by the beribboned confections. Everything about her was delectable.

She undid the lacings of her tunic so he could remove it. Then she undid the tiny buttons on her underdress, watching the hunger grow in his aquamarine eyes. She stood upon the bed naked, giving him a chance to undress, but he pulled her to him, unable to keep his hands from her. Her skin was like cream velvet against the dark pewter of his doublet. He lifted her hair, then let it fall about her in golden splendor. The thread of her pearls broke and they fell to the bed in an iridescent shower. She laughed at his look of dismay, then scooped up a handful and let them roll down her upthrust breasts and belly.

Christian joined in her laughter as he grabbed for them and caught them as they cascaded into the abundant curls between her legs. By Allah, this woman mesmerized him and held him in thrall. It was unthinkable that he give her up, she was his heart's desire, now and forever. She tugged at his doublet, wanting him to be naked with her. Christian obliged immediately, groaning as her fingertips grazed across the sable pelt on his chest. He rolled onto the bed and pulled her down on top of him. He began kissing her everywhere, searching out fragrant alcoves he'd never explored before. She was delicious to taste, intoxicating to smell.

Her hands caressed his body with equal delight until they lay enthralled, panting with desire, trembling with need, incoherent and love-drunk with unquenched passion.

The whisper and sleek slide of skin upon naked skin was so erotic Brianna was aroused to madness. When she began to bite him and her cries turned to little screams, he covered her body with his. She opened to him eagerly, thirsting for him with every pore of her body, every fiber of her being. Her thighs fell apart and she arched her body up to meet his thrust. She cried out at the pleasure-pain and Christian stopped in midthrust. She pressed her face into the warm flesh of his shoulder. His lips touched her hair and he murmured, "My darling, I didn't want to hurt you."

She was so full of him she thought she might burst with the fullness. "I love your bigness. Am I too small to give you pleasure?"

"Nay, my heart. You feel so good I could die from it."

She closed upon him so tightly he could not withdraw if he had wanted. And God forgive him, in very truth he did not want to. Brianna slowly relaxed her death grip upon the head of his shaft and whispered softly, "Come into me all the way."

Christian touched his lips to one sensitive nipple, then when it ruched, he took the whole crown into his mouth and sucked hard. She moaned with the intense pleasure of it and he plunged into her quickly until he was seated to the hilt. He began to move with small thrusts, knowing the friction would make her slippery. Gradually she became wet and sleek, enabling his strokes to slide all the way in and all the way out of her tight sheath. She felt like hot silk as he surged into her and he watched her face intently.

He saw her pupils dilate with pleasure, her nipples turn to hard little diamonds, and a flush of passion turn her throat and breasts a delicate shell-pink. Her lips parted with a deep, sensual need. She brought his hand to her mouth and began to suck on one of his fingers. It was unbelievably erotic to Hawksblood. Her pleasure was so intense she began to arch against him sensually. Quickly he withdrew his finger and crushed her lips with his, sliding his tongue into her seeking mouth and thrusting deep with the same throbbing rhythm as his manroot.

They both cried out as they spent together, then he held absolutely still as he felt the flutter of a pulse point deep within her. When every last sensation had been savored, he rolled so that she was in the dominant position. He gazed up at her in wonder that she could be so passionate. Though he was twice her size, she had almost as much sexual energy as he and she had drained him joyfully.

"You are the most glorious thing that has ever happened to me," he told her, lifting a golden tress of hair to his lips. "We will be wed soon."

Brianna looked at him aghast. Didn't he understand this would be the last time they could be together? She arose from the bed and began to dress quickly. "Christian, this is good-bye." Tears flooded her eyes, replacing the joyous laughter that had transformed her earlier. "I'm pledged to Robert."

He sprang from the bed, his face contorted with fury. "Robert is a coward; he does not want his wound to heal!" he ground out.

Brianna used anger as a defense against his arguments. "My God, you think you are the only man who thirsts for the glory of battle? You think you are the only one in England with courage enough to go to war? There's a horde out there as far as the eye can see who are willing and eager to fight! Think you we need Arabians to fight our wars for us?"

"I am more Norman than Arabian," he swore.

"Are you?" she cried. "An honorable Norman knight would never take advantage of a brother who was lame, nor call him coward because he cannot fight! It was Gnasher who bit his wound and infected him. Did you deliberately order your ferret to attack him?"

He raised his arm to strike her, then smashed his fist into the wooden bedpost, his control strained to breaking point. "I will have that son of a bitch walking on two good legs in ample time to fight for his country."

"Would to God that you could," she said fervently. "My guilt is killing me." She moved toward the door.

"Where the hell do you think you are going?" he demanded, pulling on his chausses and doublet.

"Back to Windsor. I should never have come."

"I'll not have you out in London at night! Have you taken leave of your senses?"

Brianna raised her proud, stubborn chin. "For a short time I did. Now, however, I have recovered them."

He stared at her for a full minute before he moved to the door. "Tell Edward I have returned to Windsor."

In the adjoining bedchamber, Joan of Kent said wistfully, "I wish I could stop time right this minute so we could live in this house happily ever after."

"Time seems to have speeded up the last fortnight. It's because we are going to France. Everything has an urgency about it."

She hesitated, hating to cast a shadow on their short time together. Edward was sensitive to her mood. "What is it, sweetheart?"

"The Countess of Salisbury is pressing me about the betrothal before De Montecute leaves for France."

"Goddamn it, no! I've racked my brains about how to thwart them. The only thing I can come up with is a previous contract to wed." He watched her face carefully. "What do you think of Sir John Holland?"

Holland's image came to her. He had auburn hair and a ruddy complexion. He was only of average height, but made up for it with a muscular, stocky build and a bull neck. He was one of the prince's young men who had pursued her on and off for two years. "I don't think anything about him," Joan said carefully, not wanting to make Edward jealous when there was no cause.

"He's extremely ambitious. That makes him easy to control. He continually petitions me for a royal appointment. One or two positions remain vacant because the king and I have had other matters to occupy us. I'm sure he would be willing to claim you have entered into a secret betrothal with him. It would be believable because I recall he once dangled after you, before you rebuffed him."

Joan licked lips gone suddenly dry. "But how can that help us? What is the difference being betrothed to Holland rather than De Montecute?"

"Little innocent, the betrothal to Holland would not be real. It would only be for appearances, to prevent you being contracted to De Montecute!"

"Oh, I see," Joan said, laughing nervously with relief.

Edward pulled her down to him. "Would you be willing to do this thing for me?" he demanded.

"You know I would be willing to do anything for you, Edward."

Her submission to his demands aroused him instantly. "Leave all to me; I'll arrange it." Before he had kissed her a dozen times, Joan had forgotten Holland, De Montecute, and the entire world.

John Holland couldn't get over his good fortune when Prince Edward summoned him to a private meeting. He had applied for the coveted position of Steward of the Royal Household, but did not expect to get it because he served the prince, rather than the king.

"You have always served me well in the past, John. You are ambitious and you know how to follow orders, two qualities I admire in a man. Since the king is occupied with the French campaign, I have offered to fill the appointments vacant in the royal household."

Holland held his breath.

"It is a Plantagenet practice to fill these appointments with military men, rather than clerks. The practice has worked out well for all concerned. Since you have trained under me, I know you to be intelligent, decisive, and fearless. The man I choose will need another quality: total loyalty to me."

For one dreaded moment Holland believed Edward had learned of the secret meeting he'd had with Prince Lionel.

Only a sennight ago the young prince and his first lieutenant, Robert de Beauchamp, had offered an alliance with
them if aught befell Prince Edward in the French campaign. Such an alliance was treason, of course, while the
heir to the throne lived and breathed, but the reward they
offered was worth the risk. Holland's complexion grew rud-
dier as the collar of his doublet tightened around his bull-
neck.

"There is a special lady of my acquaintance who is in
need of a husband in name only. I have summoned you to
learn if you are willing to fulfill both roles."

Holland began to breathe again. How bloody ironic!
Prince Lionel offered him Joan of Kent while Prince Edward offered him the stewardship if he kept Joan inviolate.
Holland said yes without hesitation, even though he had
already said yes to Prince Lionel. He would play both sides
against each other, and if he was clever enough, he might
achieve both his ambitions.

When Prince Edward was absolutely sure of Sir John
Holland's complete cooperation in the matter, he divulged
the lady's name and they drew up a betrothal contract,
which Holland readily signed. Edward explained haste was
necessary to prevent the lady's betrothal to William de
Montecute. When they had worked out all the details,
Prince Edward promised to see that the Council confirmed
him as Steward of the Royal Household before they departed for France.

Hawksblood, with Ali in attendance, visited Robert de
Beauchamp morning and night for a full week to tend his
wound. At the end of that time the leg was almost healed,
yet his half brother still complained of pain and still walked
with a marked limp.

Hawksblood decided a word with Warrick wouldn't be
amiss. He found him training common foot soldiers in the
most effective ways to utilize sword and shield in close
combat. Christian observed him silently for a while, not
wanting to break the older man's concentrated attention.
Hawksblood grudgingly admired Warrick's method of
teaching. He seldom told the men what to do, but rather
showed them by demonstration. It was most effective, for

none of the young warriors wanted to be shamed by the strength and ability of a graybeard.

At last Warrick saw Hawksblood watching him and bade the men practice what he had shown them. He came over to his son, grinned and wiped the sweat from his face with a brawny arm. "They shape up well. What of the men of Warrick you command?"

"Would they dare be anything but superior fighting men? All are as eager for the coming confrontation as you and I." He hesitated, then added, "All save one."

Warrick raised a wiry eyebrow, knowing Hawksblood had something sticking in his craw. "Spit it out, man," he commanded bluntly.

"Robert's leg is almost healed, yet he still limps about like an invalid."

Warrick's face turned to granite. "Ye'r not daring to hint any son of mine is a coward?" The older man's fierce countenance was terrible to behold. Hawksblood thought Warrick would smite him with his broadsword. For a moment his heart burned with envy for a father who would defend him as fiercely. As Warrick glared at him, the earl's enmity was palpable. Christian risked his abhorrence, rationalizing that there was no love to lose between them. He stood his ground. "I'll let you decide that when you've seen the leg."

"I'll come now," Warrick challenged.

They found Robert in his chamber in the Beauchamp Tower with a plump wench between his thighs.

"Ha! Never let it be said I breed aught but lusty stallions," bawled Warrick, slapping the girl's bare rump as she picked up her smock and fled the room.

Robert knew he had been fairly caught, yet the look of contempt on his bastard brother's face made him want to smash it to a bloody pulp.

Warrick flushed, not over the fornication, but over the fact that his son was wenching when he was strong enough to be training his men. "I've decided to take Prince Lionel's men to France, and since he isn't old enough to command them, the honor is yours."

"Thank you, Father. I hoped you would call on me." Robert masked his hatred behind narrowed turquoise eyes. "Did you want something, little brother?"

Hawksblood, reading his thoughts with ease, knew he was livid enough to kill. "I came to tend your leg, but now I can see you are restored to vigor, I'll take my leave."

When Hawksblood departed, a deep frown creased Warrick's brow. He had commanded men all his life and knew impending war affected them in many different ways. "War makes us face our own mortality. It is inevitable, but I advise you not to dwell on it."

Robert laughed to dispel his father's suspicions. "I am a Beauchamp. I'd rather fight than eat, but unlike you, I have no sons to follow in my footsteps should aught befall me."

Warrick studied him from beneath hooded lids. "We'd best formalize the betrothal contract. Rid yourself of yon whore's stink before I send for Lady Bedford."

That evening when Brianna, accompanied by Adele, answered the king's summons to his privy chamber, her pallor had turned her skin to pale ivory. She was aware that the betrothal ceremony was about to take place and had brought Adele as her witness. She expected Warrick and the king to be present, but she was surprised to find Prince Lionel at Robert's side. She had never liked him, even before he'd ruined Elizabeth Grey, but now the thought of him being Robert's chosen witness to her betrothal was most distasteful to her.

Brianna had chosen a deep wine gown heavily embroidered at sleeve and hem with gold thread. Her golden hair fell unbound down her back as befitted a maiden and she clasped her hands tightly before her, praying her guilty conscience would not choke her when she uttered her promise. She wished she'd picked another color now, recalling that rich hues sometimes robbed her face of life.

In the richly appointed chamber, beneath the glow of the tall tapers, she looked ethereal. The two older men, King Edward and Warrick knew a moment's sharp envy of Robert de Beauchamp. His bride-to-be was utterly lovely.

The words exchanged were secondary to the signing of the marriage contract, and so this was the first order of business. Her vision blurred as the parchment and quill were presented to her. She saw the words: Daughter of the House of Bedford and Son of the House of Warrick. She saw the king's gilt seals attached by ribbons. She saw the dotted lines for the signatures of the betrothed couple and their witnesses, but all the rest seemed to be in Latin.

Brianna's emotions were in turmoil. She knew she must cast out her longings for Christian, knew she must abandon her abhorrence for Robert, but it was easier said than done. She silently prayed for help and strength to do the honorable thing. On the surface she managed to look composed, but inside she felt as if her heart were being rent into a thousand pieces.

Everyone present attached his signature after the bride-to-be affixed hers. The exchanged verbal promise took only a fraction of the time and before she knew it, Robert pinned a heavy gold betrothal brooch to her bodice and bent to cover her lips in the betrothal kiss.

Brianna looked up beyond the tall tapers to the stained glass oriel window. A dark visaged saint stared down, pointing an accusing finger at her. It looked exactly like Hawksblood. A wave of guilt engulfed her and she felt herself going down in a swoon. When she reached out to save herself, Robert's arms swept about her to prevent her falling. The king was surprised at the tenderness in Warrick's face. It was the first soft look he had ever seen on the fierce earl's countenance.

Christian Hawksblood knew of his lady's betrothal the moment it took place. He saw it all in one of his psychic visions. He saw Brianna's hand tremble as she signed the contract, heard her whispered promise, and saw her go down in a swoon when his half brother gave her the betrothal kiss.

With a supreme effort he controlled his anger. In his rage he wanted to destroy the man who dared raise his eyes and his hopes toward *his* lady. But Hawksblood assured himself that a betrothal was not a marriage and made a sacred vow that a marriage between Brianna and Robert de Beauchamp would never come to pass.

Hawksblood was thankful that the campaign against France would begin almost immediately. He knew it would be impossible to remain at Windsor and not make love to her, even if he had to ravish her. His need was too great.

He laughed bitterly to himself. He had thought his control in all things was supreme. But that was before he had encountered Brianna of Bedford. God damn her beautiful eyes!

He paced about his chamber like a caged beast. The room imprisoned him. In desperation he began to meditate, using the ancient rituals taught him by the Templars of the Golden Dawn. Though he focused steadily, he could not achieve a state that even approached peace and tranquillity.

His mind betrayed him. It conjured a picture of his lady. She was in her bed sleeping. Her glorious golden hair trailed across the coverlet and fell to the floor. Then his body betrayed him. Her hair was ever his undoing.

He cursed and stood up to pace again. An idea came to him, but he pushed it away. He had never abused his "gifts." The idea however grew in intensity and he knew he would know no peace until he had exercised his power over her. Without analyzing it, he knew what prompted this compelling urge within him. It was pure and simple male sexual domination. Because she was pledged to another, he had to assert dominion over her to prove to both of them she would submit to him anytime, anyplace, any way he demanded.

He faced east, for he knew her chamber lay in that direction, then he gathered his powers and focused total concentration upon Brianna, exclusive of all else. The command that fell from his lips was like black velvet. "Come!"

In the curtained bed, Brianna stirred. She threw back the covers and sat up slowly. She drew on her slippers and reached for her bed-gown. She had an overwhelming need for fresh air, but did not wish to disturb Adele at such an ungodly hour. She left her chamber and walked slowly in the shadows of the stone castle. Her steps led her toward the Royal Apartments where Prince Edward had his chambers. She came to a stop before a studded door, and then it came to her that Christian's apartment was within. She lifted her hand, but not to knock, only to caress the hard wood in a loving gesture.

Suddenly the door opened and a powerful hand reached out to draw her inside.

Her eyes dilated darkly with pleasure as she gazed upon him, and her breath came out on a sigh, "Christian."

"Take off the robe," he commanded.

She lifted it from her shoulders and let it fall to the carpet. Her silk night rail clung to the curves of her lush body, accentuating its hills and valleys. He reached out ungentle hands to her, but she slid against him willingly, softly, lifting her arms to entwine them about his neck, fitting her ripe body to his hard length. Her yielding was so feminine, so generous, so submissive he felt a savage thrill that he could make her desire him with such yearning, clinging hunger. She opened her soft mouth for his ravaging tongue.

When he took his mouth away, then his arms, he heard her soft cry of loss. "Get in the bed," he ordered, and Brianna obeyed him instantly, holding out her arms to him. Perversely, he didn't want her this way! Suddenly he wanted their coming together to be *her* willing, not *his* willing.

He leashed his animal strength and drew her gently from the bed. Then he slipped her bed-robe on her and fastened it all the way up to her chin. He opened the door and gave her a gentle push. "Go back to your own chamber, Brianna."

Ali felt himself being shaken awake. "I need an opiate," came the tortured request. Without a word Ali opened his medicine chest and selected a narcotic. He knew it was not for physical pain. The pain from which Drakkar suffered was of the heart and soul.

With the dawn came the realization that he could not keep a twenty-four-hour control upon Brianna, therefore he would have to focus his power on Robert. He would have to keep him so busy, so totally occupied with problems regarding Prince Lionel's knights and men-at-arms that he would be on the point of exhaustion when and if he allowed him to seek his couch.

❧ 22 ❧

Joan of Kent was a stranger to worry. Whenever something unpleasant crossed her mind, she firmly pushed it aside in favor of happy thoughts. When Brianna told her that she had been betrothed last night, Joan wondered what she would do if the king summoned her to solemnize her betrothal to William de Montecute. She immediately sent off a note to Fish Street, then put the whole matter out of her head. Her golden prince would take care of everything.

She took out the little casket that held all Edward's love letters and sat upon the cushioned casement window seat to read and dream away the afternoon hours. When she had reread them all, she spoke to Glynis. "One of my letters from Edward is missing!"

"Are you certain, my lady?"

"Yes, 'tis my favorite. I remember his words to me after the king announced my betrothal. He said, 'I am more angry at this moment than I have ever been in my life! . . . You are my precious love and so you shall remain.'"

Glynis asked, "Didn't you sleep with it under your pillow?"

"Yes! Oh dear, then in the morning we left for Bedford. The maids must have thrown it away."

Glynis frowned. "By Our Lady, I hope they threw it away. It would be terrible if it fell into the wrong hands." Glynis knew none at court could be trusted, least of all the maids. "You had better warn the prince that one of his letters is missing."

"Oh, Glynis, you worry too much," Joan chided.

And you don't worry nearly enough, Glynis thought darkly.

As the evening shadows were gathering, Joan was pleasantly surprised to get a visit from her brother, the Earl of Kent.

"Get your cloak, love. I'm taking you to Fish Street."

"How wonderful! Glynis, run along to Brianna's chambers and ask her if she'll accompany me."

"No!" Edmund warned. "You are to come alone, Joan. Our business is private. That's why I'm here to escort you."

Joan quickly gathered up her precious letters and put them back in their filigreed casket.

"Don't forget to mention the missing letter," Glynis reminded.

"Missing letter?" Edmund echoed.

"These are Edward's letters to me," Joan explained.

"And one is missing? God's feet, Joan, sometimes you act like seven rather than seventeen. Fetch the bloody letters with you!"

The prince was waiting in Edmund's house when they arrived in Fish Street. Though he greeted Joan tenderly, he was in a serious mood. "There is no time to lose. Lady Bedford is officially betrothed and you will be next. My father already approached Edmund about the betrothal to De Montecute, but your brother informed him you had been betrothed to Sir John Holland."

Joan's eyes flew to Edmund's face.

"The king was angered, to say the least. He demanded I produce the signed contract to marry."

Prince Edward unfurled the crackling parchment. "Holland has already affixed his signature; it only requires yours."

Joan picked up the quill. Holland's handwriting was thick and bold. She shuddered. Her brother's writing beneath it was beautiful. He had witnessed the contract and dated it three months ago. Her hand hesitated. She looked up at Edward with beseeching eyes. "I don't wish to wed Holland," she whispered.

"My sweetheart, there is no question of that. It's a delaying tactic. When Edmund produces this contract, it will be impossible to betroth you to De Montecute, no matter how earnestly the Countess of Salisbury presses my father. When they reach an impasse, my father will likely send to the Pope in Avignon to decide. It could take years."

Joan gave him a grateful smile. "You are brilliant," she said, affixing her signature with a flourish.

Edward picked up the sand-caster to blot the ink, then rolled the parchment and handed it to the Earl of Kent.

With a strong hand at the small of Joan's back, Edward moved toward the garden that led to his own house.

Edmund picked up the casket Joan had set down. "Be sure to tell His Highness of the letter," he admonished.

She snatched her precious letters from Edmund's hands and tucked them beneath her cloak.

The next four hours were among the most precious of their lives. Edward and Joan played and laughed and loved, totally carefree of what the future held for them. They shared a loving cup, brimful of wine, yet both knew it was their closeness that made them intoxicated.

It was long past the hour of midnight when they began to sober. "How long before you leave?" Joan whispered, clinging to him.

His lips brushed across her fair brow. "A week, mayhap."

Joan drew in her breath on a sob. "Edward, I cannot bear it."

He kissed her and ran his hand down her silken back in an effort to soothe her. "Hush, sweeting. I go to win my spurs. When I return I will be your true knight errant."

Joan smiled tremulously, knowing men hated tears. "I'm cold."

Edward slipped from the bed and tossed her his robe, then bent to light them a fire. The black robe, with its fierce dragon of Wales, engulfed her. She wrapped it about her twice and came to stand at his shoulder as he knelt before the fire. "I'll read your letters every night," she promised.

He slipped a protective arm about her to draw her close. "I'm afraid not, precious love. For your safety and mine, we must destroy them."

"No!" she cried, "I cannot bear to part with your love letters."

He drew her into his lap. "We'll read them together one last time, then we will burn them in the fire." He brushed her tears away with his fingertips, then crushed his mouth down on hers, mastering her, forcing her to his will.

Finally, with infinite sadness, she read his letters aloud; unshed tears making her throat husky. After each letter, she kissed it good-bye and handed it to Edward, who touched it to the flames. They watched each page flare up, turn black, then fall to ashes in what seemed a mystic ritual.

She began the last letter: *"I kiss your lips, I kiss your heart, but save the other kiss for lower . . ."* He took the letter before she finished it and threw it onto the fire. Then he pushed her back upon the fur hearth rug and unwound the robe from her pretty body. His lips proceeded to kiss the intimate places he had described in his love letter.

Each afternoon King Edward and his marshal, Warrick, held a strategy meeting with the members of the king's carefully chosen war council, comprised of earls of the realm and experienced military knights. Also present was the Prince of Wales and Warrick's sons. Warrick suggested they give the French knight Godfrey de Harcourt the rank of marshal because he knew the terrain of the coming battle better than any man in England.

In various parts of France, England had had troops fighting for the last two years. Since Queen Philippa was from Flanders, the Flemish were Edward's allies. English troops, permanently stationed in Bruges, Ghent, and Ypres were presently engaged in battles and skirmishes along the French border.

Brabant also was an ally of England, but between Flanders and Brabant lay the great city of Tournai, which was occupied by Philip of France. England's allies insisted Tournai must be the first town captured in the war. However, King Edward kept a Court at Bordeaux and the royal family spent much time there. England owned the southern provinces of Gascony, Guienne, and Poitou, collectively known as Aquitaine. As a result most Anglo-Normans owned land and castles in this southern territory, and large English garrisons of troops kept it from being overrun by the French. At the present time this standing army was being decimated and was in desperate need of reinforcements.

King Philip put his son, John of Normandy, in charge of an army so large that any day it threatened to overrun all the southern provinces that had been owned by England for two hundred years.

At King Edward's war strategy meetings opinion was divided. Most of the nobles who owned property near Bordeaux voted to land the army there. The large contingent whose interests lay in Flanders, under the leadership of Sir Walter Manny, argued that the king should join up with his allies. All clustered about a massive map table boasting miniature armies and warships that could be moved around.

The king wanted a decision. He chafed visibly to get this assault underway. He waved his arm toward the map table. "Warrick—Bordeaux or Flanders?"

When the Mad Hound spoke, all listened. "Neither! Taking an army of twenty thousand across the Bay of Biscay is foolhardy. If we land along the coast of Normandy, Philip will be forced to divide his army in the south and march them north to fight us. Before he reaches us, we can ravage across northern France collecting enough spoils to pay for the cost of the operation. Then we can join with the Flemish armies to swell our ranks. In the unlikely event the rumors are true about the size of Philip's army, we can recross the Channel quickly through the narrow Strait of Dover."

As Hawksblood listened to his father, he could not help but grudgingly admire the tactics he set forth. The Prince of Wales, who had studied strategy all his life, also agreed with Warrick's plan.

King Edward studied the faces about him. Most had their own ideas and were fairly bursting to set them forth, but the ultimate decision was his and so he approved Warrick's plan.

The king spent his last night at Windsor with his family. He visited the nursery to roughhouse with his younger children. He lavished attention upon Isabel, promising to keep his eyes open for a worthy husband for her, then admonished Lionel to help his mother administer the country in his absence.

Having done all this, he took young John of Gaunt aside for a more serious talk. "If ill should befall me, John, I want you to be loyal to the Black Prince. You have the brains of the family, John. Edward will need your advice and your support, and when you are older he will need the combined military strength of the House of Gaunt and the House of Lancaster when you marry Blanche."

"I know, Father," John said solemnly. "Lionel will be

nothing but trouble. He attracts men who will manipulate him to commit treason. Edward knows I shall always support him."

"Good man," said his father, gripping his shoulder with approval. It meant more to John than the crown jewels.

Earlier, in the hall, Katherine, Countess of Salisbury, had shown the king that she would have none of him. She was furious that the Fair Maid of Kent had been allowed to sign a contract to marry Sir John Holland, when Joan and her estates had been promised to her son.

After dinner, she swept from the hall without a backward glance, but Edward was determined to clear the air between them before he departed on the most important campaign of his life.

One look at her face when he opened her chamber door told him she intended to play the shrew. "Katherine, I like it no better than you. Lady Kent has behaved wantonly to encourage two suitors at the same time."

"You are the king, for God's sake! You can order her to marry William."

"Katherine, Sir John Holland has a valid contract signed by Joan and her brother, the Earl of Kent. It is not a matter for the crown, but for the Church to decide. I'll set the matter before the Pope."

The Countess of Salisbury was only slightly mollified. Her stony heart did not soften toward Edward.

"I have other news that should please you." He watched her face closely. Her eyes brightened, she caught her breath as hope was kindled. "Even though it was against my better judgment, I offered to exchange the Earl of Moray for the Earl of Salisbury."

Katherine clutched his hand, unable to conceal the depth of her emotions.

"Philip of France has accepted with unseemly eagerness," he said quietly.

Katherine fell to her knees before him, her face radiant, her beautiful eyes liquid with tears of joy and relief. "Edward, my love, I thank you with all my heart." Her heart and her body softened toward him. At this moment she would yield him anything.

He raised her, and feeling most virtuous, placed a chaste

kiss upon her brow. "William de Montecute is my dear friend. He is a lucky man to beget such love and devotion."

With a sigh, the king put Katherine de Montecute from his thoughts before he entered the queen's bower. Philippa would welcome him as gently and as sweetly as she had since she was a maid of fourteen. He, too, was a lucky man to beget such love and devotion.

Two other couples were saying their good-byes on this last night at Windsor. Adele and Paddy dined together in the hall, then slipped out to walk by the river. They felt the urgency in the air, felt it in their blood as well. Paddy couldn't dispel the darklings. It was ever so for him before a battle. Though he couldn't put it into words, he felt that if he made a commitment and received one in return, Fate would let him come back to fulfill that commitment.

Adele couldn't endure the thought of losing this man when it had taken her so many years to find him. She marveled that such a strong, funny, kind man wanted a woman with a plain face who was about to turn thirty. That he was Irish made her feel doubly blessed. Their coming together this night was natural and right. They shared their thoughts, their hopes and fears. When they shared their bodies, they knew a small part of them would remain with the other. Perhaps the best part.

Ali and Glynis had no difficulty translating their feelings into words. Their spirits had much in common: fatalism, superstition, mysticism. They chose the loveliest, most serene place in all of Windsor to bid adieu. In the walled garden the night-scented flowers perfumed the air, the fountain sang its silvery song, and the slumbering sundial measured only the sunny hours. Their fingers and their breath entwined as they murmured love words as ancient as time itself.

They exchanged talismans. He gave her a translucent lump of amber with a myriad of dark inclusions and radiant sun spangles imprisoned in its golden depths. Amber was an eternal, magic touchstone whose sensuous softness was warm to the skin, and Glynis knew its luster would be enhanced by her continual touch.

Glynis gave Ali an amulet set with torbernite, a form of

copper with brilliant green plates. Neither experienced the fear of the unknown, for both knew their destinies were linked.

Robert de Beauchamp knew he must speak with Prince Lionel early in the evening before he drank himself to oblivion. "This campaign could stretch into years. With the king and Prince Edward in France it is your God-given opportunity to take over the reins of the realm, take the responsibilities from your mother's shoulders, and curry favor with the Council. Never forget for one moment that if aught befalls either of them, you will become heir to the throne. If aught befalls both, you will wear the crown."

Lionel grabbed him in a playful wrestling hold, pinning Robert's great arms behind his back and bending his neck forward painfully. "What are the odds?" he demanded, laughing.

Robert resisted the impulse to bring the young giant crashing over his shoulder to the floor. He was such a brainless bastard! Still, if Lionel were intelligent, he wouldn't be able to manipulate him. "The odds are very good." Robert was more cautious than to come right out and say he would do his best to make Lionel the King of England. "I'd say the odds were definitely in your favor."

Prince Lionel stopped the horseplay, prepared to listen seriously to his lieutenant's advice.

"We have some very good men in our camp, but we'll need more. You may count on those loyal to the queen and of course the House of Warrick. I also have Wiggs and his knights from Bedford. We have John Holland and young William de Montecute is ripe for plucking. But never forget that Henry of Lancaster will back your brother, John of Gaunt."

"Lancaster is a graybeard. He could easily fall in battle."

"This war could change the face of England's nobility. There could be a complete shift of power before it's over. I want you to be prepared for any eventuality, Your Highness."

When he quit Lionel's chambers, Robert rubbed his neck. Christ, he ached all over. If he didn't get some rest, he'd be dead on his feet tomorrow. He had orders to move his men to the coast and dawn came too damned early.

He had put off his leave-taking of Brianna to the last minute. She had made it plain that she would not submit to him before they were legally wed, so he decided to make no last-minute sexual demands upon her. Instead he took her a parting gift, one calculated to please and therefore bind her to him. When he arrived at her chambers, Joan of Kent was with her.

Brianna's eyes widened in disbelief as he strode into the room. "Robert, your limp is gone!"

"Yes, it seems the king's physician was wrong. All my leg needed was exercise. Fortune has smiled upon me. I am leading the men of the House of Clarence in the French campaign."

Brianna searched his face. Had he lied to her about the leg? Nay, that was such an unworthy thought. He seemed so gallant, so eager to answer the call of duty.

Joan moved toward the door. "I'll give you some privacy for your farewells."

"No need, Lady Kent. I only wished to give my lady this parting gift of paint and brushes. Think of me, Brianna, whenever you use them." He took her hand to his lips as if he were the most chivalrous knight in Christendom.

Brianna's heart softened toward him. She must count her blessings. She knew she should be content to have Robert de Beauchamp for her husband, and would have been if she had never encountered the dark and dangerous Arabian. She went up on tiptoe to kiss him. "Go with God, Robert," she whispered. Brianna meant it with all her heart.

❧ 23 ❧

Edward III's French offensive was a massive undertaking. He assembled two hundred ships to transport his army of twenty thousand. The vessels made several crossings, for fighting men needed horses, baggage wagons needed mules, and war machinery needed ammunition.

All the leaders, the knights, and the members of noble

families wore a steel cone helmet with a nasal, a long-sleeved, hooded chain-mail shirt that reached to the knees, girded by a weapons belt that held sword, knife, and mace. Each carried a shield whose sharp metal edge and point could be used as a weapon.

Some ships carried tents, fodder for the animals, medical supplies, some staple foods, and inevitably, whores. In a flotilla of two hundred vessels, the camp followers found many places to conceal themselves.

Many of the soldiers had fought in previous French campaigns and knew what to expect, but a lot were facing war without any experience. Hawksblood passed along his knowledge to Prince Edward and the other young nobles who would command men in real battle for the first time in their lives.

Hawksblood knew he need not reiterate that courage was the highest virtue and that they must cast out their fear in the face of danger. Their training had been grueling and endless, and he had no doubts that most would lead their men magnificently. But his experience in warfare would be invaluable to them. He glanced at the faces about him and was satisfied that they understood it was kill or be killed, maim or be maimed. There was no room for squeamishness in war. Hawksblood grinned at the Black Prince. He finished by telling them, "A knight is only as good as his horse, and all warfare is based on deception."

Prince Edward said, "It seems my entire life has been in preparation for this moment."

"Then let's make it count for something," Hawksblood replied, clasping Edward's thickly muscled sword arm in a pledge of allegiance.

As the English ships dropped anchor at Cherbourg, Warrick took charge of landing the first batch of invaders. Naturally he did not include England's king, the king's son, nor his own sons in this foray. There was some opposition by the French, but soon they were disarmed and in flight.

When Warrick gave the signal, King Edward was carried ashore by an overeager young De Montecute and Robert de Beauchamp. When they reached the shore, the king fell sprawling. Before it could be interpreted as a terrible omen, quick-witted Edward held out his earth-stained hands as William the Conqueror had done when he invaded England, and he repeated his famous words: "Behold, my friends, the very land of France cannot wait to embrace me as its rightful master. It is a sign from Heaven!"

King Edward was deeply superstitious and though he himself was not convinced, he wanted his army to believe it. He took Warrick and the Prince of Wales aside. "I'm going to knight you immediately, Edward, so that if I fall in battle, the men will have another leader to follow."

"Christ, Father, no! I want to *earn* my spurs!"

Warrick silenced him. "You will earn them, Your Highness, a hundred times over, never fear."

The chests holding the regalia for those newly knighted were located and within the hour of setting foot on French soil, the king created his first knights. He bade the two young men who carried him ashore to kneel with Edward. The king bent his knee, then touched the Prince of Wales upon his shoulder with his unsheathed sword, and fastened the golden spurs at his heels. Then he did the same to William de Montecute and Robert de Beauchamp.

Godfrey de Harcourt dispatched scouts immediately, laying out the best routes for them to travel and relay information regarding the numbers and locations of French forces. Within a day of landing, the march across France began.

There was very little opposition in the first weeks. The English forces conquered the French towns one by one, taking everything they had of value. Barfleur, Valognes, and Carentan all fell. Wagon trains filled with armor, tapestries, silver flagons, gold candlesticks and crucifixes, as well as magnificent French furnishings, carpets, and paintings were sent to the coast to be loaded onto vessels sailing back to England. Wealthy prisoners were sent south to Bordeaux to be held for ransom.

Christian Hawksblood led the raid upon St. Lô. He was so familiar with the town and the castle, it fell to him like a house of cards. He took Baron St. Lô and his voluptuous sister into custody. When Paddy brought them into his campaign tent, Hawksblood was not surprised when Lisette flung herself into his arms in a desperate attempt to barter

her body for her life and that of her brother. Hawksblood
smiled cynically when she did not even try to save her husband.

"He's already had the use of your body," Paddy said with
contempt. "Offer something of value."

"Paddy," Hawksblood murmured low, but it was enough
to silence him.

"The wine cellars beneath the castle," Lisette cried eagerly. "St. Lô has a thousand tuns of wine!"

Paddy whistled. "Christ, a tun holds two hundred and
fifty gallons."

"Wipe that smile off your face, Paddy, and make arrangements to have it shipped to my villa in Bordeaux." He
removed Lisette's tempting hands from his body and put a
hand beneath her chin. "I'll send you and the baron there
also, until you are ransomed." He cocked a dark brow at
her. "If your husband does not think you worth a ransom,
I'll find other uses for you, chérie."

When they reached Caen they were surprised to find a
small army, led by the Constable of France. The fighting
was fierce in the town, but they hacked their way to the
stronghold of the castle, cleared the walls of arbalests, then
put up wooden hoardings to mount the walls.

The sun was setting before the stronghold fell to them.
King Edward went to the Constable of France's war room
and searched it top to bottom. When he discovered a plan
to invade England that had been drawn up by the
Normans, he was incensed. It showed in detail how England was to be divided among the victors. He handed it to
the Black Prince, who had inherited his father's lightning
temper. The king's eyes burned with blue fury. "Tomorrow
you will put the entire population of Caen to the sword,"
he ordered Warrick.

"We will exact revenge for this plan, never fear," thundered an infuriated prince.

Warrick's eyes rolled wildly in Hawksblood's direction.
He was familiar with the Plantagenet temper and, hardened warrior though he was, he did not relish putting
women and children to the sword. The Constable of France

and his army had already been defeated and many lay dead. It was unnecessary to spill more blood.

Hawksblood understood Warrick immediately, without words having to be spoken. "You persuade the king; I'll talk to Prince Edward," he told Warrick.

Hawksblood drew Edward out onto the ramparts. The townspeople were still putting out fires the English had set. Women wept and children wailed as Caen was systematically stripped and everything of value was piled onto the English wagons. "The success of this campaign depends upon speed, Your Highness. We must sweep across the whole of the northern coast before the French effectively organize against us. The chances for loot have been greater than we ever dreamed, but it has already slowed us considerably. Putting the entire population of Caen to the sword will take days. The men will rape the women before they kill them, then after the slaughter they will drink themselves into oblivion. We'll lose another week. It has taken us a fortnight to get this far."

Edward drew in a deep breath. The air smelled of woodsmoke, blood, and death.

"Bank the fires of your anger so you may draw upon it in battle."

The Black Prince nodded slowly. He had been knighted such a short time. He would keep his vows awhile longer.

Warrick was having a much harder time controlling the king's bloodlust. He refused again and again to give up this act of revenge. Warrick pointed out the need for speed, pointed out they should be closer to the French capital by now, but King Edward would not let go of his white-hot fury. It was only when a pair of Godfrey de Harcourt's scouts arrived after dark, reporting that Philip had fallen into a panic and was preparing Paris to withstand a siege, that the king wavered.

The scouts reported that Philip was tearing down all the buildings that touched the city walls. King Edward's laughter rolled out, to think he could put fear into the King of France. The other news was less amusing, however. Philip was gathering a huge army on the Plain of St. Denis, between Paris and Poise, which swelled in number every day. The scouts could not give exact numbers, but of one thing they were certain: the French army was much larger than the English army!

King Edward forgot his need for revenge and called a strategy meeting. They decided to press on at dawn, but instead of following the coast, they would take Lisieux and the towns that lay inland on their way to Paris.

Twenty-eight days melted away before the English reached Poise. They were a mere dozen miles from Paris, but the great river Seine still had to be crossed. Suddenly they received different numbers regarding the French army. Some scouts reported fifty thousand, but others swore the French were sixty or seventy thousand strong. One thing was clear: Philip must have withdrawn all his forces from the south.

Against such vast numbers, King Edward concluded a siege of Paris would be folly. It was decided that Sir Walter Manny would take a small force south, away from the Seine, and circle back up to Paris in a deceptive tactic while a pontoon bridge was built across the river Seine.

It took them three days, and the leaders heaved great sighs of relief to have this obstacle behind them. Only lightning speed could safeguard the English army now, for they were rumored to be outnumbered at least three to one.

This was the price they had to pay for their slow progress through Normandy while they searched out loot. The king and Warrick were aware of the danger. All the roads behind them were black with French troops. They drove their heavily laden soldiers at top speed through the Vexin of Normandy and covered an unbelievable sixty miles in four days. But the most serious obstacle to their progress still lay ahead.

The broad river Somme with marshy peat bogs on both sides was enough to spark terror in the bravest heart. The king ordered his two marshals to go ahead and secure a crossing. Warrick took both his sons, but made it clear they must follow Harcourt's orders because of the French knight's familiarity with the treacherous terrain.

They found all the bridges destroyed and the fords guarded by Picardy troops. Harcourt's men failed in two attempts to seize fords. Then Warrick sent his son, Robert, who led the Duke of Clarence's men, but they too failed.

Hawksblood was eager to try, but Warrick decided to lead the men himself. They suffered high casualties; their horses floundered in the bogs and the attempt failed. When King Edward arrived with his army, he was incensed that no way across the boggy Somme had been secured.

Hawksblood withdrew to his campaign tent with his squires. They knew he needed to achieve a trance-like state before he could experience one of his visions. Christian lay supine upon the floor while Ali lit a small incense burner. Hawksblood harnessed his mind's great power, first clearing it of all unnecessary clutter. Then, one by one, he went through the barriers of fear, time, space, finally becoming one with the elements of air, earth, and water. What was secret became known, what was distant became close, what was impossible became attainable.

Hawksblood came out of his trance to find Prince Edward standing over him. "Where is the king?"

"He has called a strategy meeting. I came to fetch you." The Black Prince's eyes were filled with questions, but he and Hawksblood were close friends who did not question each other. Before they entered the tent they heard contention in the raised voices. Their dangerous position strained the leaders' tempers to breaking point.

Hawksblood spoke. "Your Majesty, I have learned that the French cavalry has already reached Amiens and is on its way to Abbeville. Philip's army marches parallel to us. It is no exaggeration that they outnumber us at least four to one."

A babble of voices broke out. Fear could be detected in most of them. Pointing at the map, King Edward shouted, "God damn Philip! He shoves us into a triangle formed by his army, the impassable Somme, and the waters of the Channel."

Robert de Beauchamp pointed out what he thought was obvious. "We must escape across the Channel."

Prince Edward gave him such a look of contempt Robert wanted to run his sword through him.

Warrick said, "We arranged to have our fleet land in our own province of Ponthieu across the Somme. It will not have arrived yet."

Harcourt stood by helplessly. He felt he had led the English army into this trap.

Robert de Beauchamp, standing with two of Lionel's knights, gritted out, "Where does the Arabian get his information?" Immediately one of the knights shouted, "How do we know he isn't in league with the French?"

It was a terrible accusation for one knight to hurl at another, but all eyes turned upon Hawksblood now that the seeds of suspicion had been sown. Hawksblood looked straight at his father. "The information came from an informant we captured," he lied. "A little torture loosened his tongue enough to reveal a navigable ford close to the mouth of the Somme."

The King and Warrick looked vastly relieved. Robert de Beauchamp fought rising panic. "What if it's a trap? Did any other hear this Frenchman's confession?"

"I did," Prince Edward said calmly.

The king invited, "Show us on the map."

Hawksblood stepped forward, tracing the line of the river Somme with his finger. "The place is called Blanche Taque. It is possible to ford it at low tide."

"Blanche Taque means 'white stone,'" Harcourt said thoughtfully. "Perhaps Blanche Taque is a landmark of some kind."

King Edward held up his hands for silence. "You must realize it is no longer possible to join forces with our allies from Flanders. Our only hope is to get across the river Somme into our own province of Ponthieu."

The earls of Northumberland and Lancaster added their voices. "We must maintain ourselves in Ponthieu until our ships arrive and get us back on English soil."

King Edward's eyes met those of the Black Prince; Warrick's eyes met Hawksblood's. They knew the king would not leave France before he had done battle with Philip. Prince Edward stepped to his father's side. "Hawksblood and I will lead the vanguard across the Somme."

The king looked upon his son with pride. Though darkness had already fallen, he gave orders to march. By midnight the vanguard reached Blanche Taque. The tide was high and it was impossible to cross the Somme. As

Hawksblood waited for the tide to ebb, he spoke with the prince. "Thank you for your confidence, Your Highness."

"You had a vision. It is a power given to only a few." He looked out over the raging black water. "You've had them before." It was not a question.

"Yes. My knowledge of the French fleet at Sluys came to me in a vision. I was never there," he admitted.

"Did Warrick know this?"

Hawksblood replied, "I told no one. Who would believe me?"

"I believe you, friend."

They knew they had formed a bond that would last them all their lives until the day they died.

Eventually all of King Edward's army reached the banks of the Somme. Not only was it impossibly wide and impossibly deep, two thousand Picards awaited them on the far side. The troops were tense, some had given up all hope. Many raised their voices in anger at being led to a place where they would drown or be sucked into the surrounding bogs. They were tired and footweary and after seeing Blanche Taque, they felt hopeless.

As dawn began to break, the tidal waters started to recede. Hope mingled with fear showed upon every face. It was like the parting of the biblical Red Sea, but the waters were still waist-deep and the weight of the horses and war wagons would surely cause them to be sucked beneath the water by the quicksand.

The king and Warrick watched in amazement as Hawksblood and the Prince of Wales rode without hesitation into the water. Their horses' hooves struck the solid white stones of Blanche Taque.

The king immediately ordered his longbowmen into the water. They drove the men of Picardy back with a storm of arrows. Warrick ordered the rest of the army into the water and they tramped waist-deep over the solid white stones.

The French were close behind them, but just as it came to pass in the Bible tale, the tide flooded back in before they could cross. The only losses to the English were a few wagons that fell into French hands.

Every man present thought he had been part of a miracle. The king and his marshals marched their army to the village of Crécy, close by the coast. It was August 25, and knowing the French could not cross for another day, they welcomed the respite gratefully.

Now King Edward did what he did best. He rallied his troops! The Plantagenet king was nothing if not ostentatious. He did everything splendidly. He ordered that his massive azure and gold silk pavilion be erected and he raised his leopard standard quartered with the lilies of France.

He had chosen the battle site well, on gently rolling downs, upon a low ridge that could be defended against attack from the plain below. The wagons and camp were located behind his pavilion. By midday the campfires were lit and pits dug for roasting meat.

Harcourt's scouts spread out and Hawksblood's Cornishmen, with their long knives, also went reconnoitering. The information they brought back was both good and bad. The French had crossed the Somme by the bridge at Abbeville. Between the two armies stretched the forest of Crécy, a thick and impenetrable barrier that would necessitate a march around it of eighteen miles for the French. Behind the English camp, a narrow path through the heart of the forest led to the sea. It was confirmed that the French army was one hundred thousand strong and King Philip had hoisted the bloodred oriflamme above his headquarters, indicating they would neither give nor accept quarter.

The French occupied St. Peter's Monastery in Abbeville and Philip had all his allies with him, including the King of Bohemia with his German knights and mercenaries. Also he had Charles of Luxembourg, King Jayme of Majorca, the Duke of Lorraine, and the Count of Flanders. King Edward, surrounded by his noble leaders, listened to this information without any hint of fear.

Marshal Godfrey de Harcourt eyed the forest path leading to the sea. He spoke up, recommending the army retreat to the coast, where they could make a last stand. Most of the nobles concurred with this plan. Warrick and Hawksblood exchanged knowing glances.

King Edward, without a hint of uncertainty, motioned about him. "This is the land of my lady mother's. We will wait for them here."

Silence fell over those crowded about him. Incredulously, Edward was laughing. "Can you imagine the impossible task of providing food and beds for one hundred thousand? Can you envision the discord of so many proud and jealous leaders, all from different countries? Can you conceive the altercations in French, German, Wendish, and Genoese when this rain that threatens comes pouring down and they have no way to keep the strings of their intricate crossbows from getting wet?"

King Edward diffused the strain of uncertainty and fear with humor. "I venture to guess Philip will spend a sleepless night in a monastery. He has too many violent sins on his conscience to face mortal conflict with equanimity!"

Warrick ordered a barricade of tree trunks be raised behind the wagons and the squires hurried off to sort out their masters' armor. Privately, most men feared they were trapped like rats. When the relentless rain began to fall, they amended that to "drowned rats."

24

Windsor womenfolk managed admirably without their men, who had been gone for a good month now. Daily life was calmer and less demanding without the noisy presence of dominant males, but time seemed to hang heavy, and as darkness approached each night it brought with it a nagging worry and concern for the fathers, brothers, sons, husbands, and sweethearts fighting across the sea in France.

Queen Philippa and Prince Lionel received regular communiqués, relayed from the Cinque Ports, and so far the news had all been good. Confiscated French possessions were pouring into England as fast as the fleet could transport them and an optimistic queen's household began preparations for a move to the Court of Bordeaux, once King Edward had vanquished the upstart, Philip of Valois.

Brianna of Bedford enjoyed a freedom she hadn't known since the day she had become inextricably involved with the men of the House of Warrick. The ladies of Windsor had spent this particular afternoon hawking and Brianna slipped away from Isabel's party, then gave her horse its head so they could ride without constraint through the sun-washed Thames Valley.

She realized it was heartless to feel so happy and free when her men—she quickly amended the word "men" to "man"—was off fighting a war. But why should she feel guilty? War was the natural order for men. They spent their entire lives in training and dreamed only of battles, bloody sword thrusts, and knighthood. To a man, knighthood was more important than marriage. Many had more consideration for their warhorses than their wives! They wore their scars like badges of honor and thought themselves iron men, measuring their strength in tourneys when there were no wars to fight.

As she rode, her hair came tumbling down from its constraints and streamed behind her in the summer wind. It was so long, it brushed her mare's flanks as they rode in wild abandon. When she was married she would have to keep it covered, save in the privacy of the bedchamber.

Unbidden, a brilliant flash of memory came to her of Christian brushing her hair. She closed her eyes, banishing the thought instantly. When she opened them, she saw bruise-colored clouds gathering and knew there would be a summer storm this night.

Night.

She tried not to think about night.

Her days were filled with activities, her evenings with her illuminated manuscripts, but her nights were filled with erotic dreams, and none of them about her husband-to-be. The guilt made her cheeks burn; the thought of Christian made her throat ache. Reluctantly she turned her palfrey and headed back to the stables.

When she arrived, she saw Princess Isabel's mare and knew the hawking party had returned before her. She took her merlin up the stone steps of the mews and turned her over to a falconer. She hesitated for a moment, then strode inside to search out Salome. It didn't take her long to locate the magnificent gerfalcon. She spoke softly to her, admiring the subtle coloring where her shoulders curved down into powerful wings. The raptor ruffled at Brianna's crooning voice. "Do you miss him as much as I?" Her words were as soft as a sigh.

She reached out to stroke the bird. In a flash it raised its talons and grabbed her fingers. She cried out in startled alarm. Amazingly it did not draw blood, but gripped her viciously, refusing to let her go for a full minute. She knew it could have torn the flesh of her hand to ribbons and none to blame but herself. Clearly, she saw the analogy of danger between Hawksblood and hawk.

She stopped at the massive Round Tower that was being built with the beautiful stone from Bedford. She ran her hands over the roughened surface, taking comfort from its solid feel, taking pleasure in its muted shadings. "I'll be back," she whispered. "I'll have my children there. We will be a safe and happy family." She did not feel foolish talking to stone. Sharing her dreams, hopes, and wishes with an element of the earth seemed natural.

Lightning snaked down the sky and struck the tower. Brianna was awed, yet not afraid. It was a sign. Good or bad? There was no answer. From whence came the sign? God? Devil? Mother? Drakkar? Large drops of rain prevented her imagination from taking flight. She ran to her chambers for shelter from the storm, but she had nowhere to run for shelter from her thoughts or her strange mood.

Adele had already left for the hall. Brianna knew she feared storms and was glad Adele had gone to join the queen's ladies for the evening meal where the music and the company would obliterate its noise. Brianna decided to stay put for the evening. The solitude of her chamber suited her. She would sketch, then perhaps paint. The subtle colors of Salome and the Bedfordshire stone challenged her artistic talent.

With a crisp russet apple in one hand and a piece of charcoal in the other, she sat down at her worktable and began to draw. She became absorbed in her work. The stone tower materialized, then the gerfalcon swooping from the crenellated stones to the outstretched arm of a knight. Her errant thoughts began to drift. Something was calling to her. Beyond the glow of the candles, the chamber was dark, shadowed. Something waited there, just beyond the light.

Or someone.

Suddenly lightning lit the room as if it were day and she saw that there was nothing there save her own private thoughts, floating in the stilly air. She could create a scene upon parchment so real she could feel the roughness of the stones, hear the swish of the raptor's wings, smell the leather of the knight's hauberk. Could she also create a living, breathing scene in this sanctuary into which she could step and, for a short time, become a part of?

The thought intrigued her, tempted her, slowly compelled her to try. From the back of her wardrobe she drew her mother's gray velvet cloak. She had not touched it since the tournament. She stood before the mirror, hesitating. The candles bathed half of her in their golden glow, the other half was shadowed, hidden, dark. She knew the folly she was about to commit was a thousandfold more reckless than reaching out to the gerfalcon.

To Brianna, however, it was irresistible.

She lifted her chin defiantly, and with a flourish, swirled the gray velvet about her shoulders. Everything shifted, then merged. She was in a tower chamber that was surrounded by a raging storm of heavy, deafening thunder and blue lightning. She was in the arms of a knight. His big hands roamed over her body, which was completely naked beneath the gray velvet cloak.

Though her flesh shrank at the intimate things he did, she arched against him temptingly. As the lightning flashed, she saw his aquamarine eyes dilate with desire and she reached up a slender arm to bring the blond head down to her seeking mouth. "Robert . . . husband . . ." she breathed against his lips, and felt his mouth go slack with need.

He was frantic to free himself of his clothes, to slide her silken flesh over his, to bury himself deep within her. The moment he was naked he again pulled her to his hard length. Her seductive hand slid down his massive chest, stroked across his belly, then closed about his jutting manhood.

A deep, harsh cry of pleasure-pain was torn from his throat and he slipped to his knees, his mouth sliding down her body until it came to rest upon her mons. She looked down at his face. His sensual lips had blood upon them. His aquamarine eyes were closed forever. She raised her eyes to those of her lover.

"I knew you could lure him up here." His voice was a dark intoxicant. She watched, mesmerized, as Drakkar withdrew his curved scimitar from Robert's body. Now indeed they shared a bond of blood. The thought that he had murdered his brother so he could have her made her delirious with joy. His dark, savage laughter engulfed her as he lifted her and carried her to the bed.

His power was drugging to her senses. She joined in his laughter as she saw the crimson drops of blood upon her white thighs, then she was snaking them about his iron-hard body, knowing that within minutes he would transform her laughter to screams of pleasure. Nothing mattered to either of them but their blinding, intoxicating, reckless passion.

Adele found her unconscious, lying atop the gray velvet cloak as she had once before. When Adele shook her shoulder, Brianna roused and pushed her tangled hair back from her face. She was so pale, even her lips looked bloodless.

"What happened, my lamb? Are ye ill?" Adele was most disturbed.

"No, no . . . a nightmare, I think," Brianna whispered, sinking into a chair.

Adele saw her eyes were wide with horror and thought Brianna was keeping something from her. "Sweet Mary, you're not with child?"

"Nay," Brianna said firmly, the very thought making her tremble.

Adele crossed herself, thanking the Holy Mother. "I'm going to fetch Glynis. 'Tis unnatural for a healthy young woman to faint. Mayhap she can mix you a herbal potion to strengthen you."

Though the hour was late, Glynis, carrying her herbal box, and Joan, too, came to Brianna's chambers, concern on their faces.

Brianna laughed shakily. "It was just a nightmare. It was so real, it frightened me, that's all."

Glynis took out a vial of distilled lily of the valley. "Put this in some wine for her," she bade Adele. "The atmosphere is strange tonight. The very air is charged with disturbing forces. Storms are often portents of things that come to pass."

"Aye, I'm terrified of the bloody things," Adele admitted. "I though it had ended, but I still hear it rumbling in the distance."

"What sort of things?" Joan asked, fascinated by Glynis' words.

"Good or evil, sometimes both. A storm before a great battle can change the outcome. Storms have changed the course of history!"

Joan tried for a lighter note. She did not wish to dwell on battles when her beloved prince was off fighting a war. "When one side wins, the other loses. It has little to do with storms."

Joan was not a deep thinker and Adele wished Brianna were more like her at this moment, for she could tell that Glynis' words were provoking disturbing thoughts.

"Dreams too can mirror the future, especially a dream at the time of a great storm."

Brianna shuddered uncontrollably. "Christ, I hope not! Mine was a nightmare, not a dream."

"Dreams are not literal, my lady. They are highly symbolic. They must be interpreted. Tell me what you dreamed and I will show you its meaning is entirely different from what you fear," urged Glynis.

"I . . . I cannot tell you. It was wicked, nay, it was evil," Brianna admitted, sipping the wine Glynis prescribed.

"Oh, do tell us!" Joan begged.

Glynis added, "By telling us, you will purge it from your mind. It will be cathartic. It will cleanse you, purify you."

Brianna wished to be free of it, but she should go to confession for absolution. She suddenly realized the subject was too intimate for the confessional booth. She looked at the faces about her. These were her only friends in the world, the only ones who cared about her. She knew whatever she told them would go no further. Even so, she could not bring herself to confess that she had deliberately tried to use the power of her mother's gray cloak to communicate with her lover. Without her realizing it, the lily of the valley loosened her tongue. "I . . . I was in a tower chamber built from Bedfordshire stone. Robert was with me." She blushed. "He was kissing me . . . I was returning his kisses."

She stopped. To give her time to pick and choose her words, she finished the cup of wine. "His half brother, Christian Hawksblood, stabbed and killed him."

Brianna heard Adele's indrawn breath.

"That's not the worst part. I was *happy* when he killed him. I saw blood on my thighs and I was *glad*!"

Joan's eyes were wide, her bottom lip caught in pretty white teeth as she listened to the dream.

Glynis asked, "Did the dream involve intercourse?"

Brianna's cheeks flamed as she recalled the passion of the mating. "Yes . . . that is, I was about to, but . . . but I think I fainted before . . . before . . ."

"My lady, it is clearly symbolic, as I thought. You were attracted to two brothers and so you dream of them. You felt guilt, so you dream of committing a terrible act that produces guilt. A tower of Bedfordshire stone is naturally your Castle of Bedford, which will go to your husband when you marry. You dreamed about one of them dying because they are both off to war and the fear is there with you every day. Even though you bury that fear, it surfaces in your dreams."

"What about the blood on her thighs and the intercourse?" Joan whispered.

"That is the core of the dream. That is what is deeply disturbing you, my lady. You fear there will be no blood on your thighs on your wedding night after you and Robert are intimate."

Brianna sat stunned. She had never given it a thought, but Splendor of God, what would Robert do when he discovered her no virgin? Brianna's hands covered her burning cheeks. "I've been so wanton," she said wretchedly.

Adele put her arm about her. "Tush! None of us are virgins here. Women have been duping men about maidenheads since the dawn of time."

Glynis nodded her head. "It only happened recently. You will still be very small. He may not be able to tell, especially if he drinks deep at the wedding."

"Prick your finger with a rose thorn or your brooch and put some drops of blood on the sheet," Joan suggested. "There isn't a man breathing can compete with a woman when it comes to being devious," she added with pride.

Adele went down before Brianna. "I don't want you worrying yourself sick about this. 'Tis a trifle! Thank Heaven above that your courses have started and you are not with child. Now *that* would be something to worry about, my lamb."

Joan's lovely brows drew together. Now that she thought about it, it seemed a long time since she had bled. She pushed the frightening thought away and jumped up. "In the morning when the sun comes up, it will banish all tonight's darklings. The storm will pass, tomorrow will be a glorious day, and we'll all live happily ever after."

The four young women smiled at each other as they said their good nights, but alone in their beds later, Joan and Brianna lay wide awake, each far more worried than she had been earlier.

Across the Channel in Crécy, France, the King of England, his marshals, and most of his captains and nobles also lay awake. Some had a fatalistic attitude, knowing they were badly outnumbered, and offered up prayers before they met their Maker.

Both the king's son and Warrick's son, however, believed they would win the day. They arose at five in the morning. Hawksblood and Prince Edward's squire, John Chandos, helped the prince don his armor. He insisted upon wearing his distinctive black chain mail and to go over it he chose a crimson and gold surcoat.

His squire protested, "Your Highness, you will stand out from the others. Every Frenchman will know you on sight and all will lust to take the son of the King of England, dead or alive!"

Prince Edward insisted, "I *wish* to be recognized! I would despise myself if I feared to be known."

Hawksblood knew the extent of Edward's towering pride, for he himself had been blessed, or cursed, with the same self-esteem. The Black Prince went to join the king and the moment he left the tent, Hawksblood too donned black chain mail.

The king wore an equally brilliant azure and gold surcoat and together with his son, mounted on white horses, rode before the assembling ranks. He noted with satisfaction his green-jacketed archers in the front had kept their bows in their cases to keep them dry. Their faces were wreathed with assured smiles, for they, more than any in Edward's army, knew their deadly power.

In the right division he placed Harcourt, the Black Prince, Warrick and his sons, along with his very best English knights. Under Northampton, a second battalion of two thousand archers and two thousand men-at-arms formed the left flank, covering the ridge. The king himself commanded a third battalion of equal strength, which could be dispatched swiftly to any part of the battlefield where they were needed.

King Edward raised his voice. "The French must travel eighteen miles around yon forest. They will come upon us abruptly and become involved in the conflict before they are ready to fight. There is no room for them to form a battle line."

A great cheer went up.

King Edward raised his arms and continued, "The larger the French force, the greater their difficulty!"

Another cheer, louder than the first, arose.

"Never forget that *one* Englishman is worth *three* Frenchmen!"

The men cheered until they were hoarse. Cries of "Edward and St. George" and "Edward, *fils du roi*" were deafening, but heartening. Rain began to fall, but none seemed to even notice. King Edward's flashing smile came to rest upon his son. Suddenly he looked uneasy that the Black Prince was such a recognizable target.

Young Edward ground out, "I care not who comes to me. I'll give a damn good account of myself. Just remember your promise to me!"

The king grinned broadly. "May the honor of this day be yours!"

The English army heard mass and waited.

At midday, the spotted the enemy. The sky was black,

lightning forked the sky, and the rain teemed down. Genoese crossbowmen, weary after tramping eighteen miles
through the storm with their heavy equipment, were reluctant to fight that day. The French high command called
them Italian scum and scurvy cowards, and the French cavalry forced them across the wet fields until they were in
range of the English and Welsh longbows.

Suddenly the rain ceased, the clouds parted, and the sun
came out, shining in the faces of the French. As if conjured
by a sorcerer's hand, a flock of black crows rose up and flew
cawing over the heads of the French.

It was an omen!

Suddenly, the goose feathers on the English arrows
made it seem like a snowstorm had replaced the rain. The
breastplates of the Genoese bowmen were no protection
against the violent power of arrows propelled from longbows. In minutes their ranks were decimated. They turned
and fled through the knights behind them.

"Kill me these cowardly rogues," cried the King of
France.

The English were treated to the ghastly spectacle of
mounted cavalry destroying their own men with no mercy
or concern!

Philip was in a black rage because he had seen the English flag quartered with the lilies of France. He threw caution to the wind and disorder reigned. The French rode
onto the plain and up a slope, not only clogged by dead
men and horses but slippery with their blood. The road was
narrow, like a ramp to a slaughterhouse.

They came, they charged, they died!

But they came in such great numbers, the battle raged on
all afternoon. Finally, the furiously attacking French broke
through the archers and engaged the English right division.
Suddenly, the men fighting about the Black Prince were
surrounded.

For Hawksblood everything slowed so that he could focus his concentration upon every danger that threatened
him. He knew exactly where to plunge his sword into three
vital places unprotected by armor: the throat, the gut, and
beneath the raised arm. He gave no thought to his back, for

he knew Paddy and Ali protected it well. He clearly saw half a dozen French ride toward the Black Prince.

He knew John Chandos was at Edward's back, and saw that his brother, Robert de Beauchamp, was beside the prince. Both the prince and Robert would likely die if he did not cut off the Frenchmen's advance. He swerved his destrier directly into their path. He slew two and knew that Paddy and Ali slew two more. The other two French cavalrymen escaped by changing direction.

A great cry went up behind him and Hawksblood turned in the saddle to see Prince Edward go down. How could that be? It made no sense! Hawksblood was out of the saddle in a flash. He stood over his friend's body as it lay in the mud, raised broadsword in one hand, battle ax in the other. For one moment he rued the decision to wear black armor identical to Edward's, for he knew what a target he made, but he firmly set aside regret so that he could glory in becoming the target. He attracted so many of the enemy, there was a sea of blood about him before he was done.

It was a great excuse for Robert de Beauchamp and Sir John Holland to retreat to safer ground. They rode straight to the king. "The Prince of Wales is sorely pressed, Your Highness." De Beauchamp hoped he was dead, but by seeking aid for the downed prince, he would avoid all suspicion of having a hand in it.

The king looked at Warrick's son, whom he had knighted beside his own son that first day. Fear gripped the king's throat. Surely Fate would not take his son's life this day, yet spare Warrick's son. "Is he wounded?" demanded the king.

"I know not, Your Highness," swore De Beauchamp.

Holland had seen him put his sword into the prince's horse so he would go down, but kept his mouth shut.

King Edward was ready to dig in his spurs to gallop to his son's rescue. Then he remembered his promise. He did not ever want it said that Prince Edward would have failed if his father had not saved him. "I want him to win his spurs. You, too, must have a chance to acquit yourselves. Go back and aid him!" He was well pleased with these valiant young knights of his.

Hawksblood glanced anxiously to see if any of the blood gushed from Edward. He almost staggered with relief as he saw all the blood upon the Black Prince had come from the mortal wounds of his horse. The prince had merely been stunned in the fall. Now he got to his feet. He had dislocated his left shoulder when his horse fell on him, but he ignored the pain. John Chandos rode to him with a horse, as did Paddy for Hawksblood. The two knights in black mail mounted, grinning from ear to ear, then flung themselves into the thick of the fighting. A picture came full-blown into Christian's mind of Prince Lionel killing his opponent's horse in the tournament. He had no proof that Robert had copied Lionel, thrusting his sword into Edward's horse, only the suspicion of his sixth sense. He tucked it away for future use and got on with the slaughter.

❧ 25 ❧

Joan of Kent almost went out of her mind with worry that twenty-sixth day of August. When she arose at dawn, she calculated when her menses should have started and realized that she was almost two months late. She had never once been late in five years, not since the onset of her womanhood at twelve. She had no doubt whatsoever that she was enceinte; her doubts all centered about what she must do about it. She was racked with indecision.

There was only one person on earth she wanted to confide in, but her beloved Edward was across the sea in France, fighting a war. All her thoughts winged to him across the miles, begging him to return to her, begging him to send her an answer to her dilemma. Trying to commune with Edward made matters worse. Suddenly she began to worry about his safety. What if he was killed in battle? The thought was unendurable. If Edward didn't return to her, she would not want to live either. The morbid thoughts engulfed her. If he died, it would solve the problem of the baby. She would kill herself and the child inside her!

Suddenly Joan began to cry. Then she began to pray. She jumped up and dashed the tears from her face. God was much more likely to listen to her if she went to Windsor's chapel. She grabbed a head veil, for once not caring if its color enhanced her delicate beauty or matched her pretty gown.

In the chapel, Joan was surprised to see Queen Philippa and half the noble ladies of the Court. She felt ashamed of herself when she learned that they came every day to pray for victory for England and for the safety of King Edward, the Prince of Wales, and all the valiant men who had accompanied them to France. This was the first time she had attended mass, but she promised it would not be her last.

Joan's cheeks burned hotly as she thought what would happen if they knew the secret she carried. Women were so cruel, especially to one of their own sex who had fallen from grace. The gossipmongers would have a heyday. She already had a reputation for flirtatiousness which she knew she had earned, but she paled to think of what would happen if they scented that she was in trouble. They would descend upon her like a pack of ravenous hounds and rend her to bits.

She sank to her knees and began to pray in earnest. It was to her great credit that she prayed for Edward's safety and her brother's for a full thirty minutes before she moved on to her own plight. Like most of her sex, Joan made extravagant promises that she would never again ask for divine help if only the angels would aid her this once. She did not dare to presume to ask for anything specific, like Edward's marrying her, she only asked that all would turn out well in the end.

After the service she went back to her chambers. She had no intention of attending Dame Marjorie Daw's incessant lecture today. It wasn't so much Dragonface she wished to avoid, it was Princess Isabel's malicious company. The spoiled princess had listened to whispers about Lady Elizabeth Grey and she had withdrawn her friendship immediately, treating her like a leper.

Joan's burden of worry seemed no lighter after her attendance at mass. She spent the next three hours contemplating abortion. She would have to confide in Glynis, of course, because she herself had no idea what to take or what dosage was safe, if any. To rid herself of the pregnancy would be the simplest solution. That way she wouldn't have to burden Edward with the problem.

However, abortifacients were highly dangerous. Many women died trying to rid themselves of an unwanted child. If she was being truthful, this baby was not unwanted. It thrilled her to think she carried Edward's baby beneath her heart. He would have royal blood. How could she destroy the child of a prince? She knew it was wrong to destroy any child, but it seemed doubly wrong to destroy this one. Still, she was prepared to do whatever was necessary to save Edward worries.

If only he would return to Windsor, her problem would be solved. She realized all her worrying, praying, thinking, and plotting had carried her in a circle and she was back where she had begun at dawn, wishing for Prince Edward's return. Then a frightening thought intruded itself. What if he didn't return for a year? She would have to leave Court before she began to show. Where would she go?

Her brother's town house on Fish Street was not nearly far enough away from Windsor. She would have to go to the family castle in Kent. She couldn't even picture it. She had been a baby when she left there. Her brother had also inherited Wake Castle in Liddell, wherever that might be. She pushed the thought away. She could not bear to live remote from Prince Edward.

Her heart ached with loneliness. If only she hadn't destroyed all his love letters. Remembering his words brought her a small measure of comfort, but if she had them to press to her lips and press to her heart, she was sure it would take away the ache. Joan felt utterly isolated and alone. She sat inert, unable to make a decision for herself.

Glynis had been busy in the laundry all day. She had decided to take advantage of the beautiful sunny day to wash everything in Lady Kent's wardrobe before the cold winds of autumn made such chores unpleasant. Adele joined her and they decided to wash all the bed linen and heavy coverlets as well.

Brianna missed Joan at the midday meal and again at the afternoon session with the princess and Dame Marjorie. Before she went down to the hall for the evening, she went along to Joan's chambers. She found her friend sitting in the twilight gloom alone.

"Where have you been all day?" Brianna asked with concern.

"I don't remember," Joan said vaguely. "I went to the chapel this morning. Did you know that the queen and most of the Court ladies attend mass every day to pray for victory for the king and for their men's safety?"

"No, I didn't realize. I've been avoiding mass, I suppose. At one point I almost went to confession to unburden myself, but realized I couldn't expose my shameful secrets. The walls have ears, even the walls of the confessional."

"Oh, you mustn't breathe a word to the priests. Only think of poor Elizabeth Grey and how she's being ostracized!"

"Let's go to the hall," Brianna urged.

"Oh, you go without me. I don't much feel like company."

This was so unlike Joan that Brianna knew there was something wrong. Her friend wasn't given to introspection, preferring to indulge in mischief. "I'm not leaving you here alone to sit and brood. You are missing Prince Edward and you need company at the moment."

All through the meal Brianna could see that Joan's spirits slumped. She did not press her, knowing when she was ready to share her troubles, she would confide in Brianna. Sooner or later she always did. The meal dragged to a close, they walked back to their chambers in silence, but when Brianna bade Joan good night, Joan took her hand in supplication. "May I stay with you tonight?" she asked breathlessly.

"Joan, of course you may! I don't fancy being alone either."

Brianna pulled the heavy drapes across the window and barred the door. She tossed some big pillows onto the rug, poured them each a cup of mead and set out a plate of marchpane, knowing her friend's weakness for sweet comfits.

Joan gave her a misty half-smile as she nibbled the almond-flavored sweet. In a small, whispery voice she said, "Do you think Elizabeth Grey did the right thing?"

"Well, poor Elizabeth's situation was dreadful. She knew marriage to Prince Lionel was out of the question and she knew if she bore the child, her chance for any marriage was ruined, so I think she did make the right choice." Silence stretched between them. Then Brianna added softly, "I couldn't have done it though."

Joan began to cry.

"Oh, love, what's wrong?" The moment the words were out of her mouth, it dawned upon her that Joan was with child. "Oh Lord, you've been caught." Brianna sank down on the cushions and took Joan's hands. "Promise me that you won't do anything foolish!"

"Such as?" Joan asked, her eyes full of misery, her cheeks wet with tears.

Such as kill yourself, Brianna thought silently. "You mustn't abort yourself . . . it's so very dangerous."

"I know," Joan whispered.

"When I said Elizabeth did the right thing, I meant it was the right thing for her. It would be absolutely the *wrong* choice for you. Prince Edward and you love each other. He would never forgive you if you destroyed his child." Brianna had Joan's full attention now. "Edward will be home from France soon. When he learns of the child, I'm sure he'll find some way to marry you."

Joan wiped away her tears.

"For goodness' sake don't confide in anyone but me. Things usually have a way of working themselves out. Remember, *when in doubt, do nothing!*"

Joan nodded solemnly, trustingly.

Brianna cursed herself for mouthing platitudes, but her immediate concern was Joan's state of mind. At least she had managed to calm some of her fears and stop her crying. "What you need is a good night's rest. Things always look brighter in the morning." As Brianna bustled about, readying the bed, she hoped her tongue wouldn't wither from her lies.

Before the night candle burned itself out, Brianna saw that Joan slept peacefully now she had unburdened herself. She, however, lay wide awake, not only uneasy about her own situation, but desperately worried about Joan's plight.

*   *   *

The plight of the French in Crécy became more desperate by the hour. They were defeated, but their leaders refused to concede victory. Throughout the afternoon the French army continued to arrive piecemeal, and was cut down by arrows to the throat or sword thrusts to the gut. As dark began to fall the French king still shouted orders but his marshals had long since fallen.

When all the light was fully gone, Christian Hawksblood called all his Cornishmen, trained in the use of long-knives, to him. On foot they moved unhesitatingly into the French lines. Hawksblood's first target was the French royal standard-bearer. He dispatched him quickly and tore the red oriflamme from its staff. Then they proceeded to decimate what was left of the French army, executing every moving thing they came across with their long-knives until not one French knight was left on that fateful road from Abbeville.

When Hawksblood returned, he was moved to see every Englishman on his knees, offering thanks for their miraculous victory. Prince Edward's surcoat was no longer crimson, but black with mud. King Edward embraced his son with joy. "You have acquitted yourself well this day." Then he raised his voice so all could hear. "You are worthy to be the future King of England."

A great cheer went up.

The Black Prince replied, "I owe my life to many, especially this man." He indicated Christian Hawksblood.

Another cheer arose.

"*All* men contributed to the victory of Crécy!"

The English were exultant because they had won against all odds.

The king spoke again. "As long as men shall live, they will speak of Crécy!"

After that, it was impossible to be heard over the jubilant cheering.

The prince and Hawksblood immediately set about counting their losses and aiding their wounded before they ever thought of themselves. Hundreds of wounds needed to be stanched, broken bones set and torn flesh stitched back together, but miraculously most of their men were accounted for.

Hawksblood sought out his half brother. His blood was

still high from battle. "I suspect it was your sword that felled Edward's horse!"

Robert opened his mouth to protest.

"Don't bother with denials, we'll call it an accident this time. But let me warn you, Robert, if aught untoward befalls Edward, I shall seek you out and destroy you!"

Robert was almost consumed with the hatred he felt for the foreign bastard. At the first opportunity that presented itself he would rid himself of the usurper.

Christian Hawksblood and Edward Plantagenet shared a campaign tent. They had washed the blood and grime from their bodies in the river, then Ali had given them each a massage with oil of almond and frankincense. The Black Prince's courage impressed Hawksblood's squire when he discovered Edward had been fighting with a dislocated left shoulder. The pain had been excruciating, but thanks to his friend's teaching, he was learning to separate himself from pain.

Both had received cuts to their faces and torsos and Edward watched with curiosity as Ali applied plain sugar to Hawksblood's superficial wounds.

"It prevents scarring, but perhaps you wish to display your scars, Your Highness."

"Hell no, Ali. My lady is a most delicate female. I don't wish to frighten her. By all means, pass the sugar."

They wrapped themselves in their cloaks and lay down on the hard earth to rest. It had been an unbelievable day. Prince Edward knew it would be the most unforgettable day of his life. Before the battle, anticipation and fear had made his blood rush through his veins, filling him with a bursting energy that needed an outlet. When he joined the battle, he had enough zeal to carry him through for hours. When his horse went down, almost on top of him, stunning him, he realized how tenuous the breath of life was within him. It could be snuffed in an instant. To rise and fight with the agonizing pain of a dislocated shoulder had called up the years of discipline and training he had endured. Again he was filled with a divine power that transcended the fear and fatigue.

He fought on long after his sword arm was numb, long after his mind was blank from the horror of blood, maim-ing, and killing. His nose became immune to the stench of death and his ears deaf to the screams of agony from both men and warhorses. He fought on until he had expended every last ounce of strength, every last gasp of breath. But the miracle of victory had sent the blood rushing back to the brain, banishing the total exhaustion that had made his limbs so heavy that he was almost inert. He felt like a vessel that had been emptied, but was now refilled. He felt energy surge back into him, replenishing him a hundredfold.

Both Christian and Edward lay upon the ground physically tired, muscles relaxed from the oiled massage, but their minds darted about with mercurial speed. Both knew sleep was a million miles away. Their throats became hoarse as they talked themselves out.

Hawksblood questioned Edward about his fall. "Do you think it possible there was deliberate treachery?"

"I saw no treachery; sensed none. John Holland rode beside me. I've just made him Steward of the Royal Household. He's too ambitious to do me harm," Edward said, laughing.

"And your other side?" prompted Christian.

"Why, I was flanked by your brother, Robert. Warrick would have his balls if he did aught that smacked of treason."

"Aye," Christian agreed. "I'm beginning to believe my sire an honorable man. I'll reserve judgment on my brother, however."

"None of us can choose our brothers," Edward said regretfully. He knew exactly whom he would have picked for brother if the choice had been his, and hoped Christian was of like mind.

They fell to silence, each man filled with thoughts of his beloved. Edward vowed that if his sojourn in France was to be a long one, he would find some way to get his little Jeanette across the Channel. He needed her sweetness, her soft femininity, to balance the stark realities of being a military leader. He had been trained to be an iron man for his men-at-arms to look to. He was expected to perform like a well-oiled military machine. But when the battle was over and darkness fell, he needed surcease, and wanted it from none but Joan of Kent.

Christian Hawksblood became introspective. It happened more and more of late. He knew he could escape into an erotic fantasy that would blot out the horrors of carnage, but his fantasies had undergone a drastic change. His dreams were of a home of his own, a family of his making. He had wandered rudderless about the world long enough. He wanted to put down roots, needed the anchor of a mate, longed to surround himself with sons and daughters. The warmth and intimacy of a family of his own was the thing he now lusted for.

He thought of Warrick. For the first time he was glad Guy de Beauchamp was his father. It was good to share command, good to have a bond of blood with someone who cared whether you lived or died.

Finally, he allowed himself to contemplate Brianna. Robert had extracted a promise of marriage from her by manipulating her compassionate nature. How contemptible to have to be pitied to gain one's ends. Hawksblood intended to have her, no matter the cost. He and Robert knew they were rivals, and though the battle lines had not yet been drawn, Christian knew the confrontation was coming. He had not pressed matters because every instinct told him that when the clash came, the result might be total annihilation. The fatal outcome could blow the tenuous truce and fledgling relationship between him and Warrick to smithereens.

He pushed the sibling antagonism away, cleansing his mind of Robert before he concentrated upon his lady. He saw her in all her beauty, missed no detail of her loveliness. Then he focused, and whispered, "Come to me."

Brianna curled over in the bed with her back to Joan, finally luring Morpheus to carry her off. *The place was Bedford; the mood, utter contentment. She was in the castle garden with three children.*

Her children. Two sturdy sons and a droll little daughter. Their excitement level was high because they anticipated the return of their father today. Her own excitement matched theirs. Nay, it surpassed theirs if she was being truthful. Her husband was the center of her life. The sun, the life-force about whom they all gravitated.

Though she would allow the children to run to him first, to claim his attention, she knew when he arrived she would have to stop herself from dashing to him and flinging herself upon him. She savored the anticipation of the moment his eyes would seek hers over the heads of their children. Aquamarine eyes! He would make love to her with those eyes and it would suffice until they were locked in their own chamber.

Sweet Mary, he was home! She flung back her hair and picked up her skirts, unable to keep from running to his arms.

"Brianna! Brianna, wherever are you going?" Joan inquired urgently.

Brianna turned, slightly confused. She looked at Joan sitting up in the bed, a look of deep concern upon her face. "I . . . I don't know where I was going," Brianna confessed. "Mayhap I was sleepwalking."

She came back to the bed and slipped beneath the covers. Slowly, her dream came back to her. How happy she had been, surrounded by her beautiful family. She hoped with all her heart that she would have the children she had dreamed about. In a way she envied Joan her baby. With a child of her own, Brianna knew she would never be lonely again. Then the rest of her dream came flooding back.

She squeezed her eyes together tightly. Ah, God, her sons had had jet-black hair and she knew to whom her feet had wanted to run so willingly. Brianna knew she could not control her dreams, but nevertheless she suddenly felt terrible guilt. She must stop herself from thinking of him, dreaming of him! She honestly wanted to be a dutiful wife to Robert de Beauchamp. She must purge herself of the Arabian Knight!

26

When the day after the Battle of Crécy dawned, the king and his nobles took a staff of heralds to examine the bloodstained field. Though it seemed hard to believe, the King of Bohemia, ten princes, and the Count of Alençon lay dead. Philip's nephew, the Earl of Blois, and his brother-in-law, the Duke of Lorraine, were also among those slain. The Count of Flanders, who was supposed to be England's ally, had paid the price for changing his coat. In all, the English had killed more than a thousand knights and thirty thousand soldiers, while suffering the loss of only a few hundred.

Philip of Valois escaped, but his fleet had been destroyed and now his army had been vanquished by the English. No French monarch had ever been so humiliated. Philip's son, John, in charge of the army in the southern provinces, arrived too late to aid his father in battle. When he learned they had been defeated by a force smaller than a quarter the size of the French army, he was disgusted with his father's leadership.

He had more than one grievance to air. Sir Walter Manny's small force had been captured, but Prince John, an honorable leader, had given his word that Manny would have safe conduct so he could rejoin the English army. John was furious that his promise had been dishonored and Manny was still being held in close confinement at Orléans under terrible conditions. He refused to strike another blow in the French cause until Philip released the English knight. Sir Walter Manny was released immediately along with that other important hostage, William de Montecute, Earl of Salisbury.

King Edward and Warrick held a strategy meeting where it was decided to lay siege to Calais. They knew the advantage they would have if they established a bridgehead on French soil for future operations.

Calais held fast. It was impregnable and could be brought down only by starvation. Within weeks, King Edward's army built a small town of comfortable wooden buildings with a marketplace at its center that sold food and clothing from England. The ships going the other way were loaded with spoils. The lowliest soldier's wife sported jewelry and set her table with silver cups, while the nobles' castles were filled with rare objects and their stables with blooded horses.

Behind this town that grew up were miles of marshland. The beleaguered citizens of Calais saw the fires of the reduced French army beyond the marshes, but despaired of

them coming to their aid. Every road and bridge was
guarded by English bowmen and the French had had
enough of such bitter medicine.

The queen, surrounded by her ladies-in-waiting, the
princesses, and her younger children's nursemaids was
reading aloud King Edward's latest letter.

My Dearest Philippa:
*We have had Calais under siege for three weeks, yet they
show no sign of capitulating. Our position is unassailable.
It would take a leader with more resolution than Philip of
Valois to bring his army across the marshes. I believe he
and his troops are about to depart for Amiens with their
tails between their legs.*

*I am determined to take Calais, which is a scant twenty-
two miles from Dover. This port has been a hotbed of
piracy long enough and I am determined it will send out no
more ships to prey on English commerce. Already an English town has sprung up outside the walls of the city and
we are quartered most comfortably.*

*I am pleased to be able to report that your own knight,
Sir Walter Manny, has been released along with my good
friend, William de Montecute. I had the honor to knight his
son and Warrick's, and of course our own beloved son,
Edward, for bravery on the field. I have knighted so many
of my valiant warriors, I will have a difficult time choosing
those who will be included in the new Order of Chivalry.*

*My dearest Philippa, if you are in accordance, I would
like to betroth our precious daughter Princess Isabel to
Louis, the new Count of Flanders. He is a handsome youth
of an age with Isabel, and this union will cement our alliance with the Low Countries.*

*I want you to begin preparations to come to France for
the betrothal ceremony. The moment Calais falls, I will
send word. When my beloved family arrives, we will enjoy a
magnificent celebration.*

*Edward Plantagenet, Your Faithful Husband
and Devoted Father*

Philippa looked up from the letter to see Isabel's mouth looking most sulky.

"This Louis is only a count?" she asked. "I always thought I would marry a king!"

Queen Philippa was taken aback. "Darling, there are no kings available, save France, our mortal enemy. Since his father was killed at Crécy, Louis, as the new count, will rule Flanders like a monarch. Remember, Isabel, Flanders is a wealthy country and your father says he is a handsome ruler."

The queen's ladies were quite excited at the news of Princess Isabel's betrothal and that they were to make preparations to move the Court to France. Isabel suddenly began to enjoy all the attention she was receiving. "I want rich India silk for my wedding gown." She cast an envious look at Joan of Kent's dress. "I want it trimmed with ermine and embroidered with *real* gold thread!"

Joan caught her breath. She would go with the queen and princess to France! She would be with Prince Edward very soon; the moment Calais fell. Joan and Brianna had spent the day in the royal nursery because they were well aware they lacked experience with children. Now they became caught up in preparations for the move to France. Though the queen and her ladies regularly visited Ghent, Hainault, and Bordeaux, this would be the first visit for Princess Isabel and her ladies.

When they returned to Joan's chambers, she could conceal her joy no longer. "Brianna, my prayers have been answered! Edward will take care of everything. Oh, it's as if a huge millstone has been lifted from my chest."

Brianna squeezed Joan's hands. She, too, was caught up in the adventure of the sea voyage and the opportunity to visit France. She had received a letter from her betrothed that made her realize how fortunate she was. Poor Elizabeth Grey grew thinner by the week and despaired of ever finding a husband.

"You are so brave and honorable to do your duty and marry Robert. How can you bear to put aside your love for Christian?" Joan asked.

"I cannot put it aside, it is with me every moment."

Joan, sorry she had asked, tried to cheer her. "Just think,

you'll be married in France, just like Princess Isabel. We must design you a wedding gown that will put Isabel's in the shade. I can't wait to see the look on Glynis' and Adele's faces when they learn they're going to France!"

Brianna knew both young women would be over the moon knowing they would be united with Paddy and Ali. With marriage in the very air, perhaps it would be contagious. She made no comment, however. How could Joan pretend her troubles were over? The prospect of seeing Edward had erased all her worries, but Brianna knew her problems would not be solved but would be compounded when the heir to the throne learned of Joan's plight.

Brianna sighed and vowed to help her as much as she could. When she returned to her own chambers, she took out Robert's letter and reread it.

My Dearest Brianna:

I am proud to inform you that King Edward knighted me for loyal and brave service to him the first day we set foot on French soil. I hope to be included in the new Order of Chivalry, which will emulate King Arthur's Round Table.

Think how proud we will be that the Edward III Tower is built from our own Bedford stone.

I have acquitted myself well commanding Prince Lionel's men. Under my direction they have taken many prizes of war. The lion's share, of course, will go the House of Clarence, but there is so much booty, I shall profit handsomely in the way of silver plate and blooded horses. I have reserved a jeweled cap for your wedding present to complement your golden hair, which is without doubt the loveliest I have ever seen.

I am impatient to be wed and dare to hope that you feel the same.

Yours in Love and Truth, Robert de Beauchamp

Brianna refolded the parchment. It was a very nice letter. He had gone to considerable effort to find a scribe to set his feelings down for her. She was proud that he had earned his spurs and achieved knighthood. It sounded as if he missed her and loved her, and that she was foremost in his thoughts. She was indeed blessed by such devotion.

* * *

King Edward welcomed William de Montecute, Earl of Salisbury, with genuine affection. Their friendship went back a long way. It had been William who had helped him set a trap for the hated Mortimer, his mother's paramour and murderer of his father.

It was only days, however, before the king had cause to regret his friend's release. He received an urgent message that King David of Scotland had marched across the English border with an invasion force of fifteen thousand men.

When De Montecute learned of it, he was incensed. "You should never have given them back the Earl of Moray in exchange for me! Keeping him locked away was England's only safeguard, Sire."

"By Christ's holy blood, I've just defeated an army of a hundred thousand strong, think you I'll lose sleep over fifteen thousand?"

"I'm responsible," Montecute insisted. "Turn me loose on the bastards!"

The king grinned. "We'll go together. It will be like old times. The Scots believe all our fighting men are here in France, but they are in for a rude awakening. York has a few thousand under his command and so do my lords of the North, Neville and Percy."

"What about the siege of Calais, Sire?" asked De Montecute.

"I have the best marshal on earth. Warrick can take charge. By the time we return from defeating the Scots, these French fools will have eaten all the horses and dogs in Calais and will be catching rats to survive!"

At a hastily summoned war council it was decided who would make the quick trip across the Channel, and who would remain with the siege of Calais. Prince Edward was so eager to fight the Scots, his father agreed he could chose some of his best lieutenants and join him and the Earl of Salisbury.

Warrick spoke up. "We need more ships to blockade the Channel and prevent the French from revictualing Calais."

"I'll send all the vessels we have available in the Cinque Ports," Edward promised.

"I'll put Northampton and Pembroke in charge of the

fleet. By the time you return, Sire, this city will be yours," Warrick pledged.

Young William de Montecute was torn. Since his father was returning to England, it was only fitting that he stay behind to fight the goddamn French, whom he hated with a vengeance, but he was most unhappy that Prince Edward was taking John Holland back with him. It would give the new Steward of the Royal Household the advantage over him where Lady Joan of Kent was concerned. However, it wouldn't be long before she was on her way here with Princess Isabel, who was coming for her betrothal to Louis, Count of Flanders. De Montecute vowed that if the Pope ruled in his favor, he would wed Joan immediately.

Queen Philippa was vastly relieved when she received the hastily scribbled note from her husband telling her he was on his way home to deal with the Scots. That good lady had been doing what she could to gather reinforcements for Edward. Now those soldiers could aid him against Scotland before they sailed to France. As had become her custom, she read the king's letter to the ladies of Windsor.

My Dearest Philippa:
Edward and I are returning immediately to deal with David Bruce of Scotland. Warrick's son is with us as well as Salisbury, who has been released from captivity, no worse for wear, thank God. I pray you have no fear, my love. We will soon rout the barbarians back across the border.
Edward Plantagenet

Three ladies' hearts turned over in their breasts. Joan closed her eyes and offered up a prayer of thanks. Her beloved prince was on his way to Windsor.

Katherine de Montecute was weak with relief. Her husband, William, had been released from captivity, all in one piece, and was on his way home to her.

Brianna felt caught between the devil and the deep. *Which of Warrick's sons is returning?* she wondered with alarm. If it was Robert, she had best prepare herself for marriage. His letter had stated plainly that he was impatient to be wed. But if it was Christian Hawksblood, she had best put up her guard against his power. She must

never fall from grace again. His very presence was dangerous; he could mesmerize, hypnotize, lure, and entice her to
commit folly with his irresistible, magnetic attraction. Her
only hope was to avoid him like the plague.

When the king and his party arrived in Dover, they did
so in secrecy, disembarking at night and riding straight to
Windsor. This was not done because of the Scots' invasion,
it was done to avoid cheering crowds gathering to welcome
the victors home.

Time was precious. They would sleep at Windsor one
night only, then with fresh mounts be on their way to the
great northern city of York. They came so swiftly, they arrived one day after the king's letter, surprising the queen
and her ladies at the evening meal.

King Edward strode to Philippa and kissed her heartily
before the entire household. There was not one lady in the
hall who was immune to her king's virile charm. Now he
shared the limelight equally with his broad-shouldered son,
Prince Edward. They had returned as conquering heroes,
and tomorrow they would be on their way to vanquish the
Scots. Many a lady thought she might swoon at the sight of
them.

Joan was gripped by such overwhelming emotions when
she saw Edward, she feared she might faint. When their
eyes met, he saw that her pretty cheeks were wet with tears
and his heart twisted that he should cause her anguish.

Katherine de Montecute wept openly when her husband,
William, swept her up in strong arms. He had been fighting
in France for the better part of two years and she could not
believe he had come home to her at last. Because he would
be leaving her again almost immediately, they slipped from
the Banqueting Hall with no thought of any but their two
selves.

Brianna fiercely told herself she was disappointed that it
was Hawksblood who had returned rather than Robert, but
what she felt was closer to relief. In truth, she was not quite
ready to marry, but assured herself she would be by the
time she traveled to France. She knew she should quit the
hall before there could be any exchange between herself
and Hawksblood, for when they were under the same roof,
his powerful presence was so compelling, she could actually

feel herself being drawn to him. When the king's minstrel began to pluck his lute, she left the table intending to slip out the closest exit.

Christian Hawksblood was acutely aware of Brianna's every move, every thought. When she reached the vaulted archway, he was there before her, blocking her way. One hand went out to stop him from coming closer, the other covered her heart as if to protect it from him. "Please, let me pass. You know there can be nothing more between us."

"Do not delude yourself, Brianna," he said quietly.

"Don't work your powers on me!" she cried desperately.

His eyes were like brilliant chips of aquamarine. *Ah, lady, 'tis you who have the power. You have enchanted me.* His body quickened at her closeness. His blood surged and throbbed in his groin. He clenched his fists at his sides to keep from snatching her up and abducting her. Years of being in control of himself came to his rescue.

"What do you want?" she cried.

Everything!

"Nothing," he replied softly. "I am merely a messenger. Prince Edward would like Joan of Kent to meet him in the new Round Tower, at the top of the steps. If you would be kind enough to convey the message, His Highness will be forever in your debt, Lady Bedford."

Color rose to her cheeks. He only sought her out at the request of the prince! She curtsied formally and her lashes brushed her cheeks as she murmured, "I shall inform the lady." When she raised her lashes, he was gone. Brianna went back into the hall to seek her friend.

Joan was breathless by the time she climbed the one hundred steps in the newly built tower, but it wasn't entirely from exertion. When Prince Edward stepped from the shadows and held out his arms, she went into them with a little cry of joy.

"Sweet, sweet," he murmured against her hair. She raised her face to him, needing the feel of his firm mouth on hers, needing the feel of his powerful arms about her, the feel of his strong, hard body against her small one. "We only have till dawn," he said thickly.

Suddenly she felt too shy to reveal her secret to him. Their time together would be so brief, how could she spoil it by burdening him with her problem?

He drew her deeper into the tower room where the magnificently carved round table that the king had commissioned for his Arthurian Order of Chivalry stood. Though it was lit only by moonlight at the moment, its great beauty was a thing to behold. Without hesitation Edward lifted Joan by the waist until she stood upon the table, her beloved face just above his. Her silvery hair fell about his throat and shoulders as she looked down at him in awe. "I mustn't stand on the table, Edward. Won't that desecrate it?"

He laughed deep in his throat, too hot to care about a mere table. "We are going to do more than stand on it, we're going to lie upon it. We won't desecrate it, we'll anoint it . . . with love!"

The hallowed table in the tower added spice to their lovemaking. When Joan lay naked, it seemed they performed a sacrificial ritual upon a sacred altar. He adored the way she had of clinging to him, making him feel omnipotent. She seemed so delicately fragile, he silently vowed to always be gentle with her. In truth, with his little Jeanette, he always felt more love than lust. When they had slaked their first great thirst for each other, he cradled her against his heart and stroked her hair.

"When I return from Scotland, I'll take you to France. You were planning to accompany Isabel for her betrothal, weren't you?"

"Of course. Coming to you in France was all I could think of."

He bent his lips to touch the rosebud tips of her breasts and they bloomed in his mouth.

"You are my own perfect knight with golden spurs." She sighed with her deep love and pride.

"And you are my own perfect princess with golden tresses."

Suddenly, the call of a night heron stole to them and Edward was on his feet, dressing Joan with urgent hands.

"What's wrong?" she whispered.

"Someone approaches. Christian just sent me a signal.

The last thing I want is for my father to find us together again."

When they were dressed, he led her toward the rear entrance. "Good-bye, sweetheart, I'll return from Scotland the moment we claim victory."

"May God keep you safe for me, Edward."

By the time the king was halfway up the hundred steps, his son was halfway down. "Ha, Edward! You beat me to it. Is the round table as spectacular as I hoped?"

"It fair took my breath away, Father."

"Come back up with me. Light some torches. How can you appreciate such a thing in the dark?"

"I managed to enjoy its finer points," Edward replied, amused at his own words.

The king's enthusiasm for the Round Tower of Bedford stone, housing the magnificent round table, showed no bounds. Prince Edward almost had to drag him away. "Father, we'll be in the saddle the entire day tomorrow. This tower will be standing long after we are both in our graves."

"That's the whole idea, Edward. Why you young people like to spend half your lives in bed is beyond me."

The queen was already abed by the time the king entered her chamber. The topic she wished to pursue was neither towers nor wars. The thing in the forefront of Philippa's mind was marriage. "Edward, I am so pleased that Isabel is to wed Louis of Flanders. Strengthening the bond between your English and my Flemish will add to the prosperity of both countries. It will increase trade a hundredfold. All the wool used by their weavers must come from England and in return, we can import all the articles they manufacture." Philippa indicated the new bed hangings. "This exquisite diaphanous material was woven in Ghent. All my ladies are buying it to make night rails. 'Tis a new fashion that is sweeping England and scandalizing the clergy. They have proclaimed the garments provoke lust and that pure-minded ladies should sleep naked." She did not tell him that Isabel was disappointed that Louis was only a count.

The king, too, kept a few things to himself. Louis was dragging his feet in agreeing to wed an English princess. His father had died at Crécy with an English arrow in his heart, and Louis hated them with a vengeance. His ministers in Flanders, who badly wanted this English alliance, had set guards about the palace so Count Louis could not escape and run to the King of France.

"I'm sorry to be leaving you so quickly, my dearest, but those goddamn barbarians to the north need a lesson. I promise to be as quick as I can about the business, and in the meantime I want you to ready yourself so that I can escort you to France. I trust you are feeling well enough to travel?" He alluded to their tenth child, which she carried.

"You know me, Edward. I'm Flemish! Are we not noted for our good Flanders mares? I always feel my best with one of your long-limbed Plantagenets kicking inside me."

King Edward thought his queen a veritable earth mother. He had certainly made the right choice in wedding Philippa. They had produced a dynasty! "I hope the administration of the realm has not sat too heavily on your shoulders while I've been off in France."

"My love, you've only been gone just over a month. Not much has transpired while you've been away except the Pope has sent his ruling about the two claimants for Joan of Kent's hand. In his wisdom, he has decided in Sir John Holland's favor. I didn't say anything to Katherine de Montecute," she said sweetly. "I thought I'd let you break the bad news to her."

The king had little experience with fear, but for once in his life he turned coward. "I'll let my good friend William break the news to her. It cost me a war with the Scots to gain her husband's release. That must be her consolation."

"I hope young William de Montecute won't be too disappointed."

King Edward knew the lad would be devastated. He sighed and began to undress. "My love, let's think about ourselves tonight."

🐝 27 🐝

It took the king and his party three days to ride the hundred and seventy miles to York. Prince Edward and Christian Hawksblood, however, rode day and night and did it in half that time. Prince Edward told his friend, "These Scots are inhuman. Each man carries a griddle and a bag of oats so they won't have to forage for food."

"I've heard they are fierce fighters," Hawksblood remarked.

"Aye, especially the Highlanders. They are like wild men on ponies. Our churches and abbeys mean nothing to them. They leave them in ruins just for the fun of it. They are totally undisciplined. They burn everything, raping and carrying off Englishwomen."

"They sound like the mad Turks," Hawksblood commented, while Paddy and Ali exchanged alarmed glances.

At York, they joined the English army that had been mustered by the northern barons. Their destination was Durham, sixty miles north. On October 16, William Douglas, in charge of the Scots, rode over a hill and saw the English army encamped at Neville's Cross. He rode straight back to give the news to King David.

David roared with laughter. "The English army is in France, mon. There are no men left in England, save monks, swineherds, tailors, and tanners!"

At dawn on the morning of October 17, he learned otherwise when the English attacked. King David was furious. When he called for his armor, his cavalry leaders tried to restrain him. "You have no idea what their longbowmen can do. They whittle magic into their bows and arrows. At Crécy 'tis rumored these bowmen won the war!"

David ground his teeth. "I will have the head of the next mon who talks tae me of Crécy!" he roared, then rode into the thick of the battle.

King David took two arrows himself, then his horse went down. As he stumbled to his feet, he looked into the darkest, fiercest face he'd ever seen. In fear, King David smashed the warrior in the mouth with his gauntlet. Christian Hawksblood merely grinned. He knew exactly who he had at the end of his sword.

When Douglas came to his king's rescue, Prince Edward took him prisoner. By day's end the English also captured Sir Malcolm Fleming and the earls of Fife and Monteith.

When Christian Hawksblood handed the King of Scotland over to the King of England, Edward Plantagenet knighted him on the spot.

When Christian protested that he had already been knighted, Edward asserted proudly, "Not by my hand, you have not."

Prince Edward and Hawksblood's squires stood by grinning as he went down on one knee to receive his English knighthood.

Brianna visited Joan after the king and his men departed for Scotland. "What did Edward say when you told him about the child?" Brianna asked softly, mentally prepared for either good or bad news from Joan.

"I didn't tell him," Joan said in a small voice.

"You didn't tell him?" Brianna cried in disbelief.

"Don't be fierce with me. I just couldn't bring myself to say the words. Our time together was so short. I'm going to France with Princess Isabel, so everything will be all right, Brianna. I just know it will."

"Oh, love, of course everything will be all right, but you must tell him. You have no choice."

"I know. I promise. Let's work on your trousseau, Brianna. I do so want your wedding gown and your clothes to put Princess Isabel's in the shade."

Brianna sighed, then began to laugh softly. Joan only ever wanted to think about the pleasant things in life. She often wished she herself could be that way. It would be so much more pleasant to let others do the worrying.

Before the month of October drew to a close, a victorious king and prince returned to Windsor. An air of rejoicing prevailed at the castle. In the evenings the hall rang with balladeers singing their praise for their mighty warrior king, and their new hero, the Black Prince. The days were spent in hurried preparation for the voyage to France. The Plantagenets felt truly invincible.

When Joan of Kent was summoned by the queen, she was filled with apprehension. She begged Brianna to accompany her. "What if she has guessed my condition?"

"Of course she has not," Brianna assured her, "you are slim as a reed. Only the four of us know and we would never betray you, love."

Brianna went with her, but stayed at the back of the solar while Philippa spoke privately to Joan.

"The king sent to the Pope to straighten out the tangle of your betrothals, Lady Kent." The queen's tone was censorious. She could not hide the fact that she disliked the beautiful young woman.

Joan waited for her to continue. She felt utterly detached from the matter Philippa spoke of, as if it had nothing to do with her in reality.

"The Pontiff has ruled in Sir John Holland's favor, so that settles the matter, and settles, I hope, any further gossip about your unorthodox affairs."

Joan made her curtsy, whispered some vague reply, then hurried back to the haven of Brianna. "Please, let's leave," she whispered.

"What's wrong?" Brianna asked with concern as they left the solar and walked toward the gallery.

"Nothing . . . it's just that I wish Edward's mother liked me."

"Joan, you have other things to worry about. You must tell Prince Edward of your plight."

Coming toward them, along the gallery, was none other than the new Steward of the Royal Household. He bowed formally to Joan of Kent. "My lady, the news has made me the happiest man in the realm."

Joan offered him her hand as if she were in a trance and murmured, "My lord Holland."

He took her hand to his lips, but scrupulously avoided contact with her skin. He then took a letter from his doublet and placed it in her hand with another formal bow.

Brianna immediately knew what the queen had told her. Joan was now legally contracted to John Holland. Try as she might, she could not picture the bull-necked Holland penning a love letter. Brianna's heart sank. Joan's predicament grew worse by the moment. If only she would come out of her trance and do something to help herself!

Joan didn't open the note until they were in her rooms. Brianna watched her face light up. "It's from Edward. He wants me to go to the house in Fish Street!"

"But your brother is in Calais, what possible excuse can you have to go into London?"

"We need to go shopping before we go to France. We'll take Adele and Glynis."

Brianna groaned, silently preferring to be excluded from this rendezvous, but Joan was her friend and who else would help her? If Brianna was honest, she didn't want to go to Prince Edward's town house for fear of encountering Christian Hawksblood. "I'll come, Joan, but only on condition that you confess all to Edward."

"Oh, I will, I will," she vowed.

And at last Joan found the courage to speak of it when they were private in their upstairs chamber in the tall house. She seized her opportunity when Edward spanned her waist with his hands to lift her for his kiss. "Sweetheart, I always forget how tiny you are until I have my hands on you."

"I won't be tiny for long, Edward . . . I'm having your child."

"Truly?" He swung her high, overjoyed. Concern turned his face serious. "I'm such a brute, I haven't hurt you, have I?"

"No, no." She laughed down into his handsome face, tears of joy threatening to spill over. "Oh, Edward, I've been so worried, I didn't know what to do."

"Who knows of this, sweeting?"

"Brianna of Bedford and my maid."

"Good, good. My enemies could use this against me."

"Enemies?" she echoed, bewildered. "Edward, you have no enemies."

He laughed at her innocence. "None that concern you, Jeanette." He removed her cloak and drew her into his lap before the warm fire. "You will come to France with me. We'll have a house. It will be heaven to have you with me."

He lifted a handful of her pretty hair and buried his face in it. "You always smell like fresh flowers."

Joan's brow was creased. "Edward, how can we live openly like that?"

"My own darling, it won't be openly. The Pope has ruled in favor of John Holland."

"Yes, I know. He brought me your letter, but I don't quite see what that has to do with us."

He couldn't believe her naiveté; sometimes she was like a little girl. "John is to be your husband; in name only. He will take a house in France, but he will live in a separate wing. The house will in actuality be ours. Darling, don't you see, it doesn't matter how many babies we have. They will all be legitimate. No scandal will touch you as Lady Holland."

"I see," Joan whispered.

"It's the perfect solution to our dilemma. I'm a tactician. It wasn't easy to outmaneuver the king and queen." Edward could see that Joan wasn't overjoyed at the idea. He was glad he hadn't told her he had bribed the Pope to favor Holland. "Joan, you know I want to marry you, but you also know that is impossible."

She nodded miserably.

"Since you are enceinte, you must have a husband. Married women have much more freedom, love. John Holland is my man. I have made him Steward of the Royal Household so I am sure of his absolute loyalty. In public you will have to pay occasional lip service to this empty marriage, but it's a price I'm willing to pay and I hope you are too, love."

"I will do anything to be with you, Edward. It's just that it frightens me to marry a man I barely know and don't even like."

Edward chuckled. "And that's exactly the way we are going to keep it. My love, he will be your humble servant. I want the ceremony to take place immediately."

"Why?" she asked, still most reluctant.

"So we can be together right away. Don't be afraid, my little Jeanette, I will protect you always."

She buried her face in his shoulder. "Hold me, Edward. Hold me."

* * *

All the Plantagenets were present in the chapel at Windsor when Sir John Holland married Lady Joan of Kent. The bride was so exquisitely adorned, it was assumed she had spent months preparing for this wedding, when in actuality it had been hours. Her undergown was her favorite pink, then over it came three layers of the white diaphanous material from Ghent. The result was just a hint of blush-pink. Her silvery hair was unadorned, as custom decreed, and fell to her hips in a silken cascade. She wore her pearls looped about her tiny waist. Pearls were reputed to symbolize tears, and today they did so for Joan.

Brianna of Bedford was her only attendant, wearing a gown of rose velvet to complement the bride's dress. Most of her other clothes and Joan's also had been packed for the journey to France.

When the stocky figure of Sir John Holland stepped to Joan's side, she feared she might faint, but Prince Edward stood beside him as best man and Joan seized upon this in a game of fantasy. In her heart she made her vows to Edward and knew that God in His wisdom would understand.

Brianna's conscience sat all awry. To her the plan was shocking and deceitful and therefore wrong. When Joan first confided in her she almost wished she had urged her friend to abort the child; then there would have been no need for marriage, but that too would have been wrong. A grave sin, in fact. So in the end she agreed to stand up with her friend, knowing how easily Prince Edward had beguiled Joan.

Because the royal family was in the midst of preparations to move the Court to France, a small wedding supper was held for the newlyweds, rather than a banquet. Sir John, as Steward of the Royal Household, occupied a luxurious suite of rooms. When he retired with his bride, Prince Edward was there to receive her and Holland departed down the backstairs.

It was only then that Joan's happy, carefree nature was restored and she went into her lover's arms with joy. To be able to spend an entire night together in secret bliss was enough to banish all the dark clouds from Joan's horizon.

From his seat at the back of Windsor's chapel, Christian

Hawksblood watched the nuptials with cynicism. What the heir to the throne was doing was morally wrong, but perhaps in the long run it would be the lesser of two evils. It was rare for royalty to have happy marriages, for one could seldom please the state and please oneself at the same time. He knew that the delightful Joan of Kent was good for the prince, who had inherited the volatile Plantagenet temper. The Black Prince was ever in a lighter, happier mood after he had spent a few hours in Joan's enchanting company. Hawksblood knew he would do all in his power to aid them in their secret relationship.

His glance touched on Princess Isabel, who was to wed Louis, Count of Flanders. Hawksblood sensed trouble in that direction. He stopped himself from probing the future. The future was based upon the present. Sequence and consequence. It was ever thus.

With that thought in mind, his glance traveled to Brianna of Bedford. He pictured her at some altar in France being wed to his brother, Robert. Sequence and consequence. He would have to do something in the present to alter the future.

At the wedding supper Christian tried to get Brianna alone, but she kept Adele at her side at all times. When he pressed her for a private word, she refused point-blank and retired shortly thereafter, taking Adele with her.

Next, Christian tried writing notes, asking her to meet him, but he received no reply. The remaining days before they departed for France melted away until only one remained. Hawksblood found a spot where he could keep vigil on her door, unobserved. He concealed himself before the first light of dawn. Leaning against the stone wall, he prepared himself to wait until night fell, if that was necessary.

Brianna and Adele made lists of the things they must pack for France. Eventually everything was done, every article folded or wrapped, or laid flat in their traveling trunks. Brianna's wedding gown, in which Joan had taken such delight, had been carefully packed with lavender sachets between the layers.

Brianna picked up a russet apple from a bowl as a treat for her white mare. She hated the thought of leaving Papillon behind, but for practical reasons they would all have to acquire new mounts when they arrived in France. She took up her cloak and made her way to the stables. She fed Papillon the apple and stroked her velvet nose lovingly. "I'll miss you, my beauty," she murmured low, and laughed when the palfrey's ears pricked at the sound of her voice. "I wish I could take you with me. I don't know when I shall see you again," she murmured wistfully. She couldn't resist one last ride. "Come on, beauty, we'll just ride out into Windsor's park." A groom saddled the horse for her and she trotted out into the crisp, frosty air.

Christian Hawksblood followed her to the stables. He waited patiently until she emerged, then he slipped inside to saddle his own mount.

As she glanced across the park, Brianna saw another rider. She knew immediately who it was. Though he was too far away to recognize, some instinct told her Christian Hawksblood had followed her. She was not afraid, but she was annoyed with herself for forgetting how persistent he could be. She did the first thing that came into her head; she rode away from him as quickly as she could.

The Arabian's mouth curved. She had made a tactical mistake. She should have ridden directly toward him and toward the haven of Windsor's stables.

Brianna gave Papillon her head, urging her to a gallop. As she entered the edge of the forest, she glanced back and saw with dismay that Hawksblood was rapidly gaining on her. She took a path that led to the left, hoping the trees would slow his progress. He turned to the left unerringly.

Brianna came to a clearing and spurred her palfrey across it toward the trees, glancing back quickly to see if she had lost him. She had not! There was something about the horse and rider behind her that evoked a flicker of fear. She was swept with the urge to flee from her pursuer. To avoid him, she galloped faster at a speed that was reckless.

Her hunter was relentless. She received the distinct impression that he was riding her down. He was a raptor, and she, his prey! She felt a bubble of terror in her chest as she heard the pounding of the massive destrier's hooves behind her. She half-turned to see the dark rider loom up, larger than life, then swoop down upon his captive, taking her in his talons. She struck out against him, but it was hopeless to escape someone who was all-powerful.

28

Hawksblood lifted Brianna, legs kicking, arms flailing, tongue protesting, until she sat before him on the blooded stallion. His eyes blazed like chips of ice. She closed her eyelids fast so he could not mesmerize her and steal her will. She clawed at his dark face, realizing the danger she was in.

Christian Hawksblood was not in the least surprised that she fought him like a wildcat. He had always known Brianna had keen instincts and they were telling her she was in imminent danger. Her instincts did not lie, he thought grimly. He pinned her arms down, not escaping her fingernails entirely. When he held her hands captive, she used her tongue to lash him, calling him every foul thing, among which *bastard* was the least offensive.

By dint of superior physical strength he subdued her. He could not do it gently; she made that impossible. The moment he loosened his cruel grip on her wrists, she attacked him again. She intended to do him an injury if she could and rather than injure her in return, he decided to maul her pride instead.

Brianna stared at him, horror and loathing mingled together as she realized he would master her, no matter how fiercely or how long she struggled. His muscled arms held her immobile, while his knees urged his horse forward. Her own mare trotted after the stallion in a sweetly docile way that made Brianna want to scream. She decided she *would* scream! Perhaps someone would come to her rescue.

He saw her intent, and as the scream gathered in her throat, his mouth swooped down to cover hers. His mouth was as cruel as his hands had been and she knew it was capable of its own violence. When he released her mouth, she blazed, "Why are you doing this?"

His gaze was steady, his voice implacable. "For your own good." As they emerged from the trees, he held his hand out to her palfrey.

She cried, "Papillon, go back, go back," but the perverse creature trotted to him trustingly and allowed him to catch hold of the long rein. He attached it to his saddle, then placed Brianna's hands over the pommel and murmured, "Hold fast."

Christian Hawksblood spurred his destrier then and it surged forward with an excess of strength and energy usually reserved for the battlefield. Brianna decided she would never speak to him again. She imagined he was abducting her to some private trysting place where he would seduce her into letting him make love to her. Christian Hawksblood de Beauchamp had a lot to learn! If he thought subjugating her to his will would make her receptive to his amorous overtures, he was dead wrong! That might be the way men treated women in Arabia, but this was England where freedom meant everything.

Brianna thought he was heading northward and when he didn't slow the pace, she wondered wildly just how far he was taking her. Questions almost dropped from her lips, but she bit them back, remembering that she had vowed not to speak to him. After an hour or so had passed, she stole a surreptitious glance at him. His face was dark, closed, set in determined lines. His silence was as complete as hers.

Brianna's mind darted here and there to seek her own answers. Her imagination flashed about like quicksilver. She feared that silently, with some dark power, he was overwhelming her. The hair on the nape of her neck rose up. She became aware of the material of her undergarment whispering against her skin. A subtle fragrance wafted to her nostrils in the chill air and she realized it was his male scent that teased her senses.

She stopped railing against him and allowed calmness to possess her. He could not make her do anything against her will, if she remained in control of herself. Her eyes were drawn to him. She studied his hawklike visage and could not deny his noble beauty. Every line spoke of power, as did his body. In such proximity she imagined she felt his male beauty burning into her soul. She had been one with him once, and the memories evoked the faint stirring of desire to be one with him again.

Brianna fought against the sensations, but she could feel her resistance slowly ebbing. The Castle of Berkhamsted loomed into view and Brianna wondered why on earth he had brought her to Prince Edward's castle. Had it something to do with Joan? But he did not slow his pace, he rode on past Berkhamsted without a glance. Things were vaguely familiar and Brianna felt she had passed this way before. After her long hours in the saddle she became weary and longed to stop and rest. Then suddenly it came to her. He was taking her to Bedford. He was taking her home!

She looked at him in disbelief. "We depart for France tomorrow. You cannot take me to Bedford!"

He looked down at her lovely face with its dimpled chin and hazel eyes. "The *Court* departs for France," he corrected.

Then she understood. This abduction was to keep her from going to France . . . from going to Robert!

"You cannot do this!" she cried in alarm.

"I have done it," he replied calmly.

She lifted her hands and beat them against his chest in anguish. She might have beat against Bedford stone for all the impression she made. When she had expended all her energy and sat quietly, he stopped at a stream to water the horses. He took bread and cheese and meat, carefully wrapped in a white cloth, from his saddlebag, then lifted her down.

The moment her feet touched the ground Brianna began to run. He loped after her and carried her back. His dark face searched hers. "Where were you running to?"

"Running *from*," she spat.

"You cannot run from your fate."

"A fate worse than death!" she cried.

Her words amused him. "I thought a fate worse than death was supposed to be rape. I shan't rape you, Brianna."

"Am I supposed to be grateful?" she sneered.

"Gratitude is the last thing I want from you," he said quietly.

"What do you want from me?" she demanded.

Everything! Heart, soul, love eternal.

"I want you to eat something," he said.

She closed her lips firmly. If he thought she would eat with him he was mistaken.

"I am a prisoner. It is my duty to try to escape," she vowed, eyes blazing. "What a poor creature I should be if I were craven!"

He wanted her just as she was, proud and high-handed as a queen.

Though Brianna was only slightly hungry, she was extremely thirsty. She reasoned that if he offered her a drink, she would be honor-bound to refuse it, but if she demanded one, he would have to do her bidding. "I want you to get me water from the stream. Do it in full view of me so you cannot put one of your evil potions in it."

Hawksblood couldn't help himself. He grinned at her fancies. "Is that the potion that compels you to fall in love or the one that makes you indulge in sinful deeds?"

"Stop laughing at me, Arabian. This is my life you are ruining!"

He pressed his lips together. He must not taunt her further. It was cruel to do so. He bent and filled the cup with water, then he placed it in her hands.

As they rode on mile after mile, he wondered if she would ever forgive him for what he did this day. Though he was optimistic, he knew it would take a long, long time.

When darkness fell, he felt the tension go out of her and knew she dozed. He realized how weary she must be to let down her guard enough to sleep. His face softened in the darkness. She was so precious to him.

About an hour's ride from Bedford, the rain began. The first big drops upon her face roused her from slumber, and then it began to pelt down. It was an extremely cold rain, so he wrapped his cloak about her, but it was so relentless it drenched them to the bone.

When they finally arrived at Bedford Castle, Hawksblood lifted her from the saddle and carried her inside. To a startled Mr. Burke he said, "She's exhausted. I'll take her to her chamber."

The plea in her eyes and her voice told her steward there was something wrong. "Come with me, Mr. Burke."

He followed the couple up the staircase, ignoring the puddle of water they left on every step. Inside her mother's chamber, which was now Brianna's, Hawksblood set her down in a chair and bent to kindle the logs in the fireplace.

"Mr. Burke, this man has abducted me. I was allowed to bring nothing. I haven't a stitch to my back. No one knows where I am, not even Adele!"

Hawksblood said over his shoulder to Burke, "Adele is on her way here with all her trunks. The Court is on its way to France. I brought Lady Bedford home, where she will be safe."

The explanation was good enough for Mr. Burke.

Brianna's anger flared. "He is a dangerous man!"

Hawksblood stood up from the fire and held Mr. Burke's gray eyes. "She is in more danger from her wet clothing than she will ever be from me."

Burke nodded and the pair departed so that she could undress. She ran across the chamber and threw the bolt home. She dragged a heavy trunk across the door for further protection. She had to sit down to catch her breath, then she peeled Hawksblood's cloak along with her own from her soaking back. Her shoes were ruined and she knew they could never be worn again. Her velvet tunic was in like case, its deep pile matted, flattened, and shabby in the extreme. Her underdress and stockings clung to her body wetly. They joined the soggy heap upon the rug and she took up a towel to dry her clammy-cold skin and rub her dripping hair.

Brianna sat naked before the welcome fire, holding the towel to her breasts. She was as much emotionally exhausted as physically, and the warmth made her drowsy. Her problem was too great to solve at this moment, so she pushed it aside until she could cope with it. Her eyelids closed, her shoulders drooped, and she tumbled into the dark abyss.

She slept until the fire burned low. When she awoke to find herself naked, she opened the wardrobe and took out a scarlet bedrobe. The sleeves and hem were embroidered with gold thread in Grecian key design. All Rhianna's clothes were vivid. Brianna slipped her arms into the sleeves and tied the golden tassels. She picked up one of her mother's brushes. Her hair had dried in hundreds of spiraling curls and looked wildly disheveled. As she caught her reflection in the polished silver mirror, she saw what a deliciously tempting picture she made: like a golden witch!

The corners of her mouth went up in a secret smile as she thought of Christian Hawksblood . . . Prince Drakkar. *He is an invading force!* The thought in no way displeased her. She walked slowly toward the curtained bed. What splendid things had been done to her in its soft depths. She stroked the coverlet . . . remembering, remembering.

Why wasn't he at her chamber door, breaking it down? She knew there was a power of the mind. Her mind as well as his. She would exercise that power! She began by creating his image in her imagination. She focused on every detail of his dark beauty. And then she called to him, whispering his name.

Desire and longing gathered inside her, overflowing her heart and running along her veins in rivulets of molten gold. Her pulses quickened, her breasts ached, her woman's center was liquid fire. Hawksblood was a mate like no other. He was a man like no other, and he was hers for the taking. What a waste it would be not to take him!

She unlocked the door, then dragged the heavy trunk to one side. No locks would ever keep him out, thank heaven, from her door or from her heart. As she sat down to await him, her longing grew deeper. She wanted him to make love to her, she wanted him to marry her, she wanted him to fill her with a babe. Together they would make Bedford their haven and it would prosper.

She could sit no longer. She stood up and began to pace the chamber, cursing him for the time they were wasting. Brianna finally decided she would go to him. She lifted the door latch, knowing where there was such passionate love, there could be no such thing as pride.

The chamber he had occupied on his previous visit was empty. In the hallway she encountered Mr. Burke. "Where is Christian?" she asked boldly.

"You said he abducted you, my lady," Mr. Burke said
tentatively.

She laughed. "He wanted me so badly, he stole me.
Wasn't that a bold, romantic thing to do? Ah, James, I
believe I've met my match."

Mr. Burke stared at her. Rhianna had always called him
James, and in the scarlet bed-gown her daughter looked
like an apparition from the past. "He has gone, my lady,"
Mr. Burke informed her.

"Gone? Gone where?" she demanded.

"Gone to the siege of Calais, I believe."

The blood drained from her face. She ran back to her
chamber and slammed the heavy door. Then in a blazing
passion she rent her bed-robe to ribbons and fell to the bed
sobbing . . . devastated.

In the morning when she awoke, the first thing she saw
was the torn robe. Everything flooded back to her. She had
been so angered at Christian Hawksblood, she had barri-
caded her door against him. Then when she had donned
mer mother's clothes, as before, her attitude and her feelings for him had undergone a dramatic reversal. She ana-
lyzed what had happened. She knew she did not become
Rhianna, but when she wore her mother's clothing, she
took on some of her mother's mystical powers and knowledge. This knowledge made her see the purity of truth. She
admitted her feelings for Christian and feared she would
always have them, but she was betrothed to his brother,
Robert, and would do her duty and try to be a faithful wife
to him. Thunder of Heaven, it was fortunate Hawksblood
had departed, for she knew she would have gone to his bed.

She examined her feelings about France. She wanted to
go to that country and yet at the same time would have
preferred more time before she wed Robert. She sighed.
Now she would have that time. She wrapped the sheet
about her nakedness and rang for a maid. "I'm afraid I will
need something to wear. A simple tunic will be sufficient.
Perhaps one of the maids will be generous enough to lend
me something."

Later in the day when Adele arrived, bringing their
trunks, her problem of clothing was solved. For a moment
she considered ordering Paddy to take them straight back

to Windsor, but upon reflection, decided to accept her fate. Perhaps this stay at Bedford Castle was meant to be.

Paddy left immediately and Brianna hugged Adele thankfully. "I'm so glad to see you. That devil Hawksblood spirited me here so I couldn't go with the Court to France. Whatever did the queen say when she thought I had run off?"

"I went to her with all sorts of excuses upon my lips, but Philippa is a wise lady. She said that you probably needed a little more time to get used to the idea of marriage. Then she didn't give it a second thought. She had Isabel to contend with and her royal brood to oversee."

Brianna opened one of her trunks and selected warm riding clothes. "Perhaps we've had a fortunate escape. I am going to enjoy playing chatelaine for a while."

Joan was almost frantic when she learned that Brianna wouldn't be going to France with her. Brianna was more than a friend; she was confidante, sister, and mother rolled into one. Joan thought of staying behind too, but under the circumstances it was impossible. She was Lady Holland now and must go with her husband, and after all, the main reason she had become Lady Holland was so that she could go to France to be with Prince Edward.

The voyage was handled most smoothly. The Black Prince sailed on a different vessel from the king and queen, and naturally since John Holland was in his service, he and his new bride sailed on Edward's ship. Joan saw little of Holland but much of her beloved Edward, which suited her to a T and filled her every waking moment with happiness.

When they arrived at Calais, Prince Edward took a large house just outside the city, which had a separate wing for Lord and Lady Holland. In actuality John Holland occupied the wing in solitude, while Joan and Edward had the rest of the spacious house to themselves.

Upon his return to Calais the king was furious to find that city still holding out against his siegers. He called a strategy meeting immediately. Warrick spoke up. "I have eighty ships blockading the harbor. Last week Philip sent forty-four vessels to revictual the city. We either captured or sank them all. One thing is certain: Calais ran out of wine, meat, and corn long ago and now I believe they have run out of cats, dogs, and horses. In three days at most, our patience will be rewarded."

Hawksblood suggested, "Why don't I take a couple of my trusty Cornishmen and slip into the surrounding French towns to see what the mood of the people is like?"

"I'll come with you," Prince Edward volunteered.

Hawksblood decided Edward and Joan should have their honeymoon. "You might be recognized, Sire. You would be more effective battering the walls of the city. They cannot hold out much longer."

Robert de Beauchamp ground his teeth in chagrin when he learned that Brianna was not among the queen's ladies. He did not seek an answer from his bastard of a brother, nor from Prince Edward. Likely they were in league against him. Instead he approached Joan of Kent and questioned her sharply.

Joan didn't know what to say to him. "I am as surprised as you, Robert. I thought she was on one of the other vessels. I . . . I am newly wed and had much to occupy me the day we departed."

Robert cursed the little slut under his breath. He should have known he wouldn't get a straight answer from her. Finally he approached the queen, but over the years Philippa had learned diplomacy. "I'm so sorry, Sir Robert, there simply wasn't room to transport all the ladies, so I chose the ones who had experience in the nursery. I can understand how anxious you are to be wed, but once Calais falls and when Princess Isabel is wed to Count Louis of Flanders, we shall all return to Windsor."

Robert had to be satisfied, so he put his energies into furthering Prince Lionel's position, which was the same as furthering his own.

The English knew it was impossible for the people of Calais to hold out much longer. But hold out they did, well into the long winter. The king's temper deteriorated to the point where he was incensed against these stubborn French dogs who defied him week after week defending "God-damn Calais," as he called it.

In the meantime, Count Louis of Flanders dragged his feet over the agreement to marry Princess Isabel. Though her mother and father diplomatically tried to hid the truth from her, explaining that these things always took an inordinate amount of time, the princess became petulant and made her ladies' lives miserable. Fortunately, the king's knights and captains had little to occupy them as they waited for Calais to surrender, and the Court devised dancing and entertainments on a lavish scale to allay the boredom.

When Hawksblood returned from infiltrating the surrounding French towns, he informed the king, "Philip has tried desperately to muster more nobles and troops, but he is growing most unpopular because of the heavy taxes he has levied. He hides in Paris, which seems the only place that still supports him."

One cold morning a few days later, the governor of Calais sent a message that he was ready to come to terms.

29

The message from Sir John de Vienne incensed King Edward. "Calais is mine for the taking! How dare he try to make terms! This harbor town has been a haven for pirates for years. Holding out against me has cost arms, money, men, and time. I'll put the place to the sword for his goddamn insolence!"

Warrick knew it was the most strategic French town they would take. He tried to keep the king from destroying it. "A lesser man would have given up long ago and earned your scorn, Sire. Set aside your wrath while we study what will best serve our cause." Warrick looked at his son Hawksblood, who immediately read his thoughts.

Hawksblood said to his friend, Prince Edward, "A little mercy can go a long way in making a king popular."

Edward spoke up. "Make the leaders pay and spare the townspeople. Make the six leading citizens come bareheaded, barefooted with ropes about their necks to turn the city keys over to you. Then hang them on the walls for all to see."

Warrick and Hawksblood looked at each other with alarm, but for the moment held their peace.

Later Edward and Joan had Christian dine with them. Hawksblood did not hesitate to discuss the matter of clemency in front of Joan because he knew she would be his ally. "They will send their most highly respected burghers. They will not be young men and they will be weak from the enforced famine. If the king butchers them, they will become martyrs."

"He cannot back down now. How would he save face?" Edward demanded.

"Oh, please, Edward. If Queen Philippa begged him to spare them, how could he refuse her? She is large with child, and he is always extremely chivalrous."

"You don't know my father's temper, sweeting. But because I can refuse you naught, I will speak to my mother about this."

Christian said, "Good! I know clemency will gain him more than revenge. No one knows how to use pageantry to better advantage. I believe you and your father should ride through the streets with a fanfare of trumpets as you take in food."

The next morning Prince Edward had a private meeting with his mother and father. It took a deal of courage to face down that blazing Plantagenet temper, but once he had convinced his father to be lenient, the king's flamboyant nature took over and he plotted a spectacle that would be remembered down through history.

The king, surrounded by his captains and best soldiers, and the queen with all her ladies in attendance, had the six leaders brought before them. Up on the wall the king's headsman stood holding his great ax. The six burghers were thin and stooped and had difficulty walking. The wealthiest, John Daire, went on his knees and the others followed suit. "We bring you the keys and put ourselves at your mercy to save the rest of the people who have suffered so hardly."

The king's handsome face was angry. He held up his hand to signal his headsman. "Upon you I will work my will. The rest I will receive to my mercy."

At this point in the pageant, Queen Philippa went down upon her knees before King Edward and begged him to show mercy. The citizens of Calais gasped, then held their collective breath to see if this king would be swayed. He took a long time to make up his mind, then lifted his hand to signal the headsman. Then he suddenly changed his mind and gave the burghers' fate into his queen's hands.

A great cheer arose from the gathered crowd for the brave queen and the compassionate king. Though they expected Edward to garrison the town, the people of Calais thought him more reliable than the French king.

John Daire, who had the biggest house in the city, offered it to the queen for as long as she remained in Calais. Philippa took over the house immediately.

Now that Calais had surrendered to the English, Count Louis of Flanders was persuaded to do likewise, albeit reluctantly. His council and the representatives from the main towns told him plainly their economy depended upon an English alliance. They needed wool from England to keep their weavers working.

"Where is this Bruges?" Princess Isabel demanded of her mother.

"It is about fifty or sixty miles up the coast from here. It is close to my beloved Ghent where your brother John was born."

"But why can't Louis come here to Calais?" demanded Isabel.

Philippa, with the patience of a devoted mother, explained, "The betrothal must take place in Flanders since that is Count Louis' country. Also, the monastery at Bruges is ancient and upon sanctified ground. A betrothal encompasses a religious ceremony as well as the signing of a civil contract."

The king spoke up. "I've decided we will sail up the coast. Your mother cannot ride sixty miles in the dead of winter in her condition. I think you and your ladies will be a lot more comfortable aboard the cog *Thomas*. I think these, too, will add to your comfort." The king signaled to an aide, who carried in some large boxes.

Isabel tore off the lid of the box marked with her name and lifted out a costly sable cloak with a warm hood. Queen Philippa received one in a lighter shade of sable. "Dearest, you shouldn't spend so much money on me. You need it to continue your campaign against France."

"Hush, Philippa. A king should be able to give his queen furs to keep her warm. Isabel harbors no such frugal notions."

"No indeed, Father," replied Isabel, already preening in hers. "But don't you think a blue fox edging about my face would be more flattering?"

"Your beauty needs nothing to enhance it, child," he said, ever gallant.

Aboard ship, however, on their way to Bruges, when Isabel saw Lady Joan Holland wrapped in blue fox with ermine tails, she wanted to scratch out Joan's eyes.

Prince Edward could not hover about his beloved on the voyage, but her comfort, safety, and welfare were of paramount importance to him. Because Holland had to stay behind to garrison Calais, Prince Edward ordered Holland to surround Joan with trustworthy servants who acted more or less as bodyguards for the ethereal young woman. She was precious to Edward, appealing to his chivalrous nature, and he always treated her with loving tenderness.

Robert de Beauchamp, on guard duty in Calais, made it his business to patrol with John Holland. Though De Beauchamp's laughing good-natured looks belied it, Holland recognized that the young blond giant was riddled with ambition. After all, he was tarred with the same brush.

"You don't accompany Lady Holland to Bruges I see, but I am sure the Black Prince will take good care of her."

Holland bristled. Deep down he coveted Joan almost as much as he coveted wealth and position, but it was his private bête noire and he wanted it kept that way. "They are royal cousins and friends since childhood," Holland replied mildly.

"There is no need to pretend with me, my friend. Though it is a closely guarded secret, I know you have a marriage in name only. That of course would change dramatically should something befall the heir to the throne."

Holland's thick bull-neck turned purple. He reasoned that Warrick's son would not dare to suggest such a thing, unless he had some evidence of proof.

De Beauchamp continued to plant seeds of destruction.

"Still, one man's misfortune will ever be another man's salvation. If aught did befall Edward, you and I would not suffer. Prince Lionel would become heir and eventually king, and our stars would then be in the ascendancy. Power and even titles could be achieved."

Holland was beginning to realize just how dangerous this affable-looking youth could be. "It pays to keep your eyes and mind open to life's opportunities. I think we understand each other. Our friendship could well be mutually beneficial."

The Plantagenets arrived at the austere monastery on a bleak day at the end of winter. They were received with much formality by Count Louis' Council and the leading burghers of Flanders. The royal family and their attendants were given rooms in the monastery, but the furnishings were in no way luxurious. They were honored with a banquet, but no lavish entertainments were provided for the royals in the sanctified air of the old monastery.

Princess Isabel's disappointment in her future husband's rank was forgotten when she met Louis. He was an extremely handsome youth with the golden coloring of her god-like brother, Edward, and when she heard her ladies sighing over his looks, Isabel was well satisfied. Louis treated the princess quite formally and she was vain enough to believe it was because he was in awe of her.

In actuality it was because his father had died with an English arrow through his heart at the Battle of Crécy and Louis' hatred knew no bounds for these Anglo-Normans. He had been brought up at the French Court and was a Frenchman at heart. King Philip of France had wanted Louis to marry Margaret of Brabant and this lady was closer to Louis' heart because they were neighbors and spoke the same language.

The day of the betrothal ceremony dawned gray and cold, but Princess Isabel's ladies were kept too busy to notice the weather. Her betrothal clothes were almost as elaborate as her wedding finery. The underdress was gold tissue, while over it came an azure tabard emblazoned with the leopards of England and the lilies of France. Upon her head she wore a gold coronet ablaze with deep blue sapphires.

At the dressing ceremony, Isabel said her clothes didn't feel right. Her ladies pinned and tucked and sewed until the gown felt better, but then she declared it didn't look right and the tucks and stitches all had to be undone. The dressing of her hair took even longer than the dressing of her person, and when the very last of her ladies lost all patience with her, she declared she was ready to be betrothed and would they please hurry along to the ceremony.

The betrothal was solemnized with all pomp and circumstance. During the ceremony, Joan and Edward's eyes met and held. They both wished with all their hearts that they could have enjoyed a formal betrothal before the whole world. Joan sighed over the exchanged vows, then sent Edward her sweetest smile. Not for the world would she have him think her sad.

Prince Edward clenched impotent fists at the wistful look he had glimpsed upon his beloved's face and made his mind up that he would go to her tonight, despite the rigid rules of the monastery that separated the sexes, including those who were married.

In spite of the austere setting, Princess Isabel expressed a wish to stay all week so that she and Louis could become better acquainted. The king and queen were only too willing to acquiesce to her wishes, for this union would benefit England's trade and make Flanders a firm ally in the war with France.

By the time darkness fell on the day of the betrothal, Louis was eager to seek his own apartments. He found no fault with Isabel's form and face. Indeed she was most attractive, but her clothes and jewels were so lavish he feared he would be in debt for a lifetime because of her extravagance. She had talked nonstop, filling him in on a lifetime of minutia which told him plainly she was vain, shallow, and spoiled beyond belief.

Back in her own apartment, Isabel was delighted by the handsome Louis, who was obviously the strong, silent type. She already fancied herself in love with him and chattered on endlessly to her long-suffering ladies, until it was obvious to all that Princess Isabel was in love with love and all the romantic details that emotion encompassed. They hid their yawns, then fell into bed exhausted when she finally dismissed them.

It was long past midnight when the shadowed figure of a monk traversed the labyrinth of corridors, then disappeared through one of the monastery's portals.

Joan gasped as a cowled figure entered her bedchamber, but her gasp turned to a sigh as Prince Edward threw back the hood of the robe and placed warning fingers to his lips, telling Joan not to speak. She nodded her understanding as she slipped out of bed and hurried into Edward's arms. With his mouth against her ear he whispered, "No one must hear us, not even the servants." He knew if there was the slightest leak about their liaison, she would be branded as harlot and whore, while he would not be censured in any way.

Before the week ended, Count Louis of Flanders escaped to the Province of Artois, then fled to Paris where King Philip welcomed him with open arms. The unthinkable had happened; Princess Isabel Plantagenet had been jilted!

The royal family sailed back to Calais immediately, but a humiliated Isabel screamed that she hated Flanders, hated France, and wanted to go home. Windsor was civilized, Windsor was safe, and spring would be arriving there any day now.

The king set about drawing up a nine-month truce with Calais. This would give him plenty of time to return to England and give his army a well-deserved rest. When he was ready to resume conquering France, his fleet would land at Calais with impunity. After their victories at Crécy and Calais, his subjects would welcome him and his son like conquering heroes. He was filled with zeal to establish his new Order of Chivalry, and then he would start recruiting the largest army England had ever known. All men would flock to join an invading force that had been victorious and had gathered such rich spoils.

Calais, of course, would be heavily garrisoned and the king left it up to Warrick to choose the best men for the job. Warrick chose Sir John Holland because he held a position of high command and had been doing an excellent job. When Warrick did not pick the king's son for garrison duty, Prince Edward went to him and volunteered to stay behind.

"You cannot be serious, Your Highness. The king wants you at his side when he returns. You are the hero of Crécy. You will go down in history as the valiant Black Prince."

The prospect of leaving his little Jeanette behind filled him with dismay. "For Christ's sake, Warrick, he's signed a nine-month truce! I can't be gone for nine months."

"Your father won't stay away that long, Your Highness. Breaking a truce never stopped him before. The crown of France has become an obsession. I'm willing to bet we'll be back fighting by summer. It is simply shrewd politics to return to Windsor to celebrate these French victories. He'll hold a great tournament, induct his top knights into his new Order of Chivalry, and then he'll be chomping at the bit to return and finish the job."

"You're right, of course, Warrick," Edward persisted, "but I can't help thinking we should leave a royal representative here."

"I agree, Your Highness. I've chosen Edmund, Earl of Kent. Sir John Holland will report directly to him. And if serious trouble should arise, we are only twenty miles across the Channel, after all."

Prince Edward knew defeat when it stared him in the face. He would have to leave Joan in her brother's care, but how in God's name would he tell her they would have to endure another separation?

He put it off as long as he could, then when they were about to retire, he made up his mind to wait no longer. As Joan began to undress, Edward was amazed to see her pregnancy had blossomed in the three weeks since they'd been together at the monastery. He approached her with concern in his eyes. "Sweetheart, are you all right?"

She glanced down at her swollen belly, her graceful hands fluttering over the mound. "I'm as big as a pig full of figs! Don't look at me."

He took hold of her hands and held them away from her body, so that she couldn't cover herself. "Sweeting, you are the loveliest little bundle I've ever seen." His heart turned over in his chest. How could he leave her? Tenderly, he gathered her against him and stroked her hair. Then it came to him exactly what he must say.

"A voyage to England would not be good for you now. As well as that, I shouldn't be making sexual demands on you when you are this far along." She was such a small, delicate female, he was suddenly afraid of childbirth.

She looked up at him with eyes large as saucers. "You have to return to Windsor, don't you?"

He made a strangled noise in his throat as he swept her up and carried her to their bed. He lay down and gathered her to his side with one massive arm. "I asked Warrick to let me stay with the garrison, but he pointed out it was my duty to return with my father." His lips feathered across her temple, his desire to protect her and his child almost choking him. "I've spoken with your brother and Edmund has agreed to move into the house here until I return."

She heard the anguish in his voice and knew she must be brave for his sake. "I'll be fine, Edward. Give me your hand . . . you can feel the baby moving."

In wonder and awe Edward placed his big hand upon the precious fruit of her womb and thought it a miracle.

Silently, Joan prayed, *Dear God, let it be a little girl . . . don't give us a son who can never wear his father's crown.*

"I can feel him kicking," Edward murmured.

"Her," she corrected, gently.

He smiled down at her, his heart overflowing with love. "If you want a daughter, then so do I."

Brianna was enjoying being at Bedford but she had never experienced such a cold winter in her life. Perhaps it was because she missed the warmth of Joan's friendship. At Court in Windsor their days had been filled with both duty and pleasure. There had been music and dancing and laughter each and every night in the hall when they dined with the royal family.

She shivered and decided she would be warmer abed. As she lay between the icy sheets, she felt colder than ever. She found it difficult to sleep alone after experiencing the smoldering heat of Christian Hawksblood's body beside hers. She pretended that she was waiting for him to come to bed. The waiting was delicious torture. Finally, he slipped in, lifted her against him, and pressed a row of kisses from her throat to her bare shoulder.

His lips discovered her skin was covered by gooseflesh. Realizing she was cold, he began to warm her flesh with his hands. He started with her feet, which were icy. He rubbed them, then he breathed his warm breath upon them and held them in his large hands until the heat from his body seeped into her. His hands moved up her slim legs and he massaged her thighs and belly. His hands covered her breasts and she could feel the delicious tautness of their pink tips. When he cupped them they fit perfectly into his warm palms.

His touch brought such pleasure she gasped over and over until he captured her lips with his to take the love sounds into his mouth. Brianna remembered when he had lifted her atop his long body. She had parted her legs so that her cleft rested on the swollen head of his marble phallus and his hands had moved up the backs of her legs to cup her buttocks. Her lips had rested upon the black mat of his chest and she had kissed his heart passionately.

Now, as then, when she felt his shaft throbbing against her woman's center she arched up and down upon him, then moved her hips in a circular motion, over and over, torturing him with her love play until Christian, with a muffled groan, clamped her hips with his powerful hands and slid deep inside her. He did not withdraw for an hour and by that time Brianna had slipped from fantasy into an erotic dream.

✌ 30 ✌

The return of the army from France was met with victory celebrations all over England. Bonfires were lit along the coast. Spring was in the air and people danced in the streets and garlanded their doorways with flowers.

The king announced that Windsor would host a week of

celebrations, beginning with a victory ball, then establishing his new Order of Chivalry and inducting his most valiant knights. The week would culminate in the greatest tournament England had ever seen. Knights from other countries were invited to come and compete in the jousts and the hastilude and partake of Plantagenet hospitality. French knights too would be welcome and safe conduct guaranteed for those brave enough to pit their skills against the flower of England's knighthood.

The gossip of Princess Isabel's aborted wedding was immediately overshadowed by the spectacular events that would begin before the month was out. If King Edward didn't miss his guess, Queen Philippa would produce a new royal baby by then, whose christening ceremony would add to the celebrations. And there was sure to be a wedding or two the day following the great tournament. A festive air gripped Windsor and everyone at Court decided they needed new clothes for the upcoming lavish entertainments.

At Bedford, Brianna had had a most enjoyable winter. At first she had missed the Court and still missed Joan, but she took her duties as chatelaine seriously and she found herself busy from morning till night.

The wool from the sheep brought in much-needed money and the royal treasury had paid handsomely for the stone for the new Round Tower at Windsor. With some of the money, Brianna purchased linen and she and Adele set the women of Bedford to sewing new sheets and bolsters for all the beds. She bought cloth from Lincoln so that all the household could have new liveries, and she showed the maids how to make scented candles and scented beeswax to make furniture polish.

Though Mr. Burke had planted all the flower gardens with vegetables, he had not neglected to gather flower seeds, pods, and bulbs and store them in the stillroom. Brianna decided to sow the seeds and plant the bulbs so that when spring arrived, Bedford would again blossom with beauty.

Her people had lots of food that winter. Even the peasants had meat on their table, thanks to Hawksblood's establishing rabbit warrens, and at Yuletide, Brianna celebrated the holy days by inviting everyone to a feast in the castle hall. They had a yule log, sang carols, played games, and presented every child with a bag of sweetmeats and a shiny penny.

They had no news from France all winter. Brianna toyed with the idea of donning a garment of her mother's to see if she could have a vision. Because of what she had seen last time, she was filled with apprehension and put it off again and again. Finally, one evening at the end of winter, with Adele beside her for security, Brianna donned the peacock gown as an experiment.

She became very still. Her eyes looked as if they were seeing something on the far horizon.

"What is it, what do you see?" Adele asked.

"It's not really a vision," Brianna tried to explain. "I just have knowledge of certain things."

"What things?" asked Adele.

"Well, I know it sounds ridiculous, almost impossible, but Princess Isabel has been jilted! Count Louis of Flanders was betrothed to her, then he fled, leaving her standing at the altar!"

"Oh no. Thank heavens we are not there to witness her tantrums. She will make someone pay for this."

"She will make everyone pay for this," Brianna predicted. "They are coming home. Even the army is returning for the present. Joan is unhappy, but she is smiling through her tears."

"She isn't ill?" Adele asked with concern.

"No, no, all is well with the child, but I think Prince Edward is returning and she must stay in France."

"What of Robert?" Adele asked.

"He . . . is well . . . he will not be put off any longer . . . help me take off the dress, Adele. I don't want to know more."

A few days later when she was admiring the first daffodils, Brianna turned to see who had just ridden into the courtyard. She was astonished to see Robert de Beauchamp.

He has come for me!

She moved to greet him as if she were in a trance. Her mind and her body seemed to separate. Physically, she felt numb, one foot moving in front of the other to propel her forward automatically, while at the same time her mind raced about, crystal clear and wary enough to sense trouble.

She recalled Robert had never been here before. "Welcome to Bedford, my lord. I had no idea you were returned from France."

He fixed her with a steely gaze. "Am I, Brianna? Am I truly welcome?" he demanded.

"But of course. You will be the new lord here when we are wed."

"We would have already been wed, if you had come to me in France. Instead, you came running to Bedford so you wouldn't have to go through with the marriage!"

"That is not true!" she cried indignantly. She dared not tell him that Christian had abducted her, there was enough bad blood between them. Her mind reached for a plausible excuse. "Princess Isabel has never liked me and she chose other ladies to attend her in France." Brianna felt she was on safe ground, for it was true that Isabel did not like her, and Robert would never be able to question the princess about leaving her in England.

His eyes narrowed. "I think you had no intention of wedding me!"

"Robert, that is not true. I even have my wedding gown."

"Show me!"

The color drained from her face. He was as good as calling her a liar. He was demanding proof. Her word meant nothing to him. "It . . . it is bad luck for the groom to see the bride's dress before the day of the wedding," she murmured.

"Is this just another one of your excuses, Brianna?"

"No. I will certainly show you the dress, Robert, if it will reassure you."

Why must I appease him? her mind cried out, but her mouth smiled prettily and she took his arm and led him into the castle.

Mr. Burke saw that two of the men with Robert de Beauchamp were knights who had served at Bedford under Neville Wiggs. He was thankful that Wiggs wasn't with them, but wondered how long that would last once De Beauchamp was the new lord.

Brianna signaled Mr. Burke. "This is Robert de Beauchamp, my betrothed. Robert, this is Mr. Burke, my castellan. I could never manage without him."

Robert scrutinized Burke closely. "Could you not?" he mocked. "Are you the one who keeps the accounts?"

"I am, my lord," Burke said evenly. "Would you care to see them?"

Robert waved a dismissive hand. "Plenty of time for that when I return." He had almost said, "You can turn them over to me," but then he thought better of it. Brianna was far too skittish. *Best get her wedded and bedded before I bring the heel of my boot down.* He smiled at Brianna. Let's see that wedding gown."

She led the way to her chamber and lifted the lid of a trunk that sat against the wall. As Brianna reached inside to lift a handful of the delicate material, Adele cried from the doorway, "Oh, my lamb, 'tis an omen of ill luck for the groom to see the bridal dress!"

But now that his eyes had seen the proof, Robert's sunny nature was restored. He bowed gallantly to Adele. "You grow more fair each time I see you. Can you pack up everything in time to leave tomorrow?"

Adele's eyes sought Brianna, who nodded imperceptibly. "Of course I can, my lord," she said with a deferential curtsy.

Brianna knew from experience the safest topic around Robert de Beauchamp was Robert de Beauchamp. "Congratulations on your knighthood, my lord. Tell us of your experiences in France." She had said the magic words that turned him into an affable, talkative companion.

The brave deeds in battle, the glory of war, the honors and more tangible rewards were recounted in detail and lasted all afternoon. Throughout the meal and the evening, Brianna listened attentively while Robert told of the week-long celebrations planned for Windsor. The topic of jousting was almost inexhaustible and then he told her with unconcealed pride that he expected King Edward would induct him into his new Order of Chivalry, since he was the first captain to be knighted on French soil. He informed her that their wedding would take place the day after the tournament, and Brianna, knowing she could have no objections, agreed with his plans.

All the roads leading to Windsor were crowded. Knights and their squires, riding to the tournament, shared the road with merchants who would set up booths to sell their wares and farmers with wagonloads of produce. Also in the crowds were jongleurs, members of the clergy, minstrels, fortune-tellers, and prostitutes by the score.

When they arrived the meadows surrounding the castle were filled with colorful tents and pavilions whose banners fluttered in the lively spring breeze. Before they parted, Robert said, "I will not be able to dance attendance upon you through the day, but we will be together each night in the Banqueting Hall."

"Thank you for the safe escort, my lord," she said dutifully, and she meant it sincerely. Robert had his faults, but he was strong, valiant, and handsome enough to set most feminine hearts racing. She would be a good wife to him and hoped fervently that once they were wed, love would blossom in her heart.

Brianna was unpacking her clothes and hanging them in her wardrobe when Adele accidentally let the lid of a trunk fall. Brianna almost jumped out of her skin.

"My lamb, I didn't mean to give you such a start."

Brianna saw that her hands were actually trembling. She knew exactly what the problem was.

Its name was Christian Hawksblood.

She feared what he would do. He had abducted her to prevent her going to France to marry Robert. What would he do this time? The Victory Ball was tomorrow night, launching the week of celebrations that would culminate in the tourney. The following day she would be wed. She fully expected to be kidnapped again. She knew she would have to be on her guard at all times and decided she must never be alone.

The lists in the jousting field were set up and a new canopy erected over the lodges where the queen and her noble ladies would sit. They extended the palisades where the crowds gathered to watch the jousts, knowing there would be twice the number of spectators as the last time.

Princess Isabel summoned all her ladies, including Brianna and Adele, to accompany her to the fair. It was a magical place with its puppet shows, acrobats, fire-eaters, and performing dog troupes. Vendors sold cups of steaming black peas, paper cones filled with winkles, roasted chestnuts, and pickled pigs' trotters.

It soon became apparent that Isabel had invited them so they would carry her purchases as she stopped at every merchant's stall, buying whatever caught her fancy without regard to cost. She bought glass beads, hair ornaments, combs, and fans. At another booth she refused to be gulled by the fake saints' bones and splinters of Christ's cross, but bought a rosary made from shiny seeds with a heavy silver crucifix, said to have been worn by St. Theresa.

One booth had every type of board game known to man. Isabel chose a game of tables, inlaid with ebony and ivory, then paid an exorbitant price for a pair of dice whose spots were purported to be diamonds. Princess Joanna voiced her doubt that the jewels were real, but Isabel silenced her. "Of course they are real, that's why the price is so high."

Joanna rolled her eyes heavenward at Blanche of Lancaster and they moved on to admire the exquisite stockings and garters displayed by a merchant who swore he supplied the French Court. The garters were delicious confections of satin and lace, some embroidered, some sequined, others bejeweled. He had others that were decorated with fur and feathers dyed every color of the rainbow. None of the ladies could resist buying a pair and Isabel bought a dozen.

The stalls that sold swords and weapons made from Toledo steel were crowded with men, but close by was a Spaniard who specialized in stilettos and ornamental daggers for ladies. Once again the princess royal purchased the most expensive item on display, a dagger in a jeweled sheath. The ladies in Europe wore ornamental daggers and Isabel decided to start the fashion here at Windsor.

Brianna's fancy was taken by a knife with a curved blade. Fashioned like a small scimitar, it drew her eye again and again. She was saving her money to buy paints, but began bargaining with the Spaniard, hoping she could get the knife for much less than he was asking. Finally she said, "If I wear this to the Victory Ball tonight, tomorrow all the

Court ladies will come to buy your dags." The Spaniard saw the wisdom in her words and let her have it for only twice what it had cost him. But Brianna was happy enough. It gave her a small sense of security. If anyone tried to take her where she didn't wish to go, she swore she would use it.

Isabel gloated, "See, I've already set the fashion. Bedford is copying me!"

When Isabel bought a lark in a cage, the cruel vendor assured her it would sing its throat out, guaranteed! Within minutes the princess regretted trusting Brianna of Bedford with her new pet bird.

"The cage door was faulty," Brianna lied, her heart soaring almost as high as the little lark as it flew straight up into the sunshine.

At the Victory Ball, the gentlemen were as brilliantly garbed as the ladies. Most had given up the hip-length tabard for the short doublet that came just to the waist. This showed off the lower half of a man's body and left nothing to the imagination. The shape of calves, thighs, and buttocks was clearly visible, but it was the bulging outline of male genitals that prompted the clergy to rail against such vanity as lewd and licentious.

Up on the dais, the Plantagenets drew every eye. The king was resplendent in cloth of gold with azure hose so tight they looked as if they had been painted on him. Of course his physique was as lithe as that of the beloved Black Prince. Tonight the prince wore his sable doublet as usual, but his hose was startling. One leg was black while the other was a stark contrast in white.

Prince John of Gaunt's short, fashionable tunic was dagged with green leaves and beside him the ethereal Blanche of Lancaster wore a tight-sleeved jacket embroidered with emeralds. Once again, her father, Henry of Lancaster, had been chosen to be grand marshal of the tournament, and he was the only soberly dressed man in the hall in a long robe, edged in miniver.

Queen Philippa was so large with child the Court held its collective breath in anticipation of her labor. Beside her, Princess Isabel looked anything but brokenhearted. She had begun a flirtation with a young noble from Gascony

who had fought with the English at Crécy. Bernard Ezi was
the son of the Lord of Albret, an English ally. Isabel did
not take her eyes from him throughout the meal and Bernard responded with zeal.

Isabel needed to inflict pain upon someone. When Louis
rejected her, she had been deliberately hurt for the first
time in her life. The only balm that would heal the wound
was revenge. She selected her victim and set out to break
his heart.

Brianna and Robert sat with Prince Lionel, who was not
yet intoxicated. *Perhaps he is maturing,* thought Brianna.
The two men talked endlessly of jousting techniques and
strategy, so Brianna was free to listen to the troubadours
who strolled about the tables with their lutes and harps. A
young minstrel bowed before her, then sang a song written
especially for her, extolling her beauty and her virtue. She
blushed hotly and stole a glance across the room where
Hawksblood sat with Warrick. His face was so impassive, he
could have been wearing a mask. For a moment she
couldn't breathe. Surely he would not send a love song to
infuriate her betrothed! Then suddenly she knew he'd had
no hand in it. Christian Hawksblood would never send another to do his wooing.

She sent Robert a smile of thanks, knowing he had paid
good coin to have the balladeer write special lyrics for her.

When the trestle tables were cleared away so the ball
could begin, Queen Philippa watched the king have the
first dance with Princess Isabel, then she retired. Her pains
had started in her back, but not by word or gesture would
she spoil her husband's Victory Ball. Every lady of the
Court looked forward to a dance with King Edward and at
least one with the divine Prince of Wales.

Brianna accepted Prince Lionel's invitation to dance and
realized immediately why he was nicknamed the Ox. It was
a relief when Robert rescued her, and though he was too
large to be graceful, Brianna thought it rather endearing
that he made the effort to dance at all, when he was more
suited to the battlefield or the joust.

Dancing was a form of courtship affording intimacies
such as touching and whispering and oftimes kissing. Not a
few of the bolder men asked ladies for a stocking or a

garter to wear as a favor in the jousting. Brianna had refused Prince Lionel's request for an intimate article and was relieved when Robert concentrated on the figures of the dance rather than personal favors.

When Brianna danced with Prince Edward, she inquired anxiously of Joan.

He grinned down at her. "She is well. We have both decided we want a little girl."

"I miss her so much," Brianna said wistfully.

Edward's hands tightened painfully on Brianna's. "By the Chalice, not as much as I. It was like cutting off my arm to leave her. Her brother, Edmund, has promised to look after her until I return and that won't be long, I swear to you."

"Will the army be returning to France soon, also?"

"Yes, Our victories have given us a great advantage. We must press on until the whole country is ours. I am returning as soon as the tournament is over; the army will follow shortly. I will be glad when you come, Brianna. I know Joan misses you."

Suddenly there was a commotion in the center of the floor. The dancing had stopped and whispers had replaced the music. The king had been partnering Katherine de Montecute, Countess of Salisbury, when suddenly a lacy blue garter, embroidered with jewels, fell to the king's feet and slithered and twirled across the polished floor.

Katherine's cheeks were bright with guilty embarrassment. Edward Plantagenet, ever chivalrous, bent to retrieve the garter and slipped it over the sleeve of his doublet. He stared down the speculative glances of those close by and said, "Shame on him who thinks ill of it!" Then he took Katherine by the hand and led her back to her husband.

A short time later the king went up on the dais to address the dancers. "The garter is an old symbol of honor in the chivalry of our land. My great ancestor, Richard Coeur de Lion, ordered the bravest of his knights to wear it at the storming of Acre. Those knights excelled in valor and bravery and were known as the Knights of the Blue Thong. I shall create the Order of the Garter and the motto writ on it shall be: *Honi soit qui mal y pense.*"

Robert claimed the next dance from Brianna. "Every man in this room burns to receive the highest honor of English knighthood, but only twenty-five of us will be chosen."

By his words Brianna realized that Robert took for granted that he would be among those chosen. She prayed that it would be so, for she had seen how sullen he could be when disappointed.

"I know someone else who burns and lusts for everything that is mine. My bastard brother watches us with his dark impassive face, but underneath that mask, he covets all that is mine. He cozies up to my father, hoping for some of Warrick's lands and castles. How it must gall him that the title will be mine!"

"Oh, Robert, I don't think he harbors any resentment toward you," Brianna protested, trying to deny her guilt, but failing miserably.

"I hope he does. I hope he lusts for you so badly it chokes him on our wedding day!" Robert threw back his head and laughed.

Desperately she tried to change the subject. "You haven't asked me for a favor to wear in the tournament."

He leered down at her. "I'll settle for nothing less than a garter."

Her emotions were in such turmoil, she could neither pretend shock nor amusement. She simply reached beneath her skirts and removed one of her garters.

"I would have preferred getting it myself," he said boldly, "but I know you are a little prude and won't allow me to undress you until we are wed."

She didn't smile, but looked at him with serious eyes. "Thank you for waiting, Robert. Thank you for not forcing me to be intimate. It is most chivalrous of you."

At that moment, Prince Lionel engaged Robert in conversation and Brianna signaled to Adele so they could make good their escape.

The next morning, all the bells began to peel as a sign that Queen Philippa had been safely delivered of another daughter. Brianna and Adele visited the queen and were allowed to peek into the magnificently carved royal cradle for a glimpse of the newest princess. Isabel, diverting attention from the baby, gathered all the ladies in the room and insisted they accompany her to the lists. The fields and meadows for miles around Windsor were crowded with competitors and spectators. Champions had arrived from all over Europe to compete in the tournament. Princess Isabel insisted they go to the lists so they could all watch Bernard Ezi practice his jousting. Brianna didn't really mind; she knew she would be safe in a crowd.

❧ *31* ❧

The morning before St. George's Day, the list was posted naming England's most valiant knights who were to be inducted into the Order of the Garter the following day. It was headed by King Edward III and Edward, Prince of Wales. Next came Sir Walter Manny, Queen Philippa's personal knight, who had accompanied her from Hainault. Then came the king's uncle, Henry, Earl of Lancaster; the Earl of Warrick, and William de Montecute, Earl of Salisbury. Also included were nineteen barons and knights who had fought at the Battle of Crécy, including the two men who had stood shoulder to shoulder with the Black Prince: Sir John Chandos and Sir Christian de Beauchamp.

Men of lower rank had been preferred to such powerful members of the aristocracy as the earls of Hereford, Pembroke, and Northampton. The younger princes and their cousin Edmund, Earl of Kent, were not included.

That day the Court almost turned into a viper's nest. Some said it was a list of favorites, others applauded that only heroes of the great Battle of Crécy were being honored. Most were consoled by the knowledge that the vast round table in the new tower would hold two hundred, so there was plenty of room for men who showed valor in the future.

The knights' costumes were put on display in the Banqueting Hall. Every garment was new. Each knight inducted into the order would wear spotless white chausses and tunic for purity, an ermine-trimmed crimson robe to show their willingness to shed blood, and spurs of gold. Twenty-five golden medallions stamped with St. George and the Dragon had been forged for the occasion, and twenty-five dark blue velvet garters emblazoned with the motto: *Honi soit qui mal y pense.*

On the eve of St. George's Day, the king led the other inductees into Windsor's chapel where each man's armor stood against the walls and his sword lay upon the altar. They sat a vigil all night long, spending hours on their knees in prayer. At dawn, their squires came in to bathe them, to wash away their sins, then dressed them in their new garments and finally their armor.

King Edward inducted them with the great Sword of State, beginning with his own son. "Rise, Edward Plantagenet, Prince of Wales. Be thou a knight of the Order of the Garter." He placed the medallion about his son's neck and the garter about his knee. Then the king gave him the kiss of peace. Prince Edward took his sword from the altar, then stepped aside for the next man.

When the religious ceremony was finished, the twenty-five celebrants mounted and rode to the new Edward III Tower. They climbed the one hundred steps and took their honored places at the round table, where they were served breakfast with all pomp and ceremony.

"Fucking whoreson bastards!" Robert de Beauchamp spat. He picked up a stool and hurled it into the wall, smashing it to splinters. It was only a momentary outlet, bringing no satisfaction. "How could they choose that stinking Arabian ahead of me?" he asked the air.

When his rage abated enough to allow him to think straight, his hatred transferred to the Prince of Wales. "It was that son of a bitch who picked his friends for the order!" That's what power did for you. It gave you the freedom to do anything you wished, Robert decided.

He made his way to Prince Lionel's apartments and found the heavy door locked. He used his key to gain entrance and saw that Lionel was consuming a liquid breakfast. "That is not the answer, Your Highness," Robert growled.

"There is no answer, Robbie," Lionel said hopelessly. "My brother is a god; I a mere mortal."

"You are a prince of the realm! You have power! You just don't exercise it!" Robert cried.

"My father is blinded by his love for his firstborn. He has raised him so high, I shall never be able to scale the heights." Lionel's voice broke on a sob. His wine cup fell from his hand and he threw himself into Robert's arms and wept like a child. As Lionel's weakness grew, so Robert's strength doubled.

"Don't get drunk, Lionel, get even!" he urged.

"How?" Lionel blubbered.

Robert seized the moment. This prince of the blood would never be more vulnerable than he was at this moment. Now was his opportunity to turn the tables. He would no longer be Prince Lionel's man; Lionel would become Robert de Beauchamp's man!

"Your brother is no god. He is mere flesh and blood and bone, just like you, just like me. If wounded, he bleeds. If mortally wounded, he dies!"

Lionel raised his head and wiped his face on his sleeve.

"Power, Lionel; power is the only thing that counts. Without it you are nothing. The hastilude that follows the jousting where everyone fights with spears is a heaven-sent opportunity to seize your destiny and make it happen!"

Lionel stared at Robert with glazed eyes. "I . . . I cannot."

"I *can*! Just give me the word."

Lionel's throat closed so that he could not speak.

"Give me a sign!" Robert urged.

Lionel nodded his head.

At last Robert had him in the palm of his hand. Prince Lionel would become heir to the throne, and then King of England, and because he had assented, Lionel would be able to refuse him nothing for the rest of their lives. Robert kept his plan to rid himself of his own brother to himself. He felt as if fate were beginning to smile upon him at last.

All those participating in the jousting spent the night in their pavilions so they could arise at dawn to begin preparations. Again, Prince Edward and Christian de Beauchamp had set up their tents next to each other. This time, however, Hawksblood had received more challenges than he could accept. Because of the number of contestants, the grand marshal had declared a limit of three jousts for each.

The melee at day's end in which all the contestants took part, was officially declared a hastilude, which meant that spears could be used. It was the king's idea because his men had tasted victory in real battle and a run-of-the-mill free-for-all would lack the thrill of dangerous anticipation.

Randal Grey came into Prince Edward's tent breathless from running. His red hair was on end and the freckles across the bridge of his nose stood out darkly against the pallor of his skin. "Your Highness, you are in grave danger!"

John Chandos picked him up bodily and deposited him outside the pavilion. "Prince Edward has no time for your games, lad."

Randal swore foully. "Let me speak with him!"

"He's halfway into his armor. You'll make him late."

Randal didn't have time to argue. He rushed into Hawksblood's tent, where he ran into Paddy, who was about to give him the same treatment as Chandos. Randal ducked under Paddy's arm and began shouting at Hawksblood. Christian removed his helm so he could hear what the page was trying to tell him.

"It's Prince Edward! They are going to kill him!"

"Who is going to kill him?" Hawksblood demanded.

"I don't know. Some men over in yon meadow. I heard them plotting!"

"Come on." Hawksblood entered Edward's tent with Randal in tow. "The boy here had heard some men talking about killing someone. He thinks it involves you, Sire."

Randal cried, "It does! I wouldn't lie to you, Your Highness!"

"I hope not, Randal," the prince said quizzically. "Tell us just what you heard."

"I was over in the east meadow . . . it was still dark. I was crawling between the tents looking for a sword or a weapon that nobody would miss, when I heard men talking."

"You were stealing," Chandos accused.

"No . . . yes," Randal admitted, knowing he must tell the truth if he was to be believed.

"How many men?" Edward asked.

"I don't know . . . I heard three different voices."

"Did you recognize any of them?"

"I'm not sure, I don't think so. I couldn't see them . . . . I couldn't let them see me."

"What did you overhear?" Edward asked.

"They said it would be easy. No one would ever suspect foul play. They said accidents always happened in a melee. They said the one who wears sable armor must die."

Hawksblood and Edward exchanged glances. "Thanks for the warning, Randal. We'll take care of it. Don't repeat this to anyone else."

"Do we believe him?" Paddy asked skeptically when Randal left.

"We cannot ignore it," Hawksblood warned.

"Well, the melee isn't until late afternoon, we have a day of jousting to enjoy first," Edward said with a grin.

The lodges where the noble ladies sat had been covered with costly red carpet. People jostled for seats because of the great number of spectators attending. The ladies of the Court vied with each other to show off their costly gowns trimmed with marten, ermine, or vair. Rich materials of sendal and samite were embroidered with gold thread and pearls. Most of the ladies carried flowers so they could toss them into the lists when a particular favorite won a joust.

The spring sunshine reflected off the trumpets of the heralds and the helms and polished breastplates of the contestants. Flags and pennons mounted all along the palisades dazzled the eye with their colorful and diverse coats of arms.

Princess Isabel presided as Queen of the Tourney because her mother was resting from childbirth. Isabel was in her element today. She would present the prizes to the champions and occupy the seat of honor in the lodges where all the spectators could feast their eyes upon her. She wore red and silver and Brianna thought she looked truly lovely.

Brianna tossed her hair back over her shoulder, thinking this was probably the last time she would wear it loose in public. After she was wed tomorrow, she would wear a scarf or headdress. A feeling was building inside her that

she could not put a name to. It was a mixture of excitement
and dread and uncertainty. It was the end of girlhood and
the beginning of womanhood. What did her future hold? If
a wizard with a crystal ball had offered her a glimpse, she
would have refused to look.

To Brianna it seemed the sands of time were running
through the hourglass with frightening speed. Before she
knew it, she would be standing in the chapel tomorrow,
pledging her sacred vows. She knew of at least two other
couples who were being wed and, of course, after the wedding ceremonies there was to be the christening of the new
baby princess.

The audience surged to its feet cheering as the contestants rode onto the field, singing a rousing battle song. The
ladies threw flowers and the cheering rose higher and
higher in a tribute to their bravery for defeating the
French. Before the first three bouts pursuivants came forward to announce the knights and revile the opponents as
had been done in ancient times. "Here is the Baron de
Bures, a brave knight of a valorous house. Watch closely all
who love brave deeds. His challenger had better find his
ransom money. All his friends will feel shame this day!"

From the opposite end of the field the challenger's pursuivant answered: "Silence your boasts. The baron will
have his spurs struck from his heels as an unworthy knight
if he survives the impact of the lances." And so the tournament progressed.

As the Black Prince in his sable armor defeated the last
of his challengers, Brianna said to Adele, "I wish Joan were
here to see him."

"Paddy says they'll be returning to France soon. This
time, we too will go."

Brianna wondered. Christian Hawksblood had done
something desperate to prevent her marriage once and she
still half-expected him to do something this time. She
prayed that he would not. She hoped that he had accepted
the fact that her marriage to Robert de Beauchamp was
inevitable.

She clasped her hands together tightly when
Hawksblood jousted. She knew he would defeat all his
challengers. He was the most skilled knight at Windsor.

She grabbed Adele's hand when Robert rode his jousts, hoping he would make a brave show, and he did not disappoint her. She blushed when the ladies about her offered her congratulations and she saw them sigh over Robert's fair countenance and tall physique.

When the elimination rounds were over, those undefeated tilted against each other. The king went down in defeat to his friend William de Montecute, Earl of Salisbury, then the crowd went wild as he in turn was beaten by their chosen champion, the Black Prince.

As time for the hastilude approached, Brianna knew the last thing she wanted to see was a re-creation of a bloody battle fought with spears. "Let's stretch our legs," she suggested to Adele.

"Yes. Let's see if we can get a cool drink. My throat is parched."

In the Black Prince's tent, Edward and Christian sat talking as their squires handed them clean dry linen tunics to wear beneath their armor. "We will exchange armor, Sire. I have an ominous feeling of foreboding about this hastilude." Hawksblood expected Prince Edward to refuse and was contemplating conspiring with John Chandos to physically restrain him from participating in the melee.

Edward nodded. "Yes. I have a plan. If I don your brass armor, I will be able to observe any who go after the man wearing sable armor. Have no fear, Christian, I am prepared to slay any who plot my death."

Christian let out a relieved breath. He had total confidence in his own ability to defend himself against any man breathing.

The roar of the crowd was so deafening that in spite of her abhorrence for violence, Brianna rushed back to her seat in the lodges, clutching a cup of cool mead. The clash of weapons and the battle cries of the knights were mesmerizing. Her hands on the metal cup turned icy and her breath caught and held as the good-natured blows became reckless and turned desperate, smiting with sword and thrusting with spear until the dust rose up to mingle with the blood and sweat of the combatants.

"Mary and Joseph, they are killing one another!"

"No, no, my lamb. 'Tis only a mock battle. You know

what men are. They cannot enjoy themselves unless they break a few bones."

Brianna's eyes were drawn to the warrior in brass armor. He stood out from the rest like a beacon. She did not have the advantage of her mother's second sight today and had no idea the man in brass was not Christian.

Prince Edward could not believe his eyes. The moment Hawksblood in his sable armor stepped upon the field, three men moved purposefully toward him with clear intent. Edward slashed his way toward Hawksblood and smote down the first man with a brutal crack to the head with his broadsword. As he fell, his helm came off and Edward saw that it was one of his brother's men from the House of Clarence.

Anger almost choked him! He cried out a warning to Hawksblood but saw with deep satisfaction that he was easily besting the second man who attacked him. Then with horror, Edward saw an enormous combatant dart behind Hawksblood, wielding both spear and sword. Bloodlust gripped the Black Prince. He would slay this treasonable swine who had murder in his heart!

Edward raised his spear, drew back his powerful arm, then sent his weapon hurtling through the air on its path of destruction. It pierced clean through the man's breastplate and the point of the spear protruded from his back. A clearing formed about the dead man, and gradually the fighting came to a halt.

The mail-clad figure was carried from the field to one of the infirmary tents. The two combatants wearing sable armor and brass armor followed. The King of England and Mad Hound Warrick disappeared into the tent and the flaps were closed.

Warrick bent over the body of his son and he knew immediately that it was too late to save him.

The king demanded, "Why in the name of Christ are you two wearing each other's armor?"

Prince Edward explained, "We were tipped off there would be an attempt on my life."

Blood drained from the king's face.

Hawksblood helped his father remove the spear from Robert's body. Warrick's face was like granite.

The Black Prince was still gripped by fury. "There were three of them—all Lionel's men!"

The king lifted the tent flap and summoned a squire. "Find Prince Lionel immediately." Master John Bray, the king's physician, rushed up and the king shook his head. "Use another tent for those wounded." Bray dropped the flap and returned to the others.

The acrid smell of sweat mingled with the metallic smell of blood and the unmistakable scent of death. Emotions hung palpably in the air . . . anger, shame, pity, sorrow. The implications were horrendous.

Lionel had to stoop before he could enter. In his chain mail he dwarfed everyone in the tent. When he saw the body, he took a clumsy step forward. "Rob? Robbie?" His face was running with tears. "Who killed him?"

Prince Edward sprang forward with upraised fist. "You did, you son of a bitch! You had to have given him the order!"

The king stepped between his two sons. "Cease! There was a plot to take Edward's life. Were you involved?" the king thundered.

"No! No, Father, I swear to you."

"You fucking liar! All three men belonged to the House of Clarence," Prince Edward shouted. "One was Fitzroy . . . I don't recall the other's name, but I'd know the swine anywhere!"

The king was incensed. "This is a black mark against the name of Plantagenet! We will be perceived as wolves, turning on each other, tearing each other's throats out for cursed ambition!"

"Father, I swear I am innocent!" Lionel cried.

"Don't you see that protestations don't matter? In the eyes of the world you will be guilty!"

Hawksblood stepped forward. "Sire, the spectators saw the knight in brass armor throw the spear. They will think I killed my brother."

The king stared at him for a full minute as the truth of Hawksblood's words sank in. "You would take the blame?"

Christian Hawksblood said, "It is best for all that I do. The Black Prince is the people's chosen champion. Real-life heroes are few and far between. Don't allow his image to become tarnished, Your Highness."

"I *would* like to keep this evil business quiet. It would destroy Philippa's happiness if Lionel had plotted his brother's death." The king saw Warrick's stony countenance. "I'm forgetting you in all this, friend. I'm sorry for your loss, Guy. Can you live with our silence in this matter?"

Warrick knew nothing could bring back his son. An investigation would probably destroy the king's son Lionel, as well. He nodded his head. "I can live with the silence, but I cannot live with the shame, Sire."

"Nay, none of us can change what our wolf cubs become." He turned to Lionel. "I want Fitzroy and the other arrested. See to it!"

Hawksblood said low to Warrick, "Are you all right?" Only the aquamarine eyes showed a glimpse of the anguish in the earl's heart and soul. Hawksblood and Warrick left the tent together and Christian led the way to his own pavilion where his squires awaited him. He sat his father down in a chair while Ali poured him a restorative drink. "Leave us awhile," he told his squires.

"We must bury him," Warrick said stoically.

"Would you like me to see to it?" Hawksblood asked.

"Nay. I'll make the arrangements." The earl drained the cup and set it down. "I know there was no love lost between you, but nonetheless I'm glad he didn't die by your hand."

"I feel exactly the same, but Prince Edward saved my life. Robert would have killed me, believing I was Edward."

Warrick shook his head in anguish. "I blame myself. I often had doubts about him, but stubbornly refused to see him for what he was. Tomorrow would have been his wedding day. Poor Lady Bedford."

"The contract that was drawn up for Warrick's son to wed Brianna of Bedford was approved by the king. I want to fullfil that contract." Warrick stared at his son, a dozen unasked questions on his lips.

"I want her. None other shall ever have her," Christian vowed.

"The people already think you killed your brother. They

will say it was no accident. They will say you murdered him to get your hands on his woman."

"I don't give a good goddamn what people say," Hawksblood emphasized.

Warrick finally said, "If the lady is willing, I have no objection. I already think of her as my daughter."

❧ *32* ❧

Brianna of Bedford felt numb. She had watched the melee in fascinated horror, her eyes fixed on the combatant clad in shiny brass armor. In spite of the pandemonium and the dust, she had seen him hurl his spear into another combatant. If the wound was not fatal, it would be a miracle!

She watched with closed throat as the felled warrior was carried from the field. Clad in plain mail his identity was unknown, yet a suspicion so terrible it shamed her rose in Brianna's mind. It couldn't be Robert. Christian de Beauchamp was incapable of such an evil deed. Yet hadn't she been waiting for him to do something that would stop the wedding?

With dread in her heart she left the lodges and made her way toward the infirmary tents. Adele trailed behind her, unsure of what had happened. A crowd milled about the tent. Brianna saw the flap was pulled down so that none could enter. Another tent was open and men with light wounds moved in and out. She entered the tent and ran her eyes over all the men being tended by Master John Bray and his assistants. The Earl of Salisbury lay with a gash in his leg, but none of the men was Robert. "Who was carried off the field?" she asked.

"It was Warrick's son, lady," a squire informed her. The nobles who knew about her relationship with Robert de Beauchamp looked at her with pity in their eyes. This told her, clearer than words, that her betrothed was dead. Brianna felt sick, her senses swam, and the floor of the tent came up to smack her in the face and she went down in a heap.

Sir John Chandos saw her swoon and carried her outside. Brianna came to almost immediately and the first thing she saw was Adele's worried face. "I'll be all right," she said. "Thank you, John."

"I'll walk with you to your chambers, Lady Bedford."

"What happened?" begged Adele, at a loss.

John Chandos said low, "Robert de Beauchamp was killed in the hastilude."

"Ohmigod," Adele whispered, crossing herself.

Brianna lay on her bed staring at the vaulted ceiling of her chamber with unseeing eyes. Her mind flew back to the moment when this ill-fated triangle had begun. The very first time they met, Hawksblood had claimed her as "his" lady.

After they had been intimate at Bedford, he had made her swear that she would renounce her betrothal to Robert. If she had done so, would it have saved Robert's life? The thought was unendurable. Hawksblood's words were indelibly etched upon her memory. He had vowed, *"Know this, lady: You will never belong to Robert de Beauchamp, not in this life or the next."*

He had made good his vow!

Brianna knew she had never loved Robert and that made it more dreadful. She had given herself wantonly to his brother, but held herself aloof from her betrothed. Yet Robert was not without blame in fostering hatred between himself and his brother. On their last night together he had said, *"I hope he lusts for you so badly it chokes him on our wedding day."* Now there would be no wedding day. Brianna turned facedown and began to sob. "Dear God, don't let me feel relief over his death. Don't let me be that wicked and shameless."

A page brought Lady Bedford a formal notice from the king that her betrothed, Sir Robert de Beauchamp, had been accidentally killed in the hastilude. An hour later a note came from the Earl of Warrick, asking if she would be good enough to attend him.

Brianna, in a black tunic over a gray underdress, her hair braided into a huge chignon, walked sadly through the

Lower Ward to the Beauchamp Tower. A servant ushered
her and Adele inside then led the way to the chamber
where the earl awaited her. Adele let her go in alone and
sat down on a carved settle to wait.

The old earl's face was craggy as volcanic rock. She had
no idea what to say to him. "My lord, I am so sorry for your
loss," she whispered.

He shook his head. "The king has declared there will be
no more hastiludes at Windsor. They are too dangerous.
We lose enough knights in war without losing them to fatal
accidents."

She opened her mouth to protest that it was no accident,
but the words would not come out. How could she tell this
man who was mourning the death of his son that his remaining son had committed the murder?

"Lady Bedford, I still want you for my daughter-in-law."

"I . . . I don't understand—"

"My son, Christian, wishes to marry you tomorrow."

"Ah God, no," Brianna cried. "Robert hasn't even been
entombed."

"My dear, 'tis a common enough practice. When a contract has been drawn up and death takes a son, another son
often takes over that contract. Usually it is because the
family doesn't wish to lose an heiress, but I swear to you
that is not our motive. I have land and castles aplenty for
Christian."

"I cannot marry Hawksblood," she whispered.

The earl's face set in stern lines. "He is determined to
have you. He is the kind of man who usually gets his way."

"I . . . I'm sorry."

"Don't give me your final answer now. Sleep on it, Lady
Bedford. Tomorrow perhaps you will see that Hawksblood
would be a wise choice."

Brianna left and she and Adele made their way through
the crowded Ward. Windsor overflowed with visitors, all
intent on celebration. The lights in the Banqueting Hall
would burn all night while the Court feasted, danced,
drank, and laughed away the hours. Life went on with a
vengeance in spite of death's presence, or perhaps because
of it.

Back in her chamber, Brianna's thoughts chased each

other in endless circles. Hawksblood had lost no time in speaking to Warrick and gaining his approval. Could he bend anyone to his will? Warrick had spoken of land and castles that would now go to Hawksblood. More motivation to eliminate the heir. And she could not deny that he had treated the people at Bedford as if they were his. Perhaps his plans had been laid long ago. Could no one else see what he had gained? With one thrust of a spear he had become heir to the Earldom of Warrick!

She was distracted from her dark thoughts by voices in the outer room. Her chamber door opened and Christian Hawksblood filled its frame.

"What do you want?" she asked coldly.

"I want you, Brianna."

"You cannot have me," she said flatly.

He took a step into the room. "I can and I will."

"Have you no guilt?" she cried incredulously.

"No, none," he said evenly.

"Robert was my betrothed!"

"You did not love Robert. In truth you shrank from the idea of becoming his wife."

Guilt washed over her. How could she in conscience deny his words? "I would have grown to love him!" she flung.

"You can grow to love me."

She stood up to face him. Her breathing was agitated, her breasts rose and fell temptingly. "I did love you. You killed that love as surely as you killed your brother."

He stepped close and took her firmly by the shoulders. "He was involved in plots you know nothing of. I am sworn to silence. Either you trust me or you do not."

She searched his dark face. It was as hard as if it were carved from mahogany. It took all her courage to defy him. A flicker of fear kindled inside her breast. She was taking her life in her hands to accuse such a physically powerful male of murder. "I do *not* trust you," she said low. She thought he flinched at her words, but then his face set in grim determination.

"A marriage without trust will prove interesting," he mocked.

"I will not marry you, Arabian!" she flared, then caught her breath at her own temerity.

"You shall, you shall!" he vowed.

She looked up at him with loathing. "You cannot make me."

"The king can make you."

"Then bring me his special writ!" she flung triumphantly, calling his bluff.

Hawksblood reached inside his doublet and took out a parchment. He lifted her hand and placed it on her open palm. Without another word he turned and left her.

Brianna pinched her nostrils against the acrid smell of melting tapers on the altar in the chapel. She had not closed her eyes all night, but spent it agonizing over today's ceremony.

It was truly a man's world. What were her wishes compared to those of the four powerful men in attendance who dominated the chapel? Warrick stood beside Hawksblood, and the king stood beside Prince Edward, who was Hawksblood's groomsman. As the priest intoned a Latin prayer, Brianna glanced down at her gown, which Joan had taken such pleasure in designing. She hated this dress!

How prophetic her words to Robert had been. *"It is unlucky for the groom to see the bride's dress before the day of the wedding."* Her thoughts wandered back to Joan. She, too, had been forced to subjugate her wishes to those of a powerful man. It was wrong! A woman should have a say in her own destiny.

Brianna jumped as the king moved beside her and took her hand. The priest had asked the age-old question, "Who giveth this woman?" King Edward Plantagenet placed her hand in Christian de Beauchamp's and said, "I do." Since she was the king's ward, it was only fitting that he give her away.

By rote Brianna repeated the words the priest gave her, plighting her troth, her future, her life until death parted them. She vowed to love, to honor, and to obey, kneeling to kiss his hand and repeating, "I submit myself to your authority, my lord husband." She had no choice but to do so.

She handed her flowers to Adele so she could receive the heavy gold wedding ring.

Christian's deep voice flowed over her. "With this ring I thee wed, with my body I thee worship . . ."

Brianna thought wildly, he has already worshiped me with his body and if I submit to him again, I will dishonor myself! Then she heard the priest solemnly intone, "I now pronounce you man and wife, in the name of the Father, and of the Son, and of the Holy Ghost."

Hawksblood loomed above her and bent his dark head to give her the kiss. She did not lift her face to receive it, but made him bend all the way to her. His eyes glittered like splinters of aquamarine in his dark face. He was too bloody proud to bend his head to any man, but she had made him do so. The kiss was brief, chaste. She took her flowers back from Adele and stood passively while each of the men present congratulated the groom and kissed the bride.

King Edward excused himself. "My friend De Montecute was wounded yesterday. His condition worsens by the hour." He and the Prince of Wales departed, but when Brianna made to follow them, Hawksblood took her wrist and said, "We remain here."

She watched in silence as two knights carried in a long coffin. There were only the three of them present to hear Robert's funeral service. She thought it shameful that Prince Lionel did not attend along with all the knights of the House of Clarence. Robert had served him so faithfully. She did not know that Lionel lay in a drunken stupor because he was being ostracized by his father and the brother he had plotted against.

Brianna reached deep and found an inner strength. She stood proud and tall while the priest intoned the interminable prayers in Latin. When at long last it was over, she moved up the altar steps to stand beside the catafalque. As she pulled a rose from her bouquet, a thorn pierced her finger and a drop of blood fell upon the white rose. She placed the lone flower upon the coffin. "Forgive me," she whispered.

Brianna blinked as she emerged from the chapel into the bright sunshine.

Adele spoke to Hawksblood, "My lord, will you send Paddy for Lady de Beauchamp's things?"

Brianna realized that she was Lady de Beauchamp. It didn't sound strange to her ears, and she thought that in itself was odd.

"Nay, Adele, I will come for my lady's things," Christian decided.

When Brianna entered her husband's chambers, she recalled that she had been here before. They once belonged to Joan's brother, the Earl of Kent, and Joan had taken her there. The rooms were lavishly appointed, for Edmund was a wealthy member of the royal family. The apartment consisted of two large chambers and a dressing room. The largest room was dominated by a massive curtained bed. Hawksblood's words sprang into her mind. *"I shall plant my seed in you, Brianna, never doubt it."* He had been so sure he would be her husband! Robert had never been an impediment to him. Had he come to England for the express purpose of seeking revenge against Warrick? His actions seemed to add up to that. Had he only ever wanted her because she was part of the spoils of the House of Warrick?

Christian carried in the last of Brianna's trunks, then turned with solicitude to Adele. "I have removed my things from the dressing room. I hope you will be comfortable here."

"Thank you, my lord, it is more than adequate."

"You are most gracious to say so, Adele. I know it is small. When we go to France I'll see that you have more than one room."

Brianna's own bed linen was of the finest quality, all embroidered with the monogram B for Bedford. Adele realized as she made up the massive bridal bed that the initial B now stood for Beauchamp.

In the other chamber they were alone for the first time since they had exchanged vows. Brianna raised her chin. "I was most content at Bedford. I would prefer to return there rather than accompany you to France."

Christian came to stand before her, though he did not yet touch her. "Brianna, I married you so that we could be together for the rest of our lives. One day we will go to

Bedford. Together. That day has not yet arrived. First we must go to France. Together."

She flung her golden hair back over her shoulders in a gesture of defiance. "You taught me well how to be devious. All I need do is disappear the day you sail!"

Now he did touch her. His powerful hands caressed her shoulders, then he drew her a little closer. He dropped his voice to a more intimate level. "By the time we are ready to sail for France, you will never wish to leave me. I will be in your blood. You will belong to me body and soul." He brought his mouth down to capture hers in a kiss that was so intimate and so possessive, it would have been the easiest thing in the world to surrender to the intoxicating male dominance of the Arabian Knight.

When he lifted his mouth from hers, she said defiantly, "If you think kisses and caresses will make us one, you know nothing about me. You may take possession of my body, you may even be able to take possession of my mind with your mystic power, but you will never have the smallest part of my soul." Even as she spoke, she knew she should not be saying these things to him. She was setting herself up as an irresistible challenge to his masculinity.

It was as if she had not spoken. His eyes caressed every detail of her hair, face, and figure. Then he murmured, "Let me help you remove your gown."

Gripped by panic that he was already demanding his marital rights while it was still afternoon, she cried, "No, I shall keep it on!"

His eyebrows elevated slightly. "You will wear your wedding gown to the royal christening? Or did you forget, chérie?"

Brianna flushed. "Of course I didn't forget. Adele will help me change my clothes." She swallowed hard. "I would like some privacy, my lord."

Christian knew it would be difficult for her to go back into the chapel for the third time on this fateful day. "I shall be back to escort you. Enjoy your privacy while you still have it," he added pointedly.

In truth she was glad to rid herself of the wedding gown. Adele helped her into a dark blue tunic with pale blue underdress. She would not wear bright colors this day in respect to Robert, but the king and queen would take it ill if she wore a mourning color to their baby's christening. It took both her and Adele over half an hour to plait and wind her golden mass of hair into a coronet.

Christian arrived for her as the last pins were set into place. "How regal you look, my love," he complimented.

Her reply held a barb. "Good enough for a prince?"

"Indeed," he nodded, refusing to be baited.

The chapel was packed to the doors, but the crowd made way for the newlyweds to pass inside. All were shocked that the Arabian had killed his brother then married his brother's betrothed, but the king apparently accepted Robert de Beauchamp's death as an accident and sanctioned the union of Hawksblood and Brianna of Bedford. All the royal Plantagenet family were present for the christening. A chair had been provided for Queen Philippa, while King Edward held the child. *Like a trophy,* thought Brianna. *All men are vain. Especially when it comes to symbols of their virility!*

Because he was so tall, she saw Prince Edward's golden head as he stood with the other princes and princesses. When Joan had her baby, he wouldn't be able to claim his child. Joan was now Lady Holland and her and Edward's child would be a Holland. Brianna's heart ached for Joan. For Edward she had no pity. He was a bloody man, and a powerful one. If he could not marry Joan honorably, he should never have had his lustful way with her!

She glanced briefly at her new husband and was surprised at the look on his face. He was so tall he could watch the christening over the heads of those in front of him. His face was so tender as he watched the baby. Wistful too. The look told her plainly he longed for a child of his own. Brianna suddenly felt faint. Instantly his eyes were on her, his arm at her back to steady her, and she could have sworn he looked at her with infinite tenderness for a fleeting moment before his mask fell back into place.

And then the ceremony was over and they were being jostled by the crowd as the entire Court made its way to the Banqueting Hall. She felt Hawksblood grip her hand so they would not get separated. A long trestle table covered with white satin displayed the christening gifts that had been presented.

"Oh dear, I gave no gift," Brianna murmured.

"I sent one from both of us."

"Which?" she asked, looking at the presents.

"The heart-shaped locket with the ruby and seed pearls," he murmured low.

Brianna almost gasped at the size of the ruby. It must be worth hundreds of pounds. Was he already dipping into Warrick's coffers, or God forbid, Bedford's?

As her husband held her chair for her, she glanced at him and said, "I don't really wish to be here."

"We'll find an opportunity to slip away soon," he assured her.

Now she was in a fever to stay!

"Have you eaten anything today?" he asked with solicitude as the toasts to the new princess began.

Brianna shook her head, realizing she had not. No wonder she felt faint in the chapel.

"Just sip the wine," he warned.

Instead, she drank it down quickly, draining the cup.

"You have already broken your vow to obey me. And done it deliberately, Brianna."

As it bloomed bloodred inside her breast, she shrugged a careless, shapely shoulder. "Since I made them under duress, I'll likely break them all before I'm done. One precious vow at a time!" As she lifted her cup as a signal for it to be refilled, he took hold of her wrist and squeezed. The cup fell from her fingers.

"You are ridiculous. There is absolutely no question about it; when I give orders, you will obey them or you will be made to obey them. The choice is yours." His eyes impaled her.

I hate you! she thought.

"You do not," he said emphatically.

My God, he read her thought. Now she hated and feared him!

The corner of his mouth went up ironically. "You do not fear me overmuch, lady, or you would not dare provoke me."

Brianna forced herself to concentrate upon the dishes

before her. She took a slice of lamb, an artichoke, and a little watercress. She managed to chew and swallow a mouthful of meat then picked the petals from the artichoke and lifted one to her mouth.

Christian bent toward her. "You do realize that is an aphrodisiac?" He kept a straight face as she pushed the plate away. When the final course was served she took a small wedge of cheese and a piece of christening cake. She timed her next move perfectly. While Ali offered rosewater to cleanse Hawksblood's fingers, she picked up her husband's wine goblet and drained it.

With sudden insight, he realized she needed courage for what lay ahead. He spoke low to Ali, but she heard every word, as no doubt he intended. "Prepare a bath for my lady, then the rest of the evening is yours."

❧ *33* ❧

"We will leave now," Christian murmured.

"We cannot offend the Plantagenets," Brianna protested low.

"All here know we were wed this morning and tonight is special to us. Come, Brianna." He stood up and took her hand. As she arose from the table she was slightly unsteady and he knew the wine affected her a little. He felt the tremor of her hand as his fingers curled about it.

As they moved down the long passage that led from the hall, she said, "If I am to bathe, I will need privacy."

He squeezed her hand and bent his dark head toward her. "We will have complete privacy, beloved. Ali knows we wish to be alone."

"That isn't what I meant!" she objected as they reached their apartment. Ali had lit a fire and set the bath in the bedchamber. The servants were just departing with their empty buckets.

"I have laid out the perfumed oils and towels, my lord. Is there anything else you desire?"

"My lady desires privacy, complete privacy. Please see that we are not disturbed this night."

Ali bowed and closed the door.

Brianna swung about. Her cheeks were flushed, her eyes brilliant. "You know exactly what I mean! Privacy from you!"

Christian moved toward her purposefully. With his eyes on hers, he lifted his hands to draw out the pins from her coronet. His fingers had been aching this past hour to touch her glorious hair, to take it down, to see it in all its glory. "I cannot understand your shyness, sweetheart. We have already been lovers and yet you needed the wine to give you courage."

"I don't need courage, I need privacy!" She tried to pull away but his fingers entangled in her hair made it painful, so she stilled.

"We have total privacy. No one will ever see what we do this night. No one will hear our love cries. None will ever know what intimacies will take place in this bath, in that bed."

She was bristling with anger now, as was his intent. Her anger would drive out her fear. Her beautiful eyes seemed filled with green sparks. "I will not undress and bathe in front of you!"

His fingers stroked her golden hair and spread it about her shoulders. "There is no need. I will undress you and bathe you." Even as he spoke his fingers had undone the lacing at the side of her tunic.

Her fury made her breathless. "You are a devil . . . an Arabian devil!"

His sure hands removed the tunic and moved to the underdress. "And you are the bride of an Arabian devil."

His words sent a tremor through her body. She could feel the heat of his powerful hands through the fine material of her underdress. One hand moved up to cup a full breast while the other moved beneath her skirt and slid up her thigh. She was all ashiver at the way he touched her.

"My beautiful, beautiful Brianna. I want to explore you until I come to know you fully. I want to see you hissing and spitting with fury, I want to see you laughing and crying and loving. I want to see you in a tower of passion that topples at my touch, and then I want to see you experience them all over again when you are naked." His hands almost succeeded in removing her underdress.

"No!" she cried, stubbornly clinging to the diaphanous material.

"No? You need a little more courage before you feel ready to embark on the journey to womanhood?"

Brianna had no ready reply to the outrageous things he said to her. He moved across the room to a cabinet and poured wine into an exquisite chalice. Then he returned to her and towered above her, far too close for her comfort. She reached out to take the golden cup, but he took her hand and placed it upon his hard muscled chest, then he himself lifted the wine to her lips. "We will share," he murmured huskily. "We will share everything as lovers."

She lowered her dark, gilt-tipped lashes and quaffed the golden wine. His hand allowed her to take all that she wanted, all that she needed. "Drink deeply of the cup of life, the cup of love," he murmured low, his voice as rich as dark velvet.

When she looked down at herself she saw that she was naked. When had he removed her last garment? He drained the last mouthful she had left him and she watched, mesmerized, as he brought his lips down to hers and gave her the wine-rich kiss. His mouth tasted like Heaven and hell. She hated him, loved him, loathed him.

Christian savored the loveliness before him. He lifted her hair and let it tumble back against her skin. Golden silk against cream satin. He cupped her face, his long fingers tenderly curving about her cheeks, then his lips brushed her brow, her cheekbone, the beauty mark. The tantalizing cleft of her chin drew the tip of his tongue to trace its shape, and then at last his mouth took possession of hers in a kiss that explored her scented, wet alcove, her wine-drenched sweetness.

The deep, sensual kiss engaged all her senses so completely that she did not feel his hand slip between her legs. She became aware of it only when the heat from his strong palm cupping her whole mons seeped up inside of her. She felt his other hand slide down the curve of her back, beneath her hair and come to rest firmly upon her rounded bottom.

And then he lifted her!

"Hawksblood, no!" she cried out, and had to cling to him to prevent herself from falling.

His wicked mouth teased hers. "Christian, say Christian. I want to taste my name upon your lips."

"Devil! Devil! Devil! What does that taste like?"

"It tastes wicked and wanton and wondrously sinful."

She gasped with exasperation and then surprise as he lifted her high, then lowered her into the warm, scented water, carefully draping her hair outside the bath. He knelt beside the tub and reached for the sponge.

"No! Please, Hawksblood, allow me to bathe myself."

"Say Christian."

"Please, Chris—" Before she had finished his name, his mouth possessed hers, savoring the feel of it upon her lips. As a reward for obeying him, he placed the sponge in her hand and stood up. A sigh of relief floated from her lips, but before the sigh was completely released, she drew in a swift breath. Jesu, he was taking this opportunity to strip naked. She dare not look away from him for fear of what he would do next, this maddening, infuriating husband of hers.

Brianna's eyes widened at the pure splendor of him. She had forgotten the physical perfection of the man. He was as darkly beautiful as some mythic god. The firelight reflected upon the sheen of his skin, highlighting every muscle and lithe sinew of his chest and iron-hard thighs.

The heat of the water and the wine combined to make her body tingle. It turned traitor on her and began to re-member the sensual sensations he had aroused in her at Bedford. A longing began, an aching that intensified relent-lessly. The emptiness inside her magnified a thousandfold. Her body needed to be filled. She was skin-hungry, needing his touch. She was ready to scream.

She watched him move about the chamber. He spread a big, thirsty towel before the fire, took the stopper from an alabaster flagon and set it beside the towel. Then he was coming for her. When he lifted her from the water, she shivered as the cool air touched her warm skin.

He laid her on the towel before the fire and spread her golden tresses in a glorious halo about her head. The water that clung to her skin slowly evaporated in the warmth from the fire. Some of the drops, however, formed tiny rivulets between her breasts, around her navel, at the vee of her thighs. Christian bent down to lick the iridescent drops from her damp body, until she was shivering from head to heels.

"Oh God, oh God," she whimpered, wanting him to stop, wanting him to continue forever.

He poured scented oil from the flagon into his palm, warmed it at the flames, then smoothed it with a sweeping, sensuous stroke down her throat, between the valley of her breasts, across her taut belly, then down to her thighs. The fragrance of myrrh and lemon almost stole her senses and her skin turned from ice to fire as he stroked and massaged her firm young flesh until it gleamed in the fireglow.

His voice, low, vibrating with dark passion flowed over her. "I want what we feel to go deeper than love, for the soul has greater depths. Love, like the symbolic wedding ring, has no beginning, no end. Deepest passion, once it starts cannot be stopped. When I take you to bed, inside the curtains, in the dark, we will trace what we feel back to the root of love. You must surrender everything you know, everything you are, with abandon."

Brianna was in a fever of need as he lifted her and carried her to the bed. But it was a purely physical need he had aroused in her, it had nothing spiritual about it. It had nothing to do with a meeting of their souls. She could feel his thick shaft rub against her thigh, hot and hard as the great iron poker that stood against the fireplace.

In the bed he rolled against her, embracing her, engulfing her with his blatant masculinity. His body was as hard as if he were mail-clad and she began to sob with her great need. What he had aroused in her was simple, downright lust! She was female, he was male, and she thirsted for his domination.

As he tongued one boldly impudent nipple until it spiked in his mouth, he slipped a finger inside her to trace her, to explore her, then he eased in a second finger and thrust deep, feeling her tighten about him, arch blindly as she began to build.

She was like hot, wet silk and though he was a master of control, Hawksblood knew an overwhelming desire to thrust his manroot deep inside her. His control shattered into a million shards. As he withdrew his fingers, Brianna moaned because of their loss.

"What, love?" he cried raggedly, towering above her.

She dug her nails into his flesh. "Christian, Christian, I want you to take me!"

He was white-hot, mad with need. He thrust home deeply, losing his heart completely to this girl with the lush woman's body and sensual woman's appetite. She met him more than halfway, taking and giving at the same time. Their lovemaking was almost violent. It was an assault of the senses.

All seven of them.

They ascended to the heights, both cried out raggedly as they peaked, then they plummeted down together, clinging tightly, in what felt very much like a small death. They lay motionless, sprawled together, drained to the last drop.

Then for Christian, the miracle of rebirth, as replenishment began. His strength and vigor swept back into him. And something else. A joy, a contentment, a peace he had never known. He rolled his weight from her, then slipped his arms about her, enfolding her against his heart, burying his face in her golden hair.

The surcease overwhelmed her. She began to sob until she bathed his heart with her tears. He had brought her pleasures that she had no right to. They had indulged in such carnal appetites, it had to be a mortal sin.

Christian knew Brianna's emotions were as tangled as her beautiful hair at this moment. He knew tears were a cathartic release for a woman. Her fulfillment was mingled with grief and guilt, love and hate. He knew, too, it would take time for her to sort them all out. Though he was a patient man, he hoped and prayed it would not take too long for her to come to the realization that she loved and adored him every bit as much as he worshiped her. He would give her time to absorb the truth that this marriage was preordained. That they had belonged to each other since the dawn of time and that they would be together throughout eternity.

Brianna, who had been emotionally exhausted, was now physically exhausted. She sank into a deep sleep, not moving for hours. When she awakened, it was still dark inside the curtained bed. She was instantly aware of the man beside her, though he was quietly sleeping. Fragments of a memory stole to her in the darkness. Was it a dream that she was trying to recall? Then suddenly she remembered.

Remembered vividly!

It was when Hawksblood had been at war and she had deliberately donned her mother's gray velvet cloak so that she could conjure a vision of him. She realized with horror it had been no dream. It had been a prophecy, a glimpse of the future. She had envisioned Christian killing Robert and she had done nothing to prevent it. She vividly remembered luring Robert to the tower so that Christian could dispose of him. Then with Robert's blood upon her, they had made love. It had all come to pass!

Brianna closed her eyes in the darkness, agonizing over the part she had played in all this. Had she in reality lured Christian to become her lover so that he would save her from marriage to Robert? Nay, she had not done so knowingly, but she admitted that she was not entirely blameless.

Her new husband turned in his sleep and his thigh brushed hers. Fear washed over her. But it was not simply fear of him. She was afraid of herself. Afraid of her deep desire for this Arabian Knight. Afraid of her dark longings that only he could assuage. Was he an immortal? Had she sold her soul to the devil? She must never let him know that he had complete power over her, that he owned her body and soul. He had put his mark upon her as surely as the brand he wore. She must keep some small part of herself from him to maintain a shred of dignity and honor. He must never know that she wanted him to touch her, that she craved sex from him. If he guessed how much she burned for him, she would be filled with self-loathing.

When Christian awoke, Brianna was still sleeping. She was lovely in her slumber. Her gilded lashes lay like tiny fans upon her cheeks and he felt a pang of regret that when they fluttered up and her green-flecked gaze rested upon him, they would be shadowed by guilt and accusation. He cursed softly that Robert's ghost would stand between them. It had been no competition at all to have a flesh and blood rival, but a dead man took on an aura of virtue that was oftimes mythical.

Christian knew full well that Brianna would hold him at arm's length and keep a part of herself inviolate from him. He knew too that he could break through her carapace anytime he desired, and of course he would do so each night, but he wanted her to close the distance between them of her own free will. She would have to learn to trust him completely. She would have to learn to give her heart into his keeping. He vowed to protect, cherish, and love her so completely, she would gradually come to know and accept that they were soulmates.

When Brianna awakened, she kept her eyes closed in feigned sleep until she felt her husband leave the bed. When she heard him pour water from the large jug into the bowl, she opened them the tiniest crack to peek through her lashes. There was so much about Christian Hawksblood she didn't know. She felt her cheeks blush warmly as she observed him. Already she had learned one thing. She learned that he shaved while still naked!

Throughout the night the king had sat vigil with Katherine de Montecute over her husband, William. The gash on the leg his friend had received in the hastilude had seemed a trifle compared to the wounds he'd taken in battle. But William's condition had worsened hourly since the tournament. Master John Bray, the king's own physician, had tended him constantly, but at a late hour he had summoned Edward from his bed because he knew the Earl of Salisbury would not last until morning. "Is there absolutely nothing more you can do?" demanded the king, his heart constricting as he saw the anguish and guilt in Katherine's eyes.

"Nay, Your Majesty. It almost seems as if the spear that wounded him was poisoned and has quickly spread its devastation through his whole body."

"Leave us private then. I want to stay with him until the end. I owe him that, at least." He took hold of William's hand, then Katherine's as well, imbuing his strength and vitality into them with his iron will. William never regained consciousness. He breathed his last a few minutes before dawn. On their knees beside him, they both wept.

"My love, we cannot be seen together," he whispered low. "Evil men will whisper that I killed him so I could have you. The wolves will tear your reputation to shreds. Rumors of poison will spread like wildfire unless we part now. I want only to honor you and William. I refuse to bring dishonor upon you."

Katherine looked at the anguish in the king's eyes. *I had them both, now I have neither!* she thought with a shock.

She veiled the double pain in her heart and soul with downcast lashes. She nodded her understanding. If William's spirit hovered, he would know that they both loved him. He would know that they would never seek his death. Alas, he would also know that they had been unfaithful, but as God knows, adultery was a human enough failing.

34

The King of England was restless. After the death of his lifelong friend, William de Montecute, it seemed that Windsor caged him. The death brought home to him how short life was and underlined his own mortality. Perhaps it was wrong to make his life's ambition the conquering of France. He was at the peak of his reign. Celebration of his great victories would go on for years. He had established the Order of the Garter for England's most chivalrous knights, and his Council and advisers were pressing for a lasting peace.

Wars cost a great deal of money and after Crécy, Calais, and the money expended on hospitality for the great tournament at Windsor, the coffers were again empty. Suddenly, events in France changed everything. King Philip died and his son, John, took the throne. Death also claimed the Pope at Avignon and a new Pope, Innocent, was chosen.

King Edward called a meeting of the Council to map out

a plan for the future. They were adamantly opposed to taking on an enormous new debt to continue the war with France. So it was decided to send the Duke of Lancaster to the new Pope in Avignon, offering peace terms if King Edward was confirmed in the full sovereignty of all his French possessions. A delegation would also be sent to King Charles of Navarre to cement an alliance between England and Navarre, because it was known he was hostile to the new King of France.

Since Princess Isabel was enamored of Ezi, son of the Lord of Albret in Gascony, a wedding contract would be negotiated, and her younger sister, Princess Joanna, would be offered to Pedro, heir to the throne of Castile. Since all of their negotiations were concerned with making allies across the Channel, Queen Philippa suggested they move the entire Royal Court to Bordeaux. It was a massive undertaking and plans began immediately.

The Black Prince, however, was determined to recall his army and return to Calais to mount another offensive. He decided to outfit and pay for his own army of ten thousand with moneys from his tin mines in Cheshire. The king, ever concerned for his family's safety and well-being, decided that the Black Prince should take his army to Bordeaux. Most of the holdings claimed by the English were in the southern provinces. Any further territory they could claim in battle should be in the south, not scattered across France.

Prince Edward could see the logic and wisdom of this, but Joan was in Calais and he could not bear to be separated any longer. When he argued that he should visit that port to see that it was still safely garrisoned, his father waved away his suggestions. "Nay, Edward, read the daily reports. Calais is now an English port for all intents and purposes. The people are far better off under English rule and well they know it. Our fleet dominates the harbor and trade is growing daily. I want you in the south and Warrick agrees with me."

Prince Edward had no choice but to capitulate. He sat down immediately to pen missives to his beloved Joan, to her brother Edmund, and to Sir John Holland.

*   *   *

Holland sat at a desk covered with paperwork and journals. Steward of the Royal Household was an appointment for which he was well paid without doing the actual work. He employed a large staff of servants to run each and every royal castle and an equally large staff of clerks to record the expenditures. Holland was quick with figures and even quicker at recognizing opportunities for profit. Hundreds of tradespeople and scores of guilds were ever eager to supply the various royal households and knew that a regular bribe in the right palm kept them ahead of their competitors.

From the window where he sat, Holland looked out at a small courtyard where his wife sat under a chestnut tree covered with spring blossoms. It was a beautiful picture, one he thought he should be part of, but her brother Edmund was with her constantly like a bloody watchdog!

His eyes narrowed as they focused on the Earl of Kent. He was a libertine who spent lavishly on himself, keeping three and four mistresses at a time. He had been left a fortune by his royal father, who had been beheaded for treason, and had never had to worry about money in his life. Holland picked up a parchment and spread it open with thick fingers. It showed that Edmund had other titles beside Earl of Kent and Lord Wake of Liddell, which encompassed much property. While he was unmarried and without issue, Edmund of Kent's legal heir was none other than Holland's wife, Joan.

He watched the pair with covetous eyes. Not only did he want Edmund's wealth, he wanted Joan too. She was filled with vitality, even in pregnancy. She appealed to Holland's deeply sensual nature. She was becoming an obsession with him because she was forbidden fruit. These days his mind constantly returned to the talk he'd had with Robert de Beauchamp. Would he be ruthless enough to assassinate Prince Edward? Would he have enough guts? Would he be clever enough to get away with it? Every day he half-expected to receive word that Edward was dead, making Prince Lionel heir to the throne.

Holland could do nothing to expedite matters but hope and pray, but there was something he could do right here in Calais to greatly enhance his own fortune. Since Fate helped those who helped themselves, he made up his mind to get his hands on the Earl of Kent's vast wealth.

As he watched Joan in the courtyard, he continually fantasized about all the things he wanted to do to her, all the things he wanted her to do to him. Her easy laughter filled the rooms and her very smile had a come-hither quality about it. Holland was swollen with lust just watching her, but all her smiles were for her goddamn brother at the moment. His hand slipped inside his chausses. He would have to ease himself before he opened the rest of his dispatches, but he vowed that soon he would ease himself on his wife's pampered body.

When Holland returned to his desk, the sun was setting on the empty courtyard. Kent had likely gone off on his nightly jaunt and Joan would be supping in her chamber with only her maid for company. He reached for the diplomatic pouch and took out a dispatch marked urgent. When he opened it, his hands shook with impotent rage. He saw it was from the Prince of Wales, informing him that the royal family and the entire Court were sailing for Bordeaux, and as Steward of the Royal Household his services would be needed there immediately.

"A pox on all princes," he muttered with hatred. So, the lily-livered De Beauchamp hadn't had enough guts to administer the coup de grace yet. Well, it took a lot of balls to assassinate a royal. He'd have to take the initiative and show Robert how it was done!

The letter gave him an excuse to seek out Joan. He made his way from his own wing into that part of the building where Joan had her private chambers. Not many of the servants were about at this hour, so he went directly to her sitting room and knocked on the door.

Glynis opened it and stared at him with hostility. She did not like John Holland with his thick bull-neck and his stocky build. She had witnessed how he had almost stalked Joan until the prince took a proprietary interest in her. "What do you want, sir?"

"My business is with Lady Joan Holland."

"She is resting," Glynis temporized.

"She is my wife. Step aside." His stance was so threatening, Glynis knew he would not be opposed.

"Who is it?" Joan called.

"It is John, my lady."

Joan came quickly to the door. "Come in, my lord." Her hand went to her breast in alarm. "Is anything wrong? Is it Edward?"

"It concerns the Prince of Wales, yes. It would be best if we could speak in private, my lady."

Glynis glared venom.

"It's all right, Glynis. I'll be fine." Joan smiled apprehensively, needing to know immediately if aught was amiss with Edward.

When they were alone, Holland turned solicitous. "Pray sit down, Joan. Your welfare is in my hands. I cannot help worrying now that your time draws close."

"Why, thank you for your concern, John, but I believe I have at least another month to go. What brings you?"

"The royal household is moving to Bordeaux and I have orders for us to travel there. However, I do not think it advisable for us to leave until after the birth of your child."

"Oh, I am feeling quite well, John. If Edward wants me, I must leave immediately."

It infuriated him that she would rush to do Edward's bidding! "It is thoughtless of him to expect you to undertake such a long, hazardous journey. He cannot realize how far along you are. It would pose a danger to both you and the child!"

"John, it is most kind of you to concern yourself with me, but you must not be critical of Prince Edward. He only wants what is best for me, and what is best for me is to be with him as soon as I may."

"Joan, you don't seem to realize that I am your legal husband and will be the legal father of your child. If aught goes wrong on the long journey to Bordeaux, I will be held responsible."

She politely ignored his words. "I shall ask my brother to provide a ship. We can sail there in comfort. I'll pack at once. If the mail pouch has arrived from Windsor, Edward must have sent a letter for me." She moved toward the adjoining door gracefully, though she was large with child. "Glynis, love, would you go with Sir John to fetch my letter?"

* * *

Brianna and Adele spent the entire day packing for Bordeaux. Paddy and Ali came in and out, taking crates and trunks that belonged to Hawksblood. Brianna glanced at her worktable set up in an alcove of the sitting room. It was covered with paints and brushes, sketches of gods from Greek mythology and a half-finished picture portraying the early Vikings who had settled in Ireland.

"I'm sorry, Paddy, I should have cleaned off my table and sorted out what I want to take with me."

"No, no, my lady, I have strict instructions to leave it be until tomorrow. Your husband says you like to paint in the evening."

"Oh, thank you." Christian was so thoughtful about everything that concerned her. He anticipated her every need, discerned her moods, knew even when she had a headache. He was gentle, tender, and loving. And yet there was a terrible barrier between them that prevented total intimacy. Until of course they were within the bed curtains. There, he had the power to forge physical intimacy and breach the chasm that stood between them. It entailed a fresh seduction each night, like a ballet of domination and submission, with Brianna yielding almost everything. Certainly more than she ever intended. Until daylight brought back her memories of how ruthless he had been in murdering his rival.

The moment they returned from the evening meal, Brianna repaired to her alcove, determined to finish her painting of the Vikings' arrival in Ireland. She had created a castle on the coast and a Viking ship with its fierce conqueror standing at the prow with covetous eyes upon the lady of the castle. It was both savage and compelling, yet to Brianna it lacked something.

Her drifting imagination was brought back to the present as she heard a chuckle. Soon she could hear Hawksblood's full-bodied laughter rolling about the chamber. A somewhat somber air had predominated in their chambers since the forced marriage. Now, however, he was clearly happy and amused over something.

Brianna marveled at how delightful it was to hear him laughing. An overwhelming desire to be included in the laughter gripped her. She laid down her brush and emerged from her alcove to see him reading a sheaf of parchments. Her heart skipped a beat. He looked so youthful in his laughter. All his dark intensity was banished by his mirth.

He saw her immediately. "I'm reading a tale by one of the king's clerks. It's so droll and amusing! Though he's changed the names to protect the guilty, I know exactly who his characters portray. You must read it, Brianna."

"I've been finishing a painting, but it still lacks something."

"The Viking warrior?"

Brianna was surprised that he knew what she was working on, yet she shouldn't be; he took a keen interest in everything, doubly so where she was concerned.

"Let me see."

She followed him to her worktable, suddenly shy to have his eyes upon her art.

He picked up the sketches of the Greek gods. "This is Proteus from *The Odyssey*. He continually changes shape from serpent to lion to tree." His eyes caught and held hers. "To be in harmony we must all change . . . transform. We have to be able to open ourselves up to people of very different cultures to experience the full sense of connection and belonging."

She knew he was speaking personally. "I will try," she murmured.

Christian hoped that when they went to Bordeaux it would be a new beginning for them. Perhaps they could leave the haunting shadows of their past behind. He tore his gaze from her to look at her painting. "Your talent is a gift from the gods. Your detail is incredible." Though their coloring was different, he recognized his own physique and features in the savage Viking conqueror. He said softly, "You know, Brianna, though they raided and eventually conquered parts of Ireland, they gave back to that land. Their customs, their strengths, their knowledge, talents, and accomplishments made Ireland a far richer culture. Their art, for instance, inspired the Celtic ribbon patterns. To the Celtic knotwork of spirals, they added the zoomorphic motif."

"Zoomorphic?"

"Animals . . . the eagle, the dragon." He began to sketch on a scrap of paper. It was a heron with a fish in its beak, its long neck curving back, entwined with the next heron to form a pattern. "Arabic art has similar intricate border patterns that utilize flowers and fruit and trees, even exotic dancers, though that kind of art is known as erotica."

Brianna blushed prettily. "I'll put a Celtic ribbon border around the painting to symbolize the Viking contribution. What do you think of dragons and shamrocks?"

His eyes held hers for long moments. "Enchanting," he murmured.

Her lashes fell and she turned back to her worktable. His arms encircled her from behind, surrounding her with his love. He dropped a kiss upon the top of her head. "Don't stay up all night, beloved. Come to me soon."

A shiver ran down the entire length of Brianna's spine. Ah, God in Heaven, how she would like to go to him and ravish him. How she would like to push his hard body back on the bed and make passionate love to him, instead of lying still, waiting until he had exhausted every trick to lure and seduce her into letting him have his way with her. Then after she'd made love to him fiercely and furiously, she would do it again playfully, calling forth his wonderful laugh, until they rolled helplessly about the bed, intoxicated with mirth and joy. And then when she had exhausted him with laughter, she would seduce him slowly, drawing out the pleasure so that it lasted throughout the night, building their desire with her tantalizing fingers, lips, and tongue. More than anything in the world she wanted to run the tip of her tongue along the entire length of the brand on the inside of his thigh. Tracing the curve of the blade, then moving upward to the thick handle . . . and beyond. It was the most erotic thought she had ever had and it stole to her often. Sometimes in broad daylight!

Brianna worked for another two hours, until her eyelids drooped from fatigue. It was so much less disturbing to sit quietly sketching and painting than to join Christian Hawksblood in his big curtained bed. It took that long for the fire in her blood to be extinguished. Finally she laid her head down on the table. She lusted for a ruthless murderer and it covered her with self-loathing.

A muffled sob escaped her lips. Then she was being lifted in strong arms. He gently undressed her and lifted her naked into the bed. He gathered her against his side and began to talk to her. "You will love Bordeaux. 'Tis one of the loveliest places in the world, Brianna." His voice was seductive, dark, enveloping. The way he whispered her name was wickedly enticing all by itself. It lured her to forget who she was, who he was, to forget right and wrong, to forget everything except that they lay naked in this bed. When he talked, it melted her antipathy faster than anything else could. "To reach it we sail down the curving river Garonne, whose silver water is wide enough for many tall ships. The buildings, surrounded by a white wall, are like spun sugar, some white, some pink, with red tile roofs.

"All is a profusion of flowers. Jasmine scents the warm air. Wait until you sip the chilled, delicate wine from Médoc. It will steal your senses." His lips touched her throat and felt her frantically beating pulse. "The sun beats down from a turquoise sky. Sometimes, in the languorous afternoon, we'll close the shutters to keep out the heat and I'll take you to bed for a siesta."

Love in the afternoon? Brianna bit down on the sheet to keep from moaning.

"I'll feed you grapes and peaches filled with nectar so that your kisses will be sweeter than they've ever been before." His mouth covered hers at last and she opened for the deep kiss for which he had made her thirst. When his fingers traced the petals of her woman's center, they unfurled for him, allowing him to plunder her until they both experienced an explosion of the senses.

Once more he had bemused, beguiled, bewitched, and bedded her!

Bordeaux was exactly as Christian Hawksblood had described it. It shimmered beneath a brilliant sun. Exotic foliage with highly scented, vivid blooms filled the senses. The port itself was a fascinating collage of wine shops, alleys, street vendors, and donkeys. Stalls and carts were filled with such diverse produce as green figs, peaches, strings of garlic and sausages. Flower-sellers offered baskets of lilies, peonies, and freesia. The women in the streets wore scarlet shawls with ornamental combs and flowers in their hair.

The magnificent royal palace had once been the Abbey of St. Andrew, but Brianna was surprised at the size and splendor of the many houses beyond it. Because Christian was needed to see to his Cornishmen and the knights from the House of Warrick, he had left Brianna and Adele in the capable hands of Paddy. Though Prince Edward's army was considered small, ten thousand men-at-arms, a third of whom were mounted, would take at least two days to transfer from ship to barracks.

All the Plantagenets had their own separate household and servants. This time Prince John had been left behind in England as regent. Though a scandal had been avoided by taking no action against Prince Lionel, nothing could alter the fact that he had plotted against his brother and the king would never trust him again. King Edward decided the Duke of Clarence and his men would accompany him to Bordeaux where he could keep an eye on his activities.

Queen Philippa had brought all the younger children and the new baby with their attendant maids, nannies, and laundresses. Because Princess Isabel and Princess Joanna were expected to be married soon, they had brought a staggering amount of baggage. Joanna, who would be going to Castile, had brought a bridal bed with Tripoli silk hangings, a chariot lined with purple velvet, chairs, tables, carpets, and gold and silver plate. Every article was emblazoned with the arms of England. Though she was only thirteen, her household consisted of over a hundred manservants, including pages, poulterers, sumpterers, chambermen, stewards, knights, and esquires.

Brianna was attached to Isabel's household, which had even more furnishings and attendants than Joanna's. Adele assured Brianna that she and Paddy would see to their trunks and crates and take everything they had brought over on the ship to Christian Hawksblood's dwelling. Brianna had to attend Isabel and knew she would be kept busy long into the night, or perhaps for days, if that spoiled princess did not give her leave to retire.

As it turned out, it was the next day before she was allowed a few hours to get settled into her own quarters. Brianna thought she had been directed to the wrong place as she walked up the steps and saw the spacious terraces and the marble floors. Then she heard Paddy's voice in altercation.

He was on a second-story balcony, arguing with someone she couldn't see, and his language was rather blue. Brianna called up to him. "This is like a palace. Does it belong to Prince Edward?"

"Indeed it does not, my lady! It belongs to Lord de Beauchamp." He almost sounded offended.

"You mean Warrick?"

"Nay, Warrick's palace is next door. This one belongs to Christian, my lady."

A dark woman came out onto the balcony and looked down. She was vividly attractive even with the derisive sneer on her lips. "Lady? What a pity. The last thing Hawksblood needs is a lady!"

❧ 35 ❧

"Shut yer mouth, bitch, before I shut it for you, and get your stuff out of here."

"What's going on? Who is that?" Brianna asked, but the man and woman were too busy exchanging threats to pay heed to her. She went up the beautifully curved staircase and turned left onto the open balcony. She found the pair inside a spacious chamber, playing tug-of-war with a trunkful of gowns. "Who is this?" Brianna repeated.

They both spoke at once, giving very different replies. Paddy said, "She's a prisoner."

The dark beauty replied, "I am Lisette St. Lô, Baroness."

Paddy made a rude noise. "She's nothing but a French whore who has taken over the master bedchamber as if she owns the place. I'll have her rubbish out of here in a jiffy, my lady."

Lisette sat down on her trunk with determination. "Hawksblood will decide which one of us shares his bed!"

Brianna stiffened. She stared at the Frenchwoman in shocked surprise. She blanched white as the blood drained from her face. Though her emotions were in chaos, her mind in total disarray, she somehow managed to look completely detached. "Come away, Paddy. I'll choose another chamber on the other side of the house. You may put my things in there."

She walked blindly in the opposite direction until she encountered Adele. Paddy was following Brianna, silently cursing Lisette, cursing himself for not rousting her from the master chamber yesterday, and cursing Hawksblood for sending the woman here to Bordeaux in the first place. The bloody cat was among the pigeons and he feared where the blame would fall. He knew Lady Brianna was almost sacred to Christian, and if she was upset by this French *poule,* he'd be in shit up to his eyeballs!

"Hawksblood has been keeping a woman here. Here, in this palace," Brianna said, wide-eyed with disbelief at what she had actually seen.

"Come and sit down, lamb. Don't be upset over a little tart like that." Adele glared at Paddy, who shrugged helplessly and asked, "Which chamber would you like, my lady?"

Brianna was moving from distress to anger. It seemed everybody knew about the baroness but her! "It doesn't matter. All the chambers are exceedingly lovely in this palace. Just be sure you choose one that has a strong lock and key."

Paddy disappeared to do her bidding. Adele said quickly, "He's holding her and her brother, the baron, for ransom. She's his prisoner . . . it's not what it seems."

"Oh? What does it seem, Adele?"

Adele flushed. "Well, you know . . . that she's his mistress."

"Exactly! Or should we say *one* of his mistresses? He's an Arabian, don't forget!"

"Oh, my lamb, don't let her spoil your pleasure in this lovely palace. It has a marble bathing pool and the gardens will take your breath away. And there's a fountain and a jade tile pond with gold and silver fishes darting about—"

"Of course I shan't let her spoil my pleasure. Did Paddy happen to tell you how in the world the Arabian came to own such a place?"

Adele knew Brianna must be furious to refer to her lord husband as "the Arabian." "Well, he did tell me about the first time they came to Bordeaux. When Hawksblood saw Warrick's palatial home, he bought this one that stood next to it. At that time, he had never met the Earl of Warrick and only suspected him of being his sire. Paddy said it was a matter of pride. He had to buy a house that was bigger and better than Warrick's."

"But where did he get the money?"

"Paddy said he bought it with *gold.*"

"Well, Paddy is a veritable treasure-trove of information. Did he happen to mention from whom he stole the gold?"

Adele bit her lip. It was unlike Brianna to be icily sarcastic. "I'll go and see where he has put your trunks. Put your feet up and have a little rest." Adele found Paddy across the hall in a pretty room that had been plastered in palest pink.

He muttered, "If she intends to lock the door against Hawksblood, she doesn't know her husband very well."

"You bloody fool, Paddy. Why wasn't she out of the master suite before Brianna arrived?"

"Because she's a sodding woman! They live just to cause trouble and aggravation."

"Well! That's a fine thing to say!"

"Now, love, I didn't mean you. I know you avoid trouble like the plague. So take my advice and make yourself scarce when himself arrives. He'll soon settle Lisette's bloody hash, and if Lady Brianna gives him any aggravation, he'll settle her hash too! Here is her bloody key, for what good it'll do her!" He gave the key to Adele. "Wish me luck, darlin' . . . I'm off to drag the Frenchie out by the scrag of her neck and lock her in a cubbyhole somewheres."

Lady Joan Holland had a ton of baggage to be taken aboard ship. Her clothes, furs, and jewelry alone filled a dozen trunks. Her own featherbed was carried aboard to assure her comfort and she would sleep aboard the night before the ship departed, so they could sail on the early morning tide.

Her good-byes to her brother were tearful. "I wish you were coming with me, Edmund."

"I'm the crown's representative here in Calais, Joan," he said regretfully.

"Don't pretend you are unhappy about it, Edmund. Your position draws females like honeybees."

He winked at her. "Position is everything, my sweet, remember that!"

"Why do men always have to be vulgar?"

"Don't tell me approaching motherhood has turned you all prim and proper?" he teased.

"It's time you thought about settling down and having children, Edmund. My little girl will need cousins to play with." She kissed him. "Good-bye, Edmund. I'll miss you."

"You will love Bordeaux. Southern France is like paradise." His careless air became serious for a moment. "For God's sweet sake, have a care for yourself, Joan." He wrapped her fur about her shoulders and squeezed affectionately.

"The angels take care of me, Edmund," she said softly.

"I believe they do, sweetheart."

Joan and Glynis had half a dozen of Holland's men escort them to the ship. It was Sir John's last night in garrison headquarters. He would come directly to the ship in time for the early morning floodtide.

Edmund of Kent made his way from Joan's house to the garrison in the center of Calais. Holland greeted him, "I'm glad you dropped in, my lord earl. I've appointed Sir Neville Wiggs to take over my command here. He's not opposed to using strong-arm tactics if and when they are required."

"Oh, I don't believe we'll have trouble in Calais. I believe we've anglicized the town. Although I do concede there are some seedy areas with pox-diseased drabs along the docks."

Holland shook his head. "We've had trouble in one of the better-heeled neighborhoods. Over on the south side there are a couple of high-priced brothels need watching. I could show you the areas that need patrolling if you fancy a walk, my lord."

"Well, by an amazing coincidence, I'm going in that direction this evening, Sir John. There's nothing like an evening stroll to work up an appetite."

The two men headed south, toward the larger houses where the richest burghers lived. They passed the imposing house where the queen had stayed, then turned a corner into what looked like an alley. "It's these back streets that need patrolling. Ah, good, I see one of our men is on the job."

As the man-at-arms approached them, Holland unsheathed a wide-bladed knife with an extremely lethal point and drove it forcefully into Edmund of Kent's back. With an agonized cry he went down between the two men, his lifeblood gushing up from the massive wound as Holland first twisted, then withdrew the blade.

"A knife in the back is not unheard of in this wealthy part of Calais. It's extremely good pickings for thieves." He bent to lighten his victim of his moneybelt. As Edmund's eyes were clouding with death, Holland smiled at him. "Don't worry yourself about my wife, she has just come into a fortune." He wiped the dripping blade on his handkerchief, then sheathed it beneath his arm. "Sir Neville, if by chance you do encounter trouble on the streets tonight, be certain to report it after the cog royal has sailed."

Wiggs saluted him smartly with his sword. "Good-bye, sir. Thank you for your confidence in me. You won't regret it."

Paddy found Hawksblood with Warrick. They were in the stables where they had just finished sewing up the wounds of half a dozen destriers injured on the voyage from England. Actually they were fortunate none had to be destroyed. When a warhorse broke loose below decks, the result could be catastrophic.

They had spent the entire day unloading horses, their most precious cargo. Those belonging to the royals and the nobles were stabled. Those of lesser knights were put into outdoor paddocks.

The moment Hawksblood saw Paddy's face, he sensed trouble. "Is there a problem?"

"In a manner of speaking, there is, my lord."

Ali, who had helped unload and calm horses for the last eighteen hours, cast him a look of disgust. "We've handled three thousand equines and you cannot handle two females?"

"*Three* females, and I guarantee they can wreak more havoc than three thousand horses!"

"Three?" Hawksblood questioned. Then he smote his forehead. "How obtuse of me. I forgot all about Lisette St. Lô."

Warrick cocked an eyebrow at his son. "I take it the French filly you hold for ransom is more mistress than prisoner?"

"Hell, no. She was never my mistress. Christ, one tumble and I have to pay for it the rest of my life!" He looked at Warrick with speculative eyes. "Will you house the St. Lôs until their ransom is paid?"

"I suppose I'd better, if you ever expect another peaceful night as long as you live," Warrick said with a grin.

The four men made their way to the two white stone palaces bathed in moonlight. As Warrick broke from the group to enter his own dwelling, Christian said, "We'll be right back."

As he opened the gate in the high wall that surrounded his own imposing palace, Christian ventured, "Is my lady very upset?"

"Mad as hellfire is my guess. Ye cannot keep two women ye've bedded beneath the same roof," Paddy explained as if Christian were an untried boy.

"We manage to do so in Arabia," Ali said in lofty tones. "It is common practice to keep four wives as well as concubines."

"We'll let you explain it all to Lady Brianna," Paddy said sarcastically.

"Where did you put the baroness?"

"I put her in her brother's rooms and threatened him with castration if he didn't keep her under control," Paddy supplied.

"Move them next door to Warrick," Hawksblood directed.

Christian Hawksblood inspected the master suite to see that all was in readiness to receive his wife. He nodded with satisfaction. Paddy had directed the servants well. The room was all white with touches of gold. The bed was low and wide, covered with snowy linen and piled with bolsters and pillows embroidered with the initials of C and B in gold thread. Filmy white silk gauze hung from ceiling to floor, surrounding the bed.

White shutters were folded back making the open balconies part of the large, airy chamber. One entire wall was a built-in wardrobe with mirrored doors. The floor of white Carrara marble veined with gold was guaranteed to provide coolness on the hottest nights.

In one corner, marble steps led down to the room below where a rectangular bathing pool ran its entire length. The room was open-ended so that the pool flowed outside into a small private garden. Beyond the pool, a turquoise tile fountain sprayed crystal drops of water ten feet into the air. The entire house was lighted by huge scented candles in round glass bowls. The effect was almost mystical and decidedly romantic.

Christian Hawksblood, however, looked anything but romantic. His clothes were soiled with the sweat and blood of his labors of the past eighteen hours, and he stank of horseflesh. He wanted a bath, but he was damned if he was going to bathe alone when Brianna was right here in this enchanting palace he had provided for her.

He pushed away his tiredness, then allowed all his annoyances to drain away. He cocked an eyebrow at Paddy. "Milady's chamber?"

His squire told him where he could find his wife, muttering, "I'll bid ye good night, I cannot stand the sight o' blood."

Hawksblood climbed the curving staircase and came to a halt outside his wife's door. In a quiet but firm voice he said, "Brianna, I welcome you to your new home. I expect you to greet me as your lord. I need bathing, feeding, and bedding, in that order. Come to me, now."

Secure inside the pink chamber with the key firmly

gripped in her palm, Brianna at last had an outlet for her fury. "You Arabian swine! I don't know how you have the unmitigated gall to even speak my name. I shall never bathe you, I shall never feed you, and I shall certainly never bed you again! I suggest you bathe yourself, ask the servants to feed you, and allow your French harlot to bed you. You have no need for a wife whatsoever, and I shall cease to be your wife until that creature is removed from my home, permanently! Is that perfectly clear, Prince Bloody Drakkar?"

It was clear to Christian that Brianna wanted a knock-down-drag-out fight. She wanted him to smash the door down and manhandle her until her teeth rattled. Christian refused to accommodate her. He took his heavy dagger from its sheath, pried the hinges from the door, and quietly opened it.

Brianna stared in disbelief at what he had done with so little effort.

His eyes glittered in his dark face. His look was so intense, a finger of fear touched her. In a voice so quiet, it was almost a threat, he said, "Since the baroness has been removed from your home, permanently, I take it you are ready to resume your role as my wife . . . or do you have more demands, madam?"

He had taken away all her arguments. Her defiance fled. She could find no more words to fling at him.

"Do you, madam?" he repeated.

Brianna shook her head.

"Then come. Now."

She looked helplessly at her boxes and trunks piled about her and knew she must obey him. He was in no mood to be trifled with.

As they emerged onto the well-lit balcony, she saw that he was covered with blood. "Are you hurt?" she asked with alarm.

"Nay. Don't touch me. It will all wash off."

She walked beside him through the house, past the bathing pool and out to the garden. In silence she watched him strip and step into the fountain. He took up a cake of soap and began to scrub himself. Immediately her feelings toward him began to thaw. He was not going to force her to bathe him. Suddenly, that was exactly what she wanted to do. She was the only woman who had the right to bathe him, feed him, and bed him, and it dawned on her that she wanted to guard that right jealously. She removed her outer garment and standing in her filmy underdress, held out her hand. "Give me the soap."

"I thank you for the wifely gesture, but you were right, I can bathe myself. However, since you are willing to get wet, will you come into the pool with me after I eat?"

Brianna blushed. "I . . . I cannot swim."

He smiled at her. "Good, then we won't swim . . . we'll play."

"I'll go and see about food," Brianna said vaguely.

"The kitchens are all the way to the back of the house. We have a superb chef, if I recall from the last time I was here. The beauty of this warm climate is the food tastes better cold than hot."

When Brianna returned with a servant in tow, Christian had set up a table in the fragrant garden. He was sitting on a double-wide chair called a loveseat, wearing only a towel, which emphasized his swarthy skin. He had lit small candles inside huge white blossoms and set them on the table. The effect was exotically romantic.

The servant emptied his tray, covering the table with platters of cold meat, soft cheese, and crusty bread, along with such a variety of fruit and nuts, Brianna could name only half. He took a stone jug of wine from a cooling pool and deftly removed the cork seal.

Brianna waited until he withdrew before she slipped into the chair beside Hawksblood. To keep her eyes from his iron-hard body, she pretended a great interest in the food. Christian named each one for her. "Figs, dates, tangerines, almonds, filberts." He dipped a crust into melted Brie and lifted it to her lips. She was pleasantly surprised at its delicious taste and helped herself liberally to the food.

"You are hungry," he said, wondering why she hadn't eaten.

She read his thoughts. "I was too angry to eat," she explained.

He exulted at her words. If she was jealous of him, her emotions ran much deeper than she admitted. He longed to hear her say she loved him, but she was such a stubborn wench, she wasn't even ready to admit it to herself, let alone to him. He wondered if he would live long enough to hear her say the words.

Christian received deep pleasure from simply looking at her. As she nibbled the fruit and sipped the wine, she seemed unconscious of her beauty. Her hair fell about her in a golden nimbus, the candleglow making it shimmer. He could see the rose tips of her breasts through the fine material of her underdress, and as she ran her tongue over her top lip to taste the sweetness of the wine, his long-simmering desire exploded into molten hot passion. He wanted her in the bed. He saw their bodies entwine, then couple, as he slid deep inside her. His loins were hot and hard and ready.

His hands moved swiftly to remove her underdress, but the moment she was naked she fled to the shadowed end of the bathing pool. He took the exotic flowers from the table with the lighted candles inside their petals, then bent down and floated them on the water. The effect was mesmerizing. As they glided toward her, she suddenly wanted them to reveal her naked beauty to him.

Brianna stepped from the shadows to the pool's edge, then she arched her body, first thrusting out her breasts, then her pelvis. She raised her arms beneath her long hair and let its golden tendrils cascade about her shoulders and down her back to her feet. Christian slipped into the pool and glided slowly toward her. The light of the floating candles filled her vision, but excitement built inside her because she knew he was coming for her, knew he was somewhere in the shadowed water.

When she looked down, Brianna realized there were steps leading into the water. Hesitantly, she took the first step down toward him. She could not see him, could not even hear him make the smallest splash. Boldly, she took the next step and felt the warm scented water swirl about her knees. Then his hands were on her ankles, slipping up her legs, his hot mouth trailing up the insides of her thighs, finally showering her pretty mons with teasing kisses.

It held him enthralled for long minutes, and Brianna, unable to resist his insistent mouth, again arched her pelvis.

His tongue licked her with long strokes until she was hot and wet. When she moaned her need and moved down toward him, he stayed her and came up out of the pool. With his lips against her ear he whispered, "I don't want your hair wet. I want to play with it. I want to take you up to bed."

She expected him to pick her up and carry her, but she did not anticipate the way he did it! He lifted her high and let her slide down his wet, sleek body. He slipped his hand between them to open the petals of her woman's center, then guided the throbbing head of his rigid shaft up inside her. Brianna wrapped her arms about his neck, and he murmured hoarsely, "Wrap your legs about me too."

As she raised her legs to wrap them about his waist, he slid deeper than he had ever been before. With his hands supporting her bottom cheeks, he walked slowly toward the stairs that led up to their bedchamber. Dear God, this man could arouse her against her will. The feel of him inside her was so potent, she could think of nothing but the pleasurable sensations like waves that built and receded, built and receded; ever higher, ever stronger. As he began to climb the stairs the sleek friction of engorged male muscle inside love-swollen female flesh became so exquisite that by the time he reached the top step she experienced a powerful orgasm that made her arch backward as she cried out her pleasure.

Her new position intensified the pure sensuality of their coupling and Christian felt the entire length of his shaft being squeezed by the pulsations of her tight, hot sheath. He stood absolutely still so they could both enjoy her climax, then when the last tremor and flicker of her swollen bud stilled, he carried her to the bed and set about arousing her all over again. Slowly, beautifully, as if they had forever.

Indeed, it seemed as if an eternity passed while she writhed and arched and gasped, then finally erupted with him. It was like a volcanic explosion, bathing each other in molten lava. His possessive arms enfolded her like bands of iron, and deep down, Brianna knew that such intensity was rare. Few lovers could possibly experience coitus as they did.

Moonlight spilled across the bed. "Christian, I was so jealous, I wanted to kill her," Brianna whispered. "I . . . I'm beginning to understand the dark evil that drove you to kill Robert."

He withdrew his arms from her, then swung his legs over the edge of the bed to sit up. She caught a glimpse of blazing eyes in a face turned to stone. He turned away from her. She saw his hard profile in the moonlight, then he was gone, swallowed by the shadows.

36

Brianna lay staring up at the silk canopy that enveloped the bed. She knew she must learn to control her tongue. She must not utter Robert's name again. And yet she knew they would never banish the dark shadow of his ghost that stood between them unless they talked it all out. She was covered with guilt and knew that Christian must be also. If he would confide in her, admit what he had done, even if he told her it was for love of her, Brianna felt she might be able to forgive him. At least she would be understanding and compassionate.

If they could talk it out so that nothing ugly and evil was hidden between them, they could make a new beginning. She heard a nightingale and its song was so poignantly beautiful, a heavy lump formed in her throat and the tears slipped down her cheeks.

The next morning Brianna was surprised by a visit from Prince Edward. "I'm sorry, Your Highness, Hawksblood isn't here."

Edward was amused. "Is that what you call him? Poor devil! He's been drilling men-at-arms since dawn. I came to tell you that Joan's ship is about to dock. Would you go down to meet her and bring her here so our reunion can be private?"

Brianna's heart lifted with joy. "Oh, I have missed her so much! Adele, Joan's ship has arrived," she called gaily.

"We'll go immediately. The servants will look after you, Sire. Please make yourself at home."

"It will be my pleasure to do so. This is a beautiful house, like a palace from a fairy tale!" he said, bemused.

The moment the vessel was secured at dockside, Brianna rushed aboard. When she saw Joan, she gasped, "Oh, my dear, you shouldn't be traveling. Your baby must be ready to be born!"

"Brianna, all I could think of was getting to Bordeaux. I wouldn't let her be born until I got here."

Brianna lowered her voice to a whisper. "He's at my house, awaiting you."

A look of alarm crossed Joan's pretty face. "I can't let him see me like this, he will fall out of love with me! I have heard Bordeaux overflows with beautiful, cultured ladies."

"We've only been here a few days. The Court hasn't held any receptions yet. Besides, Glynis and Adele here will back me up. You are absolutely blooming with loveliness."

Adele looked concerned. "I don't think she should walk."

Brianna said, "I'll get a carriage. They are pulled by donkeys, Joan. You'll just love a donkey ride."

As Brianna climbed to the deck, Sir John Holland excused himself from the ship's captain to hail her. It galled him that this beautiful, haughty bitch was privy to Joan and Edward's relationship. Whenever he saw her, he always had the urge to strike her. She made him feel less than a man. Someday he would like to have her at his mercy, then he would show her that he was far more man than she could ever handle.

"You are now Lady de Beauchamp, I assume?"

Brianna paled. "Welcome to Bordeaux, my lord. I am taking Joan to my house until her . . . I mean, until your apartments are ready."

"I shall come myself for her when all is in readiness. I have business with your husband, Robert."

Color rushed back into her cheeks. "Sir John, I am sorry to inform you that Robert de Beauchamp was killed at the tournament."

Holland looked stunned. "Prince Edward slew Robert?"

"Nay . . . he was killed by his brother, Christian

Hawksblood." She lowered her lashes, too ashamed to admit that she was married to Robert's brother. Brianna did not see the look of pure hatred in Holland's eyes. It took every ounce of his control to keep from knocking her to the ground.

Brianna and Glynis helped Joan up the white marble steps. "I've never seen anything like this . . . the flowers . . . the sunshine. This isn't a house, it's a palace," Joan declared breathlessly. "Is it yours?"

Brianna blushed. "It's my husband's."

"Darling, you are wed?" Joan exclaimed.

"It's a complicated story. Robert de Beauchamp was fatally wounded in the tournament, and the king decided to honor my betrothal contract with the House of Warrick."

"Then you are married to Christian? Oh, Brianna, you got your heart's desire! I am so very happy for you."

Brianna wanted to protest. Couldn't Joan see the cruel trick Fate had played upon her? Getting one's heart's desire was supposed to be a reward. Brianna had been rewarded when she should have been punished. But Joan was too uncomplicated for such ironic subtleties, so she simply murmured, "Thank you."

The servants brought refreshments of fruit and cool drinks and Brianna lifted Joan's feet onto the chaise longue and put cushions to her back. In spite of the heat and her advanced stage of pregnancy, Joan managed to look exquisitely cool in a pale blue gown of finespun cotton caught beneath her luscious breasts with forget-me-nots.

"You'll see that the royal palace is an enormous place. It used to be an abbey and must have over five hundred rooms. We'll go and see that your bed is set up and all your things unpacked." Brianna hurried off to find Edward. She found him pacing along an open balcony overlooking the gardens. "She's waiting for you, Your Highness, but I must seek out the queen's midwives immediately."

"My God, has her labor begun?"

"No, but it cannot be far off."

"Go then, hurry. I'll stay with her."

The moment he saw her, Edward was overcome with tenderness. He sank down on his knees before her and took her dainty hands to his lips. "My heart, it's been a lifetime. Forgive me for all the separations we must endure."

Joan's lips trembled. "Do you still love me?"

"My little Jeanette, I adore you. You have all of my heart. You should have waited to travel, sweeting."

"I couldn't wait. I wanted to be here in time for your birthday."

He bit his lip. Tomorrow a birthday celebration was to be held in his honor and naturally he would have to attend, but his heart would be with Joan. His hands gently stole to the precious mound she carried so sweetly. "You are going to have to be very brave, my love."

She smoothed the worry lines from his brow. "You mustn't be upset. Your mother has had ten children," Joan said with a little yawn.

"You're overtired. Close your eyes and try to rest."

"The heat is making me drowsy," she said, yawning again.

Edward scooped her up in his arms, then stretched out on the lounge. "I'll hold you. Try to sleep."

Safe in his arms, Joan soon drifted into slumber. Edward's lips feathered kisses across her fair brow, savoring these private moments that were few and far between, and silently praying that his beloved would be safely delivered of their child.

The Steward of the Royal Household chose an entire wing of the palace set apart from the king and queen's overflowing household by an orchard. Their ménage à trois required both space and complete privacy.

Holland was incensed at the trick Fate had played on him. The servants were quick to fill him in on all the gory details of the hastilude that had claimed the lives of Robert de Beauchamp and the king's best friend, William de Montecute. There were whispers of a conspiracy to assassinate the Black Prince, which Christian Hawksblood had thwarted by killing his own brother.

Holland cursed foully, his temper erupting at the clumsy fools who were carrying in crates and trunks. So, he had the Arabian pig to thank for his misfortune. If it hadn't been for that whoreson Hawksblood, Prince Edward would be in his grave and he'd have Joan all to himself. He swore a vow to get even. With difficulty he submerged his anger, banking his fiery temper below the surface where it could still be felt, but not seen. He knew he must report to the king and pay his respects to Queen Philippa. As Royal Steward he must make himself invaluable to them.

When Holland entered the queen's reception room, Philippa offered him congratulations on the imminent birth of his child. He accepted the gracious offer of the royal midwives, but could not keep from flushing darkly as he felt Brianna of Bedford's eyes upon him. The queen would never know Joan's baby would be her first grandchild, but that bitch Brianna knew the scandalous secret.

One by one the ladies gathered about the Steward to ask him to change their accommodation, to complain about either the size or location of their chambers, or to grumble about the high-handed servants. Finally, Queen Philippa rescued him. "Sir John, I didn't want to pounce upon you the moment you arrived, but the royal household has never needed your services as we do at this moment. We have been here at least three days, but we are in a bigger mess than the hour we arrived. Half of our baggage is missing, beds and furnishings have gone to the wrong rooms, there are over five hundred chambers in this building alone. And as if that were not enough, the food we are being served is not what we are used to. Oh, I know there are fruits and spices here from all over the world, but some of the good old English food we are used to wouldn't go amiss. Sir John, I'm afraid we already have guests arriving for the celebration tomorrow and we are in chaos. Do you suppose you can sort any of it out?"

"I shall attend to everything, Your Majesty. I should have been informed of your plans so that I could have arrived before you and had all in readiness. I shall organize the staff immediately. Leave everything in my capable hands, Your Majesty."

When Brianna returned to her house, Prince Edward told her Joan's pains had started. "I must go and order a litter to carry Joan up to the abbey. How am I to leave her?" he asked with anguish.

Brianna tried to reassure him. "I'll stay with her, I promise, and Glynis and Adele are still up there, making her chambers comfortable. Men are usually in the way at a time like this."

"Brianna, send me word how she fares. Jesu, I'd rather face the tortures of hell," he said, running distracted fingers through his golden locks.

"The litter, Sire, please!"

Joan's labor stretched through the afternoon and the long evening. Her chambers were filled with women, some offering encouragement, others predicting dire consequences because of her small size, still others ignoring her plight completely and using this opportunity to visit and gossip.

Brianna stayed at her side, holding her hand tightly whenever she was racked with a powerful contraction. Before she was done, Brianna praised her, begged her, scolded her, laughed and even cried with her, until at last the babe was born. An exhausted Brianna stepped back and let the midwives take over.

It took another two hours to bind the cord, cleanse and swaddle the child, bathe Joan, change the bed, and set the chamber to rights. Then the baby was presented for Sir John Holland's inspection. The midwives were relieved that he was not angered over the fact that it was a girl-child. Actually, Holland couldn't have been happier. Secretly he was laughing that the great Black Prince was not virile enough to produce a son!

He made a dutiful visit to his wife. It was the first time he had seen Joan in bed and he became instantly swollen with lust. How in the name of Heaven and hell did she manage to look so delectable after an ordeal like childbirth? The women finally shooed him away so Joan could rest, and Brianna in turn got rid of them, promising she would stay the rest of the night with her dear friend.

Brianna whispered to Glynis, "Try to find Edward," then she brought the tiny bundle from her cradle and placed her in her mother's waiting arms.

"I prayed for a little girl. Oh, Brianna, she's so beautiful!"

"How could she not be?" The babe looked like a pink and white cherub with silvery-gilt tendrils of hair curling about her temples.

"I can't believe I did it!" Joan whispered, bursting with pride.

Brianna heard a low scratching on the chamber door and hurried to open it so that the Prince of Wales could be put out of his misery.

Edward knelt beside the bed, love and adoration filling his heart.

"What time is it?" Joan whispered.

Edward could hardly speak. "After midnight," he murmured gruffly.

"Happy birthday, my love."

Edward was completely undone. He buried his face against her hair and tears of joy slipped silently down his cheeks.

The Black Prince's birthday feast was a lavish affair with what seemed like all of Bordeaux in attendance. The Anglo-Normans who had lived there for years put a much higher value on culture than the newly arrived English. It seemed all were accomplished in the arts. Painters, poets, writers, and minstrels were held in the highest esteem and the Royal Court was a perfect setting to display their talents.

The French influence was evident in everything from their music and dancing to their intellect and manners. In fashion especially they put the Court of Windsor in the shade.

The Banqueting Hall opened onto spacious formal gardens whose pathways were lit with torches so the guests could walk outside. An ornamental lake held small boats in the shape of swans so that a couple could glide romantically beneath the stars for an amorous interlude.

Bernard Ezi's parents, Lord and Lady Albret of Gascony, were the Plantagenets' honored guests, along with their large family of sons and daughters, and Princess Isabel put on a grand display of being madly in love with her new husband-to-be. Her younger sister, Joanna, envied Isabel her handsome young Gascon and prayed fervently that Pedro of Castile would be cast in the same attractive mold as Bernard.

Christian, at Brianna's side, was as attentive as ever but

he was so scrupulously polite she could feel a chasm opening between them and widening. It was ironic that though he was an Arabian from another culture, he blended in better than the English. He could converse on any subject, be it astronomy, the arts, or philosophy. The envious glances Brianna received from all the ladies told her plainly that he was exceedingly attractive to the opposite sex and she knew many of them would cast out their lures to him.

Brianna felt utterly wretched. Christian had offered her all of his heart, and because she was covered with guilt, she could not accept it. She watched the women flirt with him and with his friend, Prince Edward, and her heart ached for Joan as well as herself.

Whenever the king, Warrick, Prince Edward, and their lieutenants supped beneath the same roof it was inevitable that as the evening wore on, they gravitated together to discuss military matters. It seemed the French were burning and pillaging outlying English estates along the lush Garonne Valley and the Black Prince decided he could not wait for peace treaties. He would march inland to deal with the "Goddamn French."

Brianna was relieved when Hawksblood left with the army, then of course she suffered more guilt. What sort of wife would be happy to see her husband go off to face mortal danger? But the strained tension between them had become so tangible, it coiled in the air like smoke.

Brianna spent hours with Joan and the new baby, whom they had called Jenna. Joan was up and about in two days, more beautiful than she'd ever been before. She protested loudly when the queen appointed a wet nurse and a nursemaid for baby Jenna and they carried her off to the royal nursery for most of the day, but noble ladies did not look after their own babies, and wistfully Joan capitulated under all the pressure.

Her days settled into a pattern. She and Brianna spent the morning in the royal nurseries, then in the hottest part of the day, Joan retired for an afternoon nap, while Brianna returned to her white palace to take advantage of the brilliant light for her sketching and painting.

Whenever Joan was alone her thoughts were filled with Edward. After only a fortnight she had regained her slim figure and longed for him to return from the fighting so she could show it off for him. Being ungainly for months had made her insecure about her elfin beauty, or lack thereof, and she had fretted that Prince Edward would cease to be attracted to her. She was indulging in a delightful fantasy where he returned to whisper extravagant compliments, encircle her tiny waist with his big hands, and cover her now-flat belly with teasing, worshipful kisses.

Joan heard the chamber door open and close and idly wondered why Glynis had returned so soon from the cloth merchants' alley. Suddenly she sensed an invasive presence that was threatening. She sat up on the bed and grabbed the sheet to cover herself. "What do you want?" she demanded.

John Holland's eyes licked over her hotly. "That should be obvious. I want my marital rights."

Joan began to scream, but Holland backhanded her across the mouth. She fell back on the bed terrified. No one had ever physically hurt her in her life before.

He leered at her. "Go right ahead and scream if you wish. I chose this wing for us because of its privacy. No one will hear you, save me, and I rather enjoy it."

"You must be mad," Joan cried. "I'll have you arrested!"

"On what charge? Fucking my wife? If you consider for a moment, my empty-headed angel, you will realize you can complain to no one."

❧ 37 ❧

Joan lay silent, inert, wishing she could die. By agreeing to this unholy marriage she had placed herself at the mercy of a depraved monster. Edward must never, ever know what had taken place in this chamber today. No one must know!

She sat up and crawled from the bed. She poured scented water and bathed her body, then she dressed, choosing a spotless white underdress and a snowy white silk tunic to go over it. She felt clean again in the white garments. She put fresh white linen on the bed and gathered the soiled sheets inside a bolster case so that the blood-stains were not visible.

Joan sat down at her mirror and carefully covered the bruise on her face with powder and a little sandalwood rouge. Her mouth was swollen, but there was little she could do about it. Time alone would reduce the swelling. When she looked at her reflection, haunted eyes stared back at her. This was the most disastrous day of her life! Her misery was almost insurmountable. But as she sat before the mirror, she knew she must rise above what had happened to her. She must push it so far away it could not touch her. Gradually her misery diminished until she felt nothing. She was completely numb. One thing was certain, she thought, after this ordeal, nothing would ever be able to hurt her again.

Joan was wrong.

The king's face registered disbelief as he read his dis-patches from Calais. As he reread the report, his face set in grim lines. He sent for John Holland immediately.

"I have terrible news," King Edward said hoarsely, trying to control his grief. "Young Edmund of Kent was found dead in Calais."

"How did it happen?" Holland asked quickly.

"Found in an alley, stabbed in the back!"

Holland was witness to a display of Plantagenet temper. "Not enough I brought them to their knees! I should have pulled Calais down stone by stone, then crushed it to rub-ble! I should have slaughtered every living, breathing thing in that cursed city. I should have decorated the walls with the enemies' heads! I should have drowned them in their own blood. The 'Goddamn French' are like vermin. They don't know the meaning of honor!"

"Sire, I hate to say this, but Edmund of Kent frequented houses of ill repute. I often warned him about carousing in seamy bordellos."

The king gave him such a look of hauteur, Holland took a step back and swallowed any further criticism.

"Edmund of Kent was a Plantagenet! My young cousin was an honorable man, a brave warrior, and a chivalrous knight. He was obviously killed in the line of duty. He is a casualty of war, just as if he had fallen on the field of Crécy!"

"To be sure, Your Majesty. He was my own brother-in-the-law and a dear friend. We will bring his assassin to justice, never fear. I suggest you put Sir Neville Wiggs in charge of the investigation, if I may be so bold, Sire. Perhaps the patrols should be doubled, so that not one more English life will be lost."

"Great God in Heaven, how are we to break the news to his sister? They were orphaned as babies; her brother was all she had in this world."

"She has me, Sire," Holland pointed out.

"Yes, yes, of course. You must give her the tenderest loving care so she can cope with this grief." King Edward threw down the dispatch. "I shall come with you now. We will tell her together. We must do all we can to ease her sorrow!"

When Joan heard the knock on her chamber door, she went rigid and her throat closed with fear. When the door opened and King Edward strode in with Holland, she thought wildly, *The king knows he raped me and is going to arrest him!* She heard her heartbeat thudding like a drum inside her ears, deafening her to the king's words.

"My dear, we have some sad news for you. You must be very brave. Your brother Edmund has been killed in a skirmish in Calais."

Joan's hands flew to her heart as she felt it break, then she slumped down into blackness.

King Edward swept his tiny cousin up in his strong arms. "Jesu, the fall hurt her pretty face," he said, cradling the small bundle against his wide chest. "She's lost consciousness," he told Holland. "Go and fetch Master John Bray. She never was strong. Where are her women?" Edward demanded. "Tell the queen to send some of her ladies," Edward called after the departing Holland.

Edward sat down and rocked her gently until she regained consciousness. When she opened her eyes, pity filled his heart at the haunted look he saw there.

Joan clung to him and begged, "Don't leave me alone, Sire."

His compassion for this delicate girl knew no bounds.

"Hush, Jeanette, Edmund wouldn't want you to fall ill with grief. You must be strong for your little daughter's sake."

Joan nodded numbly and clung tighter. The king was so much like his son, Edward, she felt safe in his arms. Then suddenly the chamber was filled with women. Glynis arrived and close on her heels came Queen Philippa with half a dozen of her ladies. They put Joan to bed and Glynis mixed the sleeping potion the queen's physician prescribed, then she dispatched a page for Brianna.

Joan fought the effects of the strong herbs as long as she could, feeling too vulnerable to lose herself in sleep. They decided she had been up and about far too soon after childbirth. The shock of her brother's death could destroy her health unless she had complete bed rest.

Brianna was startled as Gnasher streaked across the room and climbed to her worktable. "Where on earth did you come from?" She looked up to see the freckled face of Randal Grey. "Why, Randal, I didn't know you came to Bordeaux. You've grown so tall, I hardly recognized you."

"Lord Hawksblood and Paddy are training me for squire, my lady, but they wouldn't take me with them to Carcassonne." The ferret ran back to Randal and sat on his shoulder.

"I should think not. The battlefield is no place for a boy."

"Lady Brianna, I hate being a page. I hate to be the bearer of ill tidings!"

Her hand went to her throat. "What is it?"

"It's Lady Kent, I mean Lady Holland. She's just learned that her brother is dead."

When Brianna arrived at her bedside, Joan clung to her hands beseechingly and begged, "Don't leave me alone, promise me, promise me."

"Joan, of course I won't leave you. I want you to sleep now and I swear on my life I'll be here when you open your eyes."

Gradually her frantic grip on Brianna's hands relaxed and she began to drift down into the vortex of sleep. One by one the queen and her ladies tiptoed from the chamber. After Joan had slept for two hours, Brianna told Glynis and Adele to get some rest. She would watch over her dear friend until dawn. All that mattered to Brianna was that Joan needed her.

During the long night's vigil, Brianna's active mind recalled all the happy times she had spent with Joan and Edmund. All the times he'd playfully flirted with her were but poignant memories now. Why did terrible things happen to good people? Why did tragedies happen? There was nothing more cruel than a life snuffed in the flower of youth.

Why did the French and English have to fight this continual war? Why was Prince Edward off fighting when Joan needed him! How many more lives would be sacrificed over this obsession with conquering France? What if Edward was killed? Joan's life would be over! What if Christian was killed? Brianna's eyes flooded with tears. *Dear God, don't let him be taken from me before we've had a chance for happiness,* she prayed.

When Joan awoke late the next morning, Brianna was still beside her, as she had promised. Joan was relieved to find her there and was extremely loathe to part with her. Although Brianna promised to come back later in the day, Joan became agitated. "No. I don't want to be alone, not for five minutes!"

"You won't be alone, Joan. Glynis is here and the nursemaids will bring Jenna if you feel well enough."

Joan seized upon her words. "Yes, yes, I want my daughter here with me, and her nurses. I want them to stay here, I don't want them to go back to the nursery. Brianna, you must go and make the queen understand. I cannot be alone!"

Brianna knew Joan was close to hysterics. She reasoned that it was probably apprehension that something might happen to her baby. She walked through the orchard that separated Joan's wing from the royal palace and made her way to the nursery.

It was a noisy, happy place filled with children of all ages, playing with every toy imaginable. Queen Philippa herself was rocking the cradle of her baby daughter, while Jenna's wet nurse sat beside her, holding Joan's baby.

"Your Majesty, Joan begs that her baby and Jenna's two

nursemaids be allowed to move into her chambers for a little while."

"Oh, surely Joan needs rest until she recovers from poor Edmund's death," Philippa protested.

"Your Highness, Joan is in hysterics. I think if she could see the baby and hold her, it would calm her and help her get through this terrible time."

"Why, of course. That is very discerning of you, Brianna. I remember when I lost one of my babies, they tried to keep me abed until I recovered from my loss, but my suffering didn't begin to abate until I was back in the nursery with my other babies. We'll set up the cradle right in her chamber and the baby's nursemaids in the adjoining room. Who would have imagined a little hoyden like Joan of Kent becoming a devoted mother?"

Once Joan's chambers were turned into a nursery she began to cope with the loss of her brother, Edmund. She cried a lot, but Brianna noticed that her grief was progressing to acceptance. They spoke often of Edmund and all the happy memories they had shared. However, Brianna noticed that Joan's laughter had disappeared completely and she often caught a glimpse of a haunted look of fear in her eyes.

Brianna didn't expect her fear to disappear until Prince Edward returned to her safely. The Black Prince was not only a bastion of strength to the English army, he was Joan's invincible knight in shining armor.

The king received a dispatch from his marshal Warrick that they had sacked Carcassonne and the army was returning to Bordeaux. Warrick assured him there would be no more trouble from the south. The king and queen celebrated with the formal betrothal of Princess Isabel to Lord Bernard Ezi. The feast was lavish and Queen Philippa personally thanked Sir John Holland. He was the best Steward they had ever had, arranging for the royal kitchens to overflow with produce from all the exotic ports of Europe and the East, as well as importing good old English lamb, venison, and game birds by the thousand, to say nothing of the trout, salmon, and shellfish that were the finest quality in the known world.

The very next day, Princess Isabel set the Court on its ear by calling off her wedding. The king and queen both did their best to force her to change her mind, but since they had indulged her every whim since the day she was born, their pleas had no effect whatsoever upon the willful princess.

Isabel was not only jilting her betrothed, she was deriving the greatest pleasure in the world from doing so! When Bernard was devastated, Isabel laughed. When his family protested, she gloried in the scandal. When Bernard was so heartbroken he threatened to go into a monastery, she heartlessly told him to pray for her! At last Isabel was happy. She had inflicted pain and shame on the opposite sex in equal measure to that which the Count of Flanders had inflicted upon her. Her honor was vindicated, her insufferable pride restored. The king and queen consoled themselves with plans for Princess Joanna's marriage. At least she was a biddable child who would do her duty without causing a scandal.

The Black Prince's army returned to Bordeaux bringing disquieting talk of an outbreak of black death, which was rumored to have started in Constantinople and was said to be scourging the ports on the Black Sea.

A soldier under Warrick's command died a terrible death, moaning in agony, vomiting blood, and finally turning black in the face. The prince and Warrick squashed the gossip immediately. There was no possible way something from the Far East could touch them. The soldier had obviously eaten or drunk something that poisoned him, and they threatened to punish any man who spoke about a plague.

Christian Hawksblood and Ali spoke quietly together. They had their own ideas about the man's death, but kept a wise silence for fear of causing wholesale panic.

Brianna and Adele sat sewing in the garden. As summer approached, more and more flowers had come into bloom. Pink and red bougainvillea trailed against the white walls, white jasmine and yellow roses wafted their intoxicating perfume upon the warm breeze, attracting vivid butterflies and birds never dreamed of in England.

Brianna had come to love this garden. It was an oasis of calm, beauty, and tranquillity where she could escape from the demands of the Royal Court. She had learned to enjoy the pool also and looked forward to its soothing, cooling delights each afternoon while almost everyone else in Bordeaux observed the traditional siesta. After her dip, she liked to sit in the sun and sew while her hair dried. The sun was bleaching it and she thought the effect quite pretty. Pale golden tendrils fell about her temples and shoulders, interspersed with the long silken mass of brighter gold. Brianna was sewing a short white tunic to wear in the pool, while Adele stitched upon a baby's nightgown.

"Is that for Jenna?"

Adele's face lit up with pleasure. "Well, no, actually it's for another baby . . . my baby!"

"Adele! Oh, heavens, I don't know what to say!"

"At my age! Can you imagine? It's a miracle!"

Brianna could see how happy it made Adele, and in truth she envied her. "Does Paddy know?"

"Not yet. Mary and Joseph, can't you just see him strutting about, lording it over poor Ali?"

Brianna hesitated, then plunged in, "You don't think he'll shy away from marriage?"

Adele smiled complacently, sure of her man. "I'll bludgeon him into it, never fear! Well, that sun's too hot for me," she declared, touching her belly with loving hands. "I'm going to have a rest while you have your dip."

Brianna slipped off her clothes, donned the short white tunic she had just made and slid down into the turquoise water of the inviting pool. She was pleased with herself because she could now lift her feet off the bottom and actually swim a few strokes. One end of the pool was shaded, so she made her way down to the water that was in full sunshine. She closed her eyes and lifted her face to the sun. Her long hair floated out behind her in a shimmer of gold.

It was just so that Christian caught sight of her and it held him spellbound. Her beauty always thrilled him, but in this setting, surrounded by nature, the picture she created was utterly enchanting. Brianna hadn't noticed him yet, so he stayed in the shadows, absolutely still, drinking in all her loveliness as she worshiped the sun.

His heart overflowed with love for her. Whenever he was away from her, she filled his thoughts, and the anticipation of returning to find her waiting for him was the sweetest feeling he'd ever known. He was the luckiest man alive. She was everything he'd ever dreamed of, everything he wanted, everything he needed. She was beautiful, intelligent, gifted, sensual, and above all, courageous. As well, she was idealistic, with a strong belief in honor and integrity.

His mouth curved with tenderness. He wouldn't have her any other way. Though it made life difficult for him, Brianna could not give her love to a man she thought had murdered his brother. Christian was proud of her high moral standards. She would make the perfect mother for the children he longed for. She would pass her personal code of ethics on to them and set them a magnificent example with her strong sense of morality.

Sooner or later she would come to understand that he had not killed his brother so he could have her in marriage. And if the realization came later rather than sooner, it would serve as an exercise in teaching him patience. Something he lacked occasionally.

Brianna heard the distinctive clink of chain mail as Christian divested himself. She caught her breath as she realized her husband had returned from the fighting. She was rooted to the spot as she watched him throw off his clothes and saw clearly his intent to join her in the pool.

Hawksblood dove beneath the water, gliding the entire length of the pool to surface within inches of her. He shook the water from his eyes and grinned at her. "Is this Brianna or a sea nymph from some mythic tale? I know you are no mermaid, for I've just glimpsed a pair of pretty legs and other tempting parts of the female anatomy." Christian adored the way she blushed. He drew close, enjoying the teasing. He said low, "You must have known I was coming. 'Tis a delightful way to welcome me home."

"I didn't . . . I'm not—"

"Not welcoming me?" His face fell in mock disappointment. "You wish me still off fighting battles?"

"No indeed. I am most relieved that you are safe, my lord."

Her words were so measured, so careful to say what was exactly in her heart, he experienced real disappointment. If only her heart told her to greet him inordinately, lavishly, and with abandon. He would sell his soul to have her fling her arms about him and tell him she would die without him.

"It warms my heart to see you enjoying the pool and the garden," he told her.

"It gives me a great deal of pleasure," she said with enthusiasm. "The flowers have the most heavenly scents and brilliant birds play about the fountain. And the butterflies . . . I cannot begin to describe how colorful they are. I had no idea!"

"You thought all butterflies were white."

Brianna went still. "Are you privy to all my thoughts?" she asked solemnly.

"Brianna, you named your white palfrey Papillon. That tells me you thought butterflies were white."

"Oh, I see," she said, feeling foolish, then laughing with him.

"It also tells me your French is as execrable as your biology. Papillon is a masculine noun." He bent to brush her lips with his. "I shall have to teach you the French tongue," he said outrageously, and proceeded to give her the first lesson.

Christian lifted her and climbed the steps out of the pool. When he saw her beautiful eyes become shadowed, he decided he would not carry her up to bed to slake his need. Brianna meant much more to him than that. He longed for them to be companions, friends, and partners as well as lovers. He decided to restrain himself and enjoy the anticipation of the sexual tension that had already begun to build between them.

He laid her down at the pool's edge and stretched out beside her. As he fanned out her hair so it would dry in the sun, his lips twitched with amusement. The white shift was almost transparent when it was wet and he knew she had no idea it revealed more than it concealed. "Why don't we lie here and let the sun dry us? I swear there is no more luxurious feeling in the world than giving your body up to the sun's rays. I'll get you some oil. I don't want your lovely skin to turn a repulsive color like mine."

Brianna turned her head, watching him walk the length of the pool, then disappear up the stairs to their bedchamber. Christian Hawksblood was the antithesis of repulsive. He attracted like a magnetic force, or a lunar tide. She had the urge to follow him now. All she had to do was go up those stairs to their bedchamber and he would love her so passionately, he would banish every thought from her mind. His kisses would take her to a place where they were alone in the universe. Where no others could intrude. It was their private paradise, with no shadows and no ghosts. At least for a little while.

Why hadn't he carried her up to bed? Perhaps he didn't want to make love to her! She closed her eyes to banish such a disturbing thought and when she opened them again, he was towering above her in naked splendor, pouring almond oil into his palm.

"Turn over," he ordered.

He began at her heels and with long, smooth strokes anointed her slim legs with the oil. When he reached her thighs, she decided he had the most wonderful hands in the world. They were strong and firm, and the feel of his calluses made his touch so roughly masculine, she was ashiver.

His palms encircled her round buttocks and his fingers slid wickedly into the cleft between the cheeks of her bottom, arousing unusual yet pleasurable sensations that made her quiver. She gasped and tensed as he planted a kiss upon her tempting derriere, but when his expert hands moved to her shoulders, kneading and massaging, all the tension melted from her muscles and she sighed blissfully.

He lay down beside her, watching her gold-tipped lashes flutter to her cheeks, watching her mouth curve with pleasure as the sun kissed her skin with its penetrating heat.

"We are two Sybarites," he murmured huskily, deeply content to be able to snatch a few hours of happiness in this peaceful sanctuary that kept the cruel realities of the world from touching them for a little while. His hand covered hers and they threaded their fingers together, content to simply lie drowsing in the sun, in their own private Eden, where birds flew down to the fountain and butterflies drifted from flower to flower.

❧ 𝟹𝟾 ❧

Prince Edward could not simply walk into Joan's chambers when they overflowed with nursery women and the ladies who attended his mother, so he summoned Randal Grey and scribbled a hasty note. When she read the note, Joan's emotions soared with joy, then plummeted with fear. What if Holland revealed her shameful secret to Edward? She trembled at the thought. He was such a depraved monster, she knew he was capable of any foul deed.

Then reason came to her rescue. He could not destroy her without destroying himself. Her need for Edward overcame any other emotion, so she dismissed all the women except Glynis, telling them she would take a nap.

When Glynis came to get the prince, he questioned her anxiously about the state of Joan's health. His father had told him of Edmund's death and his mother added that Edmund's sister had been so overcome with grief, they feared she would lose her sanity. Glynis wanted to tell him Joan would never recover while she was married to Holland. The Welsh girl sensed he was evil. He made her very flesh crawl when he spoke to her. Glynis even carried about a coffin nail for protection from him. But Joan had never complained about him, never even mentioned his name, and she had no evidence that Joan was afraid of him. All she had was a gut feeling.

"My lady is recovering from the sad shock of her brother's death, Your Highness, and she has regained her health and her figure after the rigors of childbirth, but something is bothering her. She is no longer carefree and she is extremely nervous about being left alone." When they reached the door, Glynis let him go in alone, saying, "I hope you are the cure she needs, Prince Edward."

"Sweetheart, can you ever forgive me for not being here when you needed me?"

"Oh, Edward, thank God nothing happened to you!"

His arms closed about her tenderly. He thought he understood what troubled her. She had lost her brother to war and she feared he might be next.

Joan clung to his hand and led him to the cradle where Jenna lay gurgling. Edward picked her up, astounded that he had created something so tiny. He cradled her on one strong arm, her Plantagenet blue eyes focusing on him in fascination. He listened with delight as Joan told him every little detail about his baby daughter, but he noted the dark smudges beneath his beloved's eyes and he saw she was no longer just slim, she was wasting away. When he realized the baby had gone to sleep, he gently laid her back in her cradle and picked up Joan.

"Little Jeanette, my heart, tell me what is wrong?"

"Edward—" Her eyes flooded with tears. Dear God in Heaven, she had almost confessed all! "Nothing is wrong . . . just hold me," she begged.

Edward sank into a deep chair and gathered her close in his lap. She laid her head against his broad chest and as his strong hand reached out to stroke her hair, the tender gesture undid her. She buried her face against him and sobbed her heart out.

They took supper in Joan's chambers, then after dark when they would not be recognized, walked in the orchard. Later, when they retired to bed, Edward made no sexual demands. He saw that she needed his strength and his comfort. When she fell asleep in his arms, Edward lay awake, consumed by regret at what he had done to the one he loved most in all the world.

He had turned a laughing, mischievous hoyden into an insecure, frightened child. Was he not the invincible Black Prince? The strongest knight in Christendom? He should have overcome the king and queen's objection to his marrying his cousin. Marrying her to another man had been the act of a coward and it covered him with shame.

Perhaps he could get the marriage dissolved. It would take years and cause a hellish scandal, but in his heart he knew it was the honorable thing to do. He would say nothing to Joan about it, until he had made some inquiries. It might do her grievous harm to raise up her hopes, then dash them to the ground if an annulment was not possible. Now that Edmund was dead, Joan had attained a much higher status. She was Countess of Kent and Lady Wake of Liddell in her own right. Her wide possessions and wealth might go a long way in persuading the Pope to dissolve her marriage.

Rumors persisted about a black death that was reportedly claiming lives in the ports along the Mediterranean. Two men-at-arms came down with a mysterious malady and were dead within twenty-four hours. Hawksblood spent the evening at Warrick's house discussing the matter.

"The bodies should be burned to prevent the contagion spreading. Any new cases should be quarantined."

Warrick nodded his agreement. "I'll set up a building as a hospital and each man-at-arms must do voluntary service."

"Nay," Hawksblood said, "that would spread it through the entire army. The hospice should be set up outside Bordeaux in a nearby village with a small population. Certainly it should be manned by volunteers, but not on a rotating basis. There should be no traffic back and forth; the entire village must be quarantined."

Warrick's forehead was deeply furrowed with worry and when Hawksblood explored his father's thoughts, he was startled to find Guy de Beauchamp's worries ran on identical lines with his own. They were both deeply concerned that this plague so rampant in the East would touch Christian's mother, Princess Sharon.

Hawksblood placed his hand on Warrick's powerful shoulder. "I, too, think of her constantly."

Warrick's aquamarine eyes looked deeply into his son's. It was a rare moment of communication between father and son. "I fear I shall never see her again. Not in this world," Warrick added with grim resignation.

Hawksblood smiled at his father to lighten his worry. "I have the advantage of being able to ask Allah for favors as well as the Christian God. I'm sure our prayers for her safety will not go unanswered." But Hawksblood was anything but sure. He had a premonition that this foul scourge would indeed touch his parent, and though he tried to rid himself of the negative thought, it persisted.

When the king and Prince Edward arrived at Warrick's with grave faces, they realized there were additional things to worry about. King Edward's spies had reported that John, the new King of France, was so eager to erase his father's disgrace over Crécy, he had emulated the King of England by forming his own Order of Chivalry, which he called Our Lady of the Noble House. His nobles were flocking to him in droves, begging to be included in the brotherhood. All reports said the ranks of the French army were swelling at a time when the English had tried to sue for peace.

King Edward flung down in disgust the dispatches he had received from the Duke of Lancaster regarding his visit to the Pope at Avignon. It seemed that the papal court was overrun with Frenchmen. French cardinals, officials, builders, and merchants had swarmed to Avignon to share the enormous wealth left by the previous Pope on his death.

The new Pope Innocent turned down the terms that Edward proposed, namely that he give up his claim to the throne of France in return for having his possessions confirmed in full sovereignty. For the first time in his life, Prince Edward saw a look of defeat on his father's face. He saw clearly that his father had had a bellyful of war and it was now up to him to pick up the gauntlet for the English cause.

He took up one of the dispatches his father had flung down and handed it to Warrick. "The news is not all black. As soon as Lancaster saw the French had a stranglehold on the Pope, he sent for his own army. It should have landed at Cherbourg yesterday."

Warrick said, "Do you think if we sent south to our ally in Navarre, he would send us troops?"

Hawksblood warned, "Navarre's close neighbor, Charles of Spain, is France's ally. My guess is Navarre will see which way the wind blows before he commits himself."

Prince Edward grimaced. "As usual, we have only ourselves to rely upon."

Hawksblood grinned at his friend. "When did that ever stop us?"

Warrick decided, "We'll send scouts to learn the size of the French army and if it's on the move."

Prince Edward nodded. "In the meantime, I'll take my army north and try to join up with Lancaster's men-at-arms."

Prince Edward would have preferred facing the French army single-handed to telling Joan he must again leave on campaign. She clung to him for strength both literally and figuratively, making him feel as if he were deserting her. He knew he must prepare her for the separation, rather than spring it upon her at the last moment.

"Sweetheart, Lancaster's army has landed at Cherbourg and is heading south. I'm taking my army north to meet it. That will double our numbers, should it come to another battle with the French." They were reclining on Joan's bed, late at night, while Jenna lay kicking and gurgling between them.

The blood drained from Joan's face, leaving her white and shaking. "B-but I thought you were negotiating a peace treaty?"

He took her hands to infuse her with some of his strength. "It seems they haven't learned their lesson, so we'll have to give them another. If I can join up with Lancaster's army, it will be a lesson they won't soon forget."

Joan's throat closed with fear. She would have begged him not to go, if she could have gotten out the words.

"Jeanette, you always had supreme faith in my ability as a warrior and leader of men. Is it because of Jenna that you are suddenly afraid? I should never have burdened you with a child."

Joan found her voice. "Oh, Edward, never say that. She isn't a burden. So long as I have Jenna, I have a part of you. She is my comfort and my strength when you are gone!"

"Good, then your fear must stem from Edmund's death. I know how close you were, sweetheart; only time will ease your grief."

She knelt on the bed and put her hands upon his shoulders. "Promise me that John Holland will never receive my brother's title!" she said in great earnest.

Edward's brow creased. "You have his title. Didn't you know? You are now Countess of Kent." He suddenly realized something about Holland was agitating her. "Has Sir John done aught to offend you, love?"

"Oh no, no," she quickly assured him. "It is just that I hate sitting in the hall with him, while he struts about pretending to be my husband and Jenna's father." Joan caught her breath and bit her tongue. Had she said too much?

Edward took her in his arms. "Would it make you happier if I took Holland on this campaign?"

"Oh yes! After all, you need every man you can get to fight the French."

"Sweetheart, this is the first time you've smiled since I returned."

"I've neglected you shamefully. Why don't I get Glynis to take Jenna and then we can say good-bye the way we used to?"

"I don't leave tomorrow, it will be the next day, but I don't believe there is any law that says we can't say good-bye two nights in a row!" Edward had already divested himself of boots and doublet by the time Glynis came in to take the baby.

Randal Grey came to the house looking for Hawksblood.

"Hello, Randal! Where's Gnasher?" Brianna never saw one without the other.

"He's off chasing female ferrets every night. One of these mornings I'm afraid he won't come back. Hawksblood thinks he'd be better off living wild, but I'd miss him. May I speak with Hawksblood, my lady?"

"I'm sorry, he isn't here. You'll probably find him next door at Warrick's, discussing military strategy."

"Then may I speak with Paddy?"

Brianna hesitated, then said decisively, "No. Paddy and Adele were married this morning. If you disturb them he'll give you a clout on the ear."

The boy looked so dejected, Brianna took pity on him. "Is there something I can do, Randal?"

"Oh yes, Lady Brianna! Please ask your lord husband to take me on the campaign."

Although Christian hadn't told her when they were leaving, she realized it was imminent when Paddy took Adele before the priest. "When are they leaving?" she asked casually.

"Tomorrow. I have a horse, a sword, and a full set of armor. If you asked a boon of him, he could never refuse you."

Brianna blinked to learn Randal's fanciful notions of chivalry. And by the way he was lusting to ride into battle, his ideas about war must be just as fanciful. "Randal, war isn't valor and glory, it's blood and death."

"I cannot be considered a man until I have bloodied my sword. Please ask him to take me this time, my lady."

"You can sleep in one of the chambers if you like, and we'll ask him in the morning. He never returns from Warrick's until late."

"My armor and sword are outside. May I bring them in so they won't be stolen?"

Brianna smiled, realizing this was the way he had acquired them himself. "You'll suffocate in all that armor! How can you stand to wear it in this heat?"

"Hawksblood is teaching me to learn control. Physical discomfort can be easily overcome. It's a state of mind, my lady."

An hour later, Brianna sat in the garden amid the night-scented blooms, in a reflective mood. The more she thought about it, the more she realized that everything was a state of mind . . . courage, fear; happiness, sorrow; love, hate. Because she kept her heart hidden from Christian, he didn't share things with her.

Had he kept his departure secret to spare her worry or did he simply consider it none of a woman's business? They shared a bed, but they did not share their hopes and dreams, their inner thoughts and feelings. They neither spoke of their past, nor their future. They had come to live together on the surface, without exploring the depths, and Brianna didn't know what to do to alter their state of mind.

Christian found her in the shadowed garden. "I'm late. I didn't mean to keep you up. Were you waiting for me?"

The question sounded merely polite. Her ear could detect no hint of longing.

"I . . . it was too hot to sleep."

"Brianna, I'm glad you are still up. There is something I must say." He sat beside her in the darkness, close but not touching. "I watched Adele marry Paddy today. I never saw a happier bride. Brianna, our marriage has brought you little happiness. I realize now that I never should have forced you. I only thought of what I wanted, and that was wrong. When you love someone, you prove that love by putting their desires before your own.

"If you want this marriage dissolved, we can do it. Where I was born, a man simply says, 'I divorce you,' and it is done." His words were distant, cool, detached.

Dear God in Heaven, that wasn't what she wanted at all! She wanted him to sweep her into his arms and vow, "I will make you love me, willing or no!" She wanted this war to be over. She wanted to live at Bedford, surrounded by her children, and more than anything in the world, she wanted Christian de Beauchamp to be the father of those children!

Silence stretched between them.

Brianna realized any happiness for the future hinged on her response. She took a deep breath. Hadn't she just concluded that courage was simply a state of mind? She gathered all of her courage now and whispered, "Give me your baby, Christian."

He swept her up in powerful arms and strode upstairs to their bedchamber. With impatient hands he threw off his clothes, needing her more than he'd ever needed her before. With difficulty he forced himself to patience, removing her garments slowly, cherishing her with his hands, adoring each part of her he uncovered, then worshiping her with his lips.

The heat of the night was fierce and he knew the fever of their passion would make their bodies too slick for sustained, drawn-out lovemaking, so he tossed a bed pillow to the marble floor. He stretched out and drew her down beside him. The marble was actually cold, making Brianna's skin so deliciously cool, she shivered for a moment.

When he straddled her and bent to press kisses on every pulse point, it felt like fire and ice. He spread his palms upon the white marble to cool them before he cupped her breasts, turning her hot and cold until she was mindless with need, shivering and burning at one and the same time.

Christian was beyond reason, beyond caution. Tonight he longed to enter more than her body, he longed to enter her blood, her heart, and her soul. His love words were so intense they held her in thrall, luring her on to give him everything he demanded . . . her body, her will, her love. She couldn't escape the power of this man; didn't want to escape it, now or ever.

Everything he said and did was blatantly erotic, drugging her senses. "Yield to me!" His voice was raw with emotion.

She arched her body to sheath him completely, opened her mouth so that his tongue could plunder her of every sensation. Both wanted their last hours to be unmarred by sadness or shadows. Both drove recklessly toward fulfillment, seeking that explosion of the senses that they alone could give each other.

Brianna was the focus of his entire existence and he longed for it to be the same for her. He knew she was closer to loving him than she had ever been before. Her lovely body was totally in his keeping, and yet he sensed that she held some small part of herself secret from him. She might even believe she had yielded all, but Christian knew there was still something just beyond his reach.

Brianna felt Christian's loins clench, buried deep inside her sleek heat, then she cried out her pleasure as he anointed her with the full honors of his manhood. His cries were dark with passion as his white-hot seed filled her with his love, his life. Brianna lay blissfully exhausted from the violence of Hawksblood's lovemaking. Who would have ever dreamed that making love on a marble floor could be the ultimate in sensuality? Hand clasped in his, she drifted off into a dream where he beckoned her beyond the moon and the stars.

Christian lay awake, fire still smoldering in the brilliant aquamarine eyes beneath his long black lashes. His craving for her was like a madness. Soon, soon, she would surrender all, he promised himself. *And if she does not?* The voice came unbidden. He pushed it away. He did not wish to make a decision to end it. Salvation or damnation? He knew if he could not have every last drop of her love, he ought not condemn them to everlasting torture.

Prince Edward felt over the moon. Joan was her old teasing self again. They had laughed and loved away the hours of their last night together, then giggling like a little girl she had lured him outside into the hot night where they slipped into a gliding swan boat. They made love one last time as it floated across the cool lake.

The pink fingers of dawn were painting the sky as he carried her back to her chamber and kissed her good-bye over and over and over again.

"Shoo," Joan whispered, "this chamber will be overflowing with nursemaids and nannies very shortly."

Edward took one last look at his sleeping daughter. "Watch over her for me."

"I will, darling. I will keep her here beside me until you come back to us."

"I love you with all my heart," he vowed.

"I love you, too, Edward. Go with God."

Hawksblood and his squires were up before dawn and while Paddy was bidding Adele a tender farewell, Brianna suddenly remembered Randal Grey. "Christian, your new squire Randal is here. He seems to think that if I ask it as a boon, you will take him on this campaign."

Hawksblood said grimly, "The young devil knows I can refuse you naught." He raised his voice and bellowed, "Randal!"

"I am here, my lord," young Grey said, stepping into the breakfast room.

Hawksblood had been about to deny him, but when he saw the squire clad in full armor, he remembered what he had felt like at his age. "Do you have a mount?" Hawksblood demanded.

"Aye, my lord," Randal said eagerly.

"Do you have a saddle?"

Randal's face fell, but he dared not lie. "Nay, my lord."

"Ali will provide one," Hawksblood said shortly.

Randal's face split into a wide grin. He fell on his knees at Brianna's feet. "Thank you, my lady. I shall never be able to repay you, but when I return, I will be your devoted slave forever!"

Hawksblood turned away. The boy was so earnest, it was painful to watch him.

"When Gnasher comes back from his roaming, will you keep him safe for me? You are the only lady he likes. He disgraced himself by biting the baroness and she wants him destroyed."

"The baroness? Do you mean Lisette St. Lô?" asked Brianna, a red veil of fury almost blinding her. She swung around on her husband. "Where is she?"

"I quartered her in Warrick's house," he said evenly, planting his feet to brace himself for the storm she was about to unleash.

"You have deliberately deceived me! I thought her gone from Bordeaux and you were happy to keep me in ignorance!" Brianna's eyes flashed green fire. "I thought her at the other side of the country, when in reality she is just at the other side of the garden wall. How convenient for you. Now I realize why you spent every night at Warrick's!"

Hawksblood was not about to make excuses. Brianna was in no mood to listen. It was the same old problem that always stood between them. Trust. Either she trusted him or she did not. And obviously she did not! Not in this matter, nor in the other, more serious matter of his brother.

When he did not deny her accusations over the French girl, she assumed him guilty. "Whoremaster!" she flung, wanting him to deny it, desperately needing him to deny it! She saw his eyes turn dark turquoise with anger. His hair fell in ebony waves to his broad shoulders. He was the most damnably attractive man she had ever seen. Had he not told her he could divorce her in a moment? "Arabian devil!" she spat. "I divorce you, I divorce you, I divorce you!"

She fled up the stairs and slammed her chamber door. Her breasts rose and fell as she sat on the bed panting. Now he would come and beat her to a jelly! She shivered in anticipation. But he did not come. By the time Brianna swallowed her pride and crept downstairs, Hawksblood and his three squires were long gone.

✵ 39 ✵

King Edward envied his son going off to fight the French. He almost decided to accompany him when he learned John of France had left Paris and was bringing his army directly south. Concern for his wife and family was the only thing that stopped him. Princess Joanna had suddenly fallen ill and Queen Philippa was so frantic it might be the dreaded black death that King Edward knew he could not leave his wife to face it alone.

Hawksblood rode between Prince Edward and Warrick. Since Lancaster's army was the same size as theirs, both would be able to cover the same distance each day. They therefore estimated they should join forces around the town of Poictiers. Since the French army was larger, they reasoned it would take King John far longer to get from Paris to Poictiers.

"Poictiers sounds like a fine place for a battle to me," Prince Edward said decisively. He grinned at Hawksblood. "It's in the heart of the wine country, so keep your men sober until the victory celebration."

Warrick winked at Prince Edward. "By the black scowl on his face, my son looks as if he already has a hangover. It's either too much wine or too much woman," Warrick baited.

"Too *many* women," Hawksblood muttered.

"What, is your lady still in a rage about the French filly? Doesn't the lass know you are besotted with her?"

"No," Hawksblood shot back at him, "but apparently everybody else knows! Am I a laughingstock then, because she has me jumping through hoops?"

"Nay, in matters of the heart, all men have the right to behave foolishly, and sooner or later manage to exercise that right!"

The three men lapsed into silence, each reflecting on his own folly. Warrick deeply regretted allowing his princess to remain behind when he left the East. There was seldom a night went by without her disturbing his dreams. Letting a woman decide her own future was a mistake. A woman had no idea what she wanted until her man showed her. He should have ridden in and carried her off on his destrier. Warrick sighed for what might have been.

Prince Edward deeply regretted marrying Joan to John Holland. He should have defied his father, king or no king, and taken her for his wife. He should have married her first, then told his parents and the Council after the fact. What could they have done about it, once it was a fait accompli? Edward sighed for what might have been.

Hawksblood regretted leaving Brianna in anger. She was right. He should have released the St. Lôs instead of merely moving them next door. The woman meant nothing to him, but unfortunately Brianna did not know that. If only his beloved wife would learn to listen to her heart, her doubts would dissolve like snow in summer.

He had learned to listen to his heart where Brianna was concerned and it had shown him the way. He knew she loved him, knew she longed for exactly the same thing from life as he did: a warm and loving family. As he galloped along, he fell into a trancelike reverie, listening to his heart, savoring his deep and abiding love for the mate who encompassed his past, present, and future.

Joan handed Jenna to her wet nurse so that Glynis could dress her hair. "Braid it tightly. Brianna and I are riding today. She's going to give me a tour of beautiful Bordeaux."

Glynis was delighted with the change in Joan. She was back to her old, happy self again. A knock on the chamber door brought Marie St. Hillary, the queen's waiting-woman. "Good morning, Lady Holland. Queen Philippa has sent me on a mission of mercy."

"Marie, sit down and catch your breath, you are white as a sheet."

Glynis poured Marie a little wine and rosewater and Marie sipped it gratefully. "Princess Joanna has fallen ill and the queen begs Glynis to come and help nurse her. She knows you have a vast knowledge of herbs and medicines."

"Why, of course I will come. Let me get my supplies."

"Queen Philippa says I must warn you that the physician

has put Princess Joanna's household in quarantine so the contagion cannot spread, if it turns out to be the dreaded plague, God forbid!" Marie said, making the sign of the cross.

"You mean Glynis will have to stay there until the princess recovers?" Joan asked.

Marie nodded. "Queen Philippa is near mad with worry and wants to nurse Joanna herself, but the king agrees with the physician that she must keep away so that she cannot carry the sickness to the other royal children."

Joan took Glynis aside. "You don't have to go, Glynis. I'll write the queen a note saying I cannot spare you."

"It's all right, my lady, I'm not afraid. But it's wise to stay there so I won't bring it back to you and Jenna."

A finger of fear touched Joan as she watched Glynis leave, but the fear was not for herself, it was all for Jenna. She watched with anxious eyes as the nurse laid Jenna in her cradle. It couldn't be the black death; only sailors in foreign ports or men-at-arms contracted such disgusting diseases. How could the contagion come right into the royal palace and choose a Plantagenet princess as its victim?

Joan swung toward the door as she saw it open. She could not have been more horrified if the Angel of Death had stepped over the threshold. It was Holland!

Her hand flew to her throat. "I . . . I thought you went on campaign with Edward," she gasped.

Holland smiled. "The queen could not possibly manage without me at a time like this."

Joan feared this man more than she feared any plague on earth. She stood frozen like a rabbit, helpless in the face of a fox. Her heart catapulted into her throat as she watched him move to the cradle and take Jenna into his arms. "I think our daughter should return to the royal nursery until the threat of this sickness passes. They are taking extra precautions with the royal children."

"No!" Joan cried. "She will be safe with me."

Holland spoke quietly to the wet nurse. "I'd like to be private with my wife. I'm sure I can explain that our child's safety is more important than my wife's irrational fear of being alone."

The nurse curtsied to Sir John and went into the adjoining room.

"You monster, put my baby down," Joan hissed.

He walked toward her with Jenna, the perfect picture of a devoted father. Joan began to tremble.

"Babies are so fragile. Many don't survive their first year. Accidents happen so quickly. One twist of Jenna's tiny leg could cripple her or one careless drop on her sweet little head could damage her brain and turn her into an idiot."

Joan's mouth went completely dry, the ache in her throat almost choking her. Joan knew she must get Jenna away from him immediately. She must tell the queen he had threatened her baby. Then she remembered Philippa was consumed with worry for her own child at this moment. Holland was supposed to be her baby's father; no one would ever believe that he was a threat to his own child. They would say she was losing her mind as they had when Edmund died. There was only one person in the entire world who would believe her. Brianna.

"I will do whatever you ask," Joan whispered.

"Oh, I know you will, my angel. When I return, I want the brat gone and the fucking nursemaids banished from our chambers permanently. We need time alone together so that we can get to know each other. Intimately! You will learn to cater to my likes and whims. I will teach you to give pleasure in ways you've never dreamed of." When he saw his subjugation of her was complete, he said, "Call the nurse back."

As Holland placed Jenna in the arms of the wet nurse, Joan tried to choose words that would satisfy his sick need to dominate her. "My husband has convinced me that our baby will be safer in the nursery. I'll bring some of her things and we'll get a servant to remove her cradle. My husband's position of Steward is so demanding, he'd like our time together to be private and undisturbed."

Holland dropped a possessive kiss upon Joan's fair brow. "Thank you, my angel. Your decision is most wise. I shall join you in an hour or so."

Joan was so weak with relief that she had gotten Jenna away from him safely, her knees almost buckled as she walked with the wet nurse to the royal nursery. The girl was as terrified of the plague as Joan was of Holland and talked about it in fearful whispers until they arrived at the nursery, where she was told in no uncertain terms to keep her mouth shut in front of the children.

Joan kissed Jenna a dozen times before she could force herself to leave her, but she knew her baby would receive round-the-clock care with the experienced royal nurses. Numb with fear, she sought out her only sanctuary. Brianna.

"Joan, have you heard the dreadful news about Princess Joanna?" Brianna asked.

Joan nodded and murmured, "Queen Philippa asked Glynis if she would help nurse her in quarantine."

"How courageous she is!" Brianna declared. "I'm not sure I could be that brave."

Joan burst into tears. "Brianna, you are the bravest woman I know. 'Tis I who am weak and afraid! My God, I'm so ashamed of what I've done, I wish it were me who had the plague instead of Joanna!"

"Darling, what in the world are you saying?" Brianna cried, putting her arms about Joan. "My God, you are trembling like a leaf. Do you feel ill?"

"No . . . yes, so ill I'm dying! John Holland is killing me!" Joan blurted.

"What did he do to you?" Brianna demanded.

Joan sank down upon the chaise longue, gripping one of its cushions tightly. Then she brought it to her breast and hugged it as if it were a shield that would protect her. "When Edward went away last time, Holland raped me."

"Jesu!" Brianna gasped. "I take it you didn't tell Edward?"

"Dear God, no. Holland threatened to tell Edward I welcomed him to my bed," Joan said in a voice so filled with misery it wrung Brianna's heart.

"That same night the king came to tell me of my brother's death and when I collapsed and the queen's ladies came, it was the only thing that saved me from Holland's insatiable lust. I begged you not to leave me alone, and then you talked the queen into letting me have Jenna and her nurses in my chamber."

Brianna poured Joan a large goblet of wine and insisted that she drink it down.

"I thought I was safe from him this time. Edward told me he was taking Holland on campaign, but he didn't go!"

"Joan, you should have told someone!"

"But how can I complain about Holland demanding his rights when he is my legal husband?"

"You should have told me!"

"I was too ashamed, and I thought it would never happen again. But it will, it will!"

"It most certainly will not! Adele"—Brianna summoned her waiting-woman—"I'm going to stay with Joan. Please pack me some things."

"I'm afraid of him, Brianna, and Glynis is so afraid of him she carries a coffin nail for protection."

"God in Heaven, I have something better than a coffin nail!" Brianna declared. "Adele, where is that curved dagger I bought at the tournament fair?"

"I'll get it for you. I'd better come with you, my lamb."

"You most certainly will not. Adele is having a baby," Brianna explained to Joan. "Paddy would have my guts for garters if anything happened to you or the child. Besides, Holland won't dare lift his filthy eyes in Joan's direction in my presence."

"What if Holland harms you?" Adele demanded.

"A monster or a bully cannot be appeased. The only escape is to confront him head-on and see him for what he is. Joan, when you love and honor who and what you are, you don't allow people to coerce you; you fight them."

Adele knew that once Brianna had made up her mind, there was no deterring her. She glanced at the ferret who was running along the open balcony. "Shall I put him on his chain or do you want to take him with you?"

"As a matter of fact, that's an excellent suggestion. Gnasher is better protection than a watchdog."

As Hawksblood galloped along, a powerful vision of Brianna came to him. He saw her reach for a curved dagger and strap it at her waist. The vision was so crystal clear, he saw both outrage and stubborn determination written on her lovely face. He knew immediately that she was in grave danger.

He turned to Warrick. "I have to go back," he told his father, with no further explanation. He spurred ahead to ride abreast of Prince Edward and his squire, John Chandos. "Brianna is in terrible danger. I must go back."

Edward knew of Christian's visions. Knew this was no coward's trick to avoid fighting the French.

"I'll return as soon as I can, Sire. I'll catch up with you on the road or at Poictiers. I swear on the Cross."

"No need to pledge me vows, Christian. I know your loyalty is absolute."

Hawksblood turned his destrier and drew rein between Paddy and Ali. "I shall return as soon as I can." He jerked his head in the Black Prince's direction. "Guard his back as if it were mine."

Joan was immensely relieved to find her chambers empty when she returned with Brianna. She hoped that Holland's duties would keep him busy the rest of the day. Brianna's presence gave her much needed courage and Joan vowed she would die before she would ever submit to Holland's degradation again.

Brianna let Gnasher off his silver leash so he could explore his new surroundings, then she took her bag into the adjoining chamber and hung the clothes she had brought in the wardrobe. The girls talked as Brianna changed the sheets on the bed that the nurse had slept in. They spoke of their anxiety for the young princess and wondered aloud why the sweet one should fall ill, while the one who played merry hell with everyone went unscathed.

They admitted how much they hated their men continually riding off to war and that they prayed every night for a lasting peace. They talked of Adele and the baby she was expecting, and Brianna confided how much she envied Joan and Adele.

Joan's eyes flooded with tears. "I didn't tell you what Holland threatened to do with Jenna. He said if I didn't send her to the nursery and banish the nurses so we could be alone, he'd twist her leg so she would be crippled or drop her on her head."

"My God, the man is insane! How could Edward have married you to such a monster?" Brianna suddenly appreciated Hawksblood's devotion.

"Edward has no idea and I never want him to find out. I wish Holland were dead! Why doesn't he catch this damned plague and die?"

Brianna put her arm about Joan's shoulders. "Life doesn't work that way. My daddy used to say, if wishes were horses, beggars would ride. And prayers can be very much like wishes, I'm afraid. Divine intervention is a rare phenomenon. Joan, there is good in the world and there is evil. If we combine our strengths and stand firm against Holland's evil, we will defeat him. If we falter, we are lost."

Joan nodded. "Brianna, I love you. How can I ever thank you for being my friend?"

"You have brought laughter and fun into my life. Things I would never have known without you. Your friendship is precious to me."

"We can tell each other anything, no matter how dreadful, and know that nothing will destroy what we feel for each other."

"We are blessed," Brianna said, wiping away the last trace of Joan's tears.

Queen Philippa could stand it no longer. Accompanied by her woman, Marie, she made her way to the large pink building where Princess Joanna's large household had taken up residence. The guard posted at the door to enforce the quarantine fell back when he saw it was the queen, not daring to deny her admittance.

Inside, all seemed under control. Half a dozen women trekked from the kitchen to the upstairs sick room with boiling water, mops, and clean linen. The rest of the household were huddled behind locked doors in their own chambers. Glynis came out of the kitchen with a poultice she had just prepared. When she saw the queen she almost panicked. "Your Majesty, I beg you to leave!"

"Glynis, I will take the risk, as you do. I must see my little Joanna!"

Glynis did not want Philippa to see her daughter's pitiful condition. Joanna had begun to vomit the most foul-smell-

ing bile, she was so fevered she was delirious and an ugly
black swelling had risen in her armpit. Glynis was going to
apply the poultice to try to bring it to a head and release
the toxic poison that was in the young girl's body. "Your
Majesty, if you touch her you can carry the sickness to the
king, to Isabel or the younger children. Perhaps even all of
them! Joanna begged me to keep you away. She knows that
you love her and she asks that you go to the chapel and
pray for her," Glynis fabricated desperately.

Philippa pounced upon the suggestion with fervor. "I will
go immediately. Please tell her how much her father and I
love her."

When Philippa and Marie left, Glynis said to the guard,
"Put the bar across the door. Let no one enter or leave."

The king received more terrible news. A wounded messenger arrived with an urgent dispatch from Lancaster's
army. They had been defeated in a fierce skirmish with the
French and had retreated back to Cherbourg. The French
army outnumbered them and they would not be joining up
with the Black Prince anytime soon.

When the king summoned a servant, it was the Steward
himself who arrived. "Sir John! I thought you rode out with
Prince Edward at dawn."

"Er . . . no, Your Majesty, I thought the queen would
have need of my services when the princess fell ill."

"Thank you, Holland. It must be Providence that you
stayed behind. I need to get a message to my son or Warrick. Lancaster's army cannot get through. It will be disastrous for them to face the French alone. They must return
to Bordeaux for the present."

Holland cursed silently, while bowing to the king.

"Come with me now while I write the dispatch."

Holland knew he must make it appear that he would
deliver the message. Inside he began to rejoice that Prince
Edward was about to go down to defeat. What a stroke of
luck that the king had asked him to take the dispatch!
Holland had a feeling that Destiny had just taken his hand.
He would bid a fond farewell to his delectable young wife,
then go for a pleasant ride along the river Garonne.

When Holland entered the apartment, the first person

he saw was Brianna. The bitch stood defiantly between him and his lawful wife. "What the hell are you doing here, she-bitch?"

"Making sure you keep your place in this household, you filthy cur!"

"If you think you are a fucking self-appointed guardian angel, you've got another think coming. You are nothing but a whore, perhaps even worse! Sleeping with two brothers, then luring one to murder the other!"

"That's not true!" cried Brianna, launching herself at him to tear his ugly face with her nails.

Holland backhanded her so brutally, her head snapped back and she slumped onto the bed, unconscious. He picked her up, carried her limp body into the adjoining room and locked the door.

Joan stood rooted to the spot, white-faced, wide-eyed, trembling like a doe cornered by a wolf.

Holland was incensed that she had told her friend what he had done and that they had actually decided to defy him. Joan cried out in terror as he anchored one thick hand in the neck of her tunic and rent it down to its hem. The exquisite material fell in shreds about Joan's delicate breasts and thighs. She shrank back from him, trying to cover her nakedness with her hair, but Holland thrust his cruel hand into the silvery-gilt mass and dragged her against him. His hand caressed her concave belly. "I want you to swell with my son. He'll be the next Earl of Kent, thanks to me."

In that moment Joan knew he had somehow murdered Edmund. She looked wildly about for something to hit him with in a vulnerable moment. Brianna couldn't help her now; she'd have to help herself. Joan's glance fell upon Brianna's knife, which had fallen to the bed from its sheath when Holland hit her. Joan knew he would soon lead her to that bed. Knew he would remove his chausses so he could ravish her, and she knew what she must do!

As Brianna slowly regained consciousness, her hand crept to her jaw, which pulsated with excruciating pain. She felt as if she had been hit with a battering ram. When she moaned, Gnasher pawed at her gently, knowing she was hurt; urging her to get up from the floor.

Brianna eased herself into a sitting position and looked about her, slowly remembering where she was. Jesu, how long had she been unconscious? Holland had Joan at his mercy in the other room and ravishing her was the least he would do to her! On her hands and knees she crawled to the door and being as quiet as she could, tried to open it. Brianna wasn't surprised to find it locked.

She racked her brain trying to recall what Adele had once used to pick a lock. Her head was beginning to ache vilely from the violence of Holland's blow. She put her hands to her head, willing the pain away. Her fingers dislodged a hairpin and immediately she remembered it was the very thing Adele had used!

Working as carefully and as soundlessly as possible, she worked the wire into the keyhole and after what seemed like an eternity, finally managed to click it open. Brianna held her breath, hoping he hadn't heard, and after a minute she let out her breath and reached for her knife. Brianna had made up her mind to kill Holland! Stunned, she saw the sheath at her waist was empty. She looked all about the floor to see if it had fallen to the floor, but to her great disappointment, it was nowhere to be found. Refusing to be defeated, she took up an iron candlestick about a foot high and softly pushed open the chamber door.

Just as Joan hoped, Holland had her pinned to the bed now. The knife fit into her palm snugly, as if it had been especially designed for her small hand. She saw once again the obscenity of Holland's genitals and lusted to slice off his thick purple phallus so it could never desecrate her again, but Joan knew she was fighting for her life and Brianna's life as well, for assuredly Holland would have to kill Brianna to silence her.

As Holland plunged down upon her, Joan jabbed the knife into his throat. At that same moment Gnasher shot through the door, flashed across the bed, and fastened his teeth into Holland's exposed nether region. A scream of agony erupted from his throat, cut off by a strangling noise as blood sputtered up and bubbled through the hole in his neck that Joan had gashed open. Brianna sprang after the ferret, crashing the iron candlestick down on Holland's skull with a sickening thud. He rolled from the bed in a pool of blood.

"Sweet Jesus, are you all right, Joan?"

Joan was on her feet, the knife in her hand dripping crimson drops. "Did I kill him?" she panted.

Brianna looked down at his caved-in skull. "I think I did," she whispered.

❧ *40* ❧

As Hawksblood rode like a madman, he received continual flashes of the danger surrounding Brianna. Though his mind was powerful enough to see, he was powerless to intervene. Then suddenly the images ceased and he became frantic. Though he despaired of reaching her in time, he knew he must try his utmost, strive to the limit of his endurance, fight to get back to her with his last breath.

The two girls clung to each other desperately, horrified at what they had done, yet knowing they would do it again. Holland had left them no choice. It was a matter of kill or be killed; destroy or be destroyed!

One danger was past, but another now presented itself. Fear for the consequences of their actions almost paralyzed them. Brianna went to the wardrobe and took out a robe for Joan, then they took one end of the carpet and rolled it to cover the blood-soaked heap that was Sir John Holland.

They had no idea what they would do with him. They feared his body was too heavy for them to move, but they had little choice in the matter. "We'll wait until dark," whispered Brianna. "Perhaps we can get him as far as the orchard."

When Brianna looked at Joan she saw she was ready to faint. She guided her to a chair by the window and sat her down. If Joan went to pieces on her now, Brianna would be lost. Panic arose in her breast; she felt as if she would suffocate, her clear thinking was becoming hopelessly muddied by the emotional trauma that threatened to overwhelm her. A feeling of hopelessness gathered in her throat and threatened to erupt into a scream any moment.

His black destrier was lathered white as Hawksblood vaulted from the saddle and rushed into his house. "Where is she?" he demanded of Adele.

"She has gone to stay with Joan," Adele told him, weak with relief, secure in the knowledge that Hawksblood would keep them all from harm.

Christian loped up the hill toward the palace. He vaulted a high wall into the orchard and took the stairs leading to Joan's apartments three at a time.

When the door crashed open, Brianna screamed, and then miraculously she was in Christian's arms. She began to cry and now it was Brianna's turn to tremble. She needed him and he had come! It was that simple; it was that miraculous. Safe in Christian's arms, she did not have to be strong anymore. She gave herself into his keeping.

Joan watched mutely as Christian Hawksblood enfolded his wife in his powerful arms, surrounding her with his love. She watched them look at each other, heard them speak in such an intimate way, their words were for each other alone.

He lifted Brianna's tear-stained face with poignant tenderness. "I want you to be strong for Joan . . . I want you to be strong for me."

Brianna nodded, trusting him totally. "How did you know?"

"I listened to my heart. Forgive me for not arriving sooner. I would have given anything to spare you the necessity of killing."

Brianna clung to him. He was her bastion, her strength. "I had to do it, Christian—"

"No explanations. My love is absolute and unconditional."

"Edward must not know that he violated Joan."

"No one will know anything about this," Christian said firmly.

"What will we do?"

"You will do nothing, save recover from the ordeal. I will take care of Holland. You two will take care of each other."

Brianna nodded, some of his strength infusing her with

calmness. Christian dipped his dark head to brush her lips with his. Then he murmured softly, "I have to leave again. Tell me you will be all right. Promise me you will be strong?"

"I promise." Brianna lifted her mouth to seal the vow with a kiss. He squeezed her hands, then bent to Joan. "I want you to be strong for Edward and for Jenna."

"I promise," Joan said, knowing this man's protection and loyalty were absolute.

He came back to Brianna. "My mind is at ease. All danger to you has passed. Trust me . . . I know these things."

"Christian, I do trust you." Silently she thought, *Now I know what it's like to kill someone to protect another. You killed your brother, Robert, to protect Prince Edward, and I almost let it kill our love.*

Christian looked at her bleakly. He had heard her thought as if she had spoken aloud. "Brianna, I beg you, listen to your heart."

He rolled the carpet firmly about Holland's body, then slung it over his shoulder, departing as swiftly as he had come.

Hawksblood rode for two hours with the body slung in front of his saddlebow. Then he dismounted to unroll the carpet and examine Holland's body. His jugular vein had been severed, which would have resulted in his death, if he had not died as a result of his caved-in skull.

Hawksblood's eyes fell on a paper in Holland's doublet. When he drew it out, it was soaked with blood, but Christian saw the official wax seal of the king and realized it had import. He broke the seal and studied the message. Some of it was obliterated, but enough words were left to convey its meaning.

Lancaster's army was not coming! The king suggested Edward's army return to Bordeaux. Fighting the French army with a force of ten thousand was tantamount to suicide. Hawksblood looked down at Holland with contempt, realizing he would never have delivered the dispatch. He wanted Joan of Kent. Keeping this vital information from the Black Prince would guarantee his death.

Hawksblood had no more time or energy to waste on the heap of offal that lay before him. He lifted his gaze to the clear blue skies and projected his wishes upon the wind. Within minutes he glimpsed a lone vulture gliding upon a hot updraft. More birds joined the first, until about two dozen gathered, making their pattern of lazy circles. It was a fitting end. Ashes to ashes, dust to dust, carrion to vultures.

Hawksblood urged his destrier to ever greater speed in his attempt to rejoin Edward's army. Though he had spent twenty hours in the saddle, his weariness fell away when he focused on his goal.

Relief swept over him when he reached Angoulême where the army had camped for the night. When he dismounted and greeted the nearest men-at-arms a cold hand gripped his vitals. He had ridden into the French camp, completely unaware! He cursed beneath his breath. Why hadn't he utilized his sixth sense to warn him of the danger? He had been preoccupied with thoughts of Brianna and of the black plague endangering his mother. How on earth had the French army reached Angoulême so quickly?

He faded back behind the trees and was swallowed by the darkness. His clothing and his horse were black. If he was worth his salt, he must treat this as a God-given opportunity to assess the size of the French army.

Hawksblood advanced with great stealth, leading his horse on foot. After two hours he had gauged how far south, west, and north the army stretched, but the unknown was the eastern boundary. It seemed to spread back across the entire country.

He stretched out full length on the warm earth beneath the trees and began to concentrate. One by one he penetrated the barriers of time, space, sound, and distance until he attained the state conducive to his visions. Unbelievable as it seemed, John of France had an army of forty thousand men! He had his four sons with him, twenty-six noble dukes and counts, and over five hundred knights belonging to the chivalric order of Our Lady of the Noble House, who had taken an oath to die in battle rather than give ground. And as if this were not enough, they stood between Edward's army and Bordeaux, cutting off any hope of retreat.

Armed with nothing but bad news, Hawksblood pressed northward until he met up with Prince Edward and Warrick a few miles outside Poictiers. "You had best call a meeting of the leaders. Your nobles must be armed with the knowledge of our precarious position."

Hawksblood related the unwelcome news that Lancaster's army had retreated to Cherbourg and would not be joining forces. He told them that they had advanced too far north, and that the French army stood between them and their home base of Bordeaux. Then, reluctantly, he told them the numbers.

Salisbury swore. "We will be defeated!"

Edward crashed his fist down on a war chest. "It is blasphemy to say I will be conquered alive!"

Warrick spoke up, "No army on earth can withstand good English bowmen!"

Pembroke said, "I will inform the men-at-arms of the great odds they must face."

Hawksblood thundered, "Nay! Battles are decided before they begin. Our men must not be handicapped by fear of greater numbers!"

Edward said with pride, "It is English tradition to face great odds—and win!"

Warrick spoke up decisively. "From here to Poictiers the hillsides are covered by vineyards. We will occupy this strategic site. The rows of vines will protect us." Warrick set the foot soldiers to digging trenches and erecting ramparts of earth behind the vines.

The next morning, the Cardinal of Poictiers, Talleiran de Périgord, fearing his beautiful town would be laid to waste, issued an edict to John of France. He told him that the plague that was now rampant in France was God's punishment for fighting. He ordered the king to sue for terms.

The French king and his nobles did not want terms, they wanted to defeat these English dogs who dared raise their eyes to the throne and crown of France. But the religious leader could not be ignored. The power of the Church was greater than the power of the crown and John of France was forced to agree to meet with Prince Edward.

Under a flag of truce, John and his nobles met with Edward, Warrick, and Hawksblood. The Black Prince, the most chivalrous knight in Christendom, generously offered to return all the prisoners they held for ransom and to give up the towns and castles they had recently taken, in return for a seven-year peace.

King John, seeing the look of contempt on his nobles' faces, demanded that Prince Edward surrender himself along with one hundred of his knights.

The Black Prince laughed in his face!

King John argued, "Your countrymen love you so well, they will soon raise your ransom."

The Plantagenet temper exploded. "What sort of knight do you think I am? I will rather die, sword in hand, than be guilty of deeds so opposed to my honor and the glory of England! *Englishmen shall never pay ransom of mine!*

Warrick, usually so stoic, was unable to suppress his indignation. "You French have no intention of making a truce! Why should you? You have four times more men than we have. We care naught for that! Here is the field and the place. Let each do his best and may God defend the right!"

Christian Hawksblood had never been so proud in his life. Warrick was indeed worth five Frenchmen. He thanked both God and Allah that this man was his sire. From this day forth he would be honored to use the name De Beauchamp!

The prince, Warrick, and Hawksblood knew the English position was hopeless if the French king used tactical skill. All he had to do in fact, was surround the small army to force its surrender. They refused to accept defeat, however, even when it stared them in the face.

On the morning of the battle, the English bowmen were positioned on the slope behind hedges and thick vines where the ditches and ramparts had been dug. It was not a fair and open field where knighthood could perform to advantage.

A scout brought Edward news that the King of France wore a white plume upon his helmet and his highest-ranking nobles had copied him. The Black Prince stationed himself at the top of the hill where he could command a view of the narrow path that wound up it. What he saw astounded him. King John had learned nothing from Crécy!

He sent his knights, four abreast, up the narrow path.

The Black Prince gave the signal and his longbowmen cut them down as quickly as they advanced. When John broadened his lines, the English archers shot down the horses of the advancing knights. Hawksblood's Cornishmen with their long-knives crept through the thick vines and dispatched the French knights before they could gain their feet.

The French marshal, trying to save the king's sons, ordered them to retreat. As a result, one division fell back on the one behind and chaos reigned. Warrick and Hawksblood with a small force of mounted knights rode headlong into a second French division. Edward's squire, John Chandos, cried, "Sire, push forward. The day is yours! God has given it into your hands."

The golden lilies of France fell to the ground with blood on them. The retreat of the French was so infectious that by afternoon only the troops under direct command of King John were still fighting. Finally, they had to either die or surrender. The King of France at last yielded himself a prisoner, saying, "I hope you take me peaceably to your prince. I am great enough to enrich you all!"

So many nobles surrendered themselves for ransom, the Black Prince could not believe his good fortune. When Randal Grey brought in the king's youngest son, twelve-year-old Philip, at the end of his sword, Edward knighted him on the spot.

When Warrick and Hawksblood tallied their gains and losses, they estimated the French had left over ten thousand dead on the field, while the English lost only hundreds. They had taken prisoner the King of France, his four sons, his brother, the Duke of Orléans, and dozens of the highest nobles in the land, all sporting the white feather!

That night the English celebrated their victory with the food and wine of prosperous Poictiers. Prince Edward, honoring the rules of chivalry and carrying them to new heights, served the King of France with his own hands.

John ground out, "This is the bitterest day of my life; I am your prisoner!"

The Black Prince lifted his goblet in a salute and said valiantly, "Nay! You are my honored guest."

* * *

Paddy, Ali, and Sir Randal slept in Hawksblood's tent, while their lord shared Prince Edward's pavilion. They could not sleep, of course, after the exhilaration of battle and knew they would have to talk it out, as had become their custom. In the darkest hour of night, just before dawn, Christian said quietly, "John Holland is dead."

"Are you sure?"

"Yes, I positively identified his body. His throat had been slashed and his skull caved in. He was dead when I came upon him," Hawksblood said truthfully.

Prince Edward crossed himself. Silence stretched between them for long minutes. Finally, Edward could contain himself no longer. "That means Joan is a widow!"

"It does, Your Highness," Christian agreed, holding his breath.

"Jesu, all I need is a dispensation from the Pope! Will you go to Avignon for me?"

"I will, Sire," he said, smiling into the darkness. In that moment they felt omnipotent as gods.

When Hawksblood finally drifted off to sleep, he dreamed of his childhood. He was the pampered darling of the harem with his silky black curls and brilliant aquamarine eyes. Then the scene changed to the night he was smuggled to safety. He felt his mother's deep anguish. Parting with him had been like death to her, but she loved him with all her heart and soul, and giving him up was the sacrifice she accepted in return for his safety.

He relived his baptism of fire. It was a cruel awakening for a spoiled seven-year-old to be thrust among hardened Norman knights, but the training had been of more value than the gold and precious jewels his mother left in trust for his future. When he awoke, he was drenched with sweat. The beautiful image of his mother was still with him, but so was her pain. He sensed a threat to her future happiness that he could not dispel.

Hawksblood roused his squires from their sleep. Ali arose quietly and dressed. Paddy complained loudly that he had only just fallen asleep. Hawksblood grinned at him. "You'd better get used to being disturbed at all hours of the night, Daddy."

"Jasus, don't give Ali-Babba ammunition or I'll be known as Daddy-Paddy for the rest of my days!"

"I am going to Avignon for Prince Edward and taking Ali. I want you, and Randal," he added glancing at the earnest-faced youth, "to watch over our ladies. The mission isn't secret in the strictest sense, but the fewer who know about it, the better."

Ali crouched down beside Paddy and said low, "Tell Glynis . . ." He hesitated. Then he realized how ridiculous it was to be reticent with a man who had saved his life and vice-versa. Paddy would be the closest friend he would ever have. "Tell Glynis to start sewing her wedding dress . . . no, that would be sheer male arrogance! Just tell her that I shall return, no matter what."

On the ride back to Bordeaux, Warrick suddenly began to feel his age. Perhaps it was no bad thing that the war with France was over. The Plantagenets now held prisoner both the King of Scotland and the King of France, and a time of peace should prevail for the next few years. When trouble started again sometime in the future, as it inevitably would, he would be too old to go to war. He had always dreaded this day arriving, but now that it was here, he felt only relief. And weariness. A great encompassing weariness that ran sluggishly along his veins and penetrated into his very bones!

Paddy was the first to notice the old warrior slump forward in his saddle. He knew things were not right with the marshal, whose back was always ramrod straight. Paddy had a quick word with Randal and the two positioned themselves to ride on either side of him. When they saw his eyes close in fatigue, they shouted and laughed to keep him awake; when he swayed in the saddle, they closed ranks so he would not fall.

Word of the Black Prince's great victory swept before the army, and by the time it neared Bordeaux the roads thronged with cheering people, making merry and celebrating. The returning conquerors were offered food, drink, kisses, and garlands of flowers as they rode homeward.

At the palace, the king and queen were in personal mourning for their sweet daughter, Joanna, who had been taken from them in the cruelest of deaths, but King Edward did not allow his private pain to overshadow the glorious welcome that his valiant son deserved. He immediately began making arrangements to send their royal prisoners to England for safekeeping, and setting the terms of their ransom.

Paddy and Randal got Warrick safely to his own house and left him with his servants. Warrick was clearly ill and Paddy wished to God that Hawksblood and Ali had not ridden off to Avignon. Both had considerable medical knowledge, while he had none at all. He very much feared Warrick had fallen victim to the black plague!

When Paddy walked through the door, Adele fell upon him, kissing him, offering prayers of thanks for his safe return, and finally bursting into very real tears. Paddy was so touched by his wife's deep concern for him, his own eyes became moist.

Brianna arrived, flushed, breathless and very beautiful. She asked eagerly, "Is he home?"

Paddy shook his head. Brianna saw his tear-filled eyes and her hand flew to her breast as she experienced the worst moment of her life.

🦢 41 🦢

"He's still in one piece, my lady. He's gone on a mission for the prince. I wish to God he hadn't, though. His old man is sick as a bloody hound. I thought he was going to stick his spoon in the wall on the journey back to Bordeaux."

"Warrick is ill? Was he wounded?" Brianna asked with alarm.

"Nay. I fear it is you-know-what," Paddy said, too superstitious to say it aloud.

"Dear God, not the plague? Princess Joanna died of it only a sennight ago."

Paddy shook his head with regret. "Hawksblood and Ali

are better than any physician, but I'm as useless as teats on a boar!"

"I must go to him. Perhaps Glynis will help. She knows what it's all about."

Glynis had only just returned to Joan's chambers the previous day, waiting a full week after the princess's death, so that she would not carry the infection to those she loved.

Joan's face was alight with hope as she greeted Brianna, yet her eyes were shadowed with uncertainty. "Edward will wait until after dark before he comes to me. Oh, Brianna, I don't think I can bear to receive him in these chambers."

"Why don't you go and stay at my house where Edward can come and go as he pleases without prying eyes watching. Unfortunately I won't be there. Warrick has fallen ill and I intend to move into his house until he is recovered. Christian hasn't return yet and I can't let him come home to a house of death."

Glynis pulled out her coffin nail to ward off evil. "Judas, you don't think it's the black death?"

"I haven't seen him yet. I pray that it is not. I am on my way there now."

Glynis turned to Joan. "If you will go to Adele, I will help Lady Brianna nurse Warrick."

"You are both so brave," Joan said with admiration.

"Nay, I am terrified," Brianna admitted.

When they arrived at Warrick's house, he was still sitting exactly where Paddy had left him. They moved to either side of him to assist him to rise. "We have to get you to bed, my lord," Brianna explained.

His face was flushed, his aquamarine eyes glazed. "No . . . hospital . . . quarantine . . ."

"There is no one in this house other than your servants. You can be quarantined here." Both Brianna and Glynis knew he was too ill to be moved to the village hospital. When he stood up, he vomited for the first time.

"And so it begins again," Glynis said, confirming what ailed him. They put him to bed on cool, clean sheets and Brianna bathed his fevered torso. His upper body was marked with the silvery traces of old, healed wounds, but it was still hard and sinewy. He was a tough old warrior and Brianna, with a flicker of hope in her heart, told him he was

strong enough and hardy enough to overcome this afflic-
tion.

Occasionally he lapsed into delirium and she did not
know if he comprehended all she told him, but that did not
stop her from giving him continual encouragement.

"The king's physician and I disagree on the best treatment for this dreaded pestilence," Glynis told Brianna.

"I would follow your advice over his, any day. You have
always had the power to heal."

"They kept Joanna's windows sealed shut to keep out the
evil in the air, but I think fresh air is beneficial. If not to the
patient, at least to the caregivers. The stench in a plague
sickroom is enough to gag a corpse."

Both girls crossed themselves at Glynis' unfortunate
choice of words. "Another thing I disagree with is overly
strong purges. They prescribe hemlock to induce vomiting.
Jesu, if the patients don't die of the plague, they die of the
cure! I think it would be better to give a soothing herbal
drink like chamomile. Chamomile is good in a clyster too.
Lord only knows the bowel is inflamed enough without
subjecting it to mustard enemas!"

They flung open the windows and vowed to keep Guy de
Beauchamp as cool and clean as was humanly possible.
They cleaned up his foul-smelling excretions immediately,
changing his bed linen and cleansing his body. They sensed
their vigil would be a long one, and so they worked out a
plan where one tended Warrick while the other rested.
Morning and night they examined his armpits and his groin
for the dreaded hard black lump that appeared in all fatal
cases.

As Brianna sat vigil through the long hours of the night,
her thoughts explored many avenues that led from past to
present to future. Christian had not returned to her and
she feared that she might never see her husband again! His
last words to her had admonished her to listen to her heart.
How did one do such a thing?

As she sat quietly contemplating, searching her mind for
answers, she reached deeper and deeper within herself. She
realized that she loved Christian more than she loved life.
Slowly it came to her that the love she felt for him was
unequivocal and unconditional. She loved him no matter

what he had done. Her love was absolute and abiding. She would love him forever!

One by one the petty barriers she had erected against him came down. And then a miraculous thing happened. Her heart began to fill with warmth and happiness. Brianna experienced a joy she had never felt before. Then suddenly, like a blinding flash, she knew Hawksblood had not killed his brother. Sweet God in Heaven, how blind she had been!

It had been before her all this time, but she had been too stubborn to see and feel the truth. Christian and Edward had exchanged armor as they had done before. Prince Edward had slain Robert de Beauchamp!

A single tear drifted down her cheek, then she was crying, sobbing out the pent-up suspicion that had poisoned her heart. Would he forgive her? The answer came back a resounding yes! He would forgive her anything. Would he return to her? Yes, a thousand times, yes! His love was absolute. Just like his honor. Brianna began to smile through her tears and her smiles changed to laughter and her laughter changed to profound, all-encompassing happiness.

She became aware of a pair of aquamarine eyes watching her from the darkness. Brianna gasped and bent closer to the bed. "Are you awake, my lord?"

"Sharon? My Rose of Sharon?" His voice was hoarse, no more than a croak, and yet it was compelling. "Why did you desert me?" he demanded. "Why did you leave my ship in the middle of the night?"

Brianna searched her thoughts. He must think her Christian's mother. Brianna took his hand.

"My little Arabian princess! Why did you deceive me?"

She saw he was hallucinating and becoming most distressed. Brianna decided to be whoever he wanted her to be, if it would calm him.

"Guy?"

"Yes, love?"

"I . . . was afraid to go with you to a strange land."

"But I was your husband, and the father of your child. Why did you conceal him from me?"

Brianna was stunned. Was Christian's mother really an Arabian princess and had Warrick actually married her?

He gripped her hands tightly, possessively, as if he would never let go.

"We were from two different worlds," Brianna murmured.

"You knew if you told me of the child I would force you to come with me!"

"Yes . . . yes. I thought it was kinder to keep you in ignorance."

"But he found me! He searched until he found me."

"Yes, he did."

"He is all I ever wanted in a son. Thank you." With Brianna holding his hand, Warrick closed his eyes and slept.

As dawn's light stole in across the open balcony, Brianna realized she had been here a whole week, and he was still alive! When Glynis came to relieve her, they pulled down the sheet to examine him for the black lump. Suddenly, Warrick grew erect.

Both girls jumped back and stared in disbelief.

"Well, what the devil do you expect with two beautiful women fingering my groin?" he demanded.

"Lord in Heaven, I think he's going to be all right," Glynis whispered.

"Do you know who I am, my lord?" Brianna asked.

"Of course I know who you are! My son's beautiful wife, Brianna. Beautiful and generous to her very bones to nurse a mad hound like me."

"I didn't do it alone. Glynis used her healing powers."

"The Welsh lass . . . another beauty."

Just by talking, he had used all his strength and fell back in an exhausted sleep. "To sleep is to heal," Glynis murmured.

Before Brianna went to rest, she went out onto the balcony. Randal waited below for news of the marshal, as he did every morning. Today for the first time, she was able to give him a positive report. Sir Randal Grey looked more like a young boy than a knight today as he broke into a grin and Gnasher ran up his arm to perch on his shoulder.

"Randal, I want you to bring my parchment and paints. I've decided to write a book." She told him exactly what to bring and he hurried off to give the Black Prince the wonderful news about Warrick.

Joan had fallen in love with Brianna's white stone palace. All her apprehension at finally being reunited with her prince had melted away in the perfumed magic of the private garden. When he opened his arms to her, Joan went into them and clung to him as if she would never release him again. She wore delicate pink silk, her silvery hair shimmering in the moonlight, and Edward was amazed that this tiny creature could play such havoc with his heart.

His fingers traced over her pretty face as gently as if she were made of porcelain and he vowed to cherish her always. There was only one bad moment between them when Edward murmured, "Holland is dead."

"How do you know?" she gasped.

"Hawksblood identified his body after the battle."

Joan sagged against him with relief, and as she did so she noticed Edward's suppressed excitement. His long fingers cupped her face so that he could watch her eyes. "Christian has gone to the Pope to get us a dispensation so we can be married."

Joan's eyes widened with delight. "Oh, Edward, I love you so much!" It mattered not to Joan that marriage could make her the future queen, and the mother of future kings. All that mattered was that she would be Edward's cherished wife.

They made good use of Christian and Brianna's magnificent bed with its transparent silk hangings. He hadn't made love to her often since Jenna's birth and he immediately noticed a difference in her lovemaking.

Joan had always received her pleasure from giving Edward pleasure, and it had always been enough for her. Now, however, with her sheath slightly stretched, the sensations his long, hard shaft aroused were new and thrilling beyond her previous experience.

With her inborn sense of fun she began to titillate and tease him in ways that were extremely sensual and lush. She was able to straddle him and take his entire length up inside her, then in the dominant position she was able to take control of their love play for long minutes at a time, reducing her lover to a quivering, moaning supplicant, begging her to have mercy on him. "Jeanette, obey me!"

"Why should I?" she teased, lifting herself then plunging down.

"Because I'm bigger than you," he gasped.

"Mmmm, so I've noticed. Quite majestic, in fact. But you will have to learn to obey me upon occasion."

"Why should I?" He gave her back her own playful words.

"Because I am older than you!"

Edward began to laugh. He was such a seasoned warrior, he felt old enough to be her sire. Yet she spoke the truth. She was the elder and had bossed him unmercifully when she was ten and he a fledgling nine-year-old. "Mmm, you have improved considerably with age."

They spent the next two hours deciding who would take precedence in their love play. The final score was three to two in Edward's favor and, of course, that was exactly the way Joan wanted it. As she lay in his arms, soft with surfeit, she became serious.

"Edward, please don't tell anyone of your plan to marry me, until we get the dispensation."

"Sweetheart, I shall not allow anyone to prevent me taking you as my wife, not this time."

Joan knew the power of kings and queens. "Please, Edward?"

"I shall bow to your wishes. But only because you are older than me, and mayhap wiser in some things," he added, brushing his lips against her temple.

Because of his age and the destructive effects of the disease he had just barely survived, Warrick was extremely weak. It was a condition he was totally unused to, so Brianna talked with him as she sat painstakingly printing her story and illustrating it with vivid sketches.

He lay propped against a bolster, watching her with his aquamarine eyes.

"I know it must be hard to speak of your son Robert. Indeed, it has been a difficult adjustment for me also, but I would like you to confirm something for me if you would, my lord."

"Call me Guy. What is it you wish to know?"

"I have given it much thought and my heart tells me that Christian did not kill Robert. It was Prince Edward, wasn't it?"

Guy de Beauchamp nodded. "Robert conspired to put Lionel on the throne. Christian and Edward exchanged armor because young Randal Grey overheard the plot to kill the heir to the throne in the hastilude. But my son and I gave the king our word that we would remain silent. The king and I have much in common. Cursed by one son, blessed by another."

"I won't betray your confidence, Guy. Not even to Christian. I am ashamed to admit it, but at one point I thought Christian murdered his brother so he could inherit your title and castles."

"His mother and I were legally wed. He would have been my heir, even had Robert lived. Christian doesn't need my castles. He is a prince in his own right."

Brianna smiled. "Prince Drakkar." She savored it on her tongue. "How did you meet your princess?"

His eyes took on a distant look as his mind recalled the past. "My grandfather went on Crusade with Edward the First. We owned much land near Acre. My father made many visits there to administer our active commerce between East and West. By the time I was grown, most of our holdings in the East had been taken back and the Knights Templar of Acre forced underground.

"I went to salvage what I could of our commercial enterprises. I met Sharon at the summer palace of her father, Ottoman. Haifa on the Mediterranean Sea was a magical city of gilded domes and minarets. In my youthful imagination it resembled the Kingdom of Heaven and there I met an angel.

"The attraction was instantaneous. She was exotic as an orchid, imperious too. I gave my heart into her keeping forever. What she saw in me, I'll never know. Perhaps I was different. A Norman knight stuck out like a sore thumb in Arabia. Being madly in love stole all my reason. She would not yield to me outside of marriage, so being an impetuous fool, I wed her. It was all done in the strictest secrecy. If we'd been found out, both of us would likely have been put to death.

"I smuggled her aboard my ship late at night and sailed on the morning tide. You can perhaps imagine my loss when I discovered she had left the ship in the night."

He fell back against his pillows, still bereft after all these years. Brianna knew she must say something to lighten his mood.

She decided to shave him, and as she held the razor to his cheek she laughed softly. "Guy de Beauchamp, you have no idea how afraid I was of you only a year ago."

His eyes sought and held hers.

"Do you recall when you approached me to marry into the House of Beauchamp?"

Warrick nodded. The golden-haired beauty had taken his breath away.

"I thought you were asking me to become your wife."

The Mad Hound gave a bark of laughter. A grin slowly spread across his face and his aquamarine eyes glittered like jewels. "And what would your answer have been?"

"It would have been *yes!*" Brianna's eyes sparkled with mischief. She would not spoil her answer by telling him she was too softhearted to refuse him.

⚝ *42* ⚝

The king and Council and Prince Edward came to consult with Warrick about the terms to be set out in the peace treaty between the French and the English. Since his pride would not allow him to receive them while he was in bed, Brianna and Glynis bathed and dressed him in his finest surcoat and helped him to a great carved chair, padded with cordovan leather.

The king and his nobles thrashed out which territories they wanted and which they were willing to concede. They argued back and forth about ransom money and debated the length of time the peace treaty would be in effect. From an open balcony above, Brianna heard them deciding their future and hers.

The Black Prince was determined to gain sovereignty over as much of southern France as possible. By listening to him, she suspected that he must have sworn a holy vow to restore all the territory that his ancestors, King John and his son, King Henry III, had lost over the last hundred and fifty years.

The single most important issue to the king was that they retain Calais. It had been the hardest won and the king's pride would not allow him to give it back to the French.

Warrick was most concerned with the size of the ransom. He suggested ten times the amount first mentioned and was adamant against all arguments that the French could not raise such vast amounts. Brianna knew that Warrick was not an avaricious man, but rather, he was practical. He knew the Plantagenets spent money on a lavish scale with no concern if the treasury was rich or penniless. The laws of chivalry, to say nothing of Plantagenet pride, dictated that the King of England entertain the King of France in an extravagant manner, and Warrick wisely decided that the French should more or less pay for it.

Lastly, they discussed the length of the peace treaty. This was the thing that most concerned Brianna. When they decided to sue for a term of seven years, she was overjoyed!

Hawksblood's absence was taking its toll on Brianna. It was hard to keep hope alive. In her heart of hearts, she knew where he had gone and doubt was beginning to raise its ugly head about his return. How foolish and fanciful she had been to think him immortal. He was a flesh-and-blood man, susceptible to all the dangers of this world . . . accident, disease . . . temptation.

Brianna's hand went protectively to her womb. What if she was carrying Christian's child, as she now suspected? Should she pray that it was so, or go on her knees to beg that she would not have a fatherless child? Her heart gave her the answer. She fiercely wanted this baby more than she'd ever wanted anything in her life. This was the only way that Christian Hawksblood could be immortalized!

Brianna wiped away a tear and smiled. She counted the months on her fingers and concluded that if indeed she was with child, it would arrive before her next birthday, which fell on July 15.

Brianna played endless games of chess and tables with her recuperating father-in-law. She knew he enjoyed her company immensely, and truth to tell, she enjoyed his too. On the outside, he was tough as boiled owl, but underneath he had a warm and tender heart and Brianna knew he suffered from loneliness. He was reluctant to see her move back to her own house, but all his excuses for keeping her at his side were exhausted now that he had regained his full vigor.

When Brianna arrived home, she discovered that Adele had acquired a tiny kitten. It was a ball of fluff she called Muffie. Gnasher chased it immediately and they all had a good laugh when it turned to spit savagely at the cheeky ferret, who immediately sat back on its haunches to bob up and down in the most amusing fashion.

It had been a long time since the four young women had been able to enjoy each other's company, so Brianna decided they should dine in the flower-filled garden beside the fountain. It was September and all the bounties of autumn graced their table. Quinces, pears, apricots, plums, and pomegranates sat beside a dish of figs, dates, and nuts.

Glynis licked a sticky date and lamented, "It has been weeks since the army came home. I cannot understand why Lord Christian and Ali have not returned."

Joan sat with a pin, daintily picking the exotic red seeds from a pomegranate. "They should be home any day. They have only gone to Avignon." They could see Joan was bursting to tell them something, so they gave her their undivided attention.

"Christian has gone to the Pope to get a dispensation for Prince Edward and me to marry. But please don't tell anyone. I know there will be many voices raised against us marrying, once the secret is out."

"Because you are second cousins?" Adele asked.

"No. Queen Philippa thinks me a shameless hussy because I was betrothed to two men at the same time, and now that I'm suddenly a desirable widow, and have a string of suitors falling over themselves in the Banqueting Hall every night, she thinks me promiscuous. Edward seethes with impatience, but he has promised me that he will keep our secret until we get the dispensation. I've told him he has no reason to be jealous. These men are only after my money."

The other girls laughed at her. There had been, and always would be, considerably more to tempt men than Joan of Kent's fortune!

"They have had time to go to Avignon and back five times over," Glynis worried. "Avignon is close to the Mediterranean Port of Marseilles, where it is rumored fifteen thousand have died of the black plague."

Brianna bit into a ripe plum, pushing back the rising tide of panic that threatened to drown her. When Christian had come to her rescue in her darkest hour, removing all the threatening clouds from her horizon, she felt certain she was done with doubting her Arabian Knight forever. Now, she thought perhaps Fate had a hard lesson in store for her. She was about to be punished for all her sins. Life was life, not a fairy tale! She had married a prince, but the chance that she would live happily ever after was almost nonexistent.

Brianna thought about the book she was making, and came to a poignant decision. She would give it a happy ending, for even if Christian never read it, his child might. "They will return, Glynis, cast all doubt from your heart."

Adele hoped Brianna's faith was justified. It seemed most odd that Hawksblood had not chosen to return. A dispensation could take months and common sense dictated that Hawksblood would simply petition the Pope, not wait about for months until it was granted. She too had begun to fear that they might never see Hawksblood and his squire again. Of course, so long as Brianna had hope in her heart, she did not wish to destroy it.

Eventually, Glynis packed away her newly sewn wedding gown along with her hopes. She had done everything to speed Ali's return, from casting spells to making a sacrifice to an ancient pagan goddess of Wales. Adele began to see a connection between Hawksblood's absence and the disappearance of Lisette St. Lô. To Adele, it was too much of a coincidence that both were missing at the same time. Brianna was not blind to the pitying looks she received from everyone, including her friend Joan.

Edward had received a dispatch from Hawksblood informing him that he had delivered the petition for the dispensation and that he would be absent from Bordeaux for some time on his own pressing business. Edward had confided this to Joan, but she was loathe to give such information to Brianna. For what could possibly be more important to Christian de Beauchamp than returning to his wife?

Brianna had received her own dispatch telling her he would be absent for some time. He gave no explanation or details but she was content because he had closed with the words: *Trust in me always.*

The peace treaty was finally drawn up and signed. King Edward abandoned his claim to the throne of France and gave up all the northern territories they had conquered in return for confirmed sovereignty over Angoumois, Bigorre, Gascony, Guienne, Guisnes, Limousin, Poitou, Ponthieu, Rouergue, and Saintonge, which collectively the Plantagenets renamed Aquitaine. It went without saying that King Edward also received Calais. In addition, the French agreed to pay three million gold crowns in six yearly payments as ransom for their king, dauphin, and nobles.

The King of England decided to turn Aquitaine over to Prince Edward along with all power of government in the French provinces. When the prince confided the good news to Joan, she had some good news of her own to impart. They had been playing a game of dalliance in Brianna's pool, away from the prying eyes of the Royal Court, but Joan wanted to wait until they were in bed before she shared her precious secret with Edward.

As his kisses grew more demanding, she covered his hand which cupped her breast, and slid it gently down to cover her belly. Then she put her lips to his ear and whispered, "Darling, you are going to be a father again, but this time I feel it will be a boy."

Edward groaned and swung his feet to the floor. Joan's fingers flew to her lips, wishing she could catch back her words. Her prince did not sound overjoyed.

"Get dressed," he murmured.

"Are you angry?" Joan asked in a small voice.

"Angry?" he questioned.

"You sound annoyed," she ventured.

"My darling little Jeanette, I am only annoyed with your timing. I am in the throes of passion and your news makes it impossible for me to continue."

"Why?" she asked softly.

"Because I am taking you before the priest so he can marry us."

"We have no dispensation."

"To hell with the dispensation."

"Edward, are you sure?"

He slid his great hands beneath her armpits and lifted her to stand on the bed so they were of equal height. "My sweetheart, I have never been more sure of anything in my life. If you are right, and you are carrying my son, he can only become king if he is legitimate. I intend to see there is absolutely no question of that. When we get the dispensation, we can be married again. At Westminster. I'll insist on it! All the royal family will be present and all England's nobility will pay you homage as the Princess of Wales. We will make it legal and binding, however, this night!"

"Whatever shall I wear?" Joan asked breathlessly.

Edward began to chuckle. "It's after midnight and only an ancient priest will see you."

"That doesn't matter. I have to look beautiful for my wedding."

Edward nuzzled her ear. "Wear something you can slip off easily, beneath one of my cloaks, for I intend to hurry back to make you finish what you started." He rubbed his swollen manroot against her soft thigh, but Joan's imagination had already taken flight.

"May I wear the crimson velvet cloak with the golden leopards across the back?"

He groaned again. "I suppose so, but that means I have to go all the way back to the palace to get it."

"Poor Edward. Am I a sore trial to you?"

He kissed her pretty nose, unable to refuse her anything. "You are my lady love and I am your knight errant. I undertake this quest for you alone."

Joan giggled. "I shall reward you, Edward Plantagenet."

* * *

The King of France, his four sons, and all his nobles who had been taken prisoner enjoyed the King and Queen of England's lavish hospitality at Bordeaux. They hoped to be able to stay in southern France until their ransoms were paid, but the Plantagenets were practical enough to realize the temptation to escape would be too great.

In late October ships were readied to transport their valuable prisoners to England, and in a magnificent burst of generosity, King Edward gave John of France the newly built palace on the Thames called the Savoy, for his sojourn on English soil. As a parting gesture of goodwill, a great hunt had been planned, which would be followed by a feast before the Plantagenets' "guests" sailed across the Channel.

Brianna and Joan had been looking forward to the hunt for days. The autumn weather was beautiful. The oppressive heat of the summer months had departed, giving way to warm sunshine, tempered by refreshing sea breezes.

The moment Brianna threw back the covers to arise, a wave of nausea washed over her. She hoped it would pass, but as she bathed, a pungent aroma coming from the kitchens did her in. She was indelicately sick in her washbowl and began to feel decidedly sorry for herself. The thought of going on a hunt would give her about as much pleasure as being buried alive, so she urged Joan to go without her. The new bride was positively glowing and she looked absolutely ravishing in an apricot velvet riding jacket.

Brianna dragged herself out to the fountain to shower away the nasty miasma of her morning sickness, then climbed the stairs to her chamber most gingerly, to ensure her stomach would settle down. To cheer herself she chose her prettiest gown in a rich peacock shade, leaving her hair unbound so that the ends could dry in the sun.

She wandered out to the balcony to watch the hunt leave the royal palace. It was like a rich tapestry springing to life. Her artist's eye appreciated the vivid colors, the glossy coats of the horses, the hawks and the hunting dogs.

Her eyes suddenly widened in disbelief, for there, as large as life, rode Lisette St. Lô, flirting outrageously with the King of France. Brianna's anger effectively chased away her morning sickness. The baroness was supposed to be a bloody prisoner, yet here she was, dressed to kill, being lavishly entertained by two kings. To Brianna, life seemed abysmally unfair. She went back into her chamber, flung herself upon the bed, and wished the world, and everyone in it, to hellfire!

Christian Hawksblood and Ali disembarked from a vessel that had just anchored at Bordeaux's busy docks. Both wore Arabian robes and turbans and between the men was a veiled woman. They helped her mount a magnificent white Arabian steed, then together they rode beside the river Garonne that wound its way toward the towering Abbey of St. Andrew.

When the trio dismounted outside Warrick's white stone palace, Ali took charge of their mounts. Then Prince Drakkar took hold of his mother's hand and led her inside.

Warrick had been polishing his broadsword, determined to keep it honed and rust-free. That he might never use it again in battle mattered not to the warrior. He looked up, instantly aware of approaching footsteps before they ever entered the room.

Hawksblood paused in the doorway, his turban almost brushing the lintel. Aquamarine eyes met, locked, then sparkled with joy at their reunion. Though he had never said so to Brianna, Warrick had been racked with worry over his son's long absence. Now he broke into a relieved grin and was startled at the whiteness of Christian's teeth against his dark face when he grinned back.

Then Hawksblood stepped to one side, revealing the figure of a small, veiled woman. As she lifted a jeweled hand to remove her veil, Christian caught a look of naked vulnerability upon Guy de Beauchamp's face, and knew that must be exactly the way his own face looked whenever his gaze fell upon Brianna.

Christian suddenly realized that this moment was so intimate, it was meant for lovers alone, with no other eyes to witness such heart-stopping tenderness. Without a word, he faded from the scene, quite certain that they were aware only of each other.

* * *

Brianna jumped as the kitten dashed through her chamber with Gnasher nipping at its tail. It ran out onto the balcony and jumped up onto the roof in a frenzied effort to escape its tormentor.

Brianna was thoroughly exasperated. She sprang up and went out onto the balcony. "This is the last straw!" The kitten cowered on the tile roof, while Gnasher debated whether to follow it and risk Brianna's fury or sit contritely while she scolded him.

"You wretched little devil . . . I'll cut off your bloody whiskers!" she threatened. The black-footed ferret took off as if he believed her. Thoroughly vexed, she called to the kitten. "Here, Muffie . . . come, Muffie . . . the bad boy has gone now . . . here, Muffie. Damn it, Adele, why did you have to give it such a sissy name? I feel like the world's biggest fool calling Muffie!" she said to thin air.

It was obvious the little cat was not going to come down on its own. Someone would have to go out on the roof for it. It was also equally obvious who that someone would be. Brianna pulled up her skirts, then aided by the lattice that ran upward from the balcony, she climbed onto the roof. On hands and knees she crawled up the pitch of the roof to where the kitten huddled.

"What the hell are you doing up there?" a deep voice demanded.

Brianna's heart lifted. "Christian!" she gasped, standing up so she could get a full view of him. All her irritation with the world wafted away with the breeze. Brianna laughed. "I climbed to the rooftop to shout to the world that I love you." Then she cupped her hands about her mouth, threw back her head, and shouted, "I love Christian de Beauchamp!"

"I married a crazy woman. Come down!" he thundered.

"Catch me," she called back.

"Brianna, for the love of Allah, don't jump; it's too high!" he said with alarm.

"Love of Allah be damned, I'm doing it for the love of Christian!" Her heart soared, her senses overflowed with happiness, making her giddy. It was a heady experience.

"I'll come up and help you down. Don't attempt to jump, it isn't safe!"

"I'll always be safe in your arms. Catch me!" Brianna scooped up the kitten, ran lightly down the tiles to the roof's edge, then flung herself down into Hawksblood's up-stretched arms. They rolled onto the grass in a tangle of cape, skirts, and golden hair. The kitten leaped away and Christian's turban rolled after it.

Hawksblood's face was fierce with fury, but Brianna's laughter was so infectious, he felt his anger melt into mirth. "Why did you do such a reckless thing?"

She laughed up into his dark face and looked deeply into his aquamarine eyes. "I listened to my heart."

Christian examined her beautiful face with intense scru-tiny. The shadow behind her eyes was gone, along with all semblance of decorum. He rolled with her until he was in the dominant position. With mock solemnity he reminded her, "When you wed me, you said: *I submit myself to your authority, my lord husband.*"

"And you said: *With my body, I thee worship,* but not on the front lawn where everyone can see, I hope," she teased, feeling his iron-hard erection against her belly.

"Is that all you think about?" he demanded in shocked tones.

"Oh, once in a while my thoughts drift off to inconse-quential things, but they always come back to the heart of the matter, the *pièce de résistance,* the *crème de la crème.*"

"Your French tongue improves."

"I still need lessons; practice makes perfect."

Christian could hold back no longer. He needed to taste the deliciously tempting morsel held captive beneath him. When his mouth took possession of hers, he was thor-oughly bemused by her passionate response. Was he imag-ining it, or was she inviting dalliance?

To test the water, he ran his lips down her throat to the delicious place where her breast rose slightly above her square neckline. She arched up like a feline when it wished to be stroked. His eyes couldn't hide his amusement. He'd give her strokes if that's what she craved!

Christian took Brianna's hand and drew her into the house. Their bedchamber was the goal he had in mind, but after two steps in that direction they encountered Adele, who was almost as overjoyed as Brianna to see the head of the household returned. Ever chivalrous, Christian could not show his impatience with Adele and answered her questions cheerfully.

Next came Paddy, equally overjoyed, but with twice as many questions. When Joan came running down the stairs to greet him and tell him her news that she and Prince Edward were secretly wed, Christian's eyes met Brianna's with a helpless, yet amused glance.

Within the next five minutes Ali and Edward arrived. The Black Prince questioned him about going to Avignon for the dispensation and from there the conversation naturally progressed to Hawksblood's other adventurous travels. When Gnasher ran in, ran up Hawksblood's leg and perched on his shoulder, he and Brianna started to laugh. Their mirth knew no bounds. They laughed until the tears rolled down their cheeks. They wanted to be alone, they ached to make love after their long separation, but both of them knew they would not be sharing their bed until after dark. Spacious though it was, it could not accommodate seven people and a ferret!

Brianna ordered food and it was a laughing Glynis who brought it from the kitchen and served it with the help of Sir Randal Grey. The four couples, all very much in love, talked the afternoon away. Before Christian could tell them why he had been so long away, Brianna took his hand. "I know where you were . . . you went home. Your father told me you were both worried about your mother. You had a premonition that the black plague might touch her in some way. I pray that you found her in good health, my lord."

Christian's eyes sparkled as he squeezed her hand. "My powers are not infallible, thank Heaven. By the time I arrived in the East, the pestilence had done its devastation there and moved West. I found my mother in the best of health." He turned to Brianna to watch her reaction. "I brought her back with me."

Brianna's reaction surprised him. Her face was suffused with delight. "Where is she?" she demanded.

"At the moment she is in my father's house. Enjoying their privacy, I sincerely hope."

The ladies all sighed at the romantic thing that Christian had done for his parents.

"It was your father who was touched by the plague." Brianna's hand went to her heart. "Oh, wouldn't it have been devastating if you had brought her all this way only to discover that Guy had not survived?"

Hawksblood was stunned. "I was just there. He looked healthy enough to me."

"The Angel of Death stood at his bedside from the moment he arrived home from the victory of Poictiers," Glynis told him.

Joan spoke up. "Brianna and Glynis quarantined themselves with him and nursed him day and night until he recovered."

Christian was almost speechless. "I thank you from the bottom of my heart for such a selfless sacrifice."

Glynis blushed at his praise. Brianna smiled her secret smile. "It was no sacrifice to look after him . . . I'm half in love with him!"

Prince Edward said, "You're back in time for a splendid reception tonight. Our honored guests are leaving for England in the next couple of days."

Hawksblood knew he'd have to grit his teeth and bow to chivalry. "We will be honored to attend."

"Oh, Edward, we'll have to move to another room. Brianna and Christian would no doubt like to sleep in their own bedchamber tonight."

"The thought hadn't crossed my mind," Christian vowed chivalrously, and all his company laughed that he made such a terrible liar!

Prince Drakkar took his wife to meet his mother before they went to the Banqueting Hall. Brianna was extremely nervous and changed her clothes three times before she was satisfied with her appearance. She finally chose a dress with a full skirt of black and gold lace and a fitted ruby red jacket that showed off the bright splendor of her golden hair. Christian insisted that she must not cover such beauty, so she chose a plain gold fillet to hold it back from her face.

When they arrived at Warrick's, he told them that Sharon was too shy to attend the banquet, that they would much rather spend the evening alone together. Christian envied them. Princess Sharon wanted to receive her daughter-in-law privately. Brianna approached the adjoining room shyly, not knowing quite what to expect.

Christian's mother was the most vividly beautiful woman Brianna had ever seen, and the darkest. Her bloodlines made her regally proud, yet at the same time she was so small and feminine, Brianna understood how Warrick had fallen under her spell. She must have aroused a fierce protectiveness in the young Norman that still blazed in the old warrior.

They approached each other timidly. Since the older woman was a royal princess, Brianna waited for her to speak first.

Finally she asked, "Do you love my son?" Even her accent was exotic.

"With all my heart," Brianna assured her.

"Then we have much in common. Only when you have a child of your own, will you understand what it cost me to give him up."

"Love for a child must be unconditional and absolute. I understand that."

"Then you will make a good mother, Lady de Beauchamp."

"How lovely," Brianna said happily, "no one has called me that since my wedding day."

"Then I hope you will return the compliment for none has ever called me by my husband's name."

Brianna smiled at her. "Welcome to Bordeaux, Lady de Beauchamp."

Sharon smiled back. "I hear Bordeaux is beautiful, but it is England I long to see."

"I, too, long to go home," Brianna confided.

"Allow me to thank you for saving my husband's life." She picked up a gold filigree casket from a table beside her. "Please accept these as a token of my appreciation . . . and my love."

Brianna opened the lid and gasped. It was filled with rubies. "Oh, I couldn't possibly—"

"Nonsense. Christian," she called, "come and adorn your beautiful wife with the rubies I brought her."

Warrick and Christian came into the room and he fastened the rubies into her ears and clasped the necklace about her throat.

"*Magnifique!* Only women who are beautiful enough to outshine jewels should ever wear them," Princess Sharon declared. Then she turned her attention to Warrick and Christian. "So. Brianna and I wish to go home to England. What do you men intend to do about it?"

Warrick winked at his son. "I'll think on it, but we won't be living at the Royal Court of Windsor. I intend to live at Warrick in my own castle."

"Then we shall be close neighbors, for I intend to take Brianna home to Bedford."

After the banquet when the floor was cleared for dancing, a handsome young Gascon by the name of Sir Bernard de Brocas petitioned Prince Edward. "Your Highness, I beg a favor of you. If you would introduce me to your enchanting cousin, the Duchess of Kent, I shall be forever in your debt."

Edward stared at him grimly, the Plantagenet temper threatening to explode. Instead, the legendary Black Prince came to a decision. He stalked down the hall, not stopping until he stood directly in Joan's path. Then he swung her into his arms and danced her to the dais. He climbed up and held his arms out for silence. Gradually the laughing, chattering, and whispering ceased and the entire room gave the Prince of Wales their undivided attention.

"Your Majesties, ladies and gentlemen, I wish to announce that upon my return to England, Joan, Duchess of Kent, and I will be married at Westminster. You are all invited!"

The King and Queen of England were stunned, but when they heard the cheering from their courtiers, they decided to accept their son's decision graciously.

Christian bent his dark head to Brianna's ear. "If Edward has enough guts to finally do as he pleases, so have I."

"And what is it you please to do, my lord?"

"It pleases me to take you home to bed!" He put one strong arm beneath her knees and swept her into his arms before the whole assembly. Brianna slipped her arms about his neck, clinging to him, her heart almost melting against his. As he strode from the hall a group of courtiers stared, outraged at his audacity.

"An old Arabian custom," he murmured haughtily, a prince to his very bones.

Everyone was at the Banqueting Hall, so when they returned to their house, they were entirely alone. They could have swum naked in their own private Eden, but their needs were too great at the moment for water play.

Again, Christian lifted her high against his heart and carried her upstairs. He set her feet to the floor and captured her lips. Then with his mouth in complete possession of hers, his hands began to unclothe her. There was magic in his fingers as he undressed her by feel alone, never lifting his mouth from hers.

Brianna started to do the same to Christian. It was a most arousing and sensual game to disrobe him by touch alone, with her eyes closed, her mouth fused to his, and her senses so heightened, she wanted to scream with desire.

When she was naked, his hands did not leave her but continued to work their magic, touching, stroking, feeling, rubbing, squeezing, sliding, caressing, teasing, encircling, and then his tongue too began to taste and stroke and thrust. She stood on her tiptoes, slid her arms about his neck, then lifted herself onto his marble shaft.

As Christian walked slowly to the bed, the velvet head of his shaft moved in and out of her with each firm step. He knew that she would allow him any intimacy. At long last, all her barriers were down. She trusted him totally, knowing he would bring her to rapture.

Her passion for him tonight knew no bounds. As he slid his hard length all the way up inside her, she had never been hotter than she was tonight. She was fevered, scalding, and highly aroused almost to madness. When he tried to prolong their pleasure, she began to move on him in a frenzy of need, and he knew she was ready for what he was about to do to her. Knew in body and soul that she would respond sensually and yield totally, so that he could take her on the journey of transformation.

He began to thrust into her with hard, slow, pulsating strokes. All semblance of gentleness fell away. She reveled in the fullness, the power, and potency of his thrusts. He was giving her everything she needed if only he would move faster. Christian knew the deliberately slow rhythm coupled with the intense force of his hard thrusts would pleasure her ten times longer than rapid strokes that would bring a quick climax.

Tonight he wanted her to know the bliss of multiple orgasm and so he used his greater strength to force her body to match his slow, endless, undulating rhythm. Brianna gave her will into his keeping and allowed him total control. The pleasurable sensations her body experienced were beyond anything she had ever known. Molten gold fire ran along her veins, melting her very bones, molding her to his size and shape. Their bodies became one, endlessly giving, endlessly taking. As he worshiped her with his body, time and place and identity fell away until they were transformed.

Finally, she could sustain the pleasure no longer, and deep within her body, she climaxed long and hard, one contraction after another, vibrating her sleek sheath until she shuddered to a stop. Christian held still for half a dozen heartbeats and then he withdrew his hard, thick length halfway, positioning the swollen head of his phallus against her hard bud, high on her mons.

For a moment she almost cried out that it was too much, but she read his thoughts as clearly as he read hers. *Stay with me, trust me for this loving.* Had he spoken aloud? Perhaps. It mattered not, she did trust him, would trust him always, forever, in this life and the next.

This time her pleasure built swiftly, exquisitely, with new and different sensations, making her so passionate she bit the smooth dark skin that stretched across his breast and shoulder. *He will have scars,* she thought, and then she lost even the ability to think as her bud exploded into a million delicious pulsations.

Christian held still once more to experience every last flutter of his beloved's body. She was learning that trusting him had untold rewards. When her last shiver stilled, he thrust into her savagely once, and to the hilt, finally spending, flooding her with his love, his life. When she felt his white-hot seed spurt inside her, she experienced her final bliss.

Brianna felt too languorous to even breathe. She was utterly content to simply be. His love surrounded her in never-ending circles that moved outward from her to infinity.

Much later when they could breathe again, and move and think, Christian untangled himself from her beautiful hair and whispered, "I have a gift for you."

Suddenly she remembered the book she had made him. "I have a gift for you too."

As they gifted each other with a book, it would have been a coincidence, except of course there is no such thing. Each opened the book and turned the pages with rapt attention. His was entitled *The Arabian Knight* and she had lovingly sketched him on each page, telling his story. She portrayed him taming a falcon, winning a joust, fighting in battle, being knighted by the king, sitting at the Round Table wearing his Order of the Garter. Christian looked up from the book, enthralled that she had made this thing of beauty for him.

Brianna sat gazing in fascination at the book he had given her. When her eyes widened in disbelief, he laughed and explained, "It is a pillow book. In the East a bridegroom gives one to his bride and they look at the erotic positions of love when they retire to bed."

"Christian! For the love of Allah, this is the wickedest thing I've ever seen. It's positively decadent and lewd!"

He closed the book so she wouldn't have to look at the depraved couplings. "I'm sorry, love. I didn't mean to shock you. I meant to amuse you. The book you have made me touches me deeply. I will cherish it forever." He turned to the last page where she had painted them both with their arms about three children. The illuminated script read: *And they lived happily ever after.*

"How do you know we will have three children?"

"I saw them in a vision once. Two strong sons and a droll little daughter."

He reached out his hand to stroke her golden hair. "You are a marvel."

"I know," she said mischievously, opening her pillow book. "I think I'd like to try page twenty-four."

As his mouth fell open, she ran giggling to the bed. Then Christian was in full pursuit. They burrowed beneath the bedcovers, laughing like lunatics. She pushed him back forcefully and rubbed her cheek along the inside of his thigh. Then her tongue came out and she traced the length of the curved scimitar branded high on his inner thigh.

She had him helpless, moaning with pleasure and laughing at the same time. "Your hair is tickling me to death!"

Soon the bedclothes were on the floor, and not long after, they followed the covers. "Mmm, imagine doing page twenty-four on a marble floor!"

"You little cocotte, what you want to do to me is too wicked to be in that book. I can't waste my seed like that if you want to get started on that family."

Brianna pushed him back again, but stopped laughing so she could be serious for a moment. "I'm already carrying your son tucked deep beneath my heart."

"My darling, I love you with all my heart." He kissed her tenderly and Brianna sighed with happiness, feeling it all the way down to her toes. Suddenly he grabbed her shoulders. "You reckless little fool. You jumped off the roof knowing you were with child!"

Brianna reached out one finger to tap his manhood. It stretched like a beast that had been sleeping, but was now fully alert. "Beat me," she invited. "Use your stout rod and beat me, my wicked Arabian Knight."